THE GOOD ENEMY

UNDER HER WHIP

BY

S.N. JEFF

AUTHORS ADDRESS

This is not a book about falling in love. Rather, it is a book about stepping out of the way and allowing love happen.

WARNINGS

DEPRESSION

GRIEF

CHILDHOOD TRAUMA

MENTIONS OF SUICIDE

VIVID BDSM SCENES

EXPLICIT SEX SCENES

MORALLY GREY BEHAVIOR

FOUL LANGUAGE

PLAYLIST

CRY — CIGARETTES AFTER SEX
AMY WINEHOUSE— BACK TO BLACK
ADELE — OH MY GOD
DPR IAN — SO BEAUTIFUL
BTS — FILTER
TROYE SIVAN — COULD CRY JUST THINKIN ABOUT YOU
JEFF SATUR — WHY DON'T YOU STAY
ISAK DANIELSON — POWER
THE WEEKND — SAVE YOUR TEARS
STEPHEN SANCHHEZ — UNTIL I FOUND YOU
ISAK DANIELSON—SHES ALWAYS A WOMAN
THE BLACK SKIRTS — TILL THE END OF TIME
BTS — BLACK SWAN
JOJI, BENEE — AFTER THOUGHT

THAI WORDS AND HONORIFICS TO KNOW

NONG: Non-binary honorific used in addressing someone younger.
PHI: Non-binary honorific used in addressing someone older.
KHUN: Formal non-binary honorific. Can be compared to:
MRS/MISS/MR.
BPAA: Older sister to your mother.
KHUN PUU/PUU: Grandfather on your father's side.
KHUN YAA/YAA: Grandmother on your father's side.
MAE: Mother.
PO: Father.

DEDICATION

To everyone who found comfort in pain and
chose not to stay.

ONE
THE INTERVIEW

"**N**ong Wine... Nong Wine?" Dr. Rueng calls my name, dragging my attention back to her.

"Yes. I'm sorry." I exhale.

I can't remember when I stopped paying attention to our session. My thoughts drifted away as I watched the heavy rain shower against the widespread tall window. The dancing trees and floating dark clouds created a captivating view that could easily be used as reference for depressing art.

I love it when it rains. I love the smell, the soothing sounds, the coziness. The storm brings me comfort and peace. Maybe because it looks a little bit like chaos, so I don't have to worry about the one inside me.

"That's okay." Dr. Rueng adjusts her glasses. "Where were you just now?"

"Thinking of my sister."

"I didn't know you have a sister."

"Had. She died when I was five... I think."

"How old was she?"

"I'm not quite sure, maybe a year."

"What was she like?"

"I don't know... a baby... she cried a lot. I remember her cries quite well."

"When you think of her, what do you think of?"

I return my gaze to the window, taking a deep breath and exhaling quietly. When we aren't speaking, the sound of the rain fills up the office, and I can think more clearly.

1

Something small to distract me from my ever-turbulent mind.

"If she'd like me if she got to know me."

"Do you think she would?"

I blink, taking a quick glance at my fingers before lifting my gaze back to her. "No."

She smiles at me, a poor attempt to hide her concern, then begins scribbling on her writing pad.

Dr. Rueng has a way about her. Very calm, collected, elegant. She mostly dresses in neutral tones that match her deep brown skin. It was one of the first things I noticed about her when our video call sessions started while I was still in the United States.

Everything else in her office is color coded as well. The dark green carpets match the dark green curtains. All the furniture are different hues of brown except the sofas, they are dark green too. She color codes her books and pens, as well as the ice-skating figurines laid out on top of her bookshelf. I like that she's that way. Highly organized and structured. In some way, it makes me feel like I can trust her process.

***

The rain has not let up since I left Dr. Rueng's office. I get down from the taxi and hurry into the bar where Plerng and Lucifer are waiting. As I step in, I move my damp hair away from my face. I have been growing it out for a while now, it's the longest my hair has ever been, with the tip now resting on my shoulders. Though it compliments my high cheekbones and soft eyes, it has become increasingly difficult to manage. My eyes dart around the bustling bar in search of my friends.

"Wine!"

I turn sharply to my left and see Lucifer's giant self cheerfully waving me over. Beside him, a grinning Plerng. My smile broadens as I squeeze myself through the crowded bar. Lucifer's charming dimples match his incredible sunshine personality. It seems he got a new hairstyle too: fluffy, curly bangs. I like it on him. Plerng looks pretty much the same; expensive and uninterested in anything.

"Gee! What did they feed you in the States!" Lucifer shakes me, pulling me into a tight hug.

"Snow and debt."

We chuckle in our embrace.

"My turn." Plerng pulls us apart.

I pick Plerng's petite body off the floor, spinning her around as we laugh wholeheartedly before putting her down and sniffing her forehead.

"Look at you! Putting suburban dads to shame with that sweater," Plerng teases.

She's never been a fan of my simple minimalistic taste in fashion, seeing as she is the complete opposite. Plerng comes from money, the kind of money that would make anyone with a hundred thousand dollar per year salary feel broke. With money like that, comes an expensive taste in everything, particularly for Plerng, fashion. She's always dressed as if the runway follows her around, an overconfident attitude to match. With Plerng, you'd need to get to know her first to see her humble sweet side.

Although Lucifer comes from old money too, his taste in life is quite mundane. However, it's probably because he comes from money that he can live as carefree and as simple as he does. Not particularly believing in anything, aspiring to anything or needing anything.

"Who knows, maybe one day I'll become a suburban dad, carrying on the daddy issues tradition," I reply.

"You have to let me take you shopping, for once," Plerng insists as we take our seats.

"Men with daddy issues are hot. Toxic, but hot," Lucifer says.

"You're saying I'm not hot?" I chuckle.

"You're hot, but in a friendly, cute way; not in a daddy issues kind of way, you know what I mean?"

"No, Lucifer, I do not know what you mean." I smack his shoulders.

3

"Women with daddy issues are hot, men with daddy issues are just toxic," Plerng says.

"You have daddy issues, Plerng," I say.

"Case in point." Plerng flips her hair. "I have you to thank for that, Luce, since you won't stop fucking my dad."

"Oh Buddha!" I shake my head with a grin.

I should be used to how blunt and vulgar Plerng gets after knowing her for over a decade, but she still manages to catch me off guard.

"I'm not fucking your dad... we're... dating, it's not casual," Lucifer stutters.

"Do you know how many men you've said that about?" Plerng continues.

"In my defense, it's been a year, the longest relationship I have ever had. Never happened with any of those people."

"Still gross, Luce."

"Plerng... you said you were cool with this."

"Yes, yes, I am, I am, sorry."

The waiter arrives and they order more wine for themselves. To keep myself sober, I order for soda.

"What do you think you're doing? We're all getting drunk tonight!" Plerng snaps her fingers.

"I have that interview tomorrow, remember? I need a job; these student loans won't pay off themselves."

"I hate that you're getting a job, it's so... grown. Please don't get a job." Plerng squeezes me from the side, sniffing my cheeks.

"We always said we'd travel after graduation, and we never did because you just had to do your masters and then a PhD, now is the time," Lucifer says.

"Seeing as I'm the only one on this table without a trust fund, I have to work to afford travel."

The waiter drops off our drink and we all thank him with a bow.

"Just us, hoping flights across the globe, the experience we'd have, the memories we'd make; Plerng and I would split the bill, you don't have to worry."

"Guys, let it go." I sip my drink. "What do you guys know about the Cheng family anyway?"

4

"They give me psychopathic vibes," Plerng says. "The second child, umm... What's her name again? Elina Cheng? There is that rumor about her murdering her ex-husband."

I choke on my drink. "Wait, what?" My eyes widen, wiping the spill off my lips.

"Plerng! Stop! You do this shit all the time!" Lucifer complains.

"I have heard stories, Luce, she's literally called the Black Widow of Chiang Mai. I'm telling you, if the family wasn't richer than God, she'd probably be in jail for murder or heaven knows what."

"Should I not go for this interview?" I ask.

"I don't think you'll fit in there."

"You should go, see what it's like for yourself," Lucifer includes.

Plerng scoffs, sipping her drink. "If you end up in a box at the bottom of the Cheng mansion, don't say I never warned you."

"Shut up, Plerng!" Lucifer shakes his head, smirking.

"I'm just saying, get off my dick, Lucifer!"

Plerng's distrust in people isn't foreign to me. It can easily be justifiable given her history with people befriending her for her wealth, then taking advantage. In the past, it saved me from multiple heartaches, I have always trusted her instincts. However, getting a masters and then a PhD in child psychology is expensive. So, my first instinct isn't to follow Plerng's gut feeling about a job that will make me debt free.

The Cheng family is one of the oldest and wealthiest families from Chiang Mai, with businesses spread across Asia, Europe, America and Africa. After Elina Cheng, the second daughter of the Cheng family moved to Bangkok five years ago, rumors spread about what went on behind those mansion doors. Theories about the sudden disappearance and death of her husband. That is as far as I know, I don't dabble in tabloid gossip, a good waste of anyone's time if you ask me. Plerng on the other hand cannot live without it.

When I discovered the Cheng household was looking to hire a psychologist for their child with a 1,500,000 Baht annual salary attached to it, there just was no way I wasn't going to try. I sent in my application and now I have an interview.

The rest of the night dazzled with events as expected. There is never a dull moment with Plerng and Lucifer. From dancing on the bar to Plerng making out with random girls, Lucifer stripping and allowing every person with a hand run it all over his eight pack like he was a go-go boy. Lucifer's body is an alluring sight. He's gorgeous and he knows it, flaunts it. His confidence and sweetness contribute greatly to his sexiness. The whole night reminded me of our university nights, we were so wild, young and careless. Well—they both still are.

I got up with the sun to do chores and make breakfast for Po, although he often insists I don't. I have missed having breakfast together. It became a big part of my daily routine before I left to study abroad, and while in the States, I found myself making breakfast for two on some days even though I lived alone.

"Witthaya," Po calls. He's the only one that still calls me that, not that I mind.

"Sawatdee krap, Po," I greet him with a wai before turning to pull out his seat. It's our first breakfast together in two years, so I'll admit, I'm being a bit extra.

"Sawatdee krap. What is all this? Don't you have an interview today?" He sits. I join; sitting opposite him.

"It's at noon, Po. I still have some time."

He takes a spoonful of the khao tom, and I watch him chew, digging in for a second spoon. My lips curve up into a subtle smile when he begins nodding his head in approval. Po is a picky eater, if he doesn't like it, he just wouldn't eat it. His approval of the things I do has always mattered to me. It made me spend long hours perfecting so many traditional dishes, a skill I am most grateful for today. Quiet breakfasts have always been our thing, Po isn't a man of many words. I might have gotten that from him. After Mae left, it changed him in a lot of ways. Sometimes I see a glimpse of the man I knew as a child, but it quickly fades away and this distant but kind man I have come to love resurfaces.

6

"You aren't sleeping?" Po asks, interrupting the comfortable silence. "Are you having nightmares again?"

"I'm sorry, Po. Did I wake you?"

"No need to apologize. This new therapist you're seeing, is she any good?"

"Yes, Po."

"I'm visiting the market today, do you need anything?"

"No, but we are out of laundry detergent."

"I'll get some then." He smiles and we continue breakfast in silence.

As soon as we are done, I call a taxi and begin to do the dishes, a way to burn time before its arrival. Normally I'd take a motorbike around town, but the Cheng mansion is on the outskirts of the city.

As I rinse off the final dishes, I contemplate walking over to Po and striking up a conversation. We've barely talked these last few months. I wrote down 'Another chance to know Po' as one of the pros of coming home. Getting to know him better is something I've wanted for years. No matter how much I try, there always seems to be a wall between him and I. Sometimes, it feels like he's afraid of me, or angry, I cannot quite put my finger on it. All my life, he's been here, but not here. It's left me with a strange kind of emptiness.

My phone rings and it's the taxi driver. I walk over to the sitting room, retrieve my bag and bid Po goodbye.

***

My friendship with Plerng and Lucifer exposed me to so much wealth over the years, I'm unshaken by the extravagance the Cheng mansion exudes as I arrive, but it's definitely a looker. I alight from the taxi, ring the bell by the gate and stand back.

"Sawatdee Krap, Khun," a strong wobbly masculine voice greets through the intercom.

"Sawatdee Krap, Khun." I bow, though I'm not sure he can see me. "I am here for the interview, Witthaya Sutthaya."

"A moment please," he says, and I nod. "Place a valid ID card in front of the monitor please."

I hurry back to the taxi and retrieve my ID card from my bag then hurry back and place it in front of the monitor. After a few seconds, the tall steel gates buzz and slowly begin to open.

"Drive straight down, take a left and stop by the main door, it's difficult to miss."

"Thank you." I walk back into the taxi, and we drive in.

The beauty of the mansion begins to dawn on me as we drive through the pathway. Widespread green land, tall trees on each side of the narrow road. A few animals roam about: rabbits, peacocks, squirrels. It's like a little town, I've never seen anything like it. We arrive at the entrance, and I alight from the taxi once again, thanking the driver.

A bright, well-dressed elegant man, who seems to be in his early sixties or late fifties opens the door and steps out.

"Khun Sutthaya, welcome to the Cheng residence." We exchange bows in greeting.

"Thank you, Khun."

"My name is Toh, this way please."

He heads back into the house, and I follow. His demeanor is colder than my father's. He almost looks like a professor, well put together and sharp, moving quickly with strong steps. He leads me into a long art filled hallway, then into what seems to be a tearoom where two other women are seated, waiting. We all exchange greetings and bows as I enter.

"Khun Cheng will see you shortly." He gestures me over to a seat. "Coffee or tea?" he asks as I sit.

"I'm good, thank you."

He nods and leaves.

My eyes begin to travel around the room. The mansion is a fine mixture of the old and new, decorated in brown and red hues. The furniture is made of wood, deep brown colored wood, multi-colored 1980's style marble and a curtain from the same era to match. Old art lines the walls in here too, these must have cost a fortune.

One by one, the ladies are escorted out, now it's just me waiting, allowing me more freedom to get up and take a closer look at the antique decorations.

"Khun."

I turn away from the art I have been studying for over five minutes. Khun Toh stands erect by the door, hands behind his back.

"I'm sorry, just taking a closer look," I inform him with a smile.

He smiles back, creeping me out a bit.

"Khun Cheng is waiting." He gestures outside the door.

"Oh." I hurry over to my seat and retrieve my leather study bag, hanging it over my shoulder and follow him out the door.

We walk down the hall and make a left turn, walking past another room before arriving at the end of the hallway. He stops by a door and knocks.

"Go in when you're ready, push not pull."

I nod and he walks away.

My eyes follow, watching him disappear into another room. I take a deep breath and exhale, turning back to the door with apprehension. This will be my first ever formal job interview. I am prepared but not confident.

I push the door and enter.

The strong stench of cigar welcomes me, I can tell it is Cuban. I recognize the smell from university days when Lucifer took me to elite clubs for high society Bangkok men. They loved to smoke their cigars; it was just as hard to breathe in there as it is for me to breathe in here. The office's tall broad walls are stacked with shelves filled with books. It is lit mostly with golden yellow aged lamps making the office dim.

I see her sitting behind her desk at the end of the office. The cigar in between her fingers causes a fog around her. She is illuminated only by the yellow light on her massive office table. As she smokes, she flips through a folder. I can't see much of her face from this distance, just her well sculpted figure pressing against her white shirt. She rolls up a sleeve, her eyes still pinned on the document as she tucks some of her straight hair behind her left ear. I haven't moved from the same spot since I entered, the sight of her is an enigma to me.

"Khun Sutthaya?" her surprisingly soft voice calls.

"Yes. Khun." I bow. "Sawatdee Krap."

She chuckles softly; it could easily pass for a purr.

"Sawatdee kha—I can't interview you from all the way over there, Khun. Please, come sit."

I walk over with slow steps. When I arrive, she looks up at me and her face is revealed to me: oval shaped, full brows, deep red lipstick on her full plum lips. Every corner of her face has well defined sharp lines. I can't clearly see her eyes, but I can tell they are almond shaped. She doesn't seem like the kind of woman to go with an office like this. Her office is a bit depressing, but she radiates wonder. This isn't a conventional person; this isn't going to be a conventional interview I think to myself as I sit.

"Would you be ok if I smoke while we chat?" she asks with that tender strong voice that vibrated through me the first time she spoke. I can tell she is crossing her legs from the way her body tilts to the side.

"S... sure," I stutter, intertwining my palms under the table.

She puts out the cigar in an ashtray sitting on the table, then picks up a remote and turns on the air cleaner.

"Sorry if that made you uncomfortable."

"It didn't."

"It did." A crooked smile stretches across her face.

I look down at my palm, unsure if I should smile back or thank her. Her stare is a bit... intimidating. I clear my throat instead.

"I was intrigued when I received your resumé, Khun. Aren't you a little bit overqualified for this job?"

"I hoped my qualifications would make up for my lack of experience which was requested."

She leans forward, placing her right elbow on the deep brown oak table to support her chin with her palm. I can see her eyes a little better now, it's even more intimidating. I flush. It's a good thing this office is barely lit.

"You would just be a companion," she says.

"I doubt that."

"Why?"

"You described Hathai as an overly confident genius, interested in classical music, arts and mathematics, lacking social skills and empathy, who is also introverted and easy to care for."

"I did."

"Khun Cheng, that doesn't sound like a twelve-year-old who needs a companion, and I think you know that."

She smirks, holding me in her piercing gaze, strumming her fingers on the table in silence. I want to look away, but I fear it will give my nervousness away.

"Why did you pick child psychology?"

"Children fascinate me. I think... if we get to humanity early and fix the damage, we might just save the world, we might just create a better future."

"You think humanity is damaged?"

"I think it's sick."

"And you want to heal it?"

I grin and look down at my palms. "I want to try."

"What if it's too late, look around you."

"I think, maybe you should have more faith."

"Maybe, you should have less faith."

Once again, I am trapped in her gaze, surrounded by nothing but silence. Only the gentle wheezing of the air cleaner, and the sound of her fingers strumming on the table can be heard. I squeeze my fingers under the table and flash a pretentious weak smile.

"Believing humanity cannot recover is just a lie people use to excuse their evil doings."

"Evil? Do you think I'm evil, Khun Sutthaya?"

"I don't think anything of you, Khun Cheng. I mean... I don't know you."

"But you've already formed an opinion about me."

I look away from her, smiling to myself.

11

I can't decide if it's the sense of debauchery I get from her, her intimidating stare, or the way she smiles each time I reply, it all makes me a little nervous. This isn't right. I have a PhD. Act like it, Wine.

"Yes, I have, Khun. But it's just an opinion."

Another round of unnerving silence looms. Is she doing this on purpose? To make it tough on me? To see how I react?

"What do you do for fun?"

"Umm..." I swallow. "I read a lot, I love sculpting, card games."

"What's your favorite genre to read?"

"I am not picky."

"Romance or fantasy?"

"Why the two?"

"Dreamers like you usually go for one of the two."

She lowers her hand, and my eyes follow, watching her intertwine her fingers. They are slender and firm. Her nails are painted a darker shade of red, making the diamond bracelet on her wrist pop.

"Fantasy," I say.

"J.K. Rowling, George R.R. Martin or J.R.R Tolkien?"

I chuckle and so does she, dragging my eyes to her perfectly shaped red lips once again, I catch myself at once and look away.

"George."

"I would have guessed Rowling," she replies.

Our eyes meet and my cheeks warm up. I squeeze my bag hard this time, she doesn't seem to want to look away, the longest she has held my gaze and I don't want to look away first. She leans in closer over her table and I hold my breath.

"I'm a George girl too," she whispers and we both giggle as she relaxes back into her broad leather seat.

She Leaves her gaze on me, like she's studying me, analyzing me, like I'm prey, and she's predator, waiting for the chance to pounce and ravish me. I don't dislike it. I'd roll over in defeat if she tries to haunt me—Or I might put up a fight, just so she doesn't win easily. I have a feeling winning comes easy to her.

"Khun Sutthaya... I will see you out." She rises from her seat and so do I.

I was right, she's so well proportioned, a bit taller than me but that might be the heels. Her white shirt accentuates her sharp straight shoulders. I try not to look but for a fleeting moment my eyes travel to her breasts, pointed under her shirt. She's left a few buttons open; I can't see any cleavage but my body tenses up regardless. A black belt holds her plain work trousers to her waist. I stare at it as she walks over but instantly return my gaze to her face.

"Khun, what do your friends call you?"

"Just... Wine."

"Suits you."

"Thank you."

"I'll be honest, you won't get this job, Khun."

I shake my head in surprise. "Excuse me? I... I don't understand. You said earlier I am overqualified."

"Yes. I'm sorry, I don't want to waste your time."

"May I ask why?"

She slides her hands into her pockets and walks closer to me, standing directly under the golden chandelier above us. I blink, swallowing. Her brown eyes glow with wonder, the yellow light makes her beautiful caramel skin shimmer. And damn! Her perfume.

"Because... I don't mix business with pleasure. And it seems, Khun, I like you... Really like you. I'd prefer to not explore that."

I stand under her gaze bewildered, dumbfounded, conflicted and drawn. She smiles, running her eyes all over my face and my heart swells.

"I'll see you out." She walks to the door.

"What if I told you I'm dating someone, I mean... I have a fiancé, his name is Lucifer, we are set to get married this summer... We are very much in love, so... there is no way anything can ever happen between us."

She turns, a smirk on her lips, walking back towards me as I hold my breath.

"You're saying... you're gay?"

"Yes... Khun."

"You only date men?"

"Yes."

She holds my gaze while closing every distance between us. I gulp. The smell of her sweet floral perfume mixed with the smell of cigar is sensually intoxicating.

"You, Khun... Wine, has to be the prettiest liar I have ever met."

Pretty?

I clench my jaw, trying to hide how nerve racking it is to be standing so close to her. I don't think I am doing a decent job. I think she can see right through me. She's been seeing right through me from the moment I stepped into this office.

"Do I make you nervous, Wine? It's ok if I call you Wine, right?"

"I prefer we stick to formal addresses, Khun. And no, you don't."

"Already drawing a line, I see." The side of her lips twitch. I clench harder, trying not to blink too much, standing firm against her gaze. She walks away, and I quietly exhale. She opens the door. "I'll let you know, Khun Sutthaya."

I bow and exit the office. She shuts the door behind me, and my legs wobble. I now realize how nervous I was.

TWO
THE LEFT WING

*L*ooking down at my legs, there is water all the *way up to my knees. It's freezing, my feet feel numb. I slowly lift my hands, gasping at the sight of all the blood they are covered in. I shudder, trembling. My lungs feel like they are shutting down on me.*

"No! Wine!" I hear Mae scream and I turn sharply as fear grips me. The loud cry of an infant fills the air, but Mae is nowhere in sight.

"Mae! Mae!" I call, frantically shaking as I take small steps towards a door where all the water and crying seems to be coming from. The once clear water begins to turn bloody red, and I struggle to move. My legs are shaky and weak. I continue to scream for Mae; squeezing my chest and gasping for air.

"Wine," Mae calls from behind me and I turn sharply to nothing but darkness. The sound of the child crying intensifies, and out of nowhere, Mae plunges towards me with a knife.

I gasp, springing up from my bed, struggling to breathe as I tremble. My shirt is soaked in sweat.

"Witthaya," Po calls from the corner of my room, startling me. "Calm down, son. It's just me." He walks over to the bed, a cup in his hand. "Some chamomile?" he offers, taking a seat beside me. With shaky hands, I take the cup and sip.

"Thank you, Po. Sorry for waking you up."

He shakes his head. "Did you have them while you were in the U.S?"

"Barely." I take another sip.

"I thought the new doctor was helping?"

"Po, we only started our sessions two weeks ago. Don't worry about it."

He exhales and taps my shoulder. "Try and get some sleep."

I nod and he gets up and leaves.

Like I said, Po isn't a man of many words.

Sleep has eluded me since my return to Thailand. My nightmares have become frequent, it hasn't been this bad since before university. Dr. Rueng's approach is quite different from other therapists I have worked with. She is keen on learning about my childhood, my day-to-day life struggles, how I handle different situations, how I react to them rather than deciphering my dreams and understanding them.

Although my dreams scare me, I feel a sense of familiarity in them. It's the same dream over and over again. Sometimes, Mae comes at me, other times the water drowns me. I feel like it's happened before, like there is something I am supposed to know, to recognize, but I don't. I take off my sweaty shirt, toss it to the ground and lay back in bed, watching the ceiling fan turn.

***

"We are the same age, I think. The way she spoke to me was kind of condescending to be honest. Like she thinks she's better than me or something," I say, looking down at the deep blue pool.

"She did get her PhD in finance at twenty-one, and I hear she has more than one PhD. She might be better than all of us," Plerng replies.

"Have you met her?"

"No, the woman rarely attends events— I met her sister once in Paris, Junta Cheng. Ugh... The way I would sell my soul for a chance to bury my head in between her legs."

I sigh, shaking my head. "Didn't you say the family gives you psychopath vibes?"

"Yes. But I love psychopaths. It never gets boring with them. So many hidden layers."

"You should try therapy."

"Is she hot?"

"I... I wasn't... paying attention, Plerng. It was an interview, for you know, a job."

"Oh, you were— Would you fuck her?"

"Plerng!"

"I'm just saying, nothing is as exciting as fucking a murderer."

"Stop calling her that."

"You're defending her now?"

"I'm not, just... just don't make assumptions about people."

Plerng lifts herself from the pool and sits beside me, staring daggers into my brain.

"Oh my, you dig Elina Cheng."

"No! Plerng, stop it."

"I'll stop if you look me in the eye and tell me she isn't hot."

I breathe a laugh, splashing the water around with my feet.

"She's not hard on the eyes, okay?"

"Meh!" Plerng teases, tickling me until I fall into the pool.

She jumps back in after me and we continue attacking each other with water, laughing. Warm afternoons in the pool with Plerng are some of my favorite moments. I've always found her careless approach to life freeing. Freeing from boundaries I have consciously or unconsciously set for myself. When I'm around her, it feels like an excuse not to hold myself accountable, not to be so grown. My phone rings and I swim out of the pool.

"Hello."

"Sawatdee krap, this is Toh calling on behalf of Khun Cheng."

I flinch, waving at Plerng and pointing at my phone.

"Khun Toh, sawatdee krap."

"Khun Cheng would love to offer you the job you applied for. Can you come in tomorrow? Just to sign some documents and familiarize yourself with the residence, how does Monday sound to begin?"

"Sounds good." I swallow, a big smile on my wet face.

"Thank you for the time, tomorrow at noon?"

"Yes, that's fine."

"Alright, thank you." He hangs up and I stare at my phone like it's a foreign object I have never seen.

"Well?" Plerng arrives, picking up her towel to dry her face.

"She offered me the job."

"Why do you look so shocked, isn't that what you wanted?"

I exhale, looking away from Plerng. I conveniently left out the part where Khun Cheng said she likes me when I narrated the whole interview to her. I have no reason not to tell her, but the words just wouldn't form.

***

I arrive at the Cheng mansion just before noon, and Khun Toh guides me to his office. A well-furnished, lavish office, classic and antique, matching the rest of the mansion's style. It isn't that different from Khun Cheng's office, which makes me wonder what exactly Khun Toh does for this family. Is he part of the family in some way? Or just an expensive employee? I take a seat across the table from him, and he hands me the documents, explaining the details. I glance through, there is an NDA attached, it's simple and easy to understand so I sign.

"I'll show you to your quarters, Khun."

"My quarters?"

"Yes, won't you be moving in?"

"No, I didn't realize this is a stay in job."

His creepy smile reappears as he nods. "I highly suggest you still bring some clothes and leave them in your quarters. Come along, I'll show you around."

He leads the way back through the hallway we came from, past the sitting room and up a wide staircase. The magnificence of the 1800s inspired decor captivates me as we ascend.

"This is the left wing." He points when we arrive at the top of the stairs. "Solely belongs to Khun Cheng. Please do not enter unless your presence is requested."

I nod and he continues down the right wing. I turn around, taking a quick look at the left wing. What does a person need all that space for? Is she like, allergic to people? The thought stays with me as we walk down the right-wing hallway.

"This is your quarters, Khun."

He opens a large door and we enter. It looks like an apartment. A modern, gray sitting room first, then behind it, what seems to be a mini dining room. To the right, a bedroom, thrice the size of my bedroom back home. It has a king-sized bed, walk-in closet, a bathroom with a tub and shower, stocked up shelves with toiletries, I stare in awe.

"My apologies about the lack of a kitchen, we can find a way to construct one if it's an inconvenience."

I chuckle at Khun Toh's words.

"Something funny?" he asks.

"I thought you were joking?"

"Why would I be?" He stares at me, confused.

I move to explain but chew my words. "Nothing. I will not be needing a kitchen."

"Very well, I will show you the common kitchen for this wing. Here is your key."

He hands me the key to my quarters, more like a presidential suite and heads for the door, I follow. We take a few more steps down the hallway and he shows me the kitchen.

"Free to use at your disposal, but we do have an in-house chef. He seems to have gone grocery shopping. I will

19

introduce you to him at a later date." He leaves the kitchen and I follow. "Cleaners are available four times a week but we have a stay-in cleaner for day to day keeps. Nong Hathai is in the middle of a lecture, so you won't be able to make her acquaintance today. Over there are her quarters and there is her library."

We walk past the library and I take a peek. Hathai is seated poised in front of a large screen, being tutored virtually at the end of the library.

"Khun Sutthaya?"

I turn at his call, and he gestures me forward to continue the tour.

For an hour, Khun Toh and I have toured around the mansion and its grounds. It's mind boggling how many rooms exist in this mansion, it won't be difficult to hide a body. There are multiple gardens and fountains, a massive pool that stretches on, a badminton and tennis court area. I don't think I will be able to remember ninety percent of this mansion by the time this tour is over.

***

Monday arrived quickly; I looked forward to it with bubbling enthusiasm. I have often wondered what the first child I work with would be like. I have so many ideas about Hathai, although we haven't met yet. Each time I think of her, lingering thoughts of Elina Cheng makes an appearance.

Po made me lunch for work which makes me feel like I'm in high school all over again. He seems proud to wave me goodbye on my first day of work, a positive way to start the day. My goal is to meet Hathai, get to know her a little bit, before deciding my approach with her. I do not have to be with her every day, but I am excited to spend every moment of my working hours with her, till I figure out just how to be in her life.

I arrive at the mansion and one of the housekeepers lets me in and escorts me to the music room. As we approach, I hear a beautiful melodious piano piece being played. He points and leaves. I take a deep breath, gripping my bag as I enter. Here we go, the first child I'll ever care for. I stop by the door, watching her play. She's quite skilled at the piano. After a few minutes she stops and turns to me.

"Don't hover, Khun?" She raises a brow.

"Witthaya Sutthaya, but you can call me—"

"Khun Sutthaya, let me just be clear. You're not here because I need an overpriced friend. You're here because the woman that is supposed to be my mother is a coward and a wuss. I could care less about what she thinks I need. So, I suggest you enjoy that free money you're earning far away from me." She turns back and continues playing. This is going to be an exciting child I think to myself as I sit on one of the cushions. "Excuse me? Did I not make myself clear?" Hathai says, not looking in my direction.

"You did, Hathai. Thanks for sharing your thoughts with me."

"Then why are you sitting?"

"Because I don't care what you or your mother think my role is here. I care what I think my role is."

"And what do you think your role is?"

"That's what I'll find out I guess."

She turns, glares at me for a few seconds, then springs up from her seat. Her steps towards me are bold with an attitude too brass for a twelve-year-old.

"Good luck with that."

She storms out of the music room. I let out a sigh. Scratch what I said earlier, this is going to be a tough child.

***

Three weeks have passed, and I still haven't been able to get through to Hathai. My intention was to take it as slow as possible, but at this point, we aren't even moving. She speaks four languages, plays five instruments, straight A's in her final year high school classes, genius runs in the family. She's always engaged, and yet she must be the loneliest child I have ever met, not a single friend and I don't think she hates it. She leans into it, excels at it. I also don't think she prefers it. How can you prefer a life when it's the only one you've ever known? I spend a lot of my time studying her behavior from a distance. In a way, it's given me a chance to see a part of her I might not have been able to get a glimpse of if she were so open. I believe beneath all that armor, is a very scared child, going through life alone.

In all my weeks here, I have not once seen Khun Cheng. There is zero interaction between mother and daughter. Each time I pass the left wing, I take a look, wondering what she could possibly be doing in there that makes her so distant, so unavailable, even to her own child.

I have so many questions about Hathai's background, and I can't seem to access anyone with the information I need.

Hathai's final class for today wraps up. She turns off her laptop, gets up and walks past me like she always does. I follow, like I always do. She walks straight to her room and slams the door in my face. It doesn't startle me anymore. I turn around and begin to leave. It's been a long day. I won't bother waiting for her to open up and share something with me, it hasn't worked in all the weeks I have been here and today, I'm a special kind of tired; worn out from constantly thinking, and not sleeping.

I turn into the stairs, feeling a bit nauseous. I swallow, pressing my head as everything starts getting woozy. I take a few more steps and before I know it, I begin to fall. I don't try to hold on to anything or catch myself, I just let it happen, falling and rolling until I reach the end of the stairs. Everything is a blur as I pass out.

THREE
AWAKE

Mae comes at me again with a knife, and I force my eyes open, panting as tears run down my cheeks. I can barely see; it still feels like I'm dreaming. I realize Po is hugging my trembling body and I squeeze tighter, my heart pounding in my ears. It's been so long since I've been hugged by him. He never lets me hold him, not since I was a child.

I shut my eyes and open them. It begins to dawn on me: this isn't my bedroom, the decorations are all different, I am still in the Cheng mansion. Wait. If I am still in the mansion—then—in whose embrace, am I in? I run my hands across the warm body. It's firm but soft; slender, warm, they smell—that scent! I jolt backwards pushing her away.

"Khun Sutthaya, it's okay," Khun Cheng says, reaching over and wiping the tears from my cheeks with her fingers. I throw my face away.

"What happened?" I ask in a tone that's almost a whisper.

"You passed out—more accurately—you fell asleep. That's what the doctor said. Would you like some water?"

She lifts a glass jug and cup from the bedside table and begins to pour.

"You didn't have to hold me like that, Khun."

"You kept crying in your sleep. I just wanted to help."

I keep my face hidden from her, dis-oriented and embarrassed. She hands me the cup and I bow slightly to thank her before receiving it, taking a big gulp.

"I better head home." I place the cup back on the table, then raise the comforter to get out of bed. She places

23

her right palm on my knee, my gaze falls to it, the warmth coming from her palm stills me.

"Call me Elina. And I don't think you can leave."

"Why not?" I lift my face to hers, getting a clear picture of her make-up free face for the first time.

Dear Buddha. She takes my breath away. Her eyes are softer without the eyeliner from the first time we met. There are a few beauty spots on her face; some freckles scattered along the upper part of her cheeks. Her lips, free of the bold red lipstick, now a soft pink tone that appears supple and soft as they curve up into a subtle smile. I catch myself staring and look away. She points at the bedside clock, and I turn to it. A little gasp escapes me at the sight of the time. It's a few minutes past 1am? What? It was just 4pm. I have been sleeping for nine hours?

"Would you like something to eat?" she says, removing her hand from my knee.

"Khun I—"

"Elina."

"Khun. I'm sorry about this, it will not happen again."

"Do not apologize, there is no need for it." She rises from the bed, revealing her full-length flower-patterned silk nightgown. It wraps around her full rich body perfectly, all her curve's protruding. "I was making some tomato soup. You will have some." Her arms drop to her sides and the long sleeves of the night gown's jacket do a little dance.

"No, thank you." My stomach growls and I fold my lips. She smiles at me again.

"I'll be in the kitchen then." She walks to the door and pauses. "I hope you don't mind; I changed your shirt; you were sweating a lot."

I don't move, my gaze remains fixed on her as she leaves. Once the door shuts, I hurry out of bed and race into the bathroom where a giant mirror hangs on the wall. I take one look at myself and cringe. I am a complete mess: dark circles under my eyes, my hair all roughed up.

I wash my face, brush my teeth and try to fix my impossible hair. I slowdown in my poor attempt at a make-over and take notice of her shirt hanging loosely on my body. Not surprising, she seems to love oversized work shirts. The

24

sweet jasmine scent from her shirt hits me, the same one from the office. I slowly dig my nose into my elbow, inhaling her scent. Something about her scent makes my body warm. It overwhelms my senses and causes a fog in my mind. I bite my lower lip and close my eyes, letting as much of it run up my nostrils.

***

This mansion feels like a haunted vampire castle in the dead of the night. It's eerie, quiet and cold. The sound of my footsteps are loud; though I'm slow and gentle as I walk to the kitchen. I arrive, and remain standing by the door, watching her move around with beautiful elegance and grace.

"You really do not have to do all this." I take a few steps into the kitchen.

"I'm just mixing things Phi Nam already made. It is not a bother at all," she says, her back to me. "White wine." She walks to the fridge and retrieves a bottle.

"No, thanks."

"I was not asking, Khun." She pops it open and begins to pour me a glass.

"Khun—"

"Elina. Sit please."

I walk to the mini kitchen dining by the window: a round wooden table as aged as this mansion with four seats. As I sit, she places the glass of wine in front of me and goes back to the stove. I leave my gaze on her. When she moves to the cabinet, I take a sip. It's sweet.

"You don't sleep much, do you?" She walks back to the stove after retrieving some plates.

"Not recently. I should probably call my father."

"I spoke to him. He was worried. I assured him you were in good hands. I also spoke to your fiancé, Lucifer."

I choke on my drink, spilling it over the table and her shirt. She walks over with a hand towel, wipes the table, then leans over and cleans off the spilled wine on my lips with her thumb. Her eyes on my lips make my cheeks warm. I feel like I'm in her office again for the first time, struggling to breathe.

"We should get you a different shirt."

"I... I'm sorry about this," I stutter.

"If you say sorry one more time..." She moves her gaze from my lips to my eyes, piercing through me. I lower my eyes to her lips and then look away. "Take off your shirt."

"What?" My eyes widen.

"I'll get you a new one, it's soaked."

"It's just a spill, I'll survive." I cling to it.

She scoffs and walks back to the stove. I watch her in silence. Her night gown flows behind her as she moves; like that of an English queen.

"Do you need assistance?" I ask.

"No."

I raise my brow at her sharp response and continue to sip my wine, stealing glances at her every now and then in silence.

Khun Cheng finishes cooking and serves the meal. After just taking a few spoons of her food, she opens a book and starts reading, sipping wine at intervals.

Every spoon tastes better than the last, I didn't realize I was practically starving. It doesn't take long for me to finish the meal. She slides me her plate, asking me to finish hers. I want to say no, call it a night, and return to my bedroom, pretend this night never happened. But my hunger is far from subdued, and I also like sitting across from her. Her presence is soothing, calming. Nothing is being asked of me, I don't have to pretend to be interested in small talk, and she's simply gorgeous to look at.

"Can I ask you something?"

She puts down the book, lifting her gaze to me. "Go on please."

"Aren't you too young to be Hathai's mother?"

"My ex-husband had her before we met. I adopted her after we got married," she replies. I nod and continue eating. "How is she doing?"

"She is struggling. But good. She thinks you're a wuss."

Khun Cheng laughs. "I know."

"Any idea why she thinks that?"

"Because I am."

"You don't strike me as one."

"What do I strike you as?"

"Not a wuss."

"Just because you think I am intimidating, doesn't mean I'm brave."

My forehead crinkles as I press my lips into a line. I've never met anyone who reads me as easily as she does. It makes me feel naked in her presence.

"You don't intimidate me."

"Then call me by my name."

"Elina."

I said it before I could even think, and as the word rolled off my lips, I froze. There I go, breaking my own rules, to prove to her my lie is the truth. Calling her by her name, so plainly, feels like crossing a line. Why is there a pressing need to impress her?

"Beautiful," she replies with a smirk, and rises from her seat. "Goodnight, Khun."

"Khun?" I ask.

"I'll address you formally, until you're comfortable with me addressing you otherwise."

I nod. "Thanks for dinner, it is delicious."

"You'll come to realize Khun Sutthaya—I am very good with my hands—in many ways," she says, standing by the doorway.

With a warm smile, she leaves the kitchen. I squeeze my spoon.

The room is dark; slightly lit by the moonlight streaming in from the floor to ceiling window. Elina sits in a corner, legs crossed. I can't see her face clearly, just her well defined body in a black pantsuit. She blows the smoke from her cigar into the air, and I tremble in anticipation of what she needs me to do.

"Spread your legs," she commands in a gentle tone. I obey. "You're already hard. I haven't even touched you. Don't you think that's a little... disrespectful?"

"Sorry... Elina."

She rises from her seat, heels clicking as she struts over to me. Her gorgeous face is now made visible by the moonlight. My shiver intensifies, making me wriggle in my tight bondage. I'm dying to be touched by her, to please her, obey her every command. She traces a finger from my lips down to my neck, spreading goosebumps all over my body. She reaches for my nipple and rubs it, I whimper quietly.

"I did not give you permission to speak, little slut," she whispers in my ear. Her tongue licks my earlobes as she presses my nipple hard, inflicting sweet pain. I moan a little louder, desperate for more.

I jolt from my bed, breathless and drenched in sweat. What was that! Was that a—a wet dream? I feel the wetness in my shorts. I throw open the duvet and pull my shorts open. It's soaked, and I am so hard. A wet dream at twenty-eight? What!

All I could think about last night after dinner was her. Her eyes, her lips, her hands. I guess I should not be surprised. I throw myself back into bed, a little bit ashamed, guilt stricken and shy. I shut my eyes, remembering her sultry voice from my dream as my body tenses up, heating up by the second. The crippling urge to masturbate surfaces.

I run my hands through my hair, taking deep long breaths to calm myself, but I'm too far gone. I slowly reach for my hard moist self, rubbing the already leaked cum all over it and begin massaging. I'm hot, pulsing, and extra sensitive. Every stroke feels like I'm thrusting into warm wetness. I try visualizing my favorite scenario, being bound and degraded while getting fucked. The pleasure kicks in and then her face shows up.

"Elina..." I whisper, stroking the girth of me. "Mo... Fuck..." *Say it wine, it's only in your head. She isn't here.* I visualize her spanking me against a wall, and the pleasure intensifies. I moan, grabbing the sheets and biting my lips as my knees shake. I want more.

"How hard do you want to be fucked?" she whispers in my ear.

I force my eyes open, breathing heavily. I cannot cum to her. She shouldn't be in my imagination? Maybe because It's been so long since I've touched myself or been with anyone. I can't even remember when last I was this aroused. I want to cum, my whole body is begging for it. But I cannot—not to her. She's my client, my employer. It takes everything in me to rise from my bed and opt for a cold shower instead.

***

My clothes were laid out for me on the sofa when I woke. I quickly slip into them and grab my bag. Thank God Khun Cheng rarely comes to the right wing, I am too ashamed to face her today. I need to go home and forget this morning ever happened. I throw the door open, immediately startled by Hathai sitting on the hallway bench.

"Hathai?"

She rises and hurries over to me. "Do you feel better?" she asks with glowing sad eyes.

"Y... yes," I stutter, surprised.

"Are you sick?"

"No."

"If you don't die, I promise I will behave better," she says, tears well up in her eyes.

FOUR
A FUNERAL AND A BELT

I watch the monks chant and pray, leading the hundredth day funeral service for Mae Noi Chaisuwan, Hathai's former nanny, whose existence I wasn't aware of until yesterday.

Everyone joins the monks in prayer, but my attention stays on Hathai, staring blankly at the picture of the woman who was once dear to her. Seated next to her, her mother, Elina—Khun Cheng. She is focused on her prayers.

I haven't been to a funeral in a while. Oddly, I find it comforting: the sadness that looms in the temple, the peaceful chants and prayer, the smell of incense and flowers. They all bring me a peculiar type of peace.

A week ago, Hathai found me passed out at the bottom of the staircase at the Cheng mansion. It must have been scary for her to see me like that. But only a day after promising to behave if I don't die, she went back to treating me like I'm invisible.

I don't think death scares her. I watch her place flowers and light her incense. Her movements are precise and fearless. I think losing people does. She's lost one of her parents, then her longtime nanny. That is a lot of grief for a child, I do not think she has even begun to process it.

And still, I think there is more—more I can't see, because she—Khun Cheng, never makes herself available to answer any questions. Today is the first time I have seen her since that night. Even when I'm not thinking about her, I am. The daughter and the mother are different sides of the same coin.

The funeral wraps up and we begin to exit the temple. It appears Hathai's former nanny worked for some of the wealthiest families in the country. The guests in attendance are all draped in black. Although simple looking with no jewelry in sight, you can tell those are expensive clothes. Different convertibles, and limousines, are packed outside the temple, waiting for the families, many of whom have formed small circles, sharing conversation that seem rather friendly.

I watch Hathai walk straight to her car, ignoring all the other children in attendance. When Khun Cheng steps out of the temple, everyone's gaze fall on her. Her face is plain and as beautiful as a sunflower field, illuminated by the setting sun. Grace radiates from her, she doesn't have to try.

Even in my current distaste for her, I am in wonder. It is not difficult to see the admiration and jealousy on the face of the guests who have come to say their final goodbye. Some whisper, some stare. Khun Cheng is highly regarded among the wealthy, it seems. She greets a few guests; short simple greetings, then walks to her car. I have not spoken to either Khun Cheng or Hathai today. Ironic, since Khun Cheng insisted I attend the funeral, only to keep me far away from them. They drive off and I turn to leave the premises.

"Khun Sutthaya." Khun Toh approaches. We both bow in greeting.

"Khun, I didn't see you inside."

"I was behind you through most of it." He smiles and I nod. "I'll drive you back to the mansion."

"That will not be necessary, I'm heading home."

"Khun Cheng insists you return to the mansion and spend the night."

"And she couldn't just tell me that herself? I was right there."

He doesn't respond, staring at me with no expression. I scoff, holding his empty gaze for a few seconds before walking to his car and slamming the door. My impatience is rumbling to the surface. For weeks I've had a lid over it;

trying hard to keep it contained. Now, I feel that lid slipping. We drive off, and I keep my eyes on the window, tapping my laps with a single finger, a bitter taste in my mouth as I grind my teeth.

"How long was she her nanny for?" I ask.

"Six years."

"That is most of her life. They must have been quite close?"

"Yes."

"How close was she with her late father?"

"Close."

I roll my eyes at his monotone responses.

"Any idea why Khun Cheng is so distant from her?" I ask, he doesn't respond. I huff, pursing my lips. "How am I supposed to do my job if nobody tells me anything? I can't help her if I don't have the tools. It's like fighting with the goddamn wall. Who am I going to tell? I signed a non-disclosure. I'm sick of it—she could be getting help right now."

I know he can hear the impatience in my voice, I am not trying to hide it, but I remain calm. He doesn't look my way, and the car goes back to being quiet. I go back to looking out the window, more pissed than before I started talking.

"They were extremely close," he says, "she and Phi Mae Noi I mean. They did everything together, including sleeping together. She was her best friend."

My anger begins to melt away.

"How did she die?" I ask in a mellow tone.

"In her sleep."

I exhale, closing my eyes for a second before turning back to the window.

"At least it was peaceful," I say.

"Khun, they did everything together, including sleeping together."

"Yes. Thanks for telling me."

"They were sleeping together the night Phi Mae Noi passed away. She died next to Nong. When we found them the next morning, Nong Hathai was still holding her," Khun Toh explains.

32

A chill of sadness travels through my body. I don't know what I was expecting, but it was not that. I can't make sense of it, the pain she must feel.

"And her late father?" I ask.

"I am in no position to discuss the late Khun Suwan with you."

I relax back into my seat with a loud sigh.

"If you want her to open up, you will have to find your way in. She really isn't as cold as she appears, neither is Khun Cheng. But there are things that they've been through, which I am not privy to share that has made it seem so. You will need lots of patience."

He looks at me through the rear-view mirror and shares a reassuring nod. I return the nod and go back to staring through the window, my unruly thoughts fighting each other for a chance to dominate my mind.

***

An hour later, we arrive at the mansion. I head straight to Hathai's quarters and knock several times, no response. She isn't in there, if she were, by now I would have gotten an earful for disrupting her peace. She must be in the music room, it's her favorite place in the mansion.

As I approach the music room, I hear her playing the violin, a rather chirpy piece for such a gloomy day. With small steps, I arrive at the doorway. She faces the floor to ceiling window, still dressed in her funeral attire: a short black gown paired with a coat and black fur scarf. Her ponytail is still neatly packed up. The light from the window pours onto her deep brown skin as she plays, a heartwarming sight.

I walk up to her slowly, taking a stand beside her. I keep my gaze out the window, letting the music run through me. She stops playing after a few minutes and joins me in silence. We stand, just looking. We can hear the breeze right outside the window. We can hear the birds in the trees. With the music gone, the mood now matches the events of the day.

"My sister died when I was five," I say. I like the silence, but I have a feeling she does not need it today. Neither do I.

"Do you remember what she was like?"

"No. I just remember crying a lot over her death."

"Men do not cry."

I exhale and take the seat beside her, hoping to get her to look at me, but she keeps her gaze out the window, turning her head further right to hide her face from me.

"You and I both know, you are too smart to believe that."

She lowers her head, gripping her violin tight.

"You can cry, you know? Or scream," I continue.

"Do you know how to play chess?" she asks after a minute of silence.

"Yes. But I always lose." I chuckle.

"I can teach you how not to."

"I'd love that."

She swallows and goes back to playing. I rest my back on the window, watching her. Each time she looks my way, I smile.

Exhausted from playing the violin for an hour, Hathai decides to retire to her room, and I escort her. She never lets me in, so I stand back as usual. She opens the door and takes only a step into the room and pauses. I wait, wondering if she might need something, but she doesn't speak or move. She remains still for a minute then turns around, walks back and hugs me, squeezing tight. Before I can return the hug, she breaks away and walks into her room, shutting the door behind her. I exhale. Progress.

A weight of fury settles over me as I stand watching the door. I take a deep breath and begin walking briskly to the left wing. I have had enough; she can't just hire me for a job and make it impossible for me to do said job. I arrive by the entrance and pause, remembering I'm not allowed into the left wing without her permission. I contemplate breaking her rule, pacing back and forth infuriated. I have so many questions, and I'm pissed at her for distancing herself from Hathai—from me.

"Khun," a voice calls and I turn, a bit startled. One of the housekeepers stands at the bottom of the staircase. "She's in her lower office," she says with a smile and walks away.

Her lower office? She has multiple offices? I rush down the stairs, bursting into the hallway. I can't quite remember the direction to her office, Khun Toh led me there the day of my interview, but it's been a month, this house is a giant maze.

I move through multiple passages, trying to find her office but I fail. I walk all the way back to the main entrance and use my memory to retrace Khun Toh's steps. I keep my focus on finding her office, but my thoughts keep racing with what I'll say when I'm finally standing in front of her. I have much to say, much more to ask, which one comes first? I turn into another hallway and there it is.

I knock on the door and push, entering at once. Khun Cheng comes out from behind a shelf, a book in her hand, still dressed in the attire from the funeral: a long-sleeved black shirt, plain trousers, her scarf loosely hanging around her neck. She's taken off her coat.

"Khun Sutthaya?"

Her voice elevates my anxiety, and my rush of anger quickly turns into nervousness.

"Khun Cheng, I need to talk to you about your daughter."

"We are back to the formalities, I see." She slides the scarf off her neck. "What do you want to talk about?" Her voice is so calm, it's unnerving. Makes me feel guilty for speaking in such a coarse tone. I pause, catching my breath, I wasn't expecting it to be this easy.

"Lack of empathy and cold, that's what you described her as. She is none of those things. She's just mirroring your behavior as a means of survival."

"I see."

I furrow my brows, making my anger more apparent. "What... what do you see, Khun?"

"That you're doing your job."

"Barely, we've barely spoken since I started working here, she won't share anything with me."

"And?" she replies, walking over behind her desk. I advance closer.

"And?" I squint.

"Khun Sutthaya, it's your job to figure out how to get through to her, not mine."

"You're her mother, you should be elated... eager to make my job easy, but instead you sit in your office— offices, and your left wing, ordering people around from the shadows, hiding. I am trying to help her, and you won't let me!"

"What exactly got under your skin? Me insisting you spend the night, or me in the left wing?"

"What? With all due respect, Khun, that's not what this is about, did you not hear anything I just said."

"I want you to spend the night because I know she'll need you. Believe me, she doesn't want me anywhere near her, especially in times like this."

"She's a child! You decide what she wants in this matter."

"So why haven't you barged into her life yet? You watch her, study her, like a book—waiting. What are you waiting for?"

"Khun—"

"I ask again, Khun Sutthaya, what are you so angry about?"

I take a step back from the table. She is nudging me towards something I can't seem to grasp, something I don't want to grasp. I know it's unprofessional to get angry at a parent this way, but why does she keep closing herself off to me?

"I just need you to be more open about her past and yours, that's all."

"Ok." She folds her arms. "What do you want to know?"

"Tell me about your late husband."

"He was a great father, Hathai misses him."

I chuckle. "That's not enough."

"Do you have any precise questions, Khun Sutthaya? Because I think you don't know what to ask, you don't know where to look. I think, you are angry at me for more than not opening up. Perhaps... me not making myself available to you?"

That condescending tone in her voice, speaking to me like I am a child, incapable of sorting through my own feelings.

"What?"

"From the shadows?" She leans over her desk, supporting her body with her fingers, holding me in her piercing gaze.

I swallow at the return of the nervousness. The room is suddenly warm. An unsettling tension looms between us. She leans back and her hands travel to her waist. I watch her unhook her belt and slide it off her waist. The sound it makes triggers a battalion of goosebumps across my body. She begins walking—slowly—towards me. With every step she takes, my breath quickens, my heart races. I let go of my bag and it falls to the ground.

"Sadist or Masochist?"

I'm thrown by the question. My lips part but the words do not form.

"Sadist?" she presses on. I step backward, holding her gaze. "Masochist?"

My gaze falters, and I look away.

She chuckles. "Beautiful."

I feel a knot tighten in my chest, it's been a long time since I have heard those words said back to me so casually, like they hold no weight, like they mean nothing.

"Both hands on the table," she commands. I don't move. I'm hesitant and unsure. "Now." She raises a brow at me like I am an insolent child. In obedience I turn, slowly, placing both hands on the table. "Lower yourself."

I obey.

"Lower."

I obey.

She runs her hand from my lower back to the middle. A shiver runs through me as she spreads her fingers. She shoves me lower and my chest and left cheek hits the table.

37

My hands knock over the books and papers, and they fly in different directions, making fluttering sounds, the only sound filling the room alongside my gasp.

One by one, she takes my arms and ties them behind my back with her belt. I squeeze my eyes shut, parting my lips to breathe easier. It hurts a little, a sensation I have missed dearly. I have no urge to stop her, from the moment she gave her first command, I felt my sense of control begin to slip from me. I let her tie me up.

When she is done, her hands travel up my back, caressing me. My body moves to her warm touch, quivering. My mind is blank, free of any resistance that might have lingered before. Her fingers slide up into my hair and she rubs gently, lowering herself behind me.

Today, she doesn't smell of cigars. I get a whiff of her jasmine perfume and feel myself throb in my trousers. She leans against my skin, her nose to my cheeks and sniffs, spreading her warm breath all over my cheek and ears.

"You've thought of me fucking you? Haven't you, Khun?" she whispers in my ear.

Her gaze catches mine, and I hold my breath. Her eyes are deep and enticing. They make me feel helpless. I have thought about them without cease, longing to stare into them again, and now, here they are, brown and stunning.

"You want to kneel before me. Feel the end of my whip. You want to know what I taste like."

I tremble at the sound of her voice, praying she doesn't take this any further. I cannot resist her, and I am not ready.

"What do you think your fiancée would think about all those thoughts you have of me?"

Her perfume makes me want to latch onto her, squeeze her, please her. I moan silently, praying she cannot hear my racing heart, it will give away my longing for her. I keep fighting to hang on to whatever shred of privacy I have. But Elina is in my head, occupying every thought, fucking with me.

She peels me off the table, and I stand, fixing my gaze on the floor. I cannot bear to look into those eyes that seek to claim me. She leans in closer, her breasts press against my chest, and my shoulders tense. She runs her hand across my back, sliding it down to the belt. As she unhooks it with her left hand, she lifts a finger to my chin and turns my gaze to her.

"On me," she says. I swallow.

Without breaking our stare, she unhooks the belt and takes it back, taking a step back. My eyes follow. I want it. By Buddha that is all I ache for in this second. I want to be tied with it, flogged by it, leashed with it.

"I'm not a home wrecker, Khun." She takes more steps backwards.

I rush over and pick my bag off the floor, sprinting to the door.

"Khun," she calls, I stop in my tracks, still trembling. I hear her footsteps and resist the urge to turn around and look. "Walk straight to your room and take care of that bulge before you implode," she commands, a calmness in her tone.

I look down at myself. A massive bulge presses against my light trousers.

I hurry to the door, pull it open and slam it as I leave. Walking briskly down the hallway, the sound of my pounding heart deafens me. I head straight for the exit. She doesn't own me, she cannot tell me what to do with my own body. This is a line, Wine, this is a line.

I reach the exit and push the handle, parting the door slightly when my body freezes. There is a force, something stopping me from pushing this door open and escaping. I need to leave and pretend this never happened. It should not have happened—nothing else can happen—that is the right thing. Instead, I turn and begin sprinting to my room in obedience.

I dash into my room, throw my bag at an unseen destination, and rush to my bed. I pull my trousers down, spit into my palm and take my hard dick into my hands.

All I want to do is cum.

I have no interest in enjoying the process, I just want to fulfill her command. I throw myself back into the softness of my bed. The smell of the lavender scented detergent, used by the cleaners for laundry still lingers. I cover my mouth with my palm to stifle my moans as I begin stroking myself steadily.

My eyes are squeezed shut; it all feels too much to leave them open. I keep stroking, quickening my pace, so much pleasure it's almost unbearable. I wriggle, squeezing my toes inside my shoes, moaning out loud into my palm.

"Elina... Mommy... please! Let me cum!" I beg with intense passion. My nipples tingle as my entire body burns.

"You wish," her voice whispers in my head.

I can smell her luscious perfume in my palm, it feels like inhaling an aphrodisiac.

"Please! Please!" I beg, stroking myself faster.

Breathless, I reach for a pillow without looking, covering my face with it and squeezing, allowing myself moan as loudly as I need to. I visualize her touching my nipple and nearly scream.

I just want to cum, but somehow, I am trapped in an unending cycle of pleasure. I press and massage the tip of my dick faster. Chills take over my body. I am a few minutes away from rolling over and finger fucking myself, nothing feels enough.

Everything in me is begging to cum, but there is a part of me that holds back. A part of me that doesn't want to give into what I want, there is a power tussle going on in my head.

"Please, Elina! I promise I'll be... I'll be good!" I beg desperately. "I won't do it again! Mommy, I won't!" I stroke faster. And finally, an intense orgasm.

I throw my pillow to the side, watching the creamy liquid splash out of me. It feels like I've been cumming for ages, my body won't stop pulsing and jerking. I moan to ease the intense pleasure, falling back into the bed.

Out of breath, I stare at the ceiling, exhausted, drained. Tears of relief and satisfaction begin to flow. I feel empty, a sense of guilt creeps in. I want to do it all over again, if it means I can feel all that rage again.

FIVE
THE INVITATION

"Rage?" Dr. Rueng asks.

I nod, lying on the sofa with one eye shut and a finger pointing towards the ceiling, playing around with a spider forming a web.

"That's an interesting word to intertwine with pleasure. Don't you think?" Dr. Rueng continues.

"That's how it felt. I was angry. Raging from the inside out." I turn to look at her, dropping my hand. "And yet... It was the first night I've had a decent night's sleep since I returned. No nightmares."

"Tell me more about her."

I sit up, dropping my head into my palm.

"She is... sometimes... she is like a blossoming flower at the peak of dawn. Beautiful, captivating, seizing every breath in your lungs. Other times, she's a blank piece of paper."

"Do you find that comforting?"

"It's uncomfortable. I've always been able to read people, decide where to place myself in their lives. With her... I just don't know."

"Maybe, that's why you are drawn to her?"

"I'm not drawn to her." I chuckle, relaxing into the sofa and throwing my head back.

"Ok. What do you think you feel?"

I let my thoughts wander in silence.

"I'm not quite sure."

I can hear Dr. Rueng's pen scratching the paper, but I don't turn to look like I always do.

"When was the last time you were dominated?"

I spring forward, shocked by her question. My submissive lifestyle was one of the first things I divulged to Dr. Rueng when I began sessions with her— More like she ripped it out of me, as if I had a sign stamped on my forehead that said submissive.

"Excuse me?"

"You heard me," she replies, unfazed by my reaction.

"I... I don't see the point to that question."

"There is a point to it, I promise."

"I have been with people, if that's what you want to know."

"You've had sex with people of course. But I mean, when last were you dominated? We both know for you those two things do not particularly mean the same thing." She leans forward. "Sex is just an act. Two bodies, stimulating certain areas of the body to achieve an orgasm. But being dominated. That's different. It requires skill, passion, attraction. It can be intoxicating, overwhelming, thrilling. You lose yourself to it, lust and desire consumes you..."

As she speaks, it begins to feel like I am in Khun Cheng's office again. A wave of heat rushes over my face, and the belt I so desperately craved appears in my mind's eye. My breath slows down as Khun Cheng's warm breath brushes against my ear. That smell of her perfume mixed with cigar. I gulp, exhaling slowly.

"You can't get enough of it, you want more, it ignites something in your soul. And when it's over, you crave it again. Like an addict. You think about it repeatedly, reliving every moment. Do you see what I mean, Nong?"

"Uh-huh," I reply, turning away from her.

"Your need for submission is a key player in unlocking so many hidden details about your life. It isn't something you should be hiding away from. After all these years working with diverse traumatic situations, I find that how a person chooses to explore sadomasochism is very telling, especially if they have a history with trauma."

"I'm not avoiding it."

"Okay, so, tell me about the last time."

I dig my nails into my palm as the thought of Phi Lamon, my previous owner, flashes through my mind.

The soothing sound of the ocean water, brushing against the yacht, paired with the subtle chatter from Lucifer and Plerng who are seated a few steps away from me, accompany the replay of yesterday's session with Dr. Rueng in my head.

In all my years of sitting across therapists, it was the first time I shared that part of my life in such grave detail, the first time I talked about Phi Lamon. I was hers only for a few months, but she changed me in so many ways, she was the opposite of her name in every way possible. Talking about her left me with a bittersweet feeling. I know Luce and Plerng are close, but they sound far away, an echo at the back of my mind as memories of Phi Lamon continue to float around in my head, dominating every single thought.

Lucifer invited us to spend the weekend on his yacht, a longstanding tradition of ours from university days. The ocean was where we came to focus on homework and projects, it was also where we came to party our hearts out and escape the bustle of Bangkok. As it seems, it still is.

With my eyes hidden behind dark sunglasses and my body spread across the soft big cushions, the sun warms my skin. I fell asleep a couple times and woke up without Plerng and Lucifer noticing, and once again, sleep is creeping back in. I'm shaken out of it by Plerng and Lucifer's loud laughter.

"Guys..." I call with a groggy voice.

"Wine, stop being a sloth and come drink with us," Plerng says, pulling my leg.

"Get up! Get up! Get up!" Lucifer rolls over, snuggling up next to me, tickling my sides and sniffing my cheeks.

One can say Luce is very touchy, I consider his love language to be physical touch. At every chance he gets, he curls up for cuddles. He loves holding hands, sharing kisses, he's huge on PDA. We met at a time when I had not fully come to terms with my bisexuality, and it was a struggle being around his overly touchy, fluffy self. It took me a year to get used to, and sometimes, I still feel like I am.

"Oh my God, Beam is getting married!" Plerng gasps.

"Braces Beam?" Lucifer asks, turning away from me and yanks Plerng's phone.

"She's marrying from the Charani family? Po would never let me hear the end of it."

"Maybe if you take over one of the companies like he wants you to, he'll stop breathing down your neck."

"Luce, I don't want to work, working is not something I aspire to in life. What I want is to live, travel, find the hottest woman on the planet, make her cum so many times she'd never want to leave, then make her have my babies. Who knows, maybe even become a suburban mum."

"Plerng at some point he has to retire."

"Then let him retire, we can live two lifetimes and not worry about money, and he can hire CEO's."

"He wants the business to stay in the family."

"He should have thought about that before deciding to have one child, it's unfair to put it on me."

"Don't you think that's a little selfish?"

"Luce, pull your head out of my father's ass for five seconds."

"Ugh," Luce mutters.

"That's gross," I concur.

"I need my friend, not my father's boyfriend right now."

"Ok ok ok, just... talk to him, okay? He's worried about you."

"When was the last time you guys had like, really great sex," I digress, sitting up.

"Last year in Dubai, she was a princess, about to marry, I think. The things that woman did with her tongue. I squirted— twice, overlooking a magnificent skyline. I don't think any woman has lived up to that since that day."

"I just asked when, Plerng."

"Your father made me call him daddy." Lucifer smirks.

"Ewww!" Plerng and I yell in unison.

"What! I like d—"

"Daddies with a heart of gold!" Plerng and I finish his sentence.

44

"We know Lucifer, we know! You never miss an opportunity to let us know," Plerng says, refilling their cups.

They go back to drinking, quietly enjoying the view.

"Doesn't anybody want to know about mine?"

"Wine, you've slept with about three people," Lucifer says.

"Oh, and Fern from sophomore year does not count, you didn't even finish." Plerng laughs.

I hiss and turn away, relaxing back on the cushions.

"Don't pout, Wine, let's say two and half if we throw in your hands." Plerng laughs harder.

I Ignore them.

"There is no shame in that. I actually regret ninety—seventy—sixty percent give or take of most of my sexual encounters."

"That's because, Luce, you'd sleep with anything that moves."

"Used to! Used to! Point of correction."

They continue to argue, their voice gradually fading, becoming background noise to my thoughts.

After a long day of basking in the sun, street food was the next thing on our minds. Lucifer isn't a fan of it, but Plerng and I are obsessed. We arrive at the night market, scanning through different food stalls; testing some to decide what to eat. The warm breeze, the smell of grilled food and sweets, and the buzzing chatter from the market ignites the children in us. With careless laughter, we stroll to a fish ball stand and the elderly woman offers us some to try.

I turn my gaze to my left, not precisely staring at anything as we wait for Lucifer to finish placing his order. At a distance, a small band of teenage friends move away from a stall and a woman appears, running her hands through her hair. My eyes fall to the bracelet on her wrist, it looks so familiar. I focus more intently on her, watching her turn to the man beside her. I catch a glimpse of her laugh from her side profile and shudder, my eyes widen in shock.

Without taking a moment to deliberate my actions, I dash towards her, pushing against the opposing crowd. I'm too scared to look away, I don't want to lose sight of her, so I keep bumping into people.

I can hear Plerng call my name, but I have no second to spare, I keep pushing on, towards the woman at a distance, picking up my pace, eager to reach her. Without looking, I crash into a trader moving items and everyone begins to yell at me. I look away from her for a split second to apologize, when I return my gaze, she's gone.

***

I arrive home worn out from the long eclipsing day. My steps are slow and weak as I enter the compound, carrying two plastic bags filled with street food. I bought way too much. I lift my head up and see Po watering the plants and my steps become even slower.

"Sawatdee Krap, Po," I greet with a wai.

"Witthaya, you look tired. Have you eaten?"

I shake my head, braving a faint smile then lift the bags to show him.

"I bought dinner, let's eat together."

"Alright. Go shower then, I'll wait." He smiles, returning his attention to his plants.

Still in disbelief of whom I saw today, or who I think I saw, I remain frozen, contemplating asking the question we have both chosen never to address. The question we both dread but continues to linger in our minds. But today, it flashed in front of my eyes.

"Po."

"Mhm?" he replies, turning to me.

Do I tell him what I think I saw? Do I ask him that daunting question? Anxiety and doubt creeps In and I look away.

"Do you need help?" I gesture to the plants instead.

"No. Go in and get ready for dinner," he says. I flash that faint pretentious smile again and move towards the door.

I enter the house, taking small steps into the passage with my head lowered, to avoid seeing the door at the end of the passageway Po and I have taught our minds to ignore. Every day I have walked past the same passageway, and every day the memory of that room has faded into a shadow, a shadow that follows us everywhere.

Standing in front of the door to my room, I ponder. By dawn will it go back to being a faded memory? Or will I still feel this weight? I know if I turn and look, I will walk to it, I might even try to open it. I should have never seen her today.

Did I really see her?

I push my door open and walk in.

***

Mondays. I love Mondays. They feel like miniature New Years. But not this Monday. This Monday, everything feels bleak. I couldn't get myself to close my eyes last night and now I have a headache. My body is worn out, too worn out to even think about the room at the end of the passageway.

The last time I was here, last Thursday, I had an orgasm in my palm to unholy thoughts of Khun Cheng. And as I step through the mansion doors, a daunting feeling of shame settles upon me. At least I won't see her today, she's never in the left wing. I climb the widespread stairs, looking through my emails, not minding my steps.

"Shit!" I drop my phone. "Khun Cheng." I swallow.

There she is, in the middle of the right-wing hallway, standing as if she's been waiting, dressed head to toe in a forest green ensemble. Her hair is packed up Audrey Hepburn style, revealing the stunning emeralds hanging on her earlobes. She walks towards me, her arms in her pockets.

"You're the jumpy type." She smiles.

I bend over and pick my phone. As I rise, my gaze meets her belt. It's the same one from the week before. I flush.

47

"Khun Sutthaya?"

I jolt up, swallowing hard and she chuckles.

"Khun Cheng, you are in the right wing."

"Yes. Not much flies past you, huh?"

I look away, wondering if I am visibly red.

"Had a book to retrieve from Hathai's library," she says.

"Right." I nod, fidgeting. "I'll be on my way."

Keeping my head low, I walk past her.

"Khun."

I turn at once at her call.

"Yes."

"This Wednesday, Hathai will be playing at the Thailand Classical Music Exhibition, you should come."

"Sounds exciting. Looking forward to it."

"Drop by my office later and pick up invitations, bring a friend."

"Y... your office?"

"Yes Khun. That's where the tickets are."

I nod and she walks away.

A sigh escapes me.

Her office? Not again, each time I'm there, common sense leaves me.

***

I make a move and Hathai shifts her gaze from the chess board to my face, the first time she's looked at me since we began playing. She stares at me for another minute and makes her move.

"Checkmate," she says.

My lips curve up into a smile.

"You are great at this."

"No, I'm just about average. Stop being so desperate to protect your king, makes you easy prey."

"I wasn't aiming to protect him too soon, I just—"

"But you do. In all the games. The reason I win all the time. It's so predictable. Not that I'm surprised. I had an inkling."

"About?"

"You are a very scared man."

I squint. "This is why you wanted to play with me, to study me?"

"Isn't that what you are doing to me?" She moves to arrange the chess board. "Someone wise once said chess is a road map to people."

"She does seem like the type to say that."

Hathai glares at me. "I don't mean the woman in the left wing."

"You mean your late father?"

Hathai nods and continues to arrange the game.

"I like scared people," she says.

"Why?"

"They don't pretend the monster isn't under the bed."

I nod, allowing another moment of silence to rest between us, unsure of what to make of those words.

"I'll be playing Ernest's Der Erlkönig on Wednesday at the Thailand Classical Music Exhibition."

"Wow, that's uh... That's an impeccable piece."

"I am an impeccable girl," she says drily. I smirk. "Will you come?"

"Yes, if you'll have me."

"Can you stand up and clap for me when I'm done playing?"

"Of course," I say, leaning forward. "I'm sure everyone will be on their feet. You play exquisitely."

"Another round?"

"Yes."

We go back to playing. It's the most conversation I've shared with Hathai since I began working with her. Although not much was said, every single sentence left me in a state of wonder, contemplating all my earlier conclusions on her and my approach.

The day rolled by as usual, escorting her through her routine, but it all felt lighter. I think a bridge has begun to form.

Taking a deep breath, I knock on Elina's door. In and out I say to myself, let's make this quick.

I enter, she is never one to answer a knock. Khun Cheng leans against the table with her hands folded across her chest, and her feet crossed. I'm quick to notice she has company. A man rises from the seat beside her. He's tall and broad, dressed in a fine dark gray suit, that's all I can see from this distance.

He leans into Khun Cheng and plants a kiss on her cheek. They whisper words to each other I cannot hear. They appear quite close. I have never seen any guests in this house, let alone around her.

He turns away from her and walks towards my direction to make an exit. We both exchange nods, acknowledging each other's presence. His facial features are strong and well defined, a sharp jawline and high cheekbones. I wasn't expecting him to be a foreigner. He looks French, maybe Italian, but certainly European. He smiles at me, his smile is quite a looker, sparkly white teeth to match his watery gray Eyes. He opens the door and leaves, and my eyes follow.

"Khun Sutthaya," Khun Cheng calls and I turn. She slides an envelope to her left side on the table and taps it. "Your invitations."

I nod and walk over, arriving just a few steps away from her. She isn't moving, or trying to hand me the envelope, so I just look on.

"Come here," she says in a soft commanding tone.

I hold her gaze for a few seconds before taking the first step, and then another, arriving just beside her. I swallow my rising excitement at the smell of her perfume. I stretch my hands to pick up the envelope, and when my fingers reach it, she slides her fingers over mine. I flush, incapable of moving away.

"You aren't sleeping," she says in the softest tone possible. Her fingers slide up and wrap around my wrist. She gently turns me towards her, leaning in so close, the scent of her shampoo travels up my nose. "Dark circles do not look good on you, Pretty Thing."

Pretty Thing? A pet name?

Though it's not mine to claim, my heart races at the thought of being addressed in such a manner. I gather the courage to turn to her, daring to meet her gaze. All her features are forcing me to throw my hands around her neck in tender embrace. She guides my hand to her neck, then her cheeks. Her skin is warm under my touch.

I take slower breaths, fighting the temptation to look down at her well-defined red lips. I know if I do, I'll kiss her. We breathe in sync as her eyes calm the storm in my ever-turbulent mind but sets my soul on fire.

"Tell me something about you," I say.

"What?" she mutters

"Anything. Just something."

Her gaze flutters to my lips and back to my eyes. Once again, I fight off the temptation to look at her lips.

"My favorite color is pink."

"Pink?" I quietly chuckle.

She spreads her legs, grips my waist, and repositions me in between her legs, pulling me close enough to feel her breath against my skin. She returns her hands to the table, leaning back a bit. I want them back. I want her hands on my waist. I want them on my body.

"Do it again," Khun Cheng demands.

"What?"

"Smile."

I flush, smiling without even trying. I slide my hands up her neck, then to her face. She lets me trace a finger over her jawline before lifting her face away from my palm.

"Your eyes are spectacular," she whispers, leaning in and placing her cheek against mine. Her warm breath caresses my ears, making me tremble. I let out quiet whimpers as I shut my eyes.

"Elina," I mutter, my voice shaky.

"Wine," she whispers, and tingling sensations spread across my skin.

SIX
THE PINK SUIT

I enter the car and shut the door, flustered from being so up close against her body in such an intense situation. My hands are sweaty and jittery. I gulp to steady my breathing, rubbing my forehead. I still feel her cheeks against mine. The smell of her sensational perfume, the warmth of her hands as she placed me in between her legs, the disappointment I felt when she rose from the table and walked away from the breath-taking moment we were sharing, taking her seat, as if our lips weren't so close to touching. The way she discarded me after she was done toying with me, thrills me.

I've never been attracted to people I cannot decipher, and she is way too slender. I have always preferred chubby cute people, with thick thighs and soft squishy tummies. Nothing about this insane attraction I have for Elina Cheng makes sense. She doesn't let me see any part of her, there is an invincible wall between us. She doesn't pretend it's not there, and I do not hate it. Maybe Dr. Rueng is right, maybe I'm drawn. But to whom? To what? I don't know her.

I let out a loud sigh, rubbing my nose.

"Khun?" the driver calls. I forgot his presence in the car. "Going home?"

"Ah! Sorry, Phi James, yes please."

He nods and drives off. I take out my phone as we drive past the mansion gates and put a call through to Plerng.

"Hey slugger! What's up?"

"Are you busy?" I ask.

"Never too busy for you."

"Can you take me shopping?"

"What! No way!" She laughs, the excitement in her voice causes a smile on my lips. "What for?"

"Some kind of classical music event. I'm guessing it's going to be very elite, sort of."

"Sounds fun, I hope to get paid in gossip. Meet me downtown, sending you an address." She hangs up.

"Phi, change of plans," I inform the driver.

***

"Sawatdee krap, Khun Kittibun," an attendant greets Plerng in a bow as we arrive at a private shopping outlet.

"Korn! You've lost the beard, good for you! Your chances of getting laid just went up." Plerng laughs. Leave it to Plerng to make everything about sex. "They are still low but no longer on the floor, good for you, good for you!" She thumbs him up.

"Champagne?" Another attendant walks up to us with two glasses of champagne sitting on a silver.

"Yes! The only way to shop is drunk!" Plerng says, lifting the glasses from the tray. She gulps down one and forces the other into my hand. "Drink! No excuses."

I drink it all in one go.

"Keep them coming," she says to the attendant.

The elegance of the decoration is outstanding for a place where only clothes are sold. The walls and ceiling are snow white, adorned with silver decorations. No surprise this is where Plerng would take me to shop, but I am starting to wonder if I can afford anything here without bankrupting myself.

One of the attendants rolls out a long train of suits and the fashion show begins. I try on different outfits so Plerng can help me decide what to wear.

"No!"

"You look like what would happen in a Benedict Cumberbatch and RuPaul fan-fiction with an omegaverse tag, take it off!"

"Oh my god, I have to wash my eyes now."

"Disgusting shit!"

From outfit to outfit, Plerng has found a problem, cursing out the design the minute I walk out the dressing room.

With about eleven outfits down and the champagne bottle empty, we are tipsy and losing all hope of finding something suitable for Hathai's performance. Another train of clothes arrives and I pull the first one off with a sigh, heading back to the changing room.

I take off the robe, unzip the suit bag and take the suit out, lifting it up. This is the one. I wear with a grin, it's well cut in every angle and fits like a glove. I hurry out from the dressing room and Plerng leaps to her feet with a loud gasp.

"Yes! Wine! This is the one! The way I'd go straight for you right now!"

I chuckle, taking a stand in front of the three-way mirror: admiring myself.

"Don't go overboard," I reply.

"No seriously, I'd totally fuck you in that. You look... so... fuckable."

"Thanks, Plerng, others would say handsome, but I'll take the F word."

"Don't be such a prude, Wine, just say fuck for once." She turns to the attendant. "This is the one, can we get a tailor to do some finishing."

"Of course, Khun."

"Can I get this in pink?" I ask, turning towards the attendant.

"That is not fuckable," Plerng graciously points out.

"Can I?" I ask again, ignoring Plerng's disapproval.

"Yes, Khun. The tailor would be right in."

"How much is this?" I inquire.

"Nine thousand dollars, Khun."

My jaw drops in disbelief. "Does the suit rob banks?" My eyes almost popping out of their sockets as I stare daggers at the attendant.

"Stop asking silly questions, Wine," Plerng says. "You really think I was going to let you pay even if it was one baht?" She waves off the attendant.

"Plerng, no way I'm letting you pay this much for a suit."

"You never let me pay for anything, let me do this for you, you deserve it."

"Plerng I—"

"Shhh, you're ruining the mood."

I smile and nod, turning back to the three-way mirror as I slide my hands over the suit's smooth surface in admiration, wondering if Khun Cheng would love me in it.

***

Plerng fixes her boobs under her dress and I turn my gaze away, tapping my knees. We are about to pull up at the grand center where the Thailand Classical Music Exhibition is set to hold.

"Breathe, Wine, you look great. Just a bunch of rich old snobs." She winks at me.

The limousine door flies open, letting in the loud chatter and flashing lights coming from the red carpet. Plerng steps out and I follow. The camera lights flash the nervousness out of me.

Although Plerng can come off as flamboyant, she is not one to crave attention from the masses, rarely ever attending elite social events. If it were not for me, she would not be here tonight, an event I have come to learn is held in the highest regard amongst Bangkok's high society.

As we walk into the spectacular auditorium, it only takes a second for me to realize I stick out like a sore thumb. Everyone is dressed in black, a sea of black suits and gowns. I turn to Plerng who is also conveniently dressed in black.

"This is a black-tie event!" I quietly scream.

"Of course. If it's classical, it's black tie," she says, I sneer at her.

"Why didn't you tell me! I'm in a freaking pink suit!"

"But you look stunning! Who doesn't love a rule breaker."

"Plerng! Are you kidding me?"

"Pipe it down, Wine, it's not a big deal. This crowd is so boring, they could use a little color."

I grunt, drenched in embarrassment.

"Khun Sutthaya," an usher calls as he approaches. It surprises me that he knows my name. "Sawatdee Krap." He bows and so do we. "May I have your invitations please, I'll escort you to your booth."

I hand the invitation over, he examines it and gestures us forward.

"We are getting the royal treatment here. A booth? A personal usher? Whose dick did you suck." Plerng eyes me.

I throw my face away, still reeling from the embarrassment of being the only one wearing pink. Plerng continues to spew ridiculousness as he leads us to our booth.

"Champagne." A waiter arrives.

"Leave the bottle, will you?" Plerng demands.

"Yes, Khun." He puts down the tray and leaves.

"To your left is the Chinese ambassador and his loser of a son. Beside them, second wealthiest woman in Asia two years ago. My point is, these seats are no joke, why would she put you in one of these?"

"I don't know, Plerng, she just gave them to me."

The waiter returns and serves us gold plated binoculars in a tray. Plerng picks one up, using it to look at me.

"What are you doing?" I scold, raising my hand to block her view.

"Trying to see things clearer since apparently, you are lying to me about something."

I lower her hand.

"Stop it."

"Wine, I'm not stupid. I don't know what's going on, but these are not the kind of people you want to fuck around with."

"Plerng, she just gave me tickets to her daughter's performance, it's not that deep. Probably thinks I'm doing an excellent job with her daughter or something, stop nagging me."

"She thinks you are doing an excellent job, so she gives you a seat that probably costs all your monthly earnings?" Plerng rolls her eyes. "If you say so. I'm just going to enjoy the view and this champagne until the shit fucking drops."

"Oh my God, Plerng! Can you not swear for like five seconds?"

"Now why the hell would I want to do that?" she snaps at me.

I sigh and my eyes wander across the auditorium in search of Khun Cheng. Everyone is still trying to take their seats so it is a bit rowdy. I find her and my lips curve up into a little smile. Using my binoculars, I aim to get a closer look at her. She sits elegantly, alone in her booth, her eyes fixed on the empty stage.

Her hair is slicked to the back, tucked behind her ear to unveil facial curves that appear to be sculpted by God themselves. Her black pantsuit is well-fitted but does her curves no justice. Most days, her make-up is bold: black eyeliner and eyeshadow, a darker shade of red-lipstick, thick brows. But not today. Today she chose a subtle rosy glow. I like it. Though if Khun Cheng painted her face with chalk, I have a feeling I'd like it too.

She lifts her wine glass to her lips, taking a sip and my eyes fall on the gold cufflink on her wrist. They are lined with diamonds, and in the middle, the letters EK are written in unique fonts.

She gulps, lowering her glass then flexes her jawline. I flush, biting my lower lip. Then pulls out a handkerchief and daps her lips. I swallow. I have thought about those lips every second since the moment we shared in her office two days ago. Imagining what it would feel like to be kissed by her. How her tongue would feel against my neck, her hands

57

touching my naked body, her breast on my back, her scent all over me like a stamp of ownership. I have thought about what pain would feel like under her, if I'm capable of pleasing her to her standards.

I adjust my tie and lower my binoculars, steadying my breathing.

The light dims, signaling the beginning of the event and the curtains roll up to unveil a full orchestra, all dressed in black suits and gowns. Right in the middle, Hathai.

The first two pieces are played, but I have struggled to pay attention. I keep fighting the urge to just stare at Khun Cheng. She has not looked my way once; I know I'm impossible to miss in this pink suit. Maybe she just doesn't care enough to look, but I wish she would. I'd love to smile at her from a distance, like in the movies.

Hathai comes forward and begins her solo performance. For such a difficult piece, she makes it look too easy. I glance over at Khun Cheng and somewhere on her blank face, there is a sense of pride.

Hathai finishes and I spring up from my seat clapping before I realize.

"What the fuck are you doing!" Plerng screams quietly.

The whole auditorium turns to me. I am the only one clapping. Slowly, I sink back into my seat, looking over at Hathai. She smirks and walks back to her seat.

"I need the ground to swallow me," I mutter as Plerng struggles to keep her laughter under wraps.

"Everyone knows you don't clap until the final performance you dweeb," Plerng mocks, more laughter taking over her.

I roll my eyes and look over at Khun Cheng's booth and she's gone. I hope she left before I embarrassed myself.

After three long hours, the performance ends, giving way to exchange of pleasantries. Hathai approaches with a smile on her face I have never seen before.

"Thank you for clapping," she says upon her arrival.

"That was not fair."

"You shouldn't believe people so easily, another reason you always lose at chess."

"That was your way of teaching me a lesson?"

She shrugs, turning her gaze to Plerng.

"This is my best friend, Plerng Kittibun. Plerng, Khun Elina Cheng's daughter, Nong Hathai."

"I know your father," Hathai states.

"Who doesn't, he's always in the news. You play wonderfully, Nong."

"I know."

"A little thank you wouldn't hurt, Hathai," I say, raising my eyebrows at her. She throws me a look, and I start to think she might just roll her eyes and walk away.

"Thank you," Hathai replies, bowing to Plerng.

"You're welcome," Plerng smiles.

"You're wearing pink," Hathai states, turning to me.

"Yes." I nod.

"It's ugly."

"Very thoughtful words."

"Goodnight." Hathai turns and leaves, escorted by her security and one of her caregivers.

"She really doesn't like you," Plerng says.

"On the contrary, I think she does."

"I'm going to go find myself a pair of boobs to bury my head in. These events are usually crawling with depressed closeted lesbians, and I need to get railed."

I chuckle. "You are such a needy bottom."

"Yes! Thank you very much, I'm quite proud of that— You know Wine, this bottom phobia thing you have going on is not cute."

"I'm not... bottom phobic."

"Yes you are! You always have to make it clear you aren't a bottom when you ooze bottom energy,"

"What does that even mean?"

"I wonder why you care so much though, no one else does—"

"Khun Sutthaya," an usher interrupts us, saving me from Plerng's grilling words.

"Yes." I turn to him.

"Apologies for the interruption. Khun Cheng requests your presence."

I smile impulsively before taking notice of Plerng, side-eying me. For a few seconds, we share awkward glances.

"Be right back," I say, stepping away with the usher, not looking back to avoid catching Plerng's judgmental stare.

When I finally turn, she is already engaged in a conversation with a woman. I scoff.

***

The usher leads me through the hallways of the conservatory. My eyes feast on the beautiful architecture. The building is home to some of the best musical and dance talents in the country. In some areas, pictures of multiple competitions, won around the world and locally, hang. We walk past multiple rehearsal rooms and finally arrive at a door labeled piano.

The usher knocks on the door and opens it. We are greeted by the melodious sound coming from a playing piano. I step in and the door closes behind me. I stand, watching Elina play for a few minutes, then she stops, rises from her seat and turns to me.

"You play wonderfully, just like Hathai." I smile.

She slides her hands into her pockets. I like when she does that. Her steps are slow towards me, the sound of her heels clicking against the marble ground fills the room.

"Why did you do that?" she speaks in a deep tone.

"The clapping? I apologize, it wasn't... Hathai—"

"You're wearing pink," she interrupts, arriving a few inches away from me.

I look over at myself.

60

"Yes I—"

She pulls me close by my jaw, our noses almost touch. I shudder, eyes wide. She shuts her eyes, breathing heavily, her grip tightening. I feel her hands tremble on my skin. Her warm champagne scented breath caresses my lips.

Slowly, I lift my hands and squeeze her suit, fighting the intense desire to kiss her, pull the clothes from her skin, run my hands across her chest, and beg her to have her way with me.

"You. Are. Driving me insane," she says under unsteady breaths. "If you want me." She opens her eyes. "Earn it. Do not. Manipulate me." Khun Cheng pulls away.

I blink uncontrollably, my breath labored. What does that mean? I'm left bewildered, jittery and desperate for her touch again.

"Don't ever wear pink again without my consent, do you understand?" she commands.

I gulp and nod in agreement. She walks past me, heading for the door.

"Khun Cheng," I call. She stops with her hands on the door knob. "I'm not gay."

She turns to me and her once fierce gaze is now calm and soft.

"You... Make me feel..." I pause.

"Feel what?"

"Everything," I confess.

We hold each other's gaze as the minutes fly by in the quietness of the piano room. I look down at my shoes.

"Isn't that what you want to hear? What else do I need to do to... earn it."

She remains silent and I begin to think I should not have spoken. I didn't plan to. It's too soon. She must think I'm—

"Hungry?" she cuts into my thoughts.

"Yes."

"Walk with me."

She pulls the door open and walks into the hallway. I follow, walking a few steps behind her. She carries herself gallantly, walking like she owns the building—maybe she does, it won't surprise me.

We walk across multiple hallways, different people bow to greet her, she returns the bow or simply nods. It is fascinating to see how people react to her presence as she walks past some of the wealthiest citizens in the country. The stares are filled with respect, jealousy, admiration. I'm sure no one notices me following behind.

She leads me out of the building, past the flashing camera lights, and straight into her waiting limo. The driver takes off the second the door is shut.

SEVEN
JUST ONCE

Since we left the conservatory, Elina has said nothing to me. Her attention has remained on her iPad, typing and scrolling.

"Khun Sutthaya," she calls, I turn to her.

"Yes."

"At some point tonight, I am going to kiss you. And I will not stop there."

I stare at her, speechless.

"Ok," I manage to say, and she turns her attention back to her iPad.

We arrive at Veus, an exclusive, upscale hotel in the heart of Bangkok. I have driven past it multiple times, fifty flights of steel and glass. At the entrance, staff members line up, bowing to greet Khun Cheng as she walks into the building.

"Welcome, Khun," a round, stout man greets with a bow. "Everything is in place, and the guests are waiting." He walks alongside Khun Cheng while I walk behind, giving them room to talk. "Will you be needing anything else, Khun?"

"No, thank you, Aat," Khun Cheng replies, still not looking away from her iPad.

The man presses down the elevator button and Khun Cheng walks in. I follow. He and the other staff members bow to her again as the elevator doors shut.

I stand beside her, watching her swipe through endless rows of documents. She signs some and keeps swiping. I can't help but wonder if she is going to kiss me here. I have never been kissed in an elevator; it's a little fantasy of mine. I smile at that thought. She should have never told me she'd kiss me tonight, now all I can think about is when.

The elevator dings and opens, zapping me out of my thoughts. Another set of employees, already bowing to her as we step off. Her eyes stay fixed on her iPad as she walks past them, I follow behind her. Behind me, the rest of the employees. She arrives at the end of the hallway and stands in front of a tall gold-plated door. An employee swipes a key card, and the door opens.

"Wut, don't you and your staff have anything better to do than follow me around?" she says to one of the employees who seems to be a manager.

"Sorry, Khun Cheng. We just wanted to welcome you properly, it's been a while since you visited."

"I'd feel a lot more welcome if you all were out there making our clients feel welcome," she replies, calmly but authoritatively.

"Of course, Khun." He bows and turns to leave with the rest of the staff.

Elina holds the door open for me, and I walk in. My eyes travel across the exquisitely furnished penthouse with an impeccable skyline.

"Your room is this way," she says, turning to the left and leading the way. We walk into a master bedroom, artfully arranged and dimly lit. "Change, eat. I'll have someone come get you in an hour."

She turns and I watch her leave.

It is already past 8pm, where could she possibly be taking me? I thought this would be the part where she'd finally kiss me---or ask me to kiss her. I turn my attention back to my room and find a black suit laid out on the bed. I run my hands over it and lift it up. The tag says Armani.

A quick change later and I'm seated in the dining room, with different meals laid out in front of me and no appetite, just nerves.

A knock comes at the door, and I hurry to open it. I'm met by the smiling face of a female employee.

"Sawatdee Kha, Khun." She bows and I return the bow. "Khun Cheng sent for you."

"A moment please." I walk back in and retrieve my suit, sliding it on as I walk back to the door.

We start down the hallway and head into the elevator. The door closes and I intertwine my palms, nervous and curious about what awaits at the end of the elevator's descent. The elevator dings and the doors open. We walk off and arrive at a large black door. She opens it and leads me in.

I step into a mini hall with everyone seated, and a man addressing the audience, standing on a podium, with a large screen behind him.

"Going once, going twice. Sold! To Mr. Ricardo," he says in English.

Everyone claps.

It's a private auction from what I can tell. I take a seat behind and watch the bids come and go. It does not take long to realize what is being bid on isn't art or rare jewelry but rather buildings. Some, I've seen in the city. I cannot see much except the silhouettes of people in attendance, the only place illuminated is the podium. To make a bet, attendants raise their glow in the dark sticks

A bell rings and everyone rises and begin pouring into another room by the left. Khun Cheng is nowhere in sight. I rise from my seat, glancing around as I walk towards the podium. I see her standing up front, having a conversation with an elderly man. I stand back and wait. They exchange bows and he continues into the next room, she returns her attention to her iPad and I walk over.

"Interesting event," I say as I arrive in front of her.

She turns to me.

"You look good in Armani," she replies.

A coy smile forms on my lips.

She takes a few steps closer, leaning in. This is it; she is going to kiss me. Excitement rushes through me at the thought. She lifts her left hand to my shoulder, I gulp, my eyes following her lips. She brushes off some lint and leans back. I exhale.

"Come on." She leads the way into the next room.

It's an after party. Not the kind Lucifer and Plerng have taken me to in the past. This is sophisticated, gentry, made for a certain class of people. The type of people you never see in tabloids. Gentle laughter and the vocals of a soprano singer fill the air. Cigar trays are being moved around with tall glasses of champagne.

"Mingle," she simply says with a smile and walks away before I can protest.

Mingle? Is she kidding? I don't know anyone here. Even in an Armani, I am obviously an outcast.

She walks to a table with five guests. I recognize one of them, the foreigner from her office the other day. He slides his hands across Khun Cheng's waist. I squint and swallow. They exchange air pecks before he pulls her seat for her.

I turn and walk to the bar, not knowing where to place myself in such a classist environment. My gaze stays pinned on her. It's easy to see how quickly the table swoons over her. She laughs and they all laugh, when she turns to something, so do they. She sticks a cigar in her mouth and Mr. Foreigner lights it for her. What a simp. I roll my eyes and turn around.

I should take Plerng's advice, back away from whatever this is, it's the smarter thing to do—But at least once, I'd love to know what her lips taste like, what it feels like to be kissed by her. It will only happen once. How wrong could that be?

I order a glass of white wine.

"Sawatdee krap," a young feminine man with bubbly eyes, and a little too much hair gel approaches with a wai.

"Sawatdee Krap," I return the greeting.

"Only losers hang by the bar," he says.

I chuckle. "Interesting."

"Come join our table, all the good stuff is over there."

"Uh... I err..." I turn my gaze to Elina's table.

"Don't worry, she sent me."

"Elina?"

"Khun Cheng—yes. You call her by her first name? No one calls her by her first name. How did you two meet?"

"She's a client."

"A working man? That's new." He smiles.

"I'm sorry, that came out wrong."

He raises a brow.

"I'm not an escort," I clarify.

"Of course. Escorts are not Khun Cheng's type."

I lean off the bar, straightening myself. "What's her type?"

"Men who don't have to work to earn, if you know what I mean."

I nod. "Right."

"So, join us?"

"What's your name?"

"Thawit."

"I'm Witthaya, but you can call me Wine."

"Pleased to meet you. Now come along, she'd hate to see you moping around."

We both chuckle.

I follow him to his table, it is a circle of young fabulously dressed people, playing card games while smoking enough cigarettes to cause a heavy fog. The table is littered with scotch glasses and money. Two of the men seated seem to be digging for gold in each other's mouth, kissing like it's their last day on earth. They all welcome me cheerfully, then subject me to a game of fuck or kill with the attending guests. I'm quite sure Plerng would love this game, right up her alley.

At first, I would turn over to catch a glimpse of Khun Cheng every minute, but now, after an hour with the most talkative people on the planet, and four glasses of scotch, I am all talked out and too tipsy to care.

I step away from the table and stagger to the balcony. The fresh air, a wonderful break from the stuffy, foggy table. I lean over, taking a deep breath as I close my eyes for seconds, opening them up with an exhale. The beautiful skyline of Bangkok laid out before me. What a wasted night.

"Not going to jump, are you?" I hear Khun Cheng say.

She walks up beside me. I don't bother looking in her direction. The skyline has not treated me like a sculpture all night.

"You are a busy woman, Kh... Elina," I say with a sigh.

"Selectively," she replies and puffs smoke into the air.

"Why did you bring me here tonight?" I turn to her, a bit dazed.

"You looked stressed; thought you could have some fun."

I scoff and turn away.

"Unless you have other theories." She leans on the railing.

"You like that don't you?" I return my gaze to her and our eyes meet. "Making me wait, pinning over you from afar like a lost puppy."

"I do like to be admired. But that was not my intention tonight. I thought you'd have more fun without the unending clamoring of business talk." She puts the cigar back in between her lips and sucks, then blows the smoke away from my face. She moves to search for a trash can to put out the rest of it.

"Wait," I stop her. "Let me try."

"Cigar? You won't like it."

"That is for me to decide, isn't it?"

She smirks. "Have you ever smoked before?"

"No."

She laughs and moves closer towards me. Gently, she sticks it in between my lips. The second the smoke hits my lungs; I cough and my eyes fill with water. It's bitter and uncomfortable. She grins as I go in for a second one, sucking in the bitter smoke and releasing it from my mouth with a soft cough.

I try again, sucking slowly. She pulls it away and brings her lips to mine. I exhale through my nose; she isn't sparing me a chance to breathe. She drops the cigar and throws her hands around my waist.

Elina kissed me. Dear Buddha, she kissed me.

Her lips feel exactly how I imagined them: firm but soft, bitter from the cigar but also minty. Her kisses are deep and intense, triggering goosebumps and warmth across my skin. I let her movements guide mine, sinking into the warmth of her embrace.

She takes off my suit jacket, tosses it to the ground and moves to my neck, pushing me against the wall behind the curtains, away from the view of the rest of the guests.

Elina is a selfish kisser; she claims each lip with much vigor and infects me with devilish lust. I can't think straight as she runs her hand through my hair, pulling and inflicting sweet pain. Her hand travels down my neck and squeezes my chest. My skin is hot and sensitive all over. She begins unbuttoning my shirt as I moan in her ear. I am not one to have sex of any type in public, but if she wants to, I'd let her.

Her warm hands caress my bare skin and I bite my lower lip in an intense shiver, letting out a soft moan and holding onto her waist. She takes my lips back in her warm mouth. I guide her hands to my ass, and she squeezes, pressing me hard against her crotch. I break away from the intense kiss to moan.

She returns to my neck, rendering kisses while her right-hand journeys back to my chest and finds my left nipple and squeezes. I gasp, hot pleasure surges through me.

"Khun Cheng," a voice cuts in and I shudder, pulling away.

She smiles at me, her body blocking the view of the man behind her from seeing my half naked self.

"Yes, Toh," she replies, staring intensely at my lips while I watch her chest rise and fall as she catches her breath.

"The governor is here." He clears his throat.

"Tell him to wait."

"Khun I—"

"Tell. Him. To wait," she repeats, making my nipple tingle.

"Yes, Khun."

I hear his footsteps walk away.

"You should prob—" I try to speak but she shuts me up with a tender kiss.

She tilts my head to the left and sucks on my earlobes. I moan.

I kiss her again, rubbing myself against her, desperate to feel her naked body against mine, to touch her bare skin, fondle her soft breasts. I reach for her button, and she stops me, pulls away and lifts my palm to her lips, kissing it. She leans against my cheeks, kissing me and I close my eyes. The soft kisses are warm and sensational.

"I left something on the bed. Put it on and wait," she orders, then looks into my eyes. I nod in obedience. She kisses me again and turns away. Without turning back, she returns to the private club, leaving me hard, shirtless and red.

This will be the last time. I'm crossing so many lines letting this go on—just this once.

***

A silk robe and shorts paired with silk socks? That's it? It looks like I am about to go to bed! Nonetheless, I take a shower and slip them on.

It's been well over an hour since she asked me to wait, it is almost 1am. I have walked round the penthouse several times, replaying our moment on the balcony, eager to continue. The impatience has begun to wear me out. I want to end it all today, come sunrise, this should all be over. I will have her out of my system for good.

If Elina isn't going to show up, I should go lay on her bed, I'm sure it's covered in her scent. No wait, she has not laid in it yet. She's also touchy about her space. I sigh. I really want to. I walk to her room and place my hand on the doorknob. The main door opens and I run back into my room at the speed of light.

I jump into bed, pull the duvet over my body, and squeeze my eyes shut. A few minutes later, the door to my room opens and the sounds of her footsteps follow. She lifts the duvet and slides under. The strong smell of cigar on her clothes travels up my nose, and my body remembers the sensations I felt on the balcony, as if under command.

"I apologize for being late," she says.

I pretend not to hear, leaving my eyes shut. She readjusts and her warm breath brushes up against my nose, triggering more arousal and commanding goosebumps. Her fingers gently move the hair away from my face and I struggle not to move.

"Please, open your eyes," Elina whispers.

I hesitate, taking a moment before opening my eyes and meeting her soft tired gaze. She smiles and I smile back, completely taken by her gracious beauty.

"You're so adorable, Khun Sutthaya."

"Call me Wine—but only for tonight," I say, she smirks.

"You don't want anything to do with me tomorrow?" she says, making my heart flutter.

She is the adorable one.

She leans in and softly kisses my lips, sucking the lower lip then the upper one before burying her nose into my cheeks, sniffing me. I inhale deeply, every scent of her.

"Your eyes haunt me," Elina whispers and I exhale a quiet laugh.

"Why?"

She stays still for a moment then lifts her face off my cheeks and climbs over me.

"They are captivating." She stares into my eyes.

How can she say that, she hasn't stared into them long enough.

Elina unhooks her belt, and my eyes follow, staring at her hands, waiting, anticipating.

She is slow, never taking her eyes off me. I offer her my wrist before she even demands it and she smirks, satisfaction in her eyes. She ties me up and hooks it to the bed panel, then sits back, watching me as the seconds fly by. She stretches her hand and caresses my cheeks, rubbing my lips with her thumb.

"Can I bite you?" she asks.

I swallow. "Yes."

"At any moment you want me to stop, your safe word is cross."

I nod.

"Please say the word."

"Cross," I mutter with a smile, she smiles back.

"Shut your eyes."

I obey, gulping.

She blindfolds me with a piece of clothing I had not seen earlier, then lowers herself to me. I part my mouth to welcome her lips as they brush against mine. In desperate thirst, I move for a deeper kiss, she pulls away, getting off me. I suck my lips in between my teeth instead.

She walks out of the room, leaving me to lie in wait, bound and blindfolded. My imagination runs wild with ideas, things I hope she does to me though I know I'm not entitled to anything. I am not hers, I might never be hers.

The sound of her footsteps re-entering the room sends shivers across my body and silences my thoughts.

She kisses me deeply, sucking my lips delicately, her tongue caressing mine. She pulls away and before I can ask for more, takes my sensitive nipple into her mouth, I gasp a deep moan. She licks it, continuously flicking it with tongue while her free hand plays with my right nipple, squeezing and pressing. When she pleases, she bites my nipple and I shake at the sensation

"Elina..." I mutter.

She frees it. Before I can breathe, she whips it. I stifle a loud moan. It doesn't hurt, it tingles and so do my feet for some reason. She whips it again and then my other nipple. I whimper. She whips my upper groin area, then my thighs. I lick my lips and exhale.

Harder Elina, please!

She bites my nipple again, it hurts more than the whipping, a different kind of pain I've not experienced before. The more she bites all over my chest, stomach and thighs, the more claimed I feel, slipping deeper into a submissive headspace. She bites, she kisses. She bites, she sucks. And then it comes, a painful whip on my groin that sends me spiraling with pleasure, I moan out-loud in ecstasy.

She whips every sensitive region of my upper body, descending to my waist and continues, draining me of any form of control I have left.

It all stops, and she runs her soft hands all over my trembling thigh, ascending towards my groin. She spanks me right on top of my groin, making me cry a loud moan. It is an intense feeling that sends me spiraling with desire. She does it again and I continue shaking, burying my face in my arm. Her hand slides into my shorts, gently grips my hard erection at the base and slips it out.

My heavy breathing does not help with the overwhelming sensation of having the tip of my cock rubbed and teased by Elina's warm hands. She is slow and gentle with me, pressing my tip when she plays with my balls. A feather-like item begins tickling the tip of my cock, immersing me in the kind of pleasure that travels everywhere.

I moan and groan, biting my lips and shaking my legs, struggling to keep still. She spanks my thigh each time I try to move away to collect my senses, and I move back into place. It is an endless cycle of being pleasured to the edge, and then dragged back to the beginning, moaning and reaching for an orgasm that will never come. Tears begin to pour down my cheeks amidst the intense pleasure, a substitute for my lack of release.

"Elina, p... please, let me cum," I beg in between breaths, wriggling.

Ignoring my plea, she continues driving me crazy with the feathers then gives my dick a little suck. I cry harder. She drives me to the edge once more and stops, pressing the tip of my cock and kissing my waist, biting me, and softly stroking me. Her bites and kisses travel down to my thigh, she licks me and bites some more, harder. I wince and she takes my dick into her mouth, sucking it tenderly as I cry and shake.

She stops, let's go of me and leaves the bed. I can only hear my heart pounding inside my trembling, sensitive body. For a few minutes, she is gone. Out of nowhere, she unhooks me, takes off the blind fold and pulls me into a hug. I cry some more into her shoulders, squeezing her, soaking her silk robe.

"I want more," I demand amidst the tears flowing freely down my warm cheeks.

"That's enough for today," she replies and kisses my cheek.

I pull away to look into her warm, care filled eyes. It calms me, makes me feel safe.

"You won't let me cum, would you?"

She kisses my lips softly. "Do you really want to?"

I look away, feeling sort of ashamed.

"No." The tears come again.

She pulls me back into a hug, patting my back.

"It's okay," she says and for some reason, I cry harder.

EIGHT
SHATTERED

My eyes part as I wake, squinting to adjust my sight to the fairly lit bedroom with a stretch, letting out a soft purr. My body is sore but rested. It was a nightmare free slumber. I remain in bed, staring at the skyline with an empty mind for minutes and minutes.

Sluggishly, I lift my body and find Elina sitting on the long sofa in the center of the room, dressed prettily in a free-flowing ox-blood red gown with her hair packed up in a ponytail with a similar colored ribbon.

Her attention remains on the book as she flips through the pages. I like this view of her. I don't say a word. I won't be the reason the elegance of this moment comes to an end.

She exhales and raises her gaze towards my direction. Seeing I'm awake, a little smile forms on her lips and she rises from the sofa.

"Sawatdee kha," she greets, taking a seat beside me on the bed. "Sleep well?" She stretches her hand and rubs my cheek with a finger.

I nod. "Were you watching me sleep?"

"Only for about an hour. Your breathing is quite soothing," she says, and I lower my gaze. She retrieves a tiny paper bag from the bedside table and hands it to me.

"Some cream to help you not scar."

"Thanks." I collect the bag. "You're up early."

"I'm a morning person."

"Of course you are."

75

"Do I not look it?"

"Not really."

"Really?"

"You don't wear a lot of bright colors."

"I didn't know there was a dress code for morning people." She laughs beautifully with a rare lightness in her eyes. My eyes follow her lips, as if trying to memorize the lines of her laughter.

"You're quite charming in the morning, Elina." My gaze finds hers.

"Hmm... flattery..." She tucks a stray strand of hair behind my ear. "Flattery will get you breakfast." She chuckles and I join. "Clean up, I'll wait in the sitting room." She ruffles my hair and rises from the bed, picks up her book from the sofa and exits the room.

I drag my weak body out of bed, stretching as I move towards the bathroom. I take notice of the clothes laid out for me on one of the sofas, an all-white light cotton ensemble, only giving it a quick study before continuing into the bathroom.

I catch my reflection in the mirror and my brows rise in surprise. All the areas where Elina bit and whipped are red. I did not realize her bites were that deep amidst all the sensations I felt. I touch my nipple slightly and it tingles, it's the most sensitive my nipples have been in a long time. A happy laugh finds its way to my throat. The memory of last night flashes through my mind and my caramel cheeks turn a rosy pink. With Phi Lamon, those sensations were a rarity.

Everything reminds me of last night: the water running over my skin, my shirt sliding over my nipples, the belt squeezing my waist, the smell of the room. I can't stop thinking about every kiss, every bite, every touch, every whip, replaying it repeatedly in my mind. Every sensational emotion she made me feel consumes my thoughts.

We step into the elevator, and I press the ground floor button and lean on the wall behind her. My eyes are fixed on her hair, admiring its rich darkness. Straight and clean.

"Have you ever been kissed in an elevator?" Elina inquires.

I smirk. She's such a tease. She turns to me, a soft smile on her face.

"Yes," I say.

"Liar."

We both chuckle.

"Do you want to be?" She takes small steps towards me and I press my back to the wall.

"Yes." My gaze falls to her lips.

"One day..." She places her cheeks against mine. I close my eyes, letting her sweet scent occupy my lungs. "I will," she whispers.

I exhale, smiling to myself as she leans on the wall beside me, our shoulders slightly touching. It's silly, but I'm so smitten by this simple closeness.

We step out of the building and a black Bentley pulls up front. The driver hands Elina the key with a bow.

"You're driving?"

"I do own a driver's license," she replies with a cocky smile I could easily get used to seeing.

We get in and she drives off.

It feels different having her drive. Not just because I have never seen her drive, but also, I have never been driven by someone who has seen me naked, or someone who I liked romantically—not that I like her in that way. Her phone keeps ringing, on and off business calls. It doesn't take me long to realize she talks to her subordinates the same way she talks to me.

"No deal." Hangs up. "Call my secretary." Hangs up. "I decline the offer." Hangs up. Very monotonous, straight it the point. It's amusing.

We run into traffic, and she sighs. "Did you have any fun at the party?" She turns to me.

I nod. "They were a rowdy bunch, but it was mostly fun."

"If you ever need my attention at such things, you could just ask."

"But you also like your space, don't you?"

"Selectively."

The traffic clears up and she returns her attention to driving. We turn into a less crowded freeway and she begins driving with a single hand. At intervals, she'd take her hands off the wheel completely to adjust her diamond bracelet, shirt or look at her phone. I ignore it, praying and keeping my eyes steady on the road, hoping she won't do it again, but she does, again and again and again, as if tempting fate.

"Can you not do that?" I ask.

"What?"

"Take your hands off the steering wheel?"

She takes it off again with a laugh, placing them right back. "Do you drive?"

"Yes!"

"I bet you drive like a grandpa."

"If you mean in adherence to the law, then yes."

"Live a little, Pretty Thing," she says, a big grin on her face.

Although I'm still frightened for my life with the way Elina drives, hearing her call me a pet name in such a casual manner gives me a rush of excitement.

We arrive at a small cozy cafe called Flower Sun. The name is carved into a wooden panel that hangs by the entrance. On the surface, it appears simple. But as we enter, its exuberance blossoms. An upscale and secluded setting, surrounded by a luxurious garden. All the seats are painted white, occupied by guests dressed in colorful outfits. We take a seat, and a server approaches us almost instantly, greets us with a bow and hands us menus before stepping away.

"Khun Cheng," an elderly woman calls, approaching with a limp, a walking stick supports her.

"Khun Charanavat," Elina replies.

We both rise and bow, exchanging greetings.

"This is Khun Sutthaya," Elina introduces.

"A pleasure." She passes me a weak smile and turns back to Elina. "I haven't seen you around here in a while."

Elina and I sit back down, she returns her gaze to the menu.

"I'm a busy woman, Khun." Elina looks up at me from behind the menu and we exchange smiles.

"I heard you decided against Martha's recommendation."

"I decide against a lot of my employees' decisions, Khun."

"Martha was more than just an employee, we both know that."

"We mourn her every day, she was an excellent nanny. But that is all she was, contrary to what you might think."

"You have deluded your child out of proper parenting, a shame really."

"Khun Mae. I am a difficult woman to displease. You are tethering on a line. Cross it and we both know it will not end well for someone." Elina lifts her gaze to Khun Charanavat. "I am not that someone."

Khun Charanavat scoffs. "Oh... I know." She turns to me, eyeing me as if irritated by my presence, then steps away.

"Ready to order?" Elina asks.

"Did you just threaten her?"

"That wasn't a threat, it was a statement."

"Sounded like a threat to me."

"If I were threatening her, she'd know it and so would you." She raises her menu and I leave my gaze on her.

"I have heard rumors about you." I relax into my seat, folding my arms.

"The ones about me killing my husband?"

"You know?"

"I know a lot of things."

I open my mouth to speak but settle for a long pause instead, watching her read the menu. It's difficult to shape words sometimes with Elina. They always seem to deepen my curiosity, instead of helping me find answers to her mystery.

"Does anyone of those things happen to be why she thinks you've scammed Hathai out of having a decent parent?"

79

Elina lifts her gaze to me. "Do you think I did it? Killed him?" she asks politely.

"The possibility isn't dismissible."

The side of her lips twitches as she locks me into a stare that feels more like a dare, like I'm in need of discipline.

Elina rises from her seat, walks over and sits beside me, still holding my gaze in the same manner. I open my mouth to speak and she kisses me, deeply. My hands move to her shoulders to push her away, but I find myself squeezing instead, traveling downwards towards her waist. I kiss her back, sucking onto whichever lip she allows me to. I know everyone is staring, but I'm too far gone in the pleasure of her desire to stop myself.

I haven't stopped thinking about how her hands felt against my bare skin last night and in this moment, I do not want to. It feels like reliving those thrilling emotions. She pulls away and stares into my eyes, but I keep my gaze on her lips, wanting to lean in for more.

"Now everyone thinks you're fucking a killer," she whispers.

An unwelcome chill settles over me. Without sparing another second, she rises and returns to her seat, picks up her menu as if nothing happened. I blink, watching her flip through the pages.

"It's always going to be like this between you and me, isn't it? You, shrouding yourself in mystery, me trying to get in."

"I'm sorry if I come off that way."

"Come off? It... it doesn't come off that way, Elina, that's exactly what you do."

She says nothing, staring back at me in complete stillness. Not blinking, not moving a single muscle. I can hardly tell if she is breathing.

"I am going to take a day off." I turn to leave.

"Wine," she softly calls. "Don't go."

"Ok. Then answer this, Elina. Last night, when you blindfolded me, was that for me or you? You were dressed the second you were done with me."

"Both."

"How?"

"Everything is more intense when you can't see."

"And for you?"

She swallows.

"You didn't want me to see you naked, why?" I press on.

She looks away.

"Ok. Why does Hathai resent you so much?"

"Wine—"

"That's what I thought. I'm not stupid, Elina."

"I know that."

"I'll take that day off." I rise from my seat. "Last night, will never, happen, again," I say in a precise, strong but soft tone.

I turn and walk away, my stomach rumbling but not from hunger. There is a bitter taste at the back of my tongue. I am furious at myself for letting it get that far, furious at her for making it so difficult. I put a call through to Dr. Rueng.

"Sawatdee krap, Phi."

"Sawatdee kha, how can I help you?"

"I know I don't have a session today, but can you squeeze me in, I need to talk."

"I'm sorry, Nong, I have a client in less than twenty minutes."

"I can be there in ten."

"Nong, I'll see you tomorrow. If it's too much, take a day off, stay home, calm down."

We say our goodbyes and I hop into a taxi heading home.

I feel guilty for being angry and walking away. She's never concealed her lack of interest in wanting to share. I have always known, and yet I got invested. I let my whispering desires dictate my feelings and actions. As I watch the people go by from inside the car, all I can think about is how she made me feel: Free.

I resent myself for still wanting her.

Last night was not enough, it did not help me get her out of my system. If anything, quite the opposite. Every single cell in me desires nothing more than to be under her, pleasing her, being used by her. I resent myself for wishing she'd make it easier, because I know making it easy would mean crossing the line in a career I am just starting. What does that make me?

We arrive and I drag my feet to the gate. I check the mailbox and retrieve the letters, glancing through as I make my way into the compound. Most letters are for Po, some are bills. One catches my attention, there is nothing written on it. I open it and it's just a small card with a handwritten text. 'It was good to see you. Glad you are well.'

I drop the other letters in utter shock and dash into the house. It was really her at the night market that night!

"Po! Po!" I call at the top of my lungs. I check his room first before rushing behind the house where he spends most of his time molding. "Po!"

"Witthaya? Why are you shouting?" He raises his head away from the clay pot he's fixing, his brows furrowed.

"Did you know?" I ask, giving him the card. "It's her isn't it, it's Mae. Did you know?"

"Witt—"

"You knew, didn't you? You knew she was back!"

"Yes, I knew."

"Why would you not tell me!"

"I was going to tell you after you returned, but you are struggling." He stretches out his hand to hold me and I move away.

"It was not your place to not tell me! You should have told me!"

"And then what? You go see her? And she feeds you bowls of lies."

"Po! Enough! You won't answer any questions! No one does! I am not five anymore!"

"Witthaya! Things are more complicated than you think."

"Then somebody please uncomplicate it! If she doesn't want to see me, why would she send me this! Why Po?"

"I don't know."

"Maybe you've just been lying to me my whole life!"

"Then why hasn't she sent you letters over the years? Witthaya! She doesn't want you! She never has! She never will! You should be grateful that I do! After what you've done!" he screams at me. The rage in his eyes is a fire ball I have not seen in years, he got so good at taming it.

"What did I do? Huh! Tell me! What did I do!" I scream back, shaking him vigorously by the shoulders.

He shoves me hard to the ground. I wince, sitting up slowly. We hold each other's gaze in silence and I see the realization dawn on him. He bends over and tries to pull me up and I turn away, quickly getting up from the ground and storming back into the house, marching into my room.

I'm fifteen again, trapped in the web of my own emotion, wishing for affections I cannot have, playing judge, jury and executioner in my own head. I keep replaying everything that happened. I should have never yelled at him. I should have never grabbed him. I hate that I did, I hate that I got angry at Elina, that I crossed the line.

I hate it all, but most of all, I hate that Mae never wanted me and still doesn't. She could have come over; she could have at least looked my way. My neck tightens and my chest is heavy. I kneel on the ground, curling myself into a ball, the only way I have learnt over the years to survive my panic attacks.

***

I decided against going to my session today with Dr. Rueng. I don't want to sit across from her and judge my own feelings, I did a lot of that last night. I know what she'd say, "It is not your fault"—but it is.

Sitting on the dining table, I try to decide if I should leave before Po wakes and avoid apologizing, or just wait and do it now. I made breakfast, one of his favorites, khao soi. My anxiety has not eased since yesterday. I spent half the night curled on the floor, struggling to breathe and the other half walking in circles around my room, judging myself. It's been months since I've had an anxiety or panic attack. I forgot how exhausted it normally left me.

I keep strumming my fingers on my knee, shaking my legs, contemplating. It helps me cope when I'm triggered, it's been that way for years, but it leaves me exhausted too.

"Witthaya." Po walks into the dining room.

I spring up from my seat. We stare at each other for a few seconds before I remember to wai in greeting.

"I'll be back on Monday; I'm staying the weekend at the Cheng mansion." I clear my throat.

"Witthaya, I am not angry." Po takes a seat. "Take the time you need."

You're not angry? But I am. When does that start to count?

I find his calmness even more upsetting. I storm out of the house without saying goodbye.

***

It's a breath of fresh air for me to sit across from Hathai and think of nothing but the chess game before us. She loves to teach, from chess to piano to mathematics. I spent most of the day being educated. She's been warming up to me for some time now, but today is different, she laughed a lot. We talked about her passion for seventeenth century Thai art which she described as a portal to heaven. I thought it was beautifully worded.

"What do you do on Saturdays?" she asks as I escort her back to her room.

"Laundry, chores if I'm back home."

"Don't you have people for that?"

"No. My father is what you normally call... peasant people."

"Oh." She stops and turns. "You know I only say that as a joke, right?"

I laugh. "Yes, it's fine."

"Can we go hiking tomorrow?"

"Sure."

"Bright and early," she says, turning away and entering her room.

I turn and walk back to mine. I'll take a quick shower first before dinner.

***

I stretch and turn half asleep, slowly opening my eyes and catching a glimpse of Hathai staring down at me like a ghost, or even better, an evil spirit.

"Hathai!" I jerk up, turning on my bedside lamp.

"You said we'd go hiking together, it's already past 4am."

"It's too early, Hathai," I reply with a groggy voice

"If we go any later; we'd miss the sunrise."

"Ok ok, go away, give me twenty minutes."

"Please make it ten," she sharply replies and leaves the bedroom.

I exhale, getting out of bed with a grumble. Like mother, like daughter.

We arrive with her half-asleep security guard at what seems to be a hiking trail up a hill. I'm half-awake as well. I only got one hour of sleep before Hathai magically appeared in my room. When I said yes, it was not to 4am.

It is clear from the way I keep dragging myself, I need to spend more time working out, I can barely breathe while Hathai seems to be sprinting up the hill.

"Keep up old man!" she yells from a distance.

"I'm twenty-eight!"

"Exactly!"

I bend over to take a breath, panting like I ran a marathon. Her security guard walks past me with a mocking grin, chewing whatever the hell she is gauging on. I internally curse at her for being so fit.

We have only walked past two people in the thirty minutes we've been hiking. I keep whining and complaining like a twelve-year-old. It just seems to be going on forever. Yeah, I won't be doing this again anytime soon.

Finally, we arrive at the top. I gasp at the beautiful view of Greenland laid out in front of us.

"Dear Buddha! Incredible!" I say out of breath. Her bodyguard hands me my second bottle of water and I gulp it down.

"Just wait till the sun comes up, it's the best view," Hathai says. There's pure joy in her voice.

"When last were you here?"

"Five years ago."

"That's a long time, surprised you remember the trail so well."

"Po used to bring me here whenever we visited Bangkok. Sometimes we just came to the city to see it."

"Ah..." I reply, holding onto the back of my waist and looking down at her. So, this visit wasn't random.

"Phi! It's coming! It's coming!" She jumps, clapping her hands with a big smile.

"Phi?" I tease.

She rolls her eyes. "Don't make a deal out of it," she replies, a smug smile on her face, I chuckle.

As the sun rises, she continues giggling. She was right, it is the best view I've seen in a long time—aside Elina. So beautiful. I don't think I have ever woken up to see the sunrise, or waited to see the sunset.

The sight of it warms me from inside out, truly captivating. I turn to take another look at Hathai's smiling face, but it's all gone. Rather, I meet a frown. her pink cheeks all puffed up. She squeezes the edge of her shirt and I know she's fighting back tears. I do that too.

"Hathai," I softly call. She looks up at me, her eyes drowning in the tears she is holding back. I kneel to her height. "It's okay." My forehead crinkles as I reach for her.

She bursts into heavy crying. I pull her into a hug, tapping her back as she cries her heart out.

"I miss him! I miss him so much, Phi!" she cries.

I say nothing, lifting her up from the ground and holding her tight in my arms, my eyes still on the rising sun. The sun will never be just a bright orange orb to her, but a reminder that the first love of her life is no more. And finally, I'm wide awake—fully awakened by her pain.

NINE
CROSSING LINES

For over fifteen minutes, I have paced back and forth in front of Hathai's bedroom, contemplating whether to knock.

The ride back home after the hike yesterday was quiet and solemn. We were exhausted from all the hiking but that was not the reason we both felt wiped. Hathai retired to her room once we arrived and has remained there.

For most of her childhood, Hathai has been left to handle her emotions alone in moments of emotional crisis. Sharing that moment with me yesterday must have left her feeling vulnerable, or even guilty. Hathai reminds me of myself when I was her age, isolating to not be a bother. I know the implications of self-isolation as a child, and I'd hate for that to be her future. I tried checking in on her a few times but decided to leave her alone for the rest of the day. But today is Sunday, she loves Sundays.

Hathai throws her door open.

"Phi! Stop hovering, your footsteps are disturbing my meditation."

I sigh. "Hathai, I am seriously concerned."

"Why?"

"Listen, it's not just you anymore; I am hired labor, but that doesn't mean I am not deeply worried and concerned about your well-being. It hurts to see you hurt and I want to help—let me. You don't have to do it alone, it doesn't work that way anymore, ok?"

"Ok... Whatever." She shrugs.

"I'm serious, Nong. No more."

She looks away and swallows. "Ok, Phi. I promise."

"Very well. Hurry up with your meditation, let's have breakfast." I turn to leave.

"Together?"

"Yes."

"At the dining table?"

"Yes Hathai, dining table and all. I'll be waiting in the kitchen." I walk away.

***

I hear Hathai running down the hallway, slowing down her steps as she draws closer to the kitchen. With a smile, I shake my head.

"I'm here." She stands by the door.

"Come sit."

She walks over and takes a seat at the mini kitchen dining, her eyes wide and filled with excitement even though she is trying so hard to hide it. I place a bowl of oatmeal with a smiley face made from cherries and blueberries in front of her.

"Smilies? I'm not a child."

"That's literally what you are."

"I turn thirteen in a few months."

"Hathai, attending high school and loving classical music doesn't make you an adult. Eat."

She's hesitant but digs in.

"Do you believe in life after death?" she asks out of nowhere.

"That is not a traditional breakfast topic, but yes. There's just too much going on with life for it to just end here. Besides, aren't we Buddhist?"

"When was the last time you made merit?" She raises a brow at me.

I sigh, her question pricking my guilty conscience.

"Let's not go there."

"You should make merit. I think it's important to have something consistent in your life even when your faith is wavering."

"You read way too many books. You should be experiencing life outside your imagination."

"I guess that's why she brought you here." She swallows a spoonful of her meal and dig in for another.

It's not often Hathai talks about Elina in a tone not filled with complete distaste. For the last two days, I have done a rather excellent job of pretending Elina doesn't exist. It was going well till now. Elina has not sent for me either. I'll admit, a part of me wished she would, even though I said it was the last time. I daydreamed she called me, opened up to me and hugged me. I miss her. It does not make any sense how much I miss someone I barely know.

"Can I take you to see something cool after breakfast?" Hathai asks.

"Sure, what is it?"

"You'll see." Hathai smiles.

***

I sat and listened to her share her thoughts on forestry throughout breakfast. It was nice, refreshing. Meals with Po are often quiet. Meals with Luce and Plerng are often too loud. With Hathai, it was simple. I didn't have to talk. Her questions were clear and precise, only requiring short answers. I left nods and smiles that conveyed that I understood her points and that was enough for her. Most of breakfast was just me watching her eat in a kitchen overlooking a lovely garden. Such beautiful balance.

"It's a short walk," Hathai says.

"My body still aches from yesterday," I complain.

Hathai dragged me outside, leading the way down a path the minute breakfast was over.

"Ok, grandpa, it's just up ahead," she says in English.

We take a left turn and continue down another path. It doesn't take long for us to come up to the most gorgeous garden I have ever seen. A garden so pink. This certainly was not in Khun Toh's tour when I arrived.

"What do you think? Peonies and pink roses." Hathai beams.

I laugh. "Oh, Hathai, this is gorgeous."

We continue around the pink heaven of a garden, feeding my eyes with all the beauty.

"You go so well with pink," she says, and I turn to her.

"Ah, you mean my pink suit. I remember you saying it was ugly."

"Yes, it was, but the color suits you, just like Po. It reminded me of him."

"He wore a lot of pink?"

She smirks. "Rarely, but he planted this garden. He always bought me pink plushies too. I think they were more for him than me, he just won't admit it."

We chuckle as we lay on the ground, engulfed in flowers looking up at the bright blue sky. I can only imagine how pretty the view from above is.

"He got me a pink scarf once, but then the next day he said he wanted to borrow it and I never saw it again. You would have liked him, he was a very cute man."

Hathai continues to narrate more instances where her late father showed his admiration for pink. As she speaks, it begins to dawn on me—I missed it earlier, what Elina really meant to say. She told me, I just didn't hear her. It was never her favorite color.

Hathai is finally opening up and being comfortable with sharing something as important as her relationship with her father, a key factor in her life. My attention should be with her, figuring out how to help her heal. However, I am struggling to pay attention, my mind keeps drifting to Elina.

Did she want to tell me all about him? What did he really mean to her? She must have loved him more deeply than I can ever imagine. She's probably still in love with him. Is this why even though she says she likes me, there is a line? For me, the line exists because I don't want to jeopardize my career, but it seems for her it's because of him. If I crossed my line for her, I wonder if she'd do the same for me. I wonder if she thinks about me the way I think about her. Maybe, she's just too hurt to care.

"Phi?" Hathai calls.

"Yes." I smile, a weak attempt to mask how guilty I feel for being distracted.

"Are you listening?"

"Of course, I am always listening, Nong."

We stare at each other in silence. She knows I am lying. Just like her mother, she has always seen right through me.

***

We returned to the house at midday, and I retired to my quarters and hurried a shower before jumping into bed to take a nap, but sleep is far away. My head is filled with thoughts of what to say to Elina; if I should even say anything to her. I lift my phone to check the time, It's almost 4pm. Since leaving Hathai, I have remained in bed, taking in the warm afternoon and thinking the same thoughts. What if I say all the wrong things, I am of course excellent at saying all the wrong things.

I rise from my bed and leave my room heading for the left wing. Damn her goddamn rules. She didn't make them to keep people out, she made them to keep herself in. I arrive in front of the left wing's passageway and halt, contemplating the consequences of me entering without her permission.

It's one I am willing to pay for.

I put my right leg across first and then my left, taking a deep breath to come to terms with my decision before starting down the hallway. It's quite familiar even though I have never walked through it. The design and decor are pretty much the same with the right wing.

I don't know where to find her, so I aim first for the library. All the doors are shut, only dead silence looms, I can clearly hear my own footsteps. I find the library door and push it open, peeking through. She isn't here. I turn. She does have an office up here, or do I find the master bedroom first? That should be easy to spot. I move down a similar hallway to my left. There is a second hallway with a door at the end, so I go to it. I pull the handle and the door creaks as it parts.

Taking a step in, I look across the room, it's quite dim, only lit by the sunlight piercing through the tall rustic windows. This is not her bedroom, it's her second office. Not quite different from the other one, just messier—way messier.

There are stacks of books everywhere my gaze falls. The air is thick with the stench of cigar, blankets on the seats. It appears she sleeps in this office. I walk further in, the office table is on the other end, right in front of the window, her seat backs the table, facing the window.

Slowly, I move towards the table, stepping over empty bags of chips, bottles of scotch and vodka. The floor is littered with various kinds of crumbles and yet we have a cleaning crew. When I arrive by her seat, my eyes widen at the sight of her. The big black leather seat completely engulfs her, there is no way I could have seen her from the door. Her head leans against her palm, with frizzy wet hair pouring over her shoulders. Her eyes are shut and whole body is wrapped in a thick brown bathrobe. I have never seen her this way before, so small and vulnerable—but still incredibly beautiful. She has always appeared cold, distant and hard to me.

Golden rays of the setting sun sweep across her caramel calm face. I take a few steps forward, trying not to wake her up.

"You finally walked in," she says with a tender voice and I halt. She turns her gaze to me.

Those beautiful brown eyes, illuminated by the sun, instantly makes my heart flutter. I swallow, taking a few more steps further, holding her gaze. I stretch my palm towards her, placing it on her left cheek. She closes her eyes, rubbing her cheek against my palm. She looks terribly tired.

"It's not your favorite color, is it?" I ask.

"You shouldn't have come, Pretty Thing."

I kneel beside her seat and take her palm to my cheek.
"Why? So you can keep hiding?"
She moves her hand to my hair, gently patting.
"You should leave," she says, but her eyes tell me to stay.
"You wanted to tell me, that's why you said it—so tell me."
She rises from her seat, staggering over to the window and leans her body against it. I follow her to the window, leaning in front of her, leaving a little Space between us. She smells of soap, as if she walked out of the shower straight into her seat.
"Elina..." I whisper, moving the stray hair from her face and leaning in. The golden rays of the setting sun pierce between us as our noses touch. "Tell me about him."
Elina moves me, placing my back to the window then drops her head on my shoulder. She snakes her hands under my light cotton t-shirt and hugs me, sniffing the right side of my neck and then moves to the left, leaving a trail of her warm breath. Her hands rub all over my back and I exhale the arousal crawling up my skin.
"I'm trying... so hard, Wine," she says, her tone tired and groggy.
I lift her face up and put my lips to hers, gently nibbling on her lips. The sensation from her fingers tracing all over my belly makes me shiver, longing for her to squeeze me tighter, spread me across her table and have her way with my body.
"Don't I make it easy?" I ask as my lips serenade hers.
"You make it difficult." Her hands grip my waist.
"How can I make it easier?"
She lifts her face away from mine, looking into my wanton eyes as her hand travel once again to my cheeks. We hold each other's gaze in silence, I can see pain glowing in her eyes. I have been wrong about so many things so far. She's so good at making me believe the show she puts on. But now I see it more clearly, I know she's hurting—she's just hurting like the rest of us.
"Take me there," I mutter.
"Where?"

"Where it's easier."

Elina steps back, tilting her head to the side, staring back at me in thought.

A few minutes pass and she walks over to one of the shelves, presses a hidden button and the shelf pops out of the wall, revealing a door. She opens it and signals me over. I oblige, taking small steps towards her. As I arrive, I look down the doorway. It's pitch dark.

"Is this how I end up buried in a box under the Cheng mansion?"

She chuckles. "Only one way to find out."

I take a step in and the staircase is lit up by motion sensor lights revealing a path. I keep walking down and she follows behind. A few more steps down and the room lights up, revealing an alluring playroom. My lips part in surprise.

The room is a complete contrast to the rest of the house. It's very monochrome, with hues of white, black and gray only. It feels like I have stepped into some sort of sci-fi film. There is a king size bed covered in silk silver sheets, tall walls of sex toys and torture tools for pleasure. There are different sex furniture's curved into different structures that would allow for a submissive to be placed in various positions for punishment or penetration. There is also a torture rack which seizes my attention. Bondages and whips of several kinds hang off the walls. Bars for hanging and chaining. It is quite intimidating. I have never been in a playroom with such detail and diversity.

"Wine," Elina calls, and I'm startled for no reason. "Is it too much?"

"It's not. I'm just... It's different from what I have experienced."

"What do you think?"

"Very you."

She laughs softly. "You wanted to see where it gets easier for me."

"I did."

I turn and continue to feast my eyes on the toys and gadgets, walking further in and running my hand over some.

"What are you thinking?" Elina asks.

"Are you going to... umm.... umm..."

"Fuck you?" she says so matter-of-factly. It fills my skin with jitters and sends the blood running in-between my legs.

I walk towards the wall of whips, running my right hand across it before arriving at one I consider quite unique.

"It's called a Tickler Ball Chain Whip." Elina walks up beside me. "It's not for you."

"Why?"

"You're a fetus. I go slow with boys like you."

I turn to her. Her once tired eyes now vibrant as a little smile slithers across her face.

"Are there others... others who submit to you?"

Her smile broadens. "If there were, would you be jealous?"

"No. You can have as many submissive as you please."

"Hmm."

I look away, turning my attention back to the whips. "Which one are you going to use on me?"

"None."

"Why not?"

"I don't own you." She wraps her hands around my waist.

"What if I want you to?"

"You are the demanding type, aren't you? So... Needy."

"I'm not needy," I say, a bit embarrassed by the way she used that word on me.

I have never used it on others in a positive manner before. After Phi Lamon, I have always prioritized sexual independence, never depending on anyone else for my own pleasure. I don't want to feel like a burden, even when I am submitting. I never want them to think I'm demanding—I don't want to be either. She kisses my ear, and then my neck, spreading warmth all over me.

"You are," she whispers. "You just don't want to be shamed for it." She leans back, releasing me from her grip. "Come on, I'll pour you a drink, and then you should leave." She turns, heading for the stairs.

"Elina."

"Yes?" She turns.

"I want you to fuck me." I swallow.

"I'll fuck you when you've earned it." She continues to the stairs.

"I... I'm sorry." I take a step forward. She turns back, dipping her hands into the pocket of her bathrobe. "What I meant was, I'd love you to use me... to... to make it easier. You can use me for whatever you'd like, however you please."

She comes forward, holding my gaze in a familiar soft stare. "Wine, I can't."

"Can't or won't."

She takes a long pause. "Won't."

"Please."

"Don't beg."

"Does it make me look pathetic?"

"You could never look pathetic, Wine—never." Her shoulders drop as she tilts her head to side.

"Then what is stopping you? Is it because of him?"

"Wine—"

"Please... call me by my pet name."

She smiles and so do I.

"What else can I do for you?" I ask.

"Nothing."

"I can give you a massage, wash your hair."

"Wash my hair?"

"I'm really good at it."

"How did you learn?"

"Plerng really loves head massages and she has very thick curly hair. I help her deep condition and detangle."

"Plerng?"

"One of my best friends."

"And the other I'm guessing would be your fake fiancée, Lucifer?"

I laugh. "Yes."

She shuffles towards me. "Have you ever been in love, Wine?"

"I think so."

"Think?"

"I was quite young, maybe too young to know if it was real," I say.

"How old?"

"Seventeen."

"What happened?"

"He was straight."

She exhales. "I'm sorry."

"It was a long time ago. Like I said, I'm not sure if it was even real."

"It was real," she says, moving closer. "Just because you were young, doesn't mean your heart couldn't recognize what love feels like—the first ones stick with us forever."

"Was he your first?"

She nods. "Yes."

I lower my gaze and remain silent.

"Do you not want me, Elina? Even a little bit?"

"I want you more than you could ever imagine."

"Just not enough to cross your line."

She clenches her jaw. Was I too blunt? Too sharp with my words? Oh no.

"I'll take that drink now." I walk past her, heading for the stairs.

"Take off your clothes," she says.

I halt, turning.

"I should?"

She remains silent.

I obey, stripping and tossing my clothes to the ground. Her eyes feast on my nakedness as if studying a book, then she starts towards me, every step a reason for my heart to flutter.

"Are you always this hairless?" Elina asks.

"Yes."

Her fingers graze my thigh, triggering a shiver across my body.

"Why?" She slides her hands up my waist.

"My previous Domme liked me hairless. It became a habit."

"Do you like it?"

"Yes."

I can't tell if she is pleased or displeased with my nakedness. As the minutes pass with her gaze on me and her lips saying nothing, I begin to feel a little self-conscious, slowly covering my dick with my hands.

"Take it off," Elina commands. I return my hands to my sides. "Don't ever do that again." She cups my face. "You are exceptionally stunning, Pretty Thing." She caresses my cheek. I flush, folding my lips. "You're also a very difficult man to say no to."

I lower my gaze, gladdened.

She walks to one of the drawers and retrieves a blindfold, picks up a rope from the wall and walks back to me. She slides the blindfold over my eyes and leads me by my arm; tossing me onto the bed. The second I land on my belly, she climbs over me, takes my hands behind my back and ties them up with a smooth rope.

She runs her hand over each butt, gently caressing. I fold my lips, quivering in excitement. I haven't bottomed for anyone since Phi Lamon. I have craved it for so long and since meeting Elina, I have imagined all the ways she'd fuck me.

"Do you remember your safe word?" she asks.

"Yes," I mutter.

"Say it."

"Cross."

She takes a deep breath and exhales.

"Your only purpose is my pleasure. Every pulse—every moan—every sensation—For. My. Pleasure. If you're a good boy, I'll sit on your face when I'm done with it, and let you taste me— Do you understand?"

"Yes." I quiver.

She walks away from the bed, leaving me in silence for a few minutes.

Without warning, she whips my left butt and I gasp. It leaves a tingling sensation, making me shake, digging my head into the bed. I have not felt that sensation in so long. She gently kisses the area, and my arousal swells. From butt to butt, she continues whipping. I'm warm all over, whimpering, trembling and biting my lips in desperate need.

She guides my waist up, helping me get on my knees and spread my legs. I arch my back, whimpering into the sheets, hoping this is the moment she fucks me. A slimy liquid drops down my butt crack, over my butthole and drips down my balls and cock. She rubs it all over my butt, teasing my hole with her finger.

"It's a shame you don't get fucked more often. You have such a pretty butthole," Elina says, her soft hands still rubbing the liquid into my skin. It keeps getting warmer the more she rubs, teasing me.

She leaves my butt hot, eager and ready to be stretched. I swallow, swaying my hips as the warm sensation engulfs me. She whips my hole and I moan louder, shaking. She whips it again, and again, rubbing my hole each time, and each time I pray she finally drives her dildo into me and fucks me till I can't walk.

She massages my balls gently with one hand. In the other, she strokes my dick. Her hands are slow, gentle but my legs won't stop shaking vigorously from intense pleasure. I fall flat on the bed, moaning and breathing heavily.

She loosens the rope and turns me over, allowing me to lay comfortably on my back, then ties me back up, separately this time.

She leans over, her breath slowly travels from my forehead to my lips, and she kisses me. Something round and soft like cotton candy drops into my mouth. Her kisses are deep but soft. I want to lift my hands and hold her face but I'm tied up, it feels like I am banned from touching her. She kisses me until it melts and then pulls away. I keep licking my lips to hold on to the taste of her, hoping she'll kiss me again soon.

A cold clamp presses my nipple and Mt body makes a little jerk, letting out a soft moan. I have always had sensitive nipples but right now, I feel as though they are the most sensitive they've ever been. She clamps my second nipple and I let out a louder moan. Her whip runs from the tip of my nose, down to my chest, heading to my groin. She whips me right on my groin and simultaneously the cold clamps start vibrating.

I nearly scream, pulling the ropes, shaking vigorously. Elina's movement are quite sudden, taking me by surprise each time. Before my mind can take a moment, she whips me again on my groin. The vibrations on my nipples are driving me over the edge.

I need her, I need to feel her.

Just when I think I can't take it anymore, she takes the nipple clamp off and replaces it with her warm lips. I bite down, folding my lips to quiet down my moans. Her tongue flicking my nipple is intensely pleasurable.

"Please! Please!" I beg.

"What?" she whispers.

"I..." The pleasure overwhelms me.

She slides her hands down to my wet slippery hard cock and goes back to stroking me, massaging from the tip of my cock down to the base. I struggle to breathe amidst all the pleasure, my hole is still warm and tingling from being whipped. My nipples are extra sensitive after being sucked and vibrated. Her hands have always felt soft against my skin, but the warming liquid paired with them makes it all too sensual.

"Elina... please..." I tremble

"What?" She keeps stroking me.

"Let me inside you..."

She breathes a laugh, taking off one of the clamps and whips my nipple. I throw my head back, shaking. She sucks it again, giving me a little bite. I moan.

She climbs over me, slides a condom over my erection and the vibration on my nipples surge. I moan in pleasure. Slowly, she slides my hardness up into her wet warm self. We exhale a moan in unison.

She begins to ride me, slowly but making sure all of me is in the depths of her. I curl my toes and squeeze eyes under my blindfold. Every movement driving me to insanity with pleasure as I let out muffled moans. Her finger wraps round my neck as she lowers herself.

"What is your body good for?"

"Pleasing you, Elina," I mutter.

She whimpers, speeding up her pace and tightening herself on me on purpose, releasing it after a few seconds and repeating.

I accompany her whimpering with loud moans, she isn't giving my cock a break, I can't last any longer, I can hardly breathe.

I want to wrap my hands around her waist, feel her movement while she uses my dick for her pleasure, watch her face while she cums, lick every drop of her cum till she's dry. The very thought of her using me to her satisfaction is driving me over the edge, I'm close.

"Elina! I'm... I'm..." I try to speak.

She slaps me across the face and throws her palm over my lips.

"Shut up," she commands, making me desperate to orgasm.

She rides me faster, overwhelming me. The sound of her ass slapping against my thigh is the music of lust. Within minutes, I begin cumming inside her, moaning into her palm and shivering from the intense feelings of an orgasm. She tightens herself as I cum and I moan louder into her palm, shaking, pulling my chains. She frees my mouth and lifts herself off me.

"I'm sorry, Elina." My body trembles. "Elina, I am—"

She sits on my face, shutting me up.

I stick out my tongue as she grinds on it, fucking it, using it for her pleasure, rubbing her clitoris on my tongue with l seductive moans of pleasure. My dick hardens again when she pulls my hair and I steady my tongue, attempting to please her as much as possible.

Her moans grow more intense, passionate and strong as her riding slows down, giving me the chance to pleasure her. I take her clitoris into my mouth, gently sucking and running my tongue over it. She presses my head deeper into wet warmness, burying me deeper into her as she shakes. I keep sucking, pleased by her moans and trembling thighs. Fuck!

She pulls my hair, pressing my head with her thighs, letting out deep moans, shivering as she cums. She gasps, jerking, breathing heavily. She stops moving, relaxing her thighs, but I keep licking her dripping cum. It's a beautiful satisfaction, the way she leaves her pussy on my face while recovering from her orgasm.

I hope she never gets up, I want my head in between her thighs for eons.

She lets out small cooing sounds as I lick her, gently patting my head. I dig my tongue into her to lick what's left. When she lifts herself off me, my face follows in search of more, licking my lips. I draw a deep breath to keep the smell of her in my lungs.

"You look better covered in my cum," Elina says under labored breaths.

TEN
TO BE HERS

My entire body throbs as Elina loosens the ropes around my wrists. I whimper, still trying to catch my breath.

A warm towel touches my cheek and I exhale at how good it feels. With tenderness, Elina wipes her wetness off my face, traveling down to my neck then chest before taking off my condom, and wipes my groin area. She is gentle, taking her time. She takes off my blindfold and I leave my eyes closed, savoring the taste of her cum in my mouth, letting my body recover. She pecks me on my lips while patting my hair.

"I ran you a bath," Elina whispers to me.

"Thank you," I mumble, my eyes still closed.

Elina pecks me again, making me smile.

She lifts my arms around her neck and helps me sit up. I sway, still too weak to keep my eyes open.

"Try getting up," Elina says.

I'm hesitant. I want to lay back in bed and go to sleep in her arms.

We walk over to the bathroom and the bright lights hit my eyes. The sound of the running water and the flowery smell in the air is very welcoming. She lets me go and I step in, lowering my weak sore body into the relaxing warmth of the running water. The mesmerizing scent of rose runs up my nose and I let out a soft exhale. I open my eyes to catch a glimpse of her and of course, she is back in a robe, fully covered.

She caresses my right cheek and I lean into her palm, leaving soft kisses, struggling not to fall asleep. She looks just as tired as I am, but I know it will be of no use to ask her to step into the bath too. Succumbing to my tiredness, and the gentleness of her touch, I doze off.

***

My eyes open to a sight I could not have foreseen: Elina, sitting on the floor beside the tub with her head resting on the bathtub, using her elbow as a pillow. I rise slowly, trying hard not to ruffle the water too much to avoid waking her up. Her rhythmic snoring is a joy to hear. I tilt my head to see her face but can't get a clear view from this angle. I bring my legs up to my chest, allowing me to rest my head on my knees as I watch her.

She looks like a different person when she sleeps, more like the person I think she is trying so hard to hide inside the left wing. As I watch her, my mind is blank. It might be the weakening sex we just had, or it could also be the feeling of freedom I feel in this moment. The feeling that life isn't waging war against my sanity. Against my better judgment, I reach for her hair, gently moving it away from her face. She moves, and I retire my hand in haste, but it's too late, she's awake.

"Hi," she whispers with a soft smile and my heart flutters. Her fluffy hair and sleepy eyes must be the cutest look I have ever seen on her.

"Hey." I really want to reach over and smell her sleepy sweaty body. "You snore."

"Yes, sorry. Did I wake you?"

"No. I like it. It's adorable."

We hold each other's gaze and by God I want to kiss her. My eyes search for approval in her gaze to reach over, kiss her, sniff her, hug her, but she turns away, rising from the floor and I gulp down my desires.

"You should get out of the water soon. You can spend the night here if you don't mind the view of it. I'll get things out of the way for you," Elina says.

"Will you spend the night with me?"

"No." She turns to leave.

"Elina," I call, she turns back. "Will you tell me if you owned me?"

"Tell you what?"

"About him?"

She exhales, lowering her eyes. "Stop trying to run away into my world, Wine."

"Why? You are just as broken as me."

"But I'm not running."

"No—you're just hiding."

"Goodnight, Wine."

I watch her leave, shuffling her legs tiredly against the ground.

***

Too exhausted to return to my room, I contemplated taking her up on her offer and sleeping in the playroom. But lying here, surrounded by instruments of pleasure and pain, feels cold and mechanical. The warmth that she brought with her into the room is gone and all that is left is a view that reminds me of what it felt like to be whipped, kissed, touched by her.

I lift my weary body from the bed and leave the Playroom, re-entering the littered, untidy office. Elina isn't here. I continue to the door, place my hand on the door knob, ready to leave. But instead, I turn and take another look at her unsightly office. Without thinking, I begin to put the trash away.

First, I put away the stacked pile of trash on the center table: empty bags of chips, empty bottles, and several ash trays. There is so much more trash on the floor. I try picking up as much as I can, but the carpet needs to be vacuumed.

Next up, folding the blankets and clothes stacked on the couch. They need washing, their scent is quite appalling. All done, I move to her work table, scattered with documents and papers.

I begin piling them up and clearing the table. All the drawers are filled to the brim. What could she possibly need all these papers for? It's only 2:30am. I have enough time till dawn to carry out a little investigation and hopefully find something, but that will make me a menace.

I mistakenly shove a pile I already arranged, and it falls, scattering across the ground. I squat, collecting them one by one. Without giving the papers much thought, I take notice of a paper stamped EK. I've seen it before, a few days ago on Elina's wrist. I glance over at the ones I've already picked and realize; these are letters, and they all have the same stamp. The door swings open and I spring up from the floor, startled.

"What are you doing?" Elina asks, standing by the door, her tone deep and stern.

"J... just fixing up the place a bit," I stutter nervously.

I have not done anything wrong, yet I feel like I have committed some kind of crime. Like I have broken a rule.

Sluggishly, she walks over to me. She's changed into a new robe, carrying a new blanket, it seems she returned to sleep here. She arrives and looks down at my hands gripping onto the letters. She collects them and walks past me.

"Get out," Elina calmly says.

"Elina. I didn't mean to—"

"Get out!" her voice thunders.

Her eyes are nothing like the woman I woke up next to just a couple hours ago. They are cold and dark. Though I'm not threatened by her anger, I turn, walk to the door and halt, trying to decide if I should stay and make her talk to me. Ultimately, I pull the handle and leave the office. I close the door and stand still, not yet ready to move, running the whole scenario in my mind. It isn't anger or resentment I feel, it's a wave of concern.

I wish we never had sex.

When I stormed into the left wing, sex was the last thing on my mind. I wanted her to share something real with me while holding her in my arms. But then, I looked into those stunning brown eyes and my selfish desires overtook my reasoning.

At first light I got ready for the day, arriving at the kitchen to find Phi Nam making breakfast.

"Sawatdee krap, Phi," I greet with a bow.

"Sawatdee krap, Nong Wine. Sleep well? You're up quite early."

"Yes, thank you. Smells nice, Hathai loves your khao tom."

"Ah! I know." A big grin appears on his face. "My grandmother taught me how to cook, she had a very unique way of making it. Khun Cheng's late husband was hooked the first time he tasted it," he proudly says, stirring the meal.

"You have worked with the family for a long time, right?" I ask, taking my seat.

"Give or take a decade." He chuckles. "They helped me set up my restaurant, sent my kids to school, I owe them a lot, decent people."

"Phi, do you know what EK means?" I ask.

"Something to do with food?"

"No, the Cheng family."

"Never heard of it," he says with a light head shake.

"Hmm."

"Something worrying you, Nong Wine?"

"No... Just something I overheard at Martha's funeral," I lie.

"Your family member died?"

"No, Martha, Hathai's late nanny."

"You mean, Phi Mae Noi?"

"Right." I nod.

"Oh, a painful departure, she–"

"Mmh Mmh." Hathai clears her throat as she walks in. "Sawatdee kha," she greets us with a wai. Phi Nam taps her shoulder and hands her a cup of juice.

"Everyone is up early today," he cheerfully says.

"I have a quiz today," Hathai says and turns to me. "Why are you up early, you couldn't sleep?" She puts down her cup.

"Slept well, Nong. Thanks for asking."

"Should we try harvesting tea herbs later this week?"

"If you finally agree to a session with me, we can harvest all the herbs you want."

"That's manipulative, Phi."

"I agree. I learnt from the best," I reply, pointing at her. Phi Nam chuckles.

"I'll go get you both some fruits." Phi Nam exits the kitchen.

"So, what do you say, do we make the session happen?"

"How did you know her name was Martha?" Hathai asks abruptly, surprising me.

"You overheard?"

"At first. Then I stopped by the door to listen."

"That's improper, Hathai. You should not be listening in on private conversations."

"That's the only way to get information around here. Information is powerful, you'll come to see." Hathai adjusts in her seat. "You're wondering why Phi Nam doesn't know her by that name, yet I do. It's leaving an unsettling feeling in your stomach, being left on the outside. I'll tell you why he doesn't know if you tell me why you know."

I fold my arms, leaning back into my seat.

"Your mother was conversing with a friend and they both addressed her as Martha, that's how I know. And no, you don't have to give me any information back. Because Hathai, it's an extremely sad life to use information against the people that care about you."

I pat her gently on the head and turn to my food to begin eating.

"It stands for ElinaKiet," Hathai breaks the silence. "It's their initials—how they communicated when they wouldn't let her marry Po. That's what Po told me."

I smile, masking the sting of jealousy I feel.

"Thank you for telling me, Nong."

She nods.

Elina loved him enough to fight to marry him. And even after all these years, she still wears a memorabilia of him. Just like Hathai, she has not moved on. She is still mourning. There might be no space for whatever it is that can grow between us, no space for me to be hers. I know I have no right to feel this way: jealous over a man that has been dead for almost five years—*but I am.*

Not once have I considered looking Elina up in the tabloids, but it's the first thing I do after breakfast with Hathai. They are all I can think about: what they shared, what it must have felt like to be admired and loved by Elina in such an intricate way. I type their names into the search box, Kiet and Elina Cheng and multiple news articles pop up. For the first time, I see what he looks like, her ex-husband, the man between me and her.

There is an insane familiarity between us; his features and mine are quite similar. I can see why Hathai tallies me with him often, we could pass as brothers. Is this why she chose me? Why she stared into my eyes the day we met and said those words that have controlled me ever since? Does she like me because I remind her of him? I press my lips, becoming a bit nervous, maybe angry.

There is a lot of news about their dating life, they were quite public before they got married. In every article they are praised as the "IT" couple. It seems as though they were all the high-class society could talk about for a number of years. Their divorce was even more explosive, but also extremely private, filled with only speculations. Kiet had gone missing for months before his death was announced and his family did sue the Cheng family. However, they never made it to court.

Amongst all the gossip blogs filled with conspiracy theories, one blog stands out, one that is dedicated to Kiet Suwan, almost like a fan blog. The blog is filled with pictures of him without Elina, which is a rarity amongst these tabloids. It has Kiet's biography, what he liked to eat, where he liked to visit, his favorite music and books, incredibly detailed. I read every line I can make sense of, incapable of stopping myself. There are several pages and he was an interesting man. My phone buzzes, it's a text from Dr. Rueng.

'Nong Wine, hope you're well. You missed our last session and haven't returned my calls. I hope you make it to the next session, have a lovely day.'

I exhale, falling back into my bed. I have no intention of going to a session this week. I have no intention of returning home this week. It's just easier that way.

I lay in thought, wandering off to memories of last night. How good it felt when the first whip landed on my butthole. It was sensational, I felt it at the tip of my cock. I flush, breathing a little bit heavier. What do I have to do to earn being pegged by her? What would it feel like? When I slid into her, it was the most pleasurable sensation I have ever experienced. The way she touched me, held me, rode me. I felt invincible. I did not exist. I was completely hers.

She clearly held back, not wanting to do certain things to me. But I wanted everything her dominance had to offer. I ache for it even now: to serve her, please her, worship her body. I yearn to know what brings smiles to her lips and tears to her eyes. What makes her feel peace, joy, sadness. What makes her cum. I do not care whose shoes I need to walk in to make that possible. Not when she makes me feel this way.

I pull my laptop close and type in BDSM contracts. So many articles pop up with lists of do's and don'ts. Several contain written guidelines. The last one I signed was made by Phi Lamon and I have never made one myself. However, it is clear, I will never be hers if I do not fight for her dominance.

ELEVEN
THE CONTRACT

For an hour I have poured over numerous websites in search of a BDSM template that is easily editable and contains a wide range of things I can push my boundaries with. I grin when I find one that is exactly just that.

SELECT YOUR HARD AND SOFT LIMITS

- Abrasion
- Age play
- Anal sex
- Hard beating
- Soft beating
- Biting
- Choking
- Maid play
- Leather restraints
- Rope bondage
- Does the slave consent to being fisted?
- Does the slave consent to being gagged?
- Does the slave consent to flogging and whipping?
- Does the slave consent to forced masturbation?
- Does the slave consent to sensory deprivation?

It goes on and on.

The contract explores so many areas and after hours of editing, going back and forth on my decision, I am still unsure of all my choices. I let a couple of days pass by, avoiding the left wing, not that there is much to avoid, she isn't waiting on me. She hasn't missed me as much as I have missed her. She's probably half drunk, thinking about Kiet Suwan.

It's Thursday and Lucifer invited me to lunch. We haven't seen much of each other in a while, I have missed his company. Lunch at his parent's boat club was delicious and shortly afterwards, he dragged me to the market. Every now and then Lucifer loves to buy locally handmade jewelry, one can say it's a hobby. We move from shop to shop, picking out different items and finally take a break for shaved ice.

"Plerng will have our heads when she finds out we didn't bring her along."

"Yeah." I giggle, slurping my ice cream. "She told me about your new endeavors."

"Endeavors? Is that what we are calling it?"

"I don't know, Luce, you tell me. What happened to living the free life, traveling the world. Running the foundation will tie you down."

"I still want to do those, Wine. Just... I think in a way, I went along with a lot of things because of Plerng. You know I care a lot about what she thinks."

"Hmm."

"I just want to take more responsibility, Wine, that's all. Phi Dara... He makes my world bigger, he makes me want to reach for things."

"It's still weird to hear you call him by his name instead of Po," I say, and we chuckle.

"Do you think Plerng is concerned about me taking over one of the companies?"

"We didn't talk in depth about it, she only mentioned it in passing. Does she have any reason to be? She doesn't want it anyways."

"Yes, but it's still hers to inherit."

113

"Just ask her, Plerng is an open book. I think it's probably weirder for you than her."

He looks away and I go back to slurping my shaved ice, the warm breeze and the gentle chatter from the market lingers.

It came as a surprise to me when Plerng told me Lucifer's intention to take up some of her father's companies. Not once has he in the past expressed any interest in working. But more importantly, his parents have urged him for years to begin working in their company so one day he could take charge of their agricultural conglomerate. Plerng's father is a fashion and textile tycoon, this of course is more appealing to Lucifer, but certainly it will rub his family the wrong way. They've expressed their distaste in his decision to date Plerng's father and so publicly at that.

"Can I ask you something?" Lucifer asks and I nod. "Are you sleeping with Elina Cheng?"

I pause, frozen. I slowly lift my gaze to look at his face, putting down my bowl of shaved ice.

"How did you know?"

"I was at the Flower Sun last week. She kissed you."

I look away. "It's complicated, Luce—It happened only once."

"Well, are you going to let it happen again?"

"No—yes."

"Wine..."

"I know, I know, it's just..." I hesitate, swallowing.

"You never put yourself out there, I know so many people that would kill to go out with you. This puts your career in jeopardy, have you not heard anything Plerng said? She's not the kind of woman you want to fuck around with."

"It's not about the sex, Luce."

"Then enlighten me."

"Just don't tell Plerng ok? I don't want the smothering and lectures."

"I won't have to if you keep kissing her in public like that. What is it about her anyways? She's not even your type."

"I don't really want to talk about it."

"Why not?" Lucifer squints at me.

We share everything. I have no doubt me withholding information is pissing him off. My phone buzzes and I pull it out of my pocket to look at the screen. It is Dr. Rueng again.

'Sawatdee kha, Nong Wine. Looking forward to seeing you tomorrow,' the message reads.

"Are we still shopping?" I ask, ignoring the message.

"Just a few more things. Wine, what is going on?"

"Elina, umm... she's... you wouldn't understand."

"Try me."

"Luce." I lean forward. "I love you, and I trust you—I promise, me not sharing has nothing to do with you or our friendship."

"You need time."

I nod. "I need time."

"Ok... I'm always here."

We share a warm stare for a few seconds and I rise, stretching. "Let's go... bring the shaved ice along."

Lucifer is right, but nothing about the way I feel when I am with Elina is wrong.

We look through a couple more stores and Lucifer rounds off. We begin our stroll out of the market, walking past a small shop when something catches my eye: a pink scarf. It looks remarkably similar to one I saw hanging round Kiet's neck in one of those blog photos. I stop and drag Lucifer in to try it on. I squeeze it gently in my palm, studying it for a moment before paying.

***

I arrive back at the mansion just before sunset. First, I check in on Hathai who is engaged in a ballet class, then I return to my room. When I saw the scarf, I wondered what it would feel like for Elina to look at me the way she looked at Kiet in those pictures: like I am the only one that matters. Throughout the ride back to the mansion, I could not stop running theories in my mind about what must have transpired between them to lead to a divorce.

115

I wear the pretty pink scarf around my neck and his reflection appears in the mirror. Kiet Suwan. It is satisfying, conflicting and in a way, devastating. The thought that I wish in this very second to take a step in his shoes, just so I'd know what it feels like to be completely owned by her.

I toss the scarf to the bed, pick up the final contract I drafted and dash out of my room, heading for her left-wing office with hasty steps. I walk past the dining room and turn right back when I realize she is sitting in there, having dinner. She seems to have just returned home too, formally dressed in a dark blue shirt and black trouser. A beautiful diamond necklace hangs around her neck, under her shirt. Her hair is the straightest I have ever seen it. Her lips move graciously as she chews.

"Your steps were resounding, Wine," she says, not looking in my direction as she sips her wine.

I walk in, arrive by the table and take a seat. Carefully, I place the contract on the table before reaching across and picking a single grape from the bunch served, putting it in my mouth and chewing. She isn't looking at me, but she smirks.

"What's that?" Elina nods at the contract.

"A contract."

"For?"

"My ownership."

She looks up from her meal and drops her cutlery, relaxing into her seat as she folds her arms, holding my persistent gaze. I have her attention and she's trying to figure out how to take it away from me. I reach over and pick another grape off her plate as she watches me eat.

"I have no interest in owning you, Wine."

"Yes, you do. Isn't that why you hired me?"

"No."

"Liar."

She squints at me, a smile forming on her lips. She rises from her seat, walks over and leans in, holding my face up by the chin. She lowers herself and kisses me deeply, so deeply I feel the sensation all over my body. I feel myself losing to her within seconds. She breaks the kiss to stare into my eyes with her sultry gaze.

"It's admirable how you think you have any control here, Pretty Thing," she says in a mellow tone, our noses still slightly touching. She plucks a grape without looking away. "Open," she commands and I obey.

She dumps it in my mouth, using her kisses to squash it. It's sweet, soft and juicy. She sucks my lips and I resist the urge to moan but fail to stop my dick from hardening.

"Tell me, Wine... what do you want? To make love to me—or fuck me hard, over this table."

I gulp, raising my lips to receive more kisses but she withholds it.

"I want you to sign the contract," I reply, breathless.

"That isn't what your body says," she whispers in my ear, gently holding my bulge.

"My body wants a lot of things, Elina. For you to hold it, punish it, use it, tell it things you've never told anyone, kiss it, let it lay beside you."

She straightens herself and I rise to her height.

"It's at your command, it wants to be yours. Stop cowering and sign the contract."

Elina smirks. "Then I guess your body wants a lot of things it cannot have," she replies.

I lean in and kiss her softly. "That makes the two of us. You'll never feel my cock inside you again—unless you own me."

TWELVE
THE WAITING GAME

I left the left-wing feeling confident and powerful after seeing Elina speechless.

I could see it in her eyes, how much she wanted me. Her lust and thirst for me exploded like pheromones all over the room, it took over me. I craved for more than a kiss and she knew it. Even then, I knew it would be impossible for Elina to desire me more than I desired her.

The waiting game that followed the next couple of days almost drove me to insanity. She was making it difficult for me to stay true to my promise on purpose. She'd show up randomly in the right-wing kitchen she rarely visited, during breakfast or dinner, dressed to perfection in her work outfits. Without saying a word, she'd pick up something random: a cutlery, table cloth, fruit.

I'd come down to the game room in the lower floors to play snooker or arcades and a few minutes later, she'd show up too, another part of the house she rarely visited. Watching movies in the home theater became impossible. Without even looking, I'd know she was there. Her inebriating perfume would fill the theater and all of a sudden, I'd begin to lose control to thoughts of her lips.

Her presence was a plague, taunting me, weakening my defenses.

With each day, her rejection became increasingly apparent. Elina had no desire to make me her submissive and I felt discarded. A feeling that was not foreign to me.

Mae, Phi Lamon, eventually they all leave.

It hurt more when I realized how much my heart, soul and body longed for her dominance, even after she rejected me in such an ice-cold manner. I have grown used to rejection. I have learnt not ask again, when I am rejected. But not this time.

I want Elina. I would do anything to have Elina. I would be anyone to have Elina.

But my desire for her was ruining my ability to do my job. Escaping to Lucifer's home was the only way I could think straight.

"Wine!" Lucifer calls from the balcony above.

"Mhmm?" I mumble, half asleep by the pool, soaking in the afternoon sun.

"Wine!"

"What is it!"

"Your father is calling again!"

I wave him off.

Po has called a few times over the past three weeks we haven't seen each other. It's not out of resentment that I choose to not reunite with him. I miss him, our quiet breakfasts, watching him mold or water the plants together. I miss his peaceful face and soulful eyes. But I still feel the weight of our past, it's been heavier since I returned and a month away from my childhood home has lessened the weight of the unknown memories pressed upon me. An emotional game of chess with Elina Cheng will do that to you. The heavy sunlight showering over me suddenly goes dark and I open my eyes to see Lucifer standing over me.

"What's going on between you two?"

"Who?"

"You and Po?" Lucifer takes a seat beside me. I rise from the poolside chair, taking off my sunglasses.

"Nothing."

"The last time he ever called me about you was in uni, remember? When you got shit-faced, stole his bike and a cat."

"Yeah... That was fun." I giggle.

"So?"

"Why? Tired of me being here already?"

"Dude, you've only been here for a week, you could stay another five years, you know I'd never care... but I do miss having sex by the pool."

"Luce?" I shake my head.

"TMI?" he asks and I nod. "Oh please, Wine! You need to be more adventurous sexually. Don't you ever just get bored of having sex in bed, back and forth, back and forth like goody two shoes. Trust me the best orgasms are on the other side of your comfort zone, the darker side."

"Uh-huh," I mumble.

"You look starved... of orgasms."

I sigh. "Plerng is rubbing off on you."

"She could be, if she'd pick my damn calls."

"My boys!" Khun Kittibun calls, walking towards us with two glasses in his hands.

The breeze ruffles his flowery yellow shirt as his silver hair battles to stay in place. He isn't all gray, but months ago he decided to dye it all silver. Plerng was not pleased, she complained for weeks. Lucifer, however, sent me many pictures talking about how cool it looked. Lucifer embraces Khun Kittibun's age fully, and even when we didn't understand it, he was patient enough to hang on to our friendship.

I rise. "Sawatdee krap, Po," I greet with a wai.

"Sawatdee krap!" He smiles, handing me a glass of orange juice.

As I sit back down, he leans over and kisses Lucifer— on the lips! What!

I widen my eyes, my brows elevating as I raise the glass of orange juice to my lips, attempting to hide my surprise. They've been together a bit over a year now and this is my first time seeing them so intimate. Po barely comes over to Lucifer's home these days, Lucifer spends more time at his instead, I know I am the reason.

I have known him since freshman year at university as Plerng's father. He made us soup during our birthdays and once attended a PTA meeting on my father's behalf. We've gotten scolded by him several times and once he made us kneel in front of the house for an hour for crashing his Lamborghini while partying. Seeing him as Lucifer's boyfriend is alien to me.

Plerng raged when she found out Lucifer asked him out, they didn't speak for over a month. She didn't trust him. Lucifer had a popular track record of sleeping with anything that moved as long as they were men who liked other men and capable of taking his nine-inch cock.

I sip my drink and look in another direction, trying to give them some privacy as they... kiss.

"Thanks babe, it's really good," Lucifer replies after taking a sip of his drink.

"I only poured it in the cup, Nong Lamai did the rest."

"It came from your hands, it's just as sweet as you."

"Thank you." Po kisses him again. "Can I take your Ferrari out later?"

"Sure."

He kisses Lucifer some more. I falsely clear my throat, reminding them of my presence before tongues get involved. They break away from their moment. Khun Kittibun turns to me with a smile.

"Nong Wine, sorry about that. This must be a bit uncomfortable for you, haven't seen much of you since you returned from the States," he speaks warmly.

I flash a nervous smile. "No, Po."

"It's fine if it is. I'm here if you want to talk about it. You are coming for the foundation's fundraising brunch next week, right?"

"Well, I'm not—"

"Oh, you must. I will be announcing Lucifer as the new CEO for Lamai foundation, you can't miss it."

"I didn't know you both finally decided on it."

"You didn't tell him?" Khun Kittibun turns to Lucifer.

"I was going to, it's only interim C.E.O until Phi Dara finds someone else. Come, Wine."

"And I could introduce you to some new clients. A friend of mine is expanding her mental health organization, I'm sure they will need a man of your profession somewhere," Khun Kittibun includes.

"I'll be there." I rise. "I'll give you both some privacy in case you want to.... umm.... do things... by the pool."

"Things? Like what?" Khun Kittibun asks, adjusting his glasses. Lucifer glares at me

"I'm going to take a nap inside." I bow and turn away, hurrying inside.

***

I've been lying in bed for half an hour. The afternoon is warm and the silk sheets against my skin makes it even better. I lay quietly, listening to 1950's Japanese soul music, watching my thoughts travel around my mind as I caress my tummy.

I pull the soft comforter over my shoulder and turn to the window. I'm starting to get a chill. Golden rays of sunlight pierce through the white curtains as they sway slowly. Today's weather is especially kind.

I blink and Elina appears on the couch next to the window, wearing the exact same robe she wore the first and only night we spent together. She smiles and my lips follow. I close my eyes and the blanket begins to feel like her embrace. She giggles in my ear and I laugh, turning over and opening my eyes to nothing but my laptop screen.

It's the second time I've daydreamed about her since I stopped spending nights at the mansion. I don't mind the daydreams; they make me feel close to her in some way. It's more bearable than being in the same house and having her occupy my every thought, knowing fully well I can't have her.

I pull my laptop close and open my browser. The tab with the fan blog of Kiet Suwan is always open, making it easy to access it each time I get a fleeting thought about him, which is all the time.

I move straight to the photo gallery section and begin scrolling through his pictures for the umpteenth time. We have different tastes in fashion. Kiet was edgy and sharp. He wore a lot of coats and jackets everywhere for some reason,

Bangkok isn't exactly chilly. Lots of leather in red, brown and black hues. He wasn't one to shy away from his femininity too, he wore a lot of fishnets and tall boots, black eyeliner and nail polish. His style was very retro and rock, even when he dressed up formally for events.

I come across a video of Kiet and Elina at what seems to be a dinner party, I can tell from the video thumbnail. I click on it. It's the first video I've seen of them since I began obsessing over this blog. The music is loud and the person holding the camera moves through a gyrating crowd.

"Elina! Elina!" a young woman calls.

Her camera lights flash into Elina's eyes and I see her young drunk face, it takes me by surprise. Elina laughs hysterically while a bunch of people who seem to be her friends joke about something. Surprisingly, one of them is the foreigner I met in her office and that night at the after party.

"What! What!" Elina replies.

"Look at you! You're in big trouble!" the young woman's voice says with a laugh.

The foreigner throws his left arm around Elina's neck, holding up her chin with his right hand.

"If I were yours, you'd never be in trouble. I guess I don't wear enough leather for your liking," he says.

Elina pushes his hand away.

Her friends tease both of them some more. She's dressed in a simple T-shirt, jeans and a jacket, looking like a regular girl on a date. I smile at my screen. This woman is a different person I wish I had met.

"Ooi! Take your hands off!" the voice scolds when the foreigner attempts holding Elina again. "You guys shouldn't have allowed Elina to drink!" she yells

"We're not her babysitter," one of her friends points out and they laugh.

"Where is he?" Elina asks, leaning into the person holding the camera.

The screen goes black, I can only see flickering lights, she seems to be helping Elina across the hall. "Over there," I hear her say, the screen is still black.

"Phi Kiet," Elina calls.

The camera shakes as she drops Elina off then holds it up. I raise my brow at the sight of Elina on Kiet's lap, her arm around Kiet's neck.

"Cute! She's so pretty when she's drunk!" the person holding the camera exclaims, bringing it closer to Elina's face.

"He's angry with me," Elina says.

Kiet's expression remains blank, a stale smile on his face as he looks Elina directly in the eye, grinding his teeth. He's sexy, I'll give him that, especially dressed in his retro crop top and jacket. I can't see much of what's below.

"How can he be angry with the cutest person? Phi Kiet! Say hi to the camera!" She moves the camera to his face.

"You know you aren't supposed to drink," he says calmly, moving his hands to Elina's waist.

"I'm not allowed to drink or smoke, do this or that..." She swallows, pressing his cheeks. "Some would think I'm your slave instead, you know?"

"Because you are a baby, Elina!" the voice screams, laughing.

Elina and Kiet hold each other's gaze intensely as the girl holding the camera keeps laughing.

"Am I your baby?" Elina asks and Kiet's smiles.

The girl holding the camera teases them, taking the camera closer to Kiet's flushed face and he lifts his hand, covering the lens, the video ends.

I eagerly search for more videos, scrolling through different folders. Unable to find any, I slam my laptop shut and fall back into bed, letting my rumbling feelings stir up a bitter taste in my mouth.

"Hey," Lucifer calls and I turn towards the door. "Let's go pick up some groceries."

I shake my head and look away. He walks in, grabs me by the arm and pulls me up as I grumble.

We roll our carts along the shopping lines, filling them up with different groceries. I am indeed glad Lucifer made me come. I would have spent the rest of the day dying of jealousy, if I can even call it that. I can't be jealous of someone that was never mine in the first place. What they had was special, intimate, passionate, I could feel it from the way Kiet looked into Elina's eyes. He loved her. If she'd ever let me see that side of her, I know I'd look at her the same way too.

"Now, that's a healthy watermelon!" Lucifer slaps it like a grandpa, lifting it up and posing.

"Why are you so proud of a watermelon?"

"I don't know, I got a blow job and now I'm in a good mood."

"Luce."

"TMI?"

I nod. "What else do we need to get? Our cart is almost full." I glance around.

"Sausages, some fish, ah! The boyfriend and I are taking baking classes this week, I should get us those matching aprons." He turns and I follow.

"You and Po?"

"Don't call him that when we're alone," he squeezes his face, and I scoff.

"I don't know what you want me to call him, Luce, I can't call him by his name."

"Just say... my boyfriend... call him my boyfriend. Anyway, it's a date, you should come!"

"I think I'll pass."

We arrive by the shelves stacked with aprons.

"There they are! So cute!" He unhangs them excitedly and tries to put one on me. "Try this one, let's see what it looks like."

"No."

He grabs me, forcing it on me and we begin a light tussle. Of course, he wins. I have never won a wrestle with Luce. He ties it behind my back as I frown. The aprons have half hearts attached to each end and when two people stand next to each other it looks complete. I want to vomit.

"Wine! This is adorable. He'll love it! Plus, white is his favorite color!"

"You're so annoying when you're in love."

He slaps my head and I groan, I turn around to return the gesture and he blocks it, once again we enter a rowdier tussle, struggling to get at each other's head.

"Look at this! What a cute couple," a voice breaks in and we stop and look up. An elderly man, well into his seventies stands, smiling at us warmly. We tear away from each other and wai in greeting.

"Lovely aprons, newlyweds?" he asks.

I open my mouth to dispel his assumption, but Lucifer drags me into a side hug.

"Yes." He kisses my cheeks and I shrug.

"Oyi! He's a shy one, isn't he?" the elderly man says, pointing at me and stepping forward.

"Yes, Po!" Lucifer exclaims, smiling at me.

"My wife was pretty shy when we first got married too. The shy ones are the best, he'll love you deeply, you'll see."

"Thank you, Po!" Lucifer replies.

"Is she here with you?" I ask.

"Not physically, she passed away, but she's always in my heart."

The smile on our faces fades and Lucifer drops his hand. We are both lost for words. I bet Lucifer regrets lying to the old man now.

"Ooi! That was over twenty years ago, no need for those looks." He laughs. "It's just life, my sons." He walks over and pats our shoulders. "Good luck."

We bow once again as he walks away. Lucifer and I stand quietly, looking in his direction. I turn to Lucifer, taking advantage of the moment to smack him on the head in retaliation and we resume our play fight.

We finish shopping and begin our trip out of the mall, deep in conversation about his new venture as the C.E.O of Lamai foundation. Lucifer seems to be handling it all well, but sometimes it's difficult to tell with him. He's been this way for as long as I've known him, smiling through the chaos.

I drag him into a clothing store I saw earlier when we first arrived, and we begin looking through a bunch of leather jackets.

"Wine, none of these are your style."

"I want to change things up a bit," I reply.

"Why? What about the hot suburban dads," Lucifer jokes.

I chuckle, taking a couple of jackets off the hanger and we walk over to the tall standing mirror in the corner of the clothing store. Luce helps me slip on the first jacket.

"Whoa! Wine, you do go well with leather!"

"You think so?"

"Yes!"

I already knew I would, after spending all that time looking through Kiet's photos. We look so much alike down to our body types. Lucifer sniffs my cheeks and pulls up another jacket. One by one, we try them on and every single time he hugs and praises me. Nothing new, just Lucifer being Lucifer.

These jackets make me feel like in a way, I could have her. If I was more like him, more bold, more fierce, more confident.

Lucifer hugs me from behind after I slip on the final one, a dark red leather jacket, with over a billion zips.

"Wine, get this, you look so good in it," Lucifer insists.

I throw my head back onto his broad shoulders as we sway from side to side, looking back at our reflection. I can see why we are always mistaken as a couple in public. I smile at that thought, imagining I'm Kiet and he is Elina.

"Khun Sutthaya."

I turn around instantly at the sharp sound of the familiar voice. Elina standing in the clothing store, dressed in a crimson pantsuit, her hands in her pockets with her hair slicked back in a ponytail. The last person I expected to see today. I nervously glance around like I have been caught doing something wrong and my palms begin to sweat.

"Khun Cheng, this is a welcome surprise. Sawatdee Krap." Lucifer bows and so does she—more of a slight nod. "Shopping around?"

"Not exactly," she replies, keeping her eyes fixed on me.

"It is a Saturday, everyone shops on a Saturday," Luce continues.

"Seems so. Interesting choice." Elina points at my jacket. "Not very you."

"Being me hasn't gotten me much lately," I reply, avoiding her gaze.

"Can I borrow you for a moment?" she politely asks.

"Anything the matter?"

She smirks, walks over and takes me by the arm. "Just a moment."

Lucifer slides his hand across my waist and pulls me closer to him. "We are in the middle of some shopping, Khun Cheng. I think it's best if you discuss work matters on Monday."

"What's your name again?" Elina blinks at him, her forehead crinkles.

"Wang, Lucifer Charlem Wang," he proudly introduces himself.

"Please. Get your hands off him, Khun Wang," Elina demands and my eyes shoot up.

"What? I—"

"Luce," I stop him.

Elina leads me to the other end of the store and I pull away from her.

"You cannot speak to him like that," I say in a huff.

"He shouldn't put his hands on you like that, it's unsettling to watch."

"He's my best friend, he can put his hands wherever he wants and you... you're my client, you don't get a say!"

"Why did you move out?"

"You had me followed all this time?"

"Yes."

"That's absurd, Elina! Are you kidding me? Why the hell would you do that!" I scold, trying to keep my voice down.

"I like to know where my things are."

"I am not one of your things."

"Why did you move out?" she repeats.

"I never moved in."

"I need you back in the house."

"You are so entitled and selfish! And I know... I know that's your thing! Khun Mysterious. But I want things too, does that ever occur to you?"

She pulls me by the arm and shoves me into a small dressing room by the corner, pinning me against the thin wall with her fiery gaze. We keep our eyes locked on each other, our heavy breathing filling up the tiny room as she steps forward.

I move to leave and she slams me against the wall, pressing down on my chest with her elbow as her fingers grip my jaw, digging her nails into my cheek. I wince, pulling her hand away, she is quick to replace it for with her left hand, tilting my neck to the side.

"Don't. Fucking. Move," Elina commands, her breath shallow and voice deep.

I seize wriggling, holding her audacious gaze with my hand wrapped around her wrist.

"Tomorrow, before dusk, you will be back in your quarters," she says.

Drawing a heavy breath, I swallow, our stare hard on each other's faces.

"Claim me, before you command me," I dare.

She slams the wall right beside my ear and I shudder, blinking only once as she strengthens her hold on my jaw once again.

"For fuck sakes, Witthaya." She breathes, her gaze softening as she drops her forehead on my shoulder. "I am physically weakened—emotionally handicapped, in your absence," Elina says in a strong precise tone that weakens as she speaks.

I squeeze the side of my trousers, shivering under her hold, sweat dripping all over my back.

"Because of me—or him?"

She lifts her gaze to mine slowly, we share the same breath as she moves her face closer to my lips. I close my eyes, inhaling her sweet jasmine scent mixed with tobacco. Her lips move closer to mine, her body heat and soft breath warm my skin.

"You're asking for too much," she says, her voice tender but sharp.

She shoves her mouth into mine and kisses me. I inhale, holding my breath as her lips engulf mine. I slowly exhale as her lips depart from mine, my hands reach for her face, cupping her cheeks as I stare into her sad lustful eyes.

"So are you," I whisper. "I want to stand in the shadow of your memories... Let me."

She caresses my cheeks, so gently, it feels like I am being soothed to sleep. "My pretty thing..." she calls softly, and I gasp, goosebumps spread across my shivering skin.

"What did you call me?"

A little smile spreads across her lips, weakening every other defense I have left.

"My pretty—"

I kiss her back—desperately, pressing her tightly against my body as desire consumes me. I pull off the leather jacket and Elina slides her left hand under my shirt, rubbing my back. She moves to my neck and sucks it, licking me before biting. I quietly moan into her ear. I can feel her loosening her belt with her right hand and I hold onto her tightly, digging my hands into her hair.

"Your hands," she commands, her lips still attached to mine. I waste no time offering them.

She turns me over, tying me up a little tighter than usual. My wrist hurt but the pain feels damn good. Her left hand snakes under my shirt and pinches my nipple as her right hand loosens my belt. I whimper against the wall, biting my lower lip. She pulls down my trousers and roughly squeezes and kisses my ass. In a flash she is back on my earlobes, sucking it before kissing it.

"Open your mouth," she demands.

With my eyes closed, I obey. She slips in a small cold egg shaped object I can't see with her left hand, and her right travels to my butthole.

"Make it wet for me," she whispers against my ear.

Her fingers are wet and warm, massaging the surface of my butthole while I suck the object. She takes it back and before I can gulp, she shoves it into me, pressing herself against my body and I throw my head back into her shoulder.

She holds me by the chest, kissing and sucking my neck. Slight pain shoots through my hole and I wince. her finger continues to push the object until it's fully inside me. Then she spins me around, brings my face to hers and kisses me softly.

"Come back," she whispers, rendering pecks all over my face.

"Elina—"

An intense vibration explodes in my ass and I stifle a loud moan, shaking as I drop my head onto Elina's collarbone, consumed by pleasure.

"Oh my God!" I moan with a gasp, pulling the belt that has my hands bound. "Please... I... Mmh..." I squeeze tighter, struggling to stay standing.

She pulls me up and pins me against the wall, covering my mouth with her palm. I continue to moan uncontrollably.

"Shut your gorgeous mouth up and take it like a good slut," she says, and I struggle not to moan.

Holding my gaze, she releases her hold on my lips and leans back, leaving her finger on my nipple, squeezing and watching me crumble into a whimpering mess. Her free hand travels to my dick and grips it, stroking my full erection and forcing my quiet whimpers to turn into muffled moans. My body won't stop trembling, the pleasure from being stimulated both ways is overwhelming.

Someone attempts to open the door—Elina never locks a door—she slams the door shut with her right hand and increases her stroking pace. I'm convinced she wants them to hear.

The women continue talking right outside the door. I take a quick glance around and realize we are in the women's dressing room. The vibration in my ass increases and she lifts my shirt and bites my nipple.

I close my eyes, surrendering myself to every bit of pleasure she is inflicting on me. I can't fight it anymore, and fuck! I don't want to. She wants me leaking and begging, she wants to see me weak and defenseless, she wants me undone.

I am not nothing, if not hers to wreck.

I reach for the sweet release of an orgasm, trembling in euphoria when she pulls the butt plug out of my ass and stops stroking all of a sudden, pressing down in the center of my dick.

She is cutting me off!

Fuck! Fuck! Fuck!

I groan, shutting my eyes tightly to beat her to it.

Oh no! Please no Elina! I try stopping myself from cumming instead, biting my lips and stomping my feet.

I am too late. I watch the cum leak out of me in frustration and deep disappointment. My body reels from the sensation of the most unfulfilling, dissatisfying orgasm—if I can call it that—I've had in years.

I drop my head on her shoulder, breathless as she loosens the belt. The only thing worse than having my orgasm ruined, is knowing that I have no future prospects of experiencing a proper one under her till I concede.

She pulls me away from her to get a better look at my face. My focus remains with the sensations coursing through my body. I was so close to an orgasm—so close. She licks my nipple and I shiver.

"Please, Elina... Don't leave me like this? Please..." I beg with weak breaths.

"I'll never feel your cock in me again?" A smirk, cold and calm, slithers across her lips. She leans in, placing her cheek against mine and whispers: "How about now? Tell me you don't want to fuck me?"

I swallow, incapable of forming words. Fucking her is all I need right now. I need her warmth. I need an orgasm, I need a real one.

"I'll see you back at home then." She wipes the leaked cum on her hand with my face, then turns, exiting the dressing room.

I slide down to the ground, falling on my knees, emotionally and physically wrecked. I take my cock in my hand and begin stroking, hoping to pick back up where she abandoned me.

It is pointless.

THIRTEEN
A WICKED BRUNCH

"Why is it so important?" Hathai lifts her gaze to me.

"Everybody needs friends, people we can lean on, share our thoughts with."

"Phi Martha was my friend."

"Sure, she was. But I meant people your own age."

"People my age are boring, they don't understand how life works."

"How does life work?" I tilt my head to the side.

"It's mundane, vile, repetitive. People my age think Mary Poppins is in the sky and she dances on rainbows. It's so stupid." Hathai exhales.

"You don't think life can be filled with rainbows?"

"If the rain will come again, what was the point of the rainbow in the first place?"

"What did Phi Martha think about that?" I ask and Hathai looks way, taking a moment.

"She believed in the rainbows."

"Ah ha. And she was your friend."

"She always knew the rain was coming."

"I see— What was your favorite thing about her?"

"Her hair," the answer falls out of Hathai the second I asked the question. "I loved the way she packed it. It was very... neat." She smiles.

"We love neatness," I say, she exhales a small laugh. "If you could do anything differently than aunty Martha, what would you do?"

"Die sooner," Hathai replies with a cold calmness.

I recline into my seat, rubbing my lips with a finger, my elbow sits on the armrest. I can't let her see how unsettling I find her answer.

"Why is that?" I manage to say, clearing my throat.

"Spare you the pain of getting attached, caring for me."

"Hathai—"

The sound of her scheduled alarm goes off and she rises from her seat.

"I have ballet."

"Thanks for sharing today," I say.

"Phi, when are you coming back?"

"I never left."

"It's because of her, isn't it?"

"Khun Cheng?"

She nods.

"No, I just had to return home."

"You should come back." She turns.

My eyes follow her to the door as she exits the study.

It isn't how easily those words rolled out of her mouth that fills me with concern as I walk down the hallway leading to the stairs. It's the certainty in her eyes as she spoke. The eerie calmness in her tone. She's reaching for something or trying to tell me something and so far, I have failed to make sense of anything.

I turn into the staircase, not sparing a moment to glance over at the left-wing, I could care less about Elina today. It hasn't become easier to not think about her, everything is starting to feel heavy again. However, the events at the mall strengthened my resistance to her will. She wants me, or at least a part of me, the part that reminds her of Kiet. And she knows I am willing to offer it, she knows she's a drug I cannot quit. But I have come to realize—so am I to her.

I exchange greetings with the driver and enter the car. I am not eager to go home. I haven't seen her in a while, she's usually lurking around. Maybe that day at the mall, seeing me so weak and hungry for her touch reassured her I would bend to her will. I sigh at that thought. I just might—I. Miss. her.

The car takes off and I press play on my favorite sad music playlist on Spotify to go along with my self-pity.

I roll down the window glass and rest my head on the panel, letting the breeze brush against my forehead and play with my hair. I move my gaze back to my phone in search of the next music to listen to, then queue and return my gaze to the view.

Elina's car approaches from the opposite direction. I guess she hasn't been home all day if she's just returning. Our cars begin to cross, I notice her window glasses are down too.

She sees me and I see her.

Our eyes meet and my heart drops. Something turns in my stomach. We hold each other's yearning gaze as our cars drive past each other.

She looks sad—she always looks sad.

***

There is nothing the elite high-class society of Bangkok adore more than a good brunch. Khun Kittibun's brunch events are the talk of Bangkok's wealthiest every year. He is of course one of the most talked about men in Thailand, it's expected.

I arrived thirty minutes ago with Luce in one of the grandest gardens I have ever seen. The decorations look like something out of an Alice in Wonderland film: free flying butterflies and artificial ones to match, white chairs and tables lines with gold and silver, majestic tall flower stands, fountains of cakes and cute teacups. It smells like a fresh bakery in a sea of flowers.

Since my arrival, I have wandered around the dream-like garden, stuffing my mouth with sweets and cakes. I take a stand beside the chocolate fountain and watch as the fine guest's troop in with their rosy outfits, flowery hats, tight smiles and poised shoulders. Elegance is of the utmost importance amongst Bangkok's elite, and for many peasants like myself—as Hathai would say—who are 'privileged' to attend these brunches, a certain level of style and decorum is expected.

I opted for simple cross belt shorts and a white shirt, paired with a cute bamboo hat, but now it is clear that when Lucifer said, "farmers casual" he forgot to add, "but make it fashion week". It's a brunch event and they all look like they walked off a Vivienne Westwood runway. At least I am in the same hue as them, I really do not care for style or decorum.

"Hey slugger!" Plerng walks up to me, dressed in a strawberry flowing gown, a beautiful compliment to her dark glowing skin. We share a warm swaying hug. "You look like Peter Pan in that adorable hat. You also look like you could use a drink or some Advil."

"It's barely 8am."

"Exactly, what better time to get drunk." She laughs. "What's up with you and your dad anyway, he's called a couple of times."

"Just... let it cycle out."

"You both had a fight?" she presses on.

"Sort of."

"What was it about?"

"Stuff."

"What stuff?"

"Stop prying."

"Since when am I not allowed to pry? We used to tell each other everything and now you're like weird with your little weird secrets or whatever." She sips her drink.

"What secrets?"

"I don't know, Wine, you tell me. You moved in with Lucifer and then there is this talk about someone that looks like you frolicking; or just... licking, with someone that looks exactly like your client, Elina Cheng. I figured at some point you'd come tell me, but you know, I don't want to... Pry."

"Plerng..."

"Compadre's!" A cheerful Lucifer approaches and throws his arm across Plerng and I's shoulder.

"Oh, look, it's my least favorite thief." Plerng shoves his hand away.

"Plerng, you've got to stop calling me that," Lucifer complains.

"That's what you are."

"What am I missing?" I ask, throwing glances between Plerng and Lucifer.

"Lucifer, asked my father for this. I thought it was Po's brilliant idea, a way to fuck me over, but no, Lucifer was the one that asked."

"Plerng, it's not theft if you didn't want it," I say, realizing how insensitive my words were the moment it left my lips.

"You're taking his side?" her voice elevates with a stern frown on her face.

"That didn't come out right. Listen, I'm not taking anyone's side here."

"We aren't kids anymore, Plerng. I am just taking on a little responsibility to help my partner out," Lucifer says.

"Responsibility? Oh, screw you Luce!"

"Plerng you are blowing this way out of proportion, not really you," I include.

"You both. Can suck. My clitoris."

Lucifer and I sigh.

"We had a plan! Get through university, get on the plane and travel around the globe. I haven't changed! Both of you have! Now everyone is talking about responsibilities, being dodgy and shady, avoiding me like I am the problem?"

"Plerng—" I try to speak.

"You know what, Wine, you can go fuck yourself! You too, Luce! 'Not really me'? Are you kidding? If there is anyone who has remained the same, it's me! Both of you keep changing!" She turns away. "What the fuck!" Plerng slaps my arm. "Why didn't you tell me she was coming!"

"Who?" I groan.

"Junta fucking Cheng! Oh my God!" Plerng gasps, her eyes drowning in excitement.

I turn towards the entrance and see Elina, Junta Cheng and a tall brown-haired woman who looks like a pageant queen making an entrance.

"She brought that as her date?" Plerng faces wears a look a of disgust.

"That?" Lucifer asks.

"Darika Paithoon, the woman Junta is currently wasting her time on. I don't care how many fucking pageants she has won, she's not good enough for Junta. She has no style, no grace, her wealth is nothing in comparison to that of Junta's, they're not even on the same level. She's obsessed with Junta or something."

"Sounds a lot like you," Lucifer replies.

"I'm not obsessed, I know Junta quite well. She never dates anyone more than a couple months, Darika will be no different. Junta has taste." Plerng sips her drink.

"Let me guess, the taste is you?"

"Our families go back generations; we understand eloquence and power. If we were to marry, we'd run this country. Whatever she has with Darika is temporary, she knows better."

"What if it's not, what if they're in love and riding into the sunset as we speak."

"Why don't you shut the fuck up, Luce, and go find someone's company to steal!" Plerng scolds.

"Plerng, give it a rest! I'll hold the position for like five seconds! Grow up!" Lucifer retorts.

"You have some nerve on you, Luce! Grow up? You still do keg stands; you are the fucking child and..."

My eyes stay fixed on Elina as Plerng and Lucifer argue like teenage siblings, squabbling over who gets the last piece. Elina is dressed in long white free flowing trousers and a long-sleeved shirt that buttons all the way up to her neck. There is a diamond necklace underneath her collar with a purple flower crown on her head, perfectly complimenting her sleek, straight, long black hair, paired with her favorite shade of red lipstick. I have never seen her in so many bright colors, she looks ethereal and at the same time, she looks like the villain of a children's book. I'm caught in a trance.

I have avoided her during work hours at the mansion and I had no clue she'd be in attendance today. I fist my palm as the full weight of how much I have missed simply standing close to her dawns on me. Eloquently, Elina and Junta exchange greetings with other guests. Her smile is a sight I scarcely see and there she is, giving it away freely to strangers. She's indeed the most beautiful woman I have ever known.

She looks my way and our gazes lock from across the garden. My heart stops—my world stops. Elina tilts her head a bit to the right, her gaze softening like she's seen an old friend, making me melt into mush on the inside. I smile. Dammit. I must look so easy.

Claim me, Elina. Make it all stop.

"Ooi!" I exclaim, tired of their ramblings. "Both of you shut it! We have the rest of our lives to kill each other, eh! We can wait a few more hours."

They hiss and scoff at each other while I return my gaze to Elina, her attention is now stolen by her admirers. I sigh.

"There you are!" Khun Kittibun says, making his way to us. "Cheryl, this is my daughter, Plerng. Pardon that horrifying expression on her face, she's mad at me," he says in English. Khun Kittibun and the foreign lady share a laugh.

"Pleased to meet you, Plerng," the foreigner says, exchanging a wai with Plerng.

"This is Witthaya Sutthaya, the child psychologist I told you about. Nong, Cheryl Koski. Remember the mental health organization expanding into Thailand I mentioned?" Khun Kittibun asks. I nod. "Cheryl owns it, you both should talk." Khun Kittibun smiles.

"You are very much welcome to Thailand. Pleased to meet you, Ms. Koski," I say in English, and we exchange the wai.

"And my partner, Charlem, you've met."

"We most certainly have. Good to see you again Mr. Wang," Ms. Koski says.

"Good to see you again, Ms. Koski," Lucifer replies.

"Ah! Khun Cheng," Khun Kittibun hails Junta over and Elina follows. They join our circle in no time. I avoid looking in their direction.

"Cheryl, the Cheng's," Khun Kittibun introduces and they exchange the wai. "It was to my utmost surprise that they honored my invitation. The Cheng's make it a point of duty to be scarce, especially you, Nong Junta."

"My sincere apologies. I have been away in Europe, handling the family business."

"You'll age too fast if you keep at it." They exchange subtle laughter. "And your sister, Nong Hansa?"

"Still in South Africa," Junta replies.

"Well, do send her my regards."

"Of course, Khun."

"Cheryl just moved here, she's expanding one of her companies; a mental health organization into Thailand. She's also keeping an eye out for investors. I think it would be good if you both talked."

"I will be very pleased to discuss your expansion plans," Elina says.

"Thank you very much," Ms. Koski replies.

As they exchange pleasantries, I turn my gaze to Plerng who seems to be mentally undressing Junta Cheng with her eyes. What a flirt. Junta pays her no mind, focused solely on her ongoing conversation.

"Ah! Nong Wine works with one of the Cheng children, I believe yours, Nong." Khun Kittibun points at Elina. "Maybe you can pass on some recommendations?"

"Of course, for what?" Elina replies.

"I am looking for someone to head the child psychology department and Mr. Kittibun thinks Mr. Sutthaya is just the guy," Cheryl explains.

"I see. He is not taking any more clients."

"I am." I turn my gaze sharply to her.

"You are?" Elina squints at me.

"Of course, Khun Cheng. It's my job."

Elina and I share a cold stare, a muscle in her jaw twitches as she bites down whatever I know she wants to say to me.

What, Elina? Did I step on a nerve? Make me behave.

"Very well then, I'll have someone put a call through, Mr. Sutthaya," Cheryl says.

"Thank you, Ma'am," I reply with a smile, avoiding Elina's lingering stare.

"Phi Junta, we meet again," Plerng says.

Junta turns to her with a half-smile that is clearly pretentious. "We've met before?" Junta raises a brow.

"In Paris."

"This is my daughter, Plerng," Khun Kittibun introduces.

"She's grown. Last time I saw her, she was wearing black and white."

Plerng chuckles in her throat. "It's been years since I wore black and white, Phi."

"I can see that." Junta looks away.

Plerng leaves her flirtatious gaze on Junta, and I roll my eyes.

"We should probably take our seats?" Khun Kittibun suggests.

Elina won't take her eyes off me; I find it both annoying and exciting. Each time I turn my head in her direction, our eyes meet and I instantly look away with my heart racing. She is all the way on the other side of the garden, but every single stare feels like she is right beside my cheek. I need her to stop freaking staring! I can't look at her if she's looking at me.

Midday arrives and brunch begins to wind down. The guests begin saying their goodbyes with warm hugs and air kisses. The announcement of Lucifer's new appointment was met with questionable smiles and cheerful claps. It seemed he was already being welcomed into the foundation, but I could tell some of the guests were displeased.

"He's a looker," Lucifer says, smiling at one of the serving boys at the other end, clearing the table. Khun Kittibun turns away from his iPad to see whom Lucifer is referring to.

"He's not your type, Nong," Khun Kittibun replies, turning back to his iPad with a smile.

"Put him in a maid dress and he'll be." They both laugh and I bury my curiosity in my teacup.

I look up and Elina is walking hands in pocket towards our table. I squeeze the handle of my tea cup, suddenly, it is too heavy.

"Nong, leaving?" Khun Kittibun inquires.

She nods. "Lovely brunch, thank you, Khun." Elina bows.

"Hope to see more of your family," Khun Kittibun says.

Elina smiles, nodding, and turns her gaze to me. "Wine," she calls.

I choke on the tea half way down my throat, she's never called me that in front of anyone close to me, so publicly.

"Khun Cheng," I reply, wiping my mouth and blinking to avoid holding her gaze.

Everyone's eyes are on us, watching in silence for over a minute as Elina's unwavering stare pierces through me, with no words to accompany it. Elina smirks and turns away, heading for the exit. I place down my tea cup on the table with shaky hands. Every muscle in my body is too weak.

"Get up." Plerng pulls me and drags me over to them. "Phi Junta," Plerng calls.

Junta Cheng turns towards us, away from the guests she is saying her goodbyes to. "Yes?"

"I was wondering, how long will you be in Thailand for?"

"That is not information you are privy to, Nong."

"I apologize. I'd love to invite you to a dinner party, my friend, Wine," Plerng places her hand on my shoulder, "is putting together."

"I am?" I whisper. Plerng's fingers dig into my shoulder and I stifle a groan.

Junta's eyes scan me as though there is something terribly wrong with my appearance.

"I'm sorry, Nong. My schedule is full. Maybe, next time you are in Paris." Junta turns away.

"Phi..." Plerng steps forward. "How about a private dinner? We are launching the finest intercontinental restaurant that will be the best in all of Asia."

"Better than the ones run by my family?"

"Definitely, way better."

Junta laughs tightly. "Pardon me, but I must ask. Is this for business or for pleasure?"

"Why can't I have both?"

"An ambitious girl, admirable." Junta takes a few steps forward. "I don't date girls," she says, not blinking.

"You're just ten years older than me, Phi. I'm twenty-eight. I'm a woman."

"You're a girl. Still running around, spending Po's money. No responsibilities, not enough heart breaks, no care in the world. Probably doesn't know what it's like to be touched by a woman—the right way." Junta smirks. "I don't have the time to teach a girl how to be a woman. Call me when you turn thirty-five... I might indulge you." Junta turns away.

I watch her rejoin Darika and they exit the garden hand in hand. I turn to Plerng. Her face is flushed, her eyes squinted in fury. I can hear the heaviness in her breath.

"Plerng—"

"Shut the fuck up, Wine."

She storms out.

Plerng always gets what she wants, Khun Kittibun spoilt her that way. Junta will be a tough nut for her to crack, this will be the first time someone has ever turned her down and hell hath no fury like a jealous Plerng.

FOURTEEN
HERS TO OWN

I arrive at the Koski Foundation a few minutes before 10am as scheduled. A six-story grey building, fortified with smart technology and designed with sleek futuristic attributes. This might become my life after Elina, exactly what I need to pull me away from my draw to her. A new world, with new challenges, new goals, new responsibilities. I need new responsibilities, a tough challenge I can dig my mind into. That was the whole point of a PhD anyway.

Elina is set in her ways like a rock in hard earth, unmoving and solid. It's one of the many things about her that made me marvel. Someone so refreshingly confident in her choices. At the same time, I think it's one of the things that might ruin me.

I won't lay myself down for another woman that doesn't want me the way I need her. It was painful enough the first time.

But I do not exaggerate when I say this decision to breaking me. I saw the man I could become in submission to her. He was a better man than I am. Happier, bolder, brighter. Doing the right thing often taunts the heart in the beginning. This ache in my chest will melt in time.

"Sawatdee krap, Khun," I greet the receptionist and we both exchange the wai.

"Sawatdee kha, Khun," the smartly dressed young woman returns my greeting. "How may I help you?"

"I have an interview scheduled for today, Witthaya Sutthaya."

"One moment, please." She types into her computer. "I'm sorry Khun, your interview has been canceled."

"Canceled? Khun Koski set it up herself, do you mind checking again?"

"I'm very sure it's canceled, Khun. Our new management gave the instruction. Most interviews have been canceled in light of our acquisition. My apologies."

"May I ask why?"

"It's not disclosed here, Khun."

I nod. "Thank you." I turn away, exhaling my disappointment.

How could so much have changed in just five days I wonder, taking my phone out to put a call to Khun Kittibun in hopes of getting him to help me get across to Khun Koski. A thought crosses my mind. I turn, walking back to the receptionist.

"I'm sorry to bother you again, Khun."

"Please, what else can I help with?"

"You said your new management made the change?"

"Yes, we've recently been acquired, a lot of changes are going on at the moment. Sorry for the inconvenience, human resources are still trying to catch up."

"I see. May I ask what company acquired the Koski Foundation?"

"Cheng Global, Khun," she replies with a pleasant smile. "They are now our parent company. Here is a pamphlet, if you'd like to familiarize yourself with some of our new goals."

I blink, fisting my left palm in anger as I retrieve the pamphlet. "Thank you." I bow.

"You're welcome."

As I walk back to the rotating exit door, I stare down at the pamphlet. A fiery pit of anger swells in my stomach as my eyes catches the bold logo of Cheng Global: a bright white capital letter C in Latin font.

I squeeze it and swallow. In a flash, I am out of the building.

Still fuming, but battling to conceal it under a calm exterior, I storm into the Cheng mansion, squeezing my bag as I blow past the housekeepers in the common area, ignoring their greeting. I hurry up the stairs and hurry back down in one turn.

"Sorry, Phi. Sawatdee krap, where is Khun Cheng? Lower office?" My question is just as hasty as my patience.

She points up the stairs. "Upper office, Nong. Is everything alright?" Phi Chailai asks. She's the oldest of all the housekeepers in the residence, well into her forties. They all turn to her for motherly guidance, and she treats us all like her children.

I wai once more in apology for my abrupt behavior. "Yes, Phi." I pass a fading smile before dashing up the stairs and into the left wing.

Without knocking I push the door open and barge in. Elina stands by her desk, her phone to her ears, making a call. She turns to me and raises a finger, signaling me to wait and I halt. My aggrieved gaze travels across the office in one glance. I start to take notice of how clean and arranged her once disorganized office is. It doesn't smell like cigars either, just the sweet smell of her jasmine perfume lingers. I stand, waiting with my anger for her to get off the phone. Minutes and more minutes go by and I continue to wait.

"Wine," she calls softly, holding the phone away from her ear. "Why not sit."

"Why did you do that? Why did you buy Koski?" I ask under my breath, biting down my anger.

"They were looking for an investor, I was looking to buy. It was good business."

"Don't fucking play with me, Elina! You once asked me not to manipulate you. Why the fuck! Are you doing the same thing to me!"

She raises her phone back to her ear. "I'm going to have to call you back." She calmly hangs up. "Wine—"

"I want to be yours! I have made that very, very, very clear! You don't want me, so please Elina... Leave me alone! You cannot play with my life when you deem fit. I'm not for you to toss around, neither am I for your amusement. I won't tolerate it anymore... I won't—"

"Wine—"

"I won't, Elina! Do you not see what you do to me? Do you not see how I break for you? Choose me or leave me alone!"

"Those are for you." She points at the table beside me.

My head snaps down and I see two copies of the contract I made on her table. I scoff, shaking my head. "You must think I just sit around, waiting for you."

She walks up to me and lifts her hand to my burning cheek. I throw my face away and she moves it back to her gaze. My breathing is heavy, my heart is pounding. But like water, pouring smoothly out of a spring mountain, her stare moves through me, commanding me to remain still, washing away the anger that has raged through me for an hour.

"Weren't you... waiting for me?" her voice is a sweet mellow tone.

My gaze softens alongside hers and I lean into the warmth of her palm.

"I... I've done more than wait for you, Elina. I've been stuck... you left me with the pain of your rejection... alone. It hurt." I swallow.

She caresses my cheek with her thumb. "You will never have to wait again, Pretty Thing," she says.

I raise my brow in surprise, my anger easily giving way to coyness.

To completely give myself to Elina in submission, sink into her world, see myself through her eyes, gladdens my heart in more ways than words can express. I want to stay mad, yell at her for leaving me wanting for too long, for toying with me all these weeks. The loneliness I felt from her rejection haunted me through sleepless nights.

But—she is Elina Cheng.

"Aren't you going to sit?"

Bewildered, I didn't notice Elina take a seat on the sofa. I pick my copy of the contract and her eyes follow me as I sit opposite her. She smiles at me. I hate—love when she does that: silently watch me. It makes me nervous as I try to decipher what she is thinking, at the same time, it feels good to be seen. She leans forward and picks up her copy of the contract from the coffee table, opening a few pages.

"I noticed you ticked fisting as a soft limit?" Elina begins, before I am even settled into my seat.

"Yes."

"You've never done it?"

"No."

"Why not?"

I draw a deep breath, my nerves are still trying to collect themselves, anger makes me jittery. "I've always preferred pegging... and milking."

"You've never seen my strap; it might be bigger than my hands," she jokes and I let out a breathy smile, so does she. "Hard limit to golden showers?" she continues.

"Yes."

"Me too. Soft limit for triple penetration?"

"Yes."

"Interesting."

"Why?"

"Just is. You consented to verbal humiliation?"

I lower my gaze, feeling slightly judged. "Only if you want to."

"I'd love to do a lot of things to you, Wine. Unholy, sinful things." She smirks. I fold my lips, holding back a smile. "Wrestling is an interesting one. You think you can take me?" She winks at me and I chuckle. "I'm glad you consented to shaving, I'm quite skilled. Hot waxing soft limit?"

"Yes— Why do you keep reading my choices back to me, aren't we going to negotiate?"

"There isn't much I didn't agree with, it's just fun watching you squirm," Elina replies. Our eyes meet and we exchange coy smiles. "Please turn to appendix 1. Rules and protocols, paragraph 3," she says. I flip through my pages. "As a general rule, the submissive's orgasms are not controlled, unless otherwise communicated. However, should the submissive have orgasms outside of the Dominant's presence, he shall communicate this to the Dominant."

"Yes."

"Your orgasms are mine; you never touch yourself without my consent and you never cum unless I verbally or otherwise grant you permission," she says.

I curl my toes inside my shoes at the sound of her distinct low tone. "Agreed," I reply. She scribbles down.

"The submissive shall be responsible for pickup, cleaning, and putting away of sex toys and so on after play."

"Yes."

"I'll do that myself—except of course when you break one of my rules. You will be cleaning the whole playroom in nothing but an apron, with a bucket and rag." Her eyes remain coy but her voice strong and stern.

"Ok," I say.

"Sexual relations with others shall be conducted in a manner that shall not expose risk to the health and safety of either partners in this agreement?"

"Yes."

"I won't share you," Elina states.

"I have these fantasies. Sexual fantasies. A lot of them involve threesomes or group sex and I'd love to explore them. With you completely in control of who and when of course."

Her fingers tap lightly on the edge of the contract. I can see the decision dancing in her mind. To share me or not share me.

"Very well. It would be fun to pass you around a room filled with long hard eager dicks. Watch them take turns on that little tight hole of yours that never gets fucked, before riding your face."

A wave of warmth showers over me and I swallow, letting out a quiet sigh. I slide my contract over my rising erection, clasping my legs together. Elina softly chuckles.

"You are too easy," she says, returning her gaze to the document. "You expressed in paragraph 11: during non-play sexual activities, the dominant is to present herself naked."

"Yes."

"There will be no non-play sexual activities."

"Why can't I see you naked," I ask. She leaves her gaze on me in silence and we share a crippling tension. I look away, conceding. "Ok."

"I'll consent to breast and pussy worship."

"Really?"

"Blindfolded."

"I'll take it." I grin.

"You consented to flogging, canes?"

"Hard limit with canes and wires. Everything else is fine."

She nods and scribbles down.

"Throat fucking?"

"Yes."

"How long can you stay in a chastity belt without release?"

"A month?"

"Are you asking?"

"A month."

"Impressive. I will push it from time to time, if it ever gets too long, talk to me."

I nod.

"Feminization?" she asks.

"Yes, in private."

"Bondage with chains, ropes, wires?"

"Yes, to chains and ropes. Wires are a hard limit. Sorry, I didn't know I had to specify."

"That is fine. You listed spanking as punishment?"

"Yes."

Elina chuckles. "Not when you love pain, Wine. We will find more interesting punishments for you as we go along. You must always communicate clearly with me, that's a rule. Never feel like you've said too much, do you understand?"

"Yes." Phi Lamon would never agree to that for sure.

"Weekly dinners with my family, I presume you mean Hathai?" she continues.

"Yes."

"No, she—"

"It's non-negotiable," I cut in.

"Monthly. If you can get her to attend, I'll be there."

"I'll get her to attend," I say, doubting that a little.

"Paragraph 14 states the dominant shall take rest in the submissive's bedroom after play?"

"Yes."

"No."

"Why not?"

"I like my space after play."

"Once a month."

She taps her fingers against the couch, contemplating. "Fine. You also stated weekly dates, let's make that monthly too."

"Ok." I sigh.

She is deliberately shredding all the chances I put in there that will allow me spend time with her in a less sexual way.

"Cuddling sessions twice a week? It's a stretch for me," Elina continues.

"Once a week?"

"Twice monthly."

"I want it, once a week," I insist.

She narrows her eyes at me. After a few minutes, she nods, and I hide my smile.

"I wondered why there were no public sexual relations stated here?"

"You're a private person, didn't think you'd want to engage."

"I'm far from private, Wine. If I wanted to fuck you over a bridge, I'd gag you and fuck you."

My cock hardens once more and I flush.

"You have your playroom in a basement, behind a hidden door, if that doesn't scream private."

"It's there because it's sexy, not because I want to hide it."

"Right."

"You are avoiding it aren't you, public sexual activities," she says. Why did I even try to slip that in? "You care too much about people's perception of you, Wine. We will change that—together."

I nod. "Alright."

"I don't mind a bratty sub every now and then, but I prefer my submissive obedient and orderly for the most part."

"Okay."

151

"I also do not wear leather."

"Fine with me."

She flips through a few more pages.

"Is there any particular title of dominance you prefer to be addressed by?" I ask.

"My name is a title of dominance." She lifts her gaze to me. "When you're screaming, begging to cum, or just— begging. You will use my name. Every time. And each time you hear someone else say my name, which... believe me won't be often. Let it be a reminder that I own you, that you're mine, every inch of you."

I swallow, holding her piercing stare.

"Go ahead, say it," she commands.

It's a long while before I can finally bring myself to say her name, "Elina." My heart races. In a blink of an eye, it holds new meaning to me.

"Good boy." She leans back into her seat, smiling at me proudly before turning back to her document.

I watch her flip through more pages and more seconds fly by.

"Can I address you as... Mommy... on occasion?"

Saying that out loud after years of thinking it instantly cripples me with embarrassment and anxiety. I avoid looking at her, squeezing my eyes shut.

"Look at me," she says and my heart drops into my stomach. I turn slowly to her soft gaze. "What are you so afraid of?" she asks in a tender tone that calms me.

"I... I... umm..."

"I'll never judge you, Wine. I need you to understand that. Not when it comes to this, not when it comes to anything. I'd love for us to build a solid trust system, and I think the first step is making you understand that. I see you, Wine. completely and I accept you, completely. I'll prove it to you, give me a chance to earn your trust."

Warmth spreads throughout my body as if I am being wrapped in a huge comforter. I feel safe—I feel really safe. When she took away those little dates, it felt as though she was avoiding getting close to me and then she goes and says something this intimate to me. My eyes water and I press my lips to stop the tears from dropping, trying so hard to be strong.

"Crawl to me," Elina commands tenderly.

Without hesitation, I descend on all fours, crawling to her in obedience. I arrive by her foot, staring down at her high heels as I sit on my legs waiting eagerly for her next command. She lifts my face to her gaze.

"You can call me Mommy when you feel like it, Pretty Thing." She kisses my left cheek softly. "Have I ever told you how beautiful you are?" she says. I shake my head and she giggles.

She reaches to the side stool, retrieves a small box and hands it over to me. I open it and it's a beautifully crafted black leather submissive collar, paired with a black leather bracelet to match. I run my fingers slowly over the collar's hard but smooth surface. My own collar. I truly can't believe it. This is real, she owns me. I flip it over and imprinted behind it, in bold italics: *ELINA CHENG'S PROPERTY*.

I flush, and finally, the tears I've fought so hard to hold back, run down my cheek.

"Do you like it?"

"Yes. Yes I do, Elina. I like it a lot. Thank you." I smile amidst the tears.

She takes it from me, leans over and wears it across my neck, smearing me with her warmth and perfume.

"Comfortable?" she asks.

I adjust it just a little bit around my neck and nod, shying away from her stare. "Yes, Elina."

"Look at me."

I slowly turn to her kind smiling face and we both giggle. She pats my head and wipes the tears off my cheeks.

"You smell good," she says.

"It's my new body oil. Do you like it?"

"Yes." She rubs my cheek. "It matches your soft skin." She holds my gaze. As if under a spell, I am mesmerized.

"I am in awe of you, Elina."

"Don't say flattering words today, Pretty Thing. I'm weak for you."

"I am always weak for you, Elina."

FIFTEEN
RAINDROPS ON SUNFLOWERS

Elina and I talk more ever since I became hers. As a matter of fact, talking is all we've done in the last three weeks. She has not kissed me yet, let alone put me in bondage.

I don't do domestic work because of all the cleaners made available, but it is something I want. I've always loved cleaning for my Domme. I have taken up cleaning up her offices and the Playroom we never use, but they are always cleaned before I arrive.

During my morning check-ins, Elina gives an assignment for the day. I never expected any of those assignments to be centered around my spiritual growth. In the past two weeks, I have visited the temple thrice, made merit twice and I've lost count of how many times I've meditated. I bet Po would be really excited about this one. For years I have avoided prayer and meditation. Self-resentment and guilt do not go well with those two things. I'm far from where I need to be, I can barely sit through a five-minute meditation session without the clamoring thoughts taking over. However, it feels great to start making an effort again. Reconnecting with my faith.

My hardest task would certainly be the self-praise text I must send Elina daily. I have no clue why she insists on receiving messages where I praise myself or share a good thought I had during the day. It's cringey and uncomfortable. But I do it anyway, not that I think there is any truth to the words I type—at least yet.

I have come to know her favorite color is actually indigo. She prefers a rainy, chilly weather to a warm one; because just like me, chaotic weathers bring her comfort. However, Elina hates snow.

Elina works out three times a week and sometimes requires me to workout alongside her. We compete on the treadmill, but she always loses. Elina takes failure very well; we lose minutes laughing and joking about it. I won't pretend I don't enjoy watching her sweat, watching her breasts bounce and imagining what it would feel like to suck and fondle them without a blindfold. I also wonder what she'd taste like after we're done. I'd really love to lick her sweat soaked pussy after a heavy workout session. I'm hoping she'll grant me permission to do so one day.

Elina has an adorable laugh. Prior to becoming hers, she rarely ever shared it with me, but now it comes regularly and with ease, I find myself waiting to hear it. I search for jokes online and send her through a voice note, just so she can reward me with that laugh. I'm whipped for it. But I'm even more whipped when she tiredly calls me by my pet name. Elina's voice becomes soft and groggy after a long day. I hate seeing her exhausted, but I love hearing her exhausted.

I wear my bracelet of ownership every day and catch myself staring at it for minutes on end, thinking of her: what she is doing, where she's going, if she's eaten, if she's smiling. She doesn't smile often. My bracelet is like a portal to her, an emotional chain that binds me to her.

It's only been three weeks, I'm still learning how to be her submissive, learning how to fit into her small, protected world. Maybe it's too soon, but I hope to become a submissive she can be proud of more than anything. Maybe, if I'm lucky, more than just a submissive. Elina is the one time I've followed my gut instincts and it turned out completely great.

I look over at Elina whose feet are on the table, relaxed into her seat as she bites her pen and reads a document. We've been sitting in silence for an hour since I arrived. I've been working on a psychological paper I need to have published by year's end and got carried away. She looks tired, she needs to stop working. She flips the page and scribbles down something. I put down my laptop and walk over.

"Hey, Pretty Thing." She smiles as I arrive.

"Hey." I lean on the table.

"What were you working on?"

"The paper I'm trying to publish by year's end."

"The one about generational trauma?"

"Yes."

"How is that going?"

"Very slow, but good progress."

"Good. Do you need something?"

"You look tired."

"It's been a long week, I am tired." She tilts her head to the side.

I roll a seat over and carry her legs onto my lap, take off her shoes and gently press. She exhales, throwing her head back.

"You should take a break," I say.

"I'll try— I'm leaving for Singapore next week."

"Hmm."

"You'll be caged while I'm gone," she says and I pause, lifting my gaze to hers.

"Ok." I grin. "How long will you be gone?"

"Two weeks."

I nod and go back to massaging her feet.

"You've barely touched me these past few weeks," I say.

"Is that a complaint?"

"No."

"Are you masturbating?"

"No."

She laughs softly but I refrain from looking at her face.

"Say it then," she demands.

"Say what?"

"What you want to say?"

I press my lips together, taking a moment before saying: "I want to take you somewhere this weekend."

"A bit too early to be cashing in your dates, don't you think?"

"It's not a date."

"Oh?"

"I want to cook for you, clean for you, do your laundry. I can't do that here where you have someone for everything."

"I see," Elina says.

"What do you see?"

She takes down her legs from my lap and rises from her seat, leaning over me. I press myself to the seat, struggling to hold her stare but eventually concede, lowering it.

"You're trying to seduce me," she says, and I breathe a laugh. "You want me to take you across my knee"—she leans into me, her cheek against mine— "reward you for being a good boy," she whispers, and I swallow. She leans back. "Eyes on me, Pretty Thing."

I turn my gaze to her.

"You haven't even kissed me," I say.

"And?"

"And I'd like to earn it."

She raises a brow. "Where exactly would you whisk me away to if I agree?"

"The countryside. My family owns a house by a river."

"Sounds like I'm getting kidnapped."

We both laugh and a knock comes at the door. Khun Toh makes an entrance.

"Sawatdee Krap, Khun." He bows.

"What is it?" Elina says, leaving her eyes on me.

"Your meeting with the board is in an hour, we need to get going."

She straightens up and I bend over and reach for her shoes, slipping them on one after the other.

"I'll have a chopper drop you off." She reaches for the documents on the table.

"I'll go by myself."

"I–"

"Wasn't asking?" I finish her sentence. "I know. But I'd rather go by myself."

She squints at me. "With a chopper, you'd be there in less than twenty minutes."

"Yes."

"If you insist then." She walks past me.

I smile, already planning the weekend in my head.

I hear her walking back and I turn in the direction of her clicking heels. She lifts my face from behind and kisses me upside down. I part my mouth and let her tongue travel deep as she holds me by the jaw. Our lips smacking until she has had her fill of me.

"You never have to earn kisses," she says. "Kiss me when you feel like it, kiss me if you're bored, kiss me simply because."

I nod.

She kisses my forehead and walks away.

***

I spent all morning shopping cooking ingredients before hopping on the bus. It's been years since I have traveled these roads, seen the city, smelt the air. I turned down the chopper because a quick flight would've robbed me of the chance to see it all. Sitting on a bus, with my head out the window is just far more rewarding.

It is noon when I arrive. Khun Puu built this house when he was my age. It has remained empty since Khun Yâa died seven years ago. Po visits a few times a year to clean it and fix anything broken. Sometimes, during those visits, he'd call me and share childhood memories with me. I could hear the joy of his youth in his laugh. His childhood home always brings him warm memories.

I climb up the wooden stairs and retrieve the key from a hidden crack in the wall. I only have about five hours to cook, clean and get the house ready before Elina's arrival. It is a three-bedroom home with wide tall windows and doors, and it still smells like all the northern dishes Khun Yâa used to make. I open them all to let in the fresh clean air, smiling at all the green. The balcony in the backyard faces the river, it used to be my favorite place to play with Khun Puu. I know Elina will like it here.

Elina is not picky with food, but she favors fish, seafood in general and I'm particularly excellent at making pla kapong neung manao. With the garlic and chilies already chopped, I begin with the cilantro and then the lemon grass. Just as I begin stuffing the barramundi with some lemon grass, I hear vehicles pulling up outside the house. I wash my hands and hurry outside.

Five cars drive in, some Toyota's, some Fords, all black. People in suits alight from them and begin spreading around the compound. I have never seen Elina with so much security, or any at all. One of the bodyguards opens her door and Elina gets down, dressed head to toe in a dark gray pantsuit, already smiling at me. I smile back and walk down the stairs. We share a warm short hug and she ruffles my hair.

"Was it difficult to find?" I ask.

"I wouldn't know, I just handed over the address," Elina replies.

"Quite an ensemble you have here." I glance over at the bodyguards who are already making their way into the house.

"Family policy. I can't leave the capital without ample security. But don't worry, they know how to keep their distance."

"I'm not worried."

"Good."

"Khun Cheng, the house is clear," a bodyguard informs her.

"Thank you," Elina replies and begins her ascension up the stairs. I follow her into the house. "This is very... cozy," she says as we step into the sitting room. "It's... humble."

I breathe a laugh. "You sound like Hathai."

"I do?" She turns to me.

"It's something she'd say to avoid sounding condescending."

"I never sound condescending."

"Sometimes, you do."
"Even with you?"
"Even with me." I nod.
"I apologize then. You should tell me if I do."
"It doesn't bother me."
She holds my gaze for a minute before continuing inside, the sound of her heels stomping against the wood floor. She examines the sitting room with long hard stares, her face tight as she tries to mask her bewilderment. I appreciate the effort. She then walks straight into the kitchen.
"Pla kapong neung manao?" She arrives by the sink.
"Yes."
"One of my favorites." She dips a finger into the lime juice and sucks it.
"You have favorites?"
"Depends on who the chef is."
We both smile.
I get on my knees and take off her shoes.
"I'm almost done with dinner. You should take a bath, change into something more comfortable. There isn't running hot water, but I can make some for you on the stove."
"Thank you." She smiles, running her hands over the wooden counter.
"I'll show you to your room."

***

I led Elina to the freshly cleaned bedroom that used to belong to my grandparents. It is the only one with a queen-sized bed. After making sure she was all set, I returned to the kitchen to finish dinner. It's been almost two hours since, and Elina has remained in her room. I set the table, lay out our meals and light some scented candles before coming to get her.

160

"Elina." I knock. She isn't one to respond to a knock but I'm not quite sure if I can go in. "Elina, are you decent?"

"Come in," she grumbles.

I open the door and walk in. Elina sits on the floor by the bed, resting her head on a pillow. Her long white nightgown hugs her beautifully, showing every curve.

"Elina?" I kneel beside her. "What is wrong?" I crinkle my forehead.

"Just cramps," she mumbles.

"You got your period?" I ask.

"It's not supposed to come for another week, but I feel it coming."

"You should lie in bed."

"It feels better this way." She cups my face without looking. "Did you come to get me for dinner?"

"Yes."

"You worked hard on it. Will you hate me if I pass?"

I shake my head with a smile. "Did you come with your period stuff?"

"Stuff?" A soft laugh escapes her.

"Pads," I say.

"No."

"I'll go get it, there is a store down the street."

"It might not come tonight," Elina says.

"And if it does you will have an option." I rise from the floor. "Do you prefer the sticky one?"

"Pads are fine."

I nod and dash out of the room, retrieve my wallet from the dining table before heading out of the house.

***

With a single knock, I open the door, Elina still sits in the same position I left her in forty-five minutes ago. She was wrong, her night gown is stained. It's small, but I see it. I watch her for a few moments before kneeling to wake her.

"Elina." I rub her shoulders, moving the hair away from her face.

Slowly, she wakes. "Hey, Pretty Thing," she mumbles and my heart flutters.

"Let's get you changed."

"Changed? Why?"

"It came." I point at the blood stain behind her.

She looks down at her dress and sees it. "Oh."

I help her up from the floor then roll out her box to retrieve another night gown. A purple silk two piece. Then I escort her to the bathroom.

"The pads, you didn't give them to me," she says as we arrive by the bathroom door.

"It's inside." I open the door and she steps in.

"What did you do?" Elina chuckles when she sees the pads I already placed on the panties.

"I fixed them for you."

She walks to the sink and starts counting. "Ten of them? We are only here for two days."

"The doctor on YouTube said you need to change three times a day."

"W... what doctor?"

"The one on YouTube."

"And you believed him."

"It was a woman." I smirk. "I'll be in the dining room."

"These are not mine." Elina tugs the panties.

"Bought some at the store, so you don't stain your fancy ones."

"You think my underwear is fancy? You've never seen them."

"Everything about you is fancy, Elina."

She holds my gaze with an adorable smile.

"Ten panties are still too much, Wine." She pouts.

"Billionaires own things in tens." I grin.

She rolls her eyes, shaking her head. I lean in and kiss her cheek.

"Take your time." I kiss her cheek again and leave, shutting the door.

I heat up some hot water and soak a little towel in it before returning to Elina's bedside. She's gone back to sleep. Her cramps got worse, but she turned down the pain meds I got. So stubborn. I retrieve the blindfold hanging in the closet, before kneeling beside her bed. I can't see her naked, but I need to place the towel on her stomach. I cover my eyes with it and gently lift her shirt, carefully placing the warm towel on her abdomen. She moves, but just a little. I cover her back up and go back to working on my paper.

The alarm goes off, it's been four hours since she went to bed, four hours since she wore her first pad. I walk back to her room, my eyes nagging me from staring at my laptop screen for too long.
"Elina... Elina." I tap her shoulder lightly.
She turns to me. "Mmh?" she grumbles.
"You have to change."
"Change what?" she mumbles, her eyes still shut.
"Your pad, it's been four hours."
"I'll do it in the morning."
"That is not what the doctor said, you have to go change."
"I'm so tired, Wine. I'll do it in the morning."
"Elina—"
Her eyes snap open. "The doctor doesn't know everything, Wine. It's too soon."
"It'll only take five minutes," I insist.
She grumbles, rising from the bed. "You are impossible." She shuffles her legs to the door.
She's stained again and so is the bed sheet and she thinks it's too soon? I shake my head as I change the sheets. When I'm done, I find her a new night wear, one of Khun Yaa's old pajamas. I lay it out on the bed and leave for her to change.
The alarm goes off and I wake. It's 2am, another four hours have gone by. I enter her room without knocking.
"Elina... Elina." I tap her shoulder.
"Wine, please go away," she grumbles, wriggling in bed.
"You have to change."

163

"I already did, remember?"
"It's been four hours."
"Wine—"
"Elina, it'll only take five minutes."
"I swear to God!" She rises from the bed and storms out of the room.

I search the bed sheet for stains but there is none.

The alarm goes off and I wake. It's 6am. I walk back to her room and enter without knocking.

"Elina... Elina." I gently rub her forehead.

"I'm up, I'm going." She rises from the bed and shuffles out of the bedroom.

I check the bed and they're no stains. I hear rumbling and lightning flashes. It's about to rain. I sit back on the bed to wait for her in case she needs extra blankets. But I'm too sleepy. I'll just close my eyes for a bit. Just until she's back.

***

Heavy thunder strikes, waking me. I leave my eyes closed as I turn, pulling the blanket over me and wrapping myself. I pull a pillow close to my chest and dig my head into another. Rainy mornings are my favorite mornings. So cozy and intimate. I smile when Elina's scent travels up my nose. It feels like she is next to me, holding me, caressing me. My memory must be playing a funny game with me this morning because I know she didn't sleep in my room last night. I smile. It is one I'm willing to play.

In seconds, I'm turned on, squeezing the pillow and quietly moaning into it. I can feel Elina everywhere, her touch, her kisses, her warmth. The pleasure shoots through me and my nipple tingles. I bite my lower lip and swallow. The walls are thin, Elina will easily hear me but with every passing second I spend wrapped in her scent, my need to moan grows. Fuck. I lower the pillow to my groin area and begin to grind myself against it, sliding my hands under my shirt to find my nipple, then gently squeeze as I moan and wiggle my toes in pleasure.

"Argh... mmh, fuck," I moan, wriggling. "Elina..." I mutter.

"Yes, Pretty Thing."

I jolt up with a gasp, throwing the pillow to the side. Elina sits on the single couch on the other side of the room, a book in her hand. She smiles at me and I look away. Shit! I dozed off in her room.

"I wasn't—"

"Don't let me stop you, Pretty Thing. I'd like to watch." Elina crosses her legs.

I look down at myself, taking notice of my erection.

"Would you prefer I take care of it for you?" she asks.

"No!" I spring up from the bed and race out of the room.

***

It's been pouring heavily all morning. After breakfast I returned to working on my paper and Elina moved to the balcony where she has remained, watching the rain create ripples on the river.

I shut down my laptop, retrieve the coconuts I bought yesterday from the fridge, and join her on the balcony. Her head rests on her palm as she sleeps with a blanket wrapped around her. She's wearing another one of Yaa's night gowns. It's over-sized and has a faded red floral print, but Elina makes it look so regal.

"I'm not asleep," she says, eyes closed.

She stretches out her hand and I hand over the coconut.

"Still getting cramps?" I ask.

She sits up, shaking her head.

"It's only bad on the first day." She sips, nodding her head like Po when he is pleased with something I made. I smile. "Aren't you going to sit with me?" She taps the seat and I join, sipping my drink.

165

She covers me with the other end of her blanket as I fold my legs on the seat. In silence, we watch the rain, the river, the dancing trees, the crawling insects on the railings. We listen to the birds, the wind, the beautiful calmness as our fingers serenade each other's.

"Would you like us to do something? You've been sitting here all day. I must be boring company," I say, turning to her.

She smiles, caressing my cheek with a single finger. "I spend most of my life doing something, Pretty Thing. I like doing nothing with you."

I take her hand and kiss it, rub my cheek all over it before returning my gaze to the river, watching the ripples.

"I like the smell of rain," I say. From the corner of my eye, I can see her smile broaden.

She runs her hand from my shoulder to my hair, gently rubbing my scalp and playing with my hair. I shut my eyes and take in the soothing sensation.

"I like the smell of you," Elina says.

I smile. "What do I smell like?"

"Me."

I laugh, turning to her. Our eyes meet, giving room for more laughter.

I lay down on her lap and she continues petting my hair. Her fingers travel to my jaw and turns my face to hers. Her lips meet mine with softness and I kiss her back in kind. She kisses my chin, then my nose, spreading warmth and tenderness all over my body. I shut my eyes and let my heart sink into the bliss of her touch, her lips, her scent.

"You smell like lilies and sandalwood," she whispers against my cheek. "You smell like raindrops on sunflowers." She kisses my ear and trails her breath to my forehead, planting another tender kiss. "You smell like joy."

"Elina," I whisper.

"Mmh?" She rubs her nose against mine.

"Elina."

"Yes."

"Elina."

She chuckles.

"My beautiful boy," she says, and I smile.

SIXTEEN
THROUGH THE CRACKS

The morning came with the smell of wet leaves and roasted nuts in the air. Elina went to bed early after we spent most of the rainy evening on the balcony. Her arms remained wrapped around me, patting my chest and stroking my hair as we talked about simple mundane things.

It has become a sort of tradition for Elina and I to converse about ordinary mundane things with delicate attention. We shared an hour-long conversation about classical music and renaissance art before deciding farming was a topic of importance. When that ran its course, Elina divulged to me her plan to develop an alternative means of transport in Thailand, using ferry boats and ships so people can ditch the unnecessarily expensive sky train.

Since we've been in the countryside, not once has Elina reached for her iPhone or iPad, two things that are always glued to her. I appreciate that she has given me all her attention, but I have a feeling it has less to do with me and more to do with her needing a break, from everything and everyone.

I cleaned the house and decided to dedicate my morning to fixing the old barn. During Po's last visit, he left behind logs of wood for the fixing of the barn, and while I am quite skilled at taking hammer to nail, splitting wood in halves is not made for these hands. Instead, I employed the efforts of Elina's bodyguards after bribing them with oliang.

They made a competition out of it, taking turns to see who'd split the most wood. It made the morning light with

167

laughter and probably provided a good distraction for them. They've had to build tents outside the house and rotate shifts. All that time spent looking into nothing. I managed to fix most of the barn before retiring into the house to take a shower.

I should be on my way to make breakfast but decided to drop by Elina's room and check in on her. I have remained leaning on the doorway for almost thirty minutes now, admiring the morning sun against her sleeping face, wondering what she is dreaming about... if she is dreaming.

She turns, rubbing her nose adorably with the back of her palm, making me swoon as a smile finds home on my lips.

"Hey, beautiful," she says faintly, her eyes fluttering open.

I deep my hands into my pockets and take a few steps into the room. She taps the bed, signaling me to sit next to her. When I do, she snakes her hand over my knee and I place my palm on it, gently caressing.

I say nothing, listening to her soft breathing and the twittering birds outside the windows fill the room with morning melodies. Her hold on my knees weakens as she drifting back to sleep. I reach over and move the hair away from her face with care. She shifts, but only a little with a soft purr in her throat.

As I take back my hand, she gets hold of my palm and plants numerous soft kisses, pulling me into her tender bosom and we breathe a laugh. My head rests on her chest as she holds me, wrapping my entire body with her hands and legs. It's an endearing warmth and tenderness I feel, I could fall asleep in seconds.

"You smell wonderful," she whispers, digging her nose into my hair.

"I took a shower."

"Mmh, good." Her hands dig into my hair, soothingly scratching my scalp.

"You're burnt out, Elina."

"It seems so." She kisses my forehead. "What's the time?"

"Past ten. Sleep some more, I was going to go make breakfast."

"Let it wait." She kisses my forehead again before squeezing me back in and caressing my back.

For a long moment, I listen to her heartbeat, and soon we are breathing in sync.

"You're not going to take this out of my cuddling time, right?" I ask.

"What?"

"I only have a couple cuddling sessions every month. You can't take this out of it. I was not the one that initiated this."

Her fingers stop stroking my hair and I press my lips into a thin line. Her silence is unnerving. I lean back to catch a better glimpse of her face, see if she is angry at me.

"Was that too needy?" I ask.

She holds up my chin. "What are you so afraid of? Mmh?"

I dig my head back into her chest, squeezing her a little tighter.

***

My mind has continued to wander as I make a simple khai jiao breakfast. Absentmindedly, I stare out the window as the eggs simmer in the frying pan. Elina's question has stayed with me since I left her bedroom. For most of my life, I have felt as though the rug would be pulled out from under me and I'd fall flat on my face for the jest of onlookers. That is why being with Phi Lamon was simpler. Our ending was inevitable. You can't fall flat on your face if you are already on the floor. With Elina, it feels like I'm getting up, like I have a cushion.

It is scary.

The egg is golden brown in all the right places, so I scoop it all into our plates, placing them carefully on the steamed rice before sprinkling extra fish sauce on Elina's and garnishing with some lettuce.

I set the table and walk to her room, knocking only once before Elina answers.

"Breakfast is set," I announce.

My lips curve up at the sight of Elina wearing another one of Yaa's clothes: a lime green oversized gown, long enough to sweep against the aged wooden floor. She stands by the wide window, looking out into the river and brushing her hair.

"Almost ready," she says.

"Yaa's clothes are growing on you."

"They are so comfortable." A soft laugh escapes her.

"You're gorgeous in them." I walk further in. "Let me." I reach for her hair brush and she let's go.

It's such a simple act, but I feel as though I am in sub heaven. If such a thing exists, then this is it. Brushing Elina's hair from tip to scalp. I can smell the rosemary and frankincense she usually rubs in, it's a luscious rich scent that is at the same time calming. Elina has her walls and I understand why she won't let me past them, I have not shown her yet what I can take. She has not seen all of the man I can truly be.

I dig my nose in her hair and inhale deeply and she laughs a light charming laugh.

I'll show you, Elina.

Till then nothing is stopping me from looking in through these cracks.

***

"That looks really good," Elina compliments as I pull her seat. She pulls me down and plants a kiss on my cheek before I sit. "Will you be working on your paper today?"

"Yes." I reach for my spoon and my phone. "I started working on the barn this morning too, will finish it this evening."

170

"You don't have to do it all day."

"Would love to finish it before we leave, so Po won't have to do it when he visits."

"Sweet of you." She takes a spoonful of her food and I search her face for approval of its taste.

With Po, there is always a nod, a smile, something to tell me I did a good job. With Elina it's blank. Should I ask her? Not that I am looking for praise or anything. It'll just be nice to know it actually tastes nice. Or if it tastes bad, she can also tell me, I don't mind the correction. I added the extra fish sauce in hers cause I know she loves seafood. Maybe I shouldn't have done that, it might have made it salty. I barely added salt to the egg, it was—

"I love it," Elina says, cutting through my thoughts. "You did great." She stretches out her hand and rubs my puffed up cheek.

A million butterflies flutter in my stomach as I reach for my phone. "Thanks."

She goes back to eating and for a minute I stare at my phone screen with no aim before coming back to my senses and swiping, checking my email and the news as I eat.

"Do you often do that?" Elina asks.

"Mhmm?" I turn to her.

"Press your phone while eating?"

"Mostly, yes." I turn back to my screen.

"Put it down, Witthaya."

My head snaps back in her direction. She isn't looking at me, but from the tone of her voice, it's clear that was a command. I lay it down on the table, rubbing my neck as I go back to eating, hiding a smile.

"I'll make dinner tonight, som tum? I'll send one of the guards to get the papayas, or even better, tom kha kai? We already have coconuts and chicken." She chews.

"I leave my bet on tom kha kai then."

"Great."

We leave our lingering gazes on each other's beaming faces before striking up another conversation.

Seated across from Elina in the sitting room, I watch her knit, her long fingers poking the yarn in and out with a medium sized needle.

The electricity went out a little over an hour ago after dinner and we turned on the old kerosene lamps and some candles. The rain returned before we sat down for dinner, so we knew it wouldn't take long before the electricity was gone.

It began as a heavy storm, banging the doors and windows, shattering the piled-up wood by the barn, making the trees dance and rippling the once calm river. It has become quite calm now, in an hour or so, it should stop, and the electricity will be restored.

I should be writing, I have only about thirty percent of battery life left on my laptop. However, the sight of Elina knitting is a welcome distraction. Her legs are folded under the heavy brown blanket with her knees brought all the way up to her chest. Her hair is in a messy bun, way too many strands fall carelessly over her face. It has been that way since we had dinner. It has to be one of the worst hair buns I have ever seen. I now know for certain Elina Cheng would make a horrible hairstylist if she were put to the test. But there is something so endearing about the messiness of it all.

Her eyes follow the yarn and needle blankly, almost as if knitting to her is now muscle memory. As if she does not need to be present in her mind to do the repetitive task. Of all the hobbies in the world, for some reason, I never pictured Elina knitting. But I can see why she does.

On most days, Elina appears to be carrying the weight of the world on her shoulders. She has a resting thinking face. When I look at her most times, I worry for her mind. Elina has a sad habit of saying very little, only letting you see what she wants you to. But not now, not when she's knitting. Her face is dull. The kind of dullness that comes with having an empty peaceful mind.

It's a refreshing sight.

"It's so bad." Elina sighs, pouting her lips to one side. "I'm getting it all wrong." She lifts what she's been knitting for over two hours to show me.

"What is it?"

"A sweater."

"I don't see what's wrong with it."

"Some holes are too big, others are too small," she complains.

I rise from the floor, going over to take a closer look. "Where?"

She points. "See?"

"No." I laugh softly. "I can't see it, no one would notice."

"Hathai would. She is a bit of a perfectionist." She goes back to knitting.

"Well, at least I know where she gets that from," I tease, and Elina giggles in her throat. "Thirsty?"

"Yes please."

I walk to the kitchen and retrieve a bottle of water from the fridge, then pour some into a glass cup and drop a slice of lemon into it. She only takes a sip when I hand it to her, placing it down on the stool and continues knitting.

"It doesn't have to be perfect," I say taking my seat. "It's the flaws that make hobbies fun."

"Try explaining that to Hathai."

"She might not get it now, but eventually, she will."

Elina raises her gaze to me, smiling as she nods. It lingers for a bit before she turns back to knitting.

I swallow, tapping the edge of the table, wondering if this is the right time to ask the question scratching my mind. There really is no right time to ask a personal question when it comes to Elina. The answer is always the same: a blank stare.

"When did it change for you and Hathai," I ask. Elina's hands stop pulling the needle, but she does not turn to me. "Was it before or after his death."

Her gaze flutters to mine and there it is, the blank stare. She says nothing and looks away. I nod, taking my answer in the silence. I turn to my laptop and resume typing.

"I was seventeen when I first met him," Elina begins calmly and my face shoots up in surprise. "It was at the royal gala that year. My parents forced me to attend, threatened to take away my black card." She breathes a quiet laugh and the side of my lips twitch as I sit up. "In a grand hall filled with stars from all over the country, he shone the brightest. Everyone was looking at him. He had a charm to him, a rare type of grace. They all wanted to be him, to know him." Her gaze flutters back to mine and holds it. "Fuck him."

Her words steal the ability to move from my body. Jealousy, curiosity, admiration all morphed into one single emotion claws through me. She uncoils herself, lowering her legs to the ground and crosses them.

"But his eyes were on me," she continues in a low precise tone. "As he danced with his wife, kissed her neck, whispered words to her. His eyes were always on me. By the end of the night, when all the dancing and cheering and gossiping was done. I was on him. Breathless. Sweating. Burning with desire so wild I almost went blind. It felt like fucking a god." She breathes. "Most people lose their virginity in very uncanny situations. But not me. I was in heaven. And when it was over, I was addicted. Incapable of moving on... incapable of thinking clearly. He took me to the Winter Olympics that weekend. I don't think I ever came back." She takes a long pause, and the air blows a little warmer on my skin. There is something in her eyes. I see a glint of unfamiliar darkness. "Tell me, Wine. Are these the kind of things you want to hear me say?"

I swallow, releasing a little breath through my nose, digging my nails into the back of my palm.

"No, Elina. And I think you know that. Telling me things I cannot bear to hear, so you don't have to tell me what I need to know."

She makes a face, picking up her yarn and needle and goes back to knitting. "Try not to use that shiny psychology degree on me, Pretty Thing."

"Sometimes, with you, I feel like I'm playing a mind game of chess."

"Who is winning?"

"I have no clue," I'm quick to reply but not from impatience. Rather an eagerness to keep the topic open.

"I was not always like this. So... calculative, detached... cold," she says.

"I don't think you are cold."

"Detached?"

174

"Private."

"Calculative?"

"Very."

She smirks a little. "The rest of the world thinks those things of me. It doesn't bother me anymore. People like you better when you are polite, nice, a push-over. And I used to be all those things. He..." Her gaze trails off, as if chasing a thought. "He murdered that version of me." She pokes the needle. "It was not a fast death. It was slow, piece by piece, like scrapping old paint off a wall. He showed me what I could become, then he showed me how to become it, and I did."

"He taught you how to take control?"

Her pause is long, and I begin to think there will not be an answer when she says, "Men are good teachers of pain. Even when they are licking your boots." She swallows. "Don't ask me anymore today, Pretty Thing. I like this weekend the way it is. Can that be enough for you?"

I nod with a little smile. "Last question?"

"Go on."

"Does knitting help you keep the thoughts at bay?"

"Not today."

"It looked like it was."

"Would you like to know what I can't stop thinking about?"

I raise my brows. *Elina wants to share her thoughts with me?* "Of course, Elina, please."

"Throwing you over that table and fucking you into the middle of Armageddon," she says so matter-of-factly, without a flinch.

"What?" I reply with a laugh.

"I've thought about finger fucking you. Watching you wriggle under me, begging me to stop while you leak. The sounds you'd make, the tears that'll follow when I don't stop pounding your ass. The pleasure I'd get from seeing you weak and worn out because you can't take it anymore. And when you finally cum, like the whore you are, I'd start all over again, letting you suck my breasts while stroking your cock. Long, even, hard strokes, making sure while you whimper with my breasts in your mouth, I drain you of every

175

cum left in you. When you've found your breath, I'd use your face to relief myself of all the pressure you caused in between my legs." She exhales and I clasp my legs together, taming my growing erection. "My menstruation is forty percent cramps and sixty percent horniness," she jokes.

I laugh nervously. Too flushed to look in her direction, I leave my gaze pinned on my dying laptop screen, my skin burning as I hold my breath.

"Relax, Pretty Thing. I don't intend on touching you. I'm not big on period sex. But it's quite tasking thinking these thoughts. I have to walk around with the result of it, while you go scot free. You would be punished for it." The side of her lips twitch playfully, and I giggle.

"You can't blame me for your own thoughts, Elina."

"Then don't be so freaking gorgeous," she snaps back.

My fluttering heart drops into my stomach. Give me a minute to breathe Elina.

"Don't say things like that. You'll shatter me."

"Did you just tell me what I can and cannot say?"

My eyes widen and before I can open my mouth to deter her assumption—

"Get on your knees," she commands, and I obey.

"Elina I—"

"Just because I can't touch you, doesn't mean you shouldn't touch yourself for me."

My forehead crinkles. "Huh?"

"Show me your waist."

I purse my lips coyly, keeping my gaze lowered. "My body is not one of your play things," I tease. I catch a quick glimpse of her narrowing eyes and look away, forcing myself not to grin.

"My patience is wearing thin with your brattiness," she says, putting down her yarn and needle as she turns to me.

"Then you should take me across you knee... and punish me." I struggle to hold her death stare, squeezing my trousers under the table.

"Show me your waist, Witthaya," her command is sharp in a low tone. I shudder, lifting my shirt up just a little bit.

I don't understand her fascination with my waist. It's nothing like Lucifer's wide handsome waist, all muscle with an eight pack, you could punch it and he'd barely feel a thing. Mine is slender and tiny. When I slouch you can visibly see my rolls. There is not much to see. I have really good hair; I think I have a pretty great back structure. Yeah, my back is one of my best features, my jaw too. It could be sharper, but I love the curves I have. My waist, however, I do not get the fascination.

"Higher," she demands.

I lift my shirt higher, above my chest, exposing my nipples. Elina blinks, swallowing, her eyes hold no reserve in making her sizzling lust known. Her sultry stare is a command in itself. A burning command, igniting flames of submission in my soul, my mind, my body.

I squeeze the helm of my shirt as she rises from her seat. She pushes my laptop to the side and seats on the table, looking down at me for a long minute.

"Do you know you have the waist of a slut."

I swallow, lowering my gaze. "No, mommy."

She holds up my chin and I part my lips to breathe a bit easier.

"Good boys don't have waists of sluts, do they?"

"No, mommy," I say with a shaky breath.

Her fingers begin traveling down, tracing a line from my chin down to my chest, running her hand all over my burning skin. She squeezes my left nipple and I gasp a little moan. Her hands continue down to my waist, caressing it before reaching into my pajama trousers and gripping my hardness.

She guides one of my hands into my pajamas, helping me grip my dick while holding my face up by the jaw. Together, we begin stroking me and I tremble from both the sensations between my legs and her tight grip on my jaw.

Her first kiss is gentle, but the second time, she is greedy with me, kissing me hard as we stroke my dick. I whimper into her mouth, quivering as the pleasure begins overwhelming me.

When she lets go of my hand, I cling onto her dress, whimpering as I stroke, our gazes locked in a passion filled stare. She caresses my lips with her thumb, desire burning in her eyes.

"What are you?" she whispers, gently patting my hair.

"Yours," I say, breathless.

She digs her thumb into my mouth, allowing me suckle on it as I stroke myself. My eyes roll back as the pleasure transcends my ability to control myself. I stroke faster, my thighs are too weak to hold my weight.

Elina takes her finger back and swats my hand away from my dick.

"Try that again."

I search her eyes for meaning in her command, the fog of pleasure still swirling around in my mind.

"What. Are. You?" she asks again.

I swallow, drawing a steady breath. "Your whore." I whimper.

SEVENTEEN
MAKING A PRINCE

It's been a week since Elina left for Singapore and I have been wearing a chastity cage ever since, waiting patiently for her return. Although I look forward to being unlocked and feeling the intense sensations of the orgasm she denied me at the countryside, it isn't the reason I'm most excited for her return next week. In simple words, I want to sit next to her and do nothing.

Elina and I have texted, face-timed and sent each other a million voice notes every day since her departure. I check in with her every morning to share my schedule for the day; as well as pictures of my outfit. Elina gets the final say on what I wear, following the rules of our contract. But some days, like today, she leaves it up to me to decide.

"—it's a shit storm, Wine," Lucifer rambles on. "It's like I am always caught between these damn government policies and the board. If Dara had told me I'd spend half my time, asking for permission to do my Job, from a bunch of people too old to see beyond their noses, I certainly would have thought twice before taking this seat. And not to mention, the staff loathes me..."

For an hour, Lucifer has complained about his new position in the Kittibun Foundation. Pretending to listen, I continue making the Spotify playlist for Elina I'd love to send her before our evening Face-time.

I Miss You by Adele.
Take It All by Adele.
I Wanna Be Yours by Arctic Monkeys.
She's Always a Woman by Isak Danielson.
I put a spell on you by Nina Simon.
Ne Me Quitte Pas by Nina Simon.
Until I Found You by Stephan Sanchez.
Dream A Little Dream of Me by Ella Fitzgerald and Louis Armstrong.
Fine Line by Harry Styles.
Till The End of Time by The Black Skirts.
Daydreamer by Adele.

"Wine!" Lucifer startles me.

"They don't loathe you, Luce; they just don't know you. Did you expect to walk in here and have everyone fawn over you just cause?"

"No... but a little respect won't hurt."

"Respect is not given, Luce."

"What am I supposed to do?"

"You're going to have to earn their respect, prove to them you can actually do the job. Right now, you are just the man that got the job because he is sleeping with the chairman."

"Ew... When you put it like that..." He leans back into his seat swaying it from side to side. "I sound like a gold digger."

"Nobody thinks you are a gold digger, Luce. Your family owns half the real estate industry in Thailand. They know that. You have to get out of your head. Love the office decor by the way."

"Thank you, I have no clue who chose it, it's hideous."

"No it's not, but you can easily change it if you wanted."

"I've had no time for that." Lucifer's phone chimes and raises it. "Shit!" Lucifer gasps

"What?"

"Darika is a swindler?" He furrows his brows at whatever he is reading.

"Darika Paithoon?" I ask.

"It's all over the news, says she stole millions from several families." He hands me the phone.

"Fucking Plerng!" I fall into my seat as I scroll through the news report.

"You think Plerng did this?"

"Of course. Didn't you see her face at the brunch event?"

Lucifer sighs. "You think it might not be true?"

"I wouldn't know, Luce, tabloid gossip is not my thing. But it's very possible Plerng made this happen just to spite her. Remember what happened sophomore year?"

"We were all kids then, Wine. We've made mistakes."

"That was not a mistake. Plerng is a very intentional person." I exhale, putting the phone down. "Her birthday is coming up."

"Ah! Let's have a surprise boat party."

"She still hates us."

"I have all these ideas: fireworks, strippers hanging off poles–"

"Her favorite thing," I say, and we both laugh.

"Can we invite Junta Cheng by any chance? Hopefully, she'll bang the hate out of her."

"That will certainly make you stepfather of the year."

"Wine!" he scolds and the laughter returns. "I'm never getting rid of the stepfather joke, am I?"

I shake my head and my phone vibrates.

"Lean into it... it suits you," I tease, sliding my fingers across my phone and reading the text message.

"Hey, Pretty Thing."

I smile at my screen.

"Do we make it an all-white event... I want to get so drunk. Dara is not going to like it," Lucifer continues.

"How is your day going?" I text back.

"He doesn't like it when you get drunk?" I ask, lifting my gaze from my phone.

"Not always. Should I get us drinks?"

"Looks like someone wants to get punished," Elina replies.

"Shit," I mutter, realizing I haven't texted her something good about myself today.

"You've been swearing a lot lately," Lucifer states.

"Shut it."

"That's new." He rises from his seat and continues ranting about Plerng's birthday.

"I'm sorry, Elina, right on it."

'Where are you?"

I furrow my brows at the question. She's never asked for an update on my location. I have always assumed it's because she is still having me followed.

"Don't you have one of your minions following me?" I text back.

"Cakes with vagina shaped chocolates, so Plerng," I reply Lucifer's suggestion with a big grin.

"Please take a look at appendix 2. Second paragraph."

I roll my eyes, opening up the eDocument for our contract. Elina has been doing this all week, referring me to the contract each time I have a question.

THE DOMINANT/SUBMISSIVE WILL EXERCISE THEIR RIGHT TO PRIVACY TO THE FULL EXTENT OF THE LAW, UNLESS OTHERWISE INDICATED BY EITHER PARTY THROUGH VERBAL OR WRITTEN TEXT.

"What a tool." I smile foolishly at my screen.

"What did I say?" Lucifer asks.

"Sorry, not you, Luce."

"I'm in Lucifer's office, why?" I text back.

"Maybe we should just get her on a plane to Maldives." Lucifer pops open a bottle of wine.

"If she wanted to travel, Luce, she would've already."

"Of course she wants to travel, that's all she's talked about since uni."

"What are you wearing?" Elina texts back.

I raise a brow, rubbing my cheeks to mask my excitement from Lucifer.

"She doesn't want to travel alone," I reply, typing.

"Why are you red all of a sudden?" Lucifer places the cups on the table.

"Am I?" I grin.

Lucifer reaches over to take my phone away and I duck.

"Who are you talking to?" he asks.

"No one."

He squints at me. I squint back.

"Chicken," he teases.

"Cow," I reply.

I turn back to my phone and he continues rambling about the party while pouring.

"Kiniki trousers and a milk-colored shirt, very light fabric, anyone can see through it. Why? Do you want to

take it off me? Maybe I should take it off myself, the weather is rather warm today," I text back.

"Are you even listening to me, Wine?"

"Yes, of course I am. Look, whatever you decide, I'm on board, just let me know when and where."

"Shouldn't we plan the whole thing together, as usual?"

"You know I'm not good at such things, Luce. But yes to a boat party."

"Please see appendix 1, paragraph 9," Elina texts back.

I return to the eDocument.

THE SUBMISSIVE SHALL REFRAIN FROM DRESSING IN A MANNER THAT OVERLY EXPOSES HIS BODY, AS WELL AS ENGAGING IN PUBLIC NUDITY FOR THE SAKE OF SEXUAL GRATIFICATION, UNLESS OTHERWISE INSTRUCTED BY THE DOMINANT. FAILURE TO DO SO WILL RESULT IN THE SEVERE PUNISHMENT OF THE SUBMISSIVE AS STIPULATED BELOW:

- **EATING OFF THE FLOOR FOR A WEEK.**
- **NO SPANKING FOR A MONTH.**
- **KNEELING BY THE PLAY ROOM DOOR FOR SIX HOURS.**
- **WEAR THE BALL GAG FOR SIX HOURS.**
- **WRITE 'I'M SORRY MOMMY, I WON'T DO IT AGAIN' TWO-HUNDRED TIMES.**

I scoff. "Is she kidding me?"

"Wine!" Lucifer scolds.

"What!"

Lucifer rushes over from behind his desk, tickling me in an attempt to take away my phone. I struggle my way out of his grasp and he chases me around the office. We are never growing up.

After an hour of constant tussle and planning with Lucifer, I bid him goodbye. I'm not worried about him being capable of handling his new position, I don't think he necessarily needs me, not that I know much about managing a foundation, I can barely manage my life as it is. Sometimes with Lucifer, you cannot tell when he's struggling, he almost always drowns before asking for help. I made it a point of duty years ago to not wait for him to ask before lending a shoulder, but this isn't one of those times.

The motion sensor door opens and I walk onto the pavement, checking my emails for an order confirmation. I ordered some new sleeping clothes for Po. Since Elina's departure, I have become less avoidant of him. I'm ready to return home. It's just been easier to get to work from Lucifer's place.

"Khun Sutthaya."

I look up from my phone and Khun Toh stands in front of his car.

"Khun?" We exchange bows in greeting. "What are you doing here?"

"Khun Cheng sent me to pick you up."

"Pick me up? For?"

He opens the back seat door. "To drop you off."

"Is she back?"

"Yes, Khun. This morning."

I smirk, walking into the car and he shuts the door.

"You could have told me you're back," I text Elina.

"Yes, I could have. But where is the fun in that," Elina replies.

"I know how to find the way to my salon."
"Mine is better."

We arrive at an upscale boutique wellness center I've never visited. I step through the high glass doors and a soothing ambience welcomes me. It feels like pure oxygen is being pumped into the air. There is an in-built wall waterfall and most of the walls are covered in mahogany to give the space a more natural feel.

I walk over to the receptionist's and a neatly styled young woman, in a white suit welcomes me.

"Sawatdee Kha, Khun," she greets with a wai and I do the same. "Do you have a reservation?"

"I'm not quite sure."

"May I have your name please?"

"Witthaya Sutthaya."

She types into the computer.

"A moment, Khun, an attendant will be with you shortly. Please take a seat."

I turn around to take a seat and all the chairs look like they'd hurt me if I sat on them. They look like tree trunks, carved into some kind of weird shape to make it fancy. They belong in a museum, not the waiting room of a beauty center.

"Khun," an attendant calls.

I'm relieved I don't have to sit down and wait in one of those. We exchange bows and he gestures me forward. He leads me down a passage that feels like walking through a cave. White led lights line each side of the wall. We make a left turn and he opens a door. I enter, welcomed by a sweet luxurious scent. The decor of the salon is very minimalistic and clean. A few guests are being tended to.

"Sawatdee Kha, Khun Sutthaya," a purple haired dark skin woman greets with a wai.

"Sawatdee Krap."

"My name is Chariya, I'll be taking care of you today."

"Thank you na krap."

"Please have a seat, any idea what style you'd like to try?"

As I sit, I find the clearest reflection of myself in the mirror. The mirror lights highlight every imperfection & beauty. I rake my hand through my hair, playing with it, a grin on my face as I admire my features.

"I want something new, different, some curls; maybe a little color."

She steps away for a few seconds and hands me a color panel upon her return.

"See anyone you like?"

"This brown." I point, lifting the paper.

"This will definitely match your eye. Shall we?"

I nod.

She throws an apron over my shoulder and I wiggle my toes. My hair has never been any shade other than black. I've never wanted to experiment either, never thought anything other than black would suit me. Seeing Kiet in brown piqued my interest. Elina loved him in brown and it looked good on him. Since we look very much alike, it should look good on me too.

The whole process was a breeze, I have never been more relaxed by a hair appointment. She took her time massaging my scalp and the hair steaming felt great. My new fluffy brown hair makes me feel very—should I say—brand new? I can't stop admiring myself in the mirror.

"Khun, we are ready for you at the spa."

"Spa? I'm only here for a haircut."

"Khun Cheng made other arrangements for you, Khun."

I nod and follow him. I only mentioned I was going to get my hair done today and she booked multiple appointments? I touch my submissive bracelet, playing with it. It's become a habit, touching it when I think of her.

First, I'm subjected to a full body massage. The masseuse's hands are a blessing to my skin, I keep dozing off. He wakes me when he is done then I receive a full facial, manicure and pedicure.

Next, they wax me all over: my legs and arms, my armpits, my butthole and groin. It's painless but somehow feels more intimate than getting railed by multiple people at the same time.

After waxing, I'm given a full body exfoliation, scrubbed from head to toe till my skin is baby soft.

Then I'm submerged in a warm lavender and milk bath. It's a soundproof room, my mind is completely blank. I can clearly hear my heart beating, my breathing, every movement the water makes. It's deeply soothing.

Once my bath is done, I'm rubbed head to toe with a body oil that smells like vanilla, then directed to the men's locker room to get changed. The floor is covered in carpets, the lockers are made of mahogany wood. When I open my assigned locker, I find a fine cleanly cut suit hanging. I smile, running my hands all over it. Elina is taking me somewhere.

I close the locker and turn. There stands Elina, startling me.

"Elina, you're in the men's locker room."

"I can see," Elina says, leaning against a locker a few steps away.

Her fingers gently tug on the key to my cage hanging around her neck. For a moment, my gaze lingers on her hands, watching her play with it, before taking notice of her beautiful emerald green dinner gown, a gorgeous necklace and red bracelet to match.

"Stunning," I say.

"You're welcome," she replies, and we both share a laugh. "Thank you. Interesting choice of hair color."

"Do you like it?"

"I do."

I hold her gaze for a fleeting moment then coyly look away, bending over to wear my briefs with my towel still wrapped around my waist.

"Ah ah." Elina waves a finger, signaling me with her eyes to drop the towel.

I untie the towel, allowing it fall to the ground. She smiles, pleased with my nakedness. I like her eyes on me, admiring me as I slip on my briefs.

"I got you something from Singapore," Elina says.

"Yeah?"

She walks over, slides her warm hand around my waist and hugs me from behind, softly kissing my shoulder. I exhale. The silk gown she has on is smooth against my exfoliated skin, making it easy for her body warmth to latch onto me. Her hands continue upwards, arriving on my chest and gently she squeezes my nipples. My lips part, letting out a quiet sigh with my eyes shut, leaning back into her. I feel a slight pinch on my nipple and I whimper, snapping my head down to look at it. Two little nipple suckers rest on each nipple.

"Bend over for me, beautiful," she whispers.

I obey, leaning into the locker.

One hand squeezes my ass and the other finds my hole. She slips in a butt-plug and I exhale at the sensation of it arriving deep inside me.

"I'll be waiting in the lobby," Elina says, letting go of me.

I watch her leave and return my gaze to my nipples.

EIGHTEEN
DANCING ON TOP OF THE WORLD.

An array of attendants bow to welcome Elina and I as we step into the tallest buildings in the city. We exchange greetings and casual conversation with a man that appears to be the manager as he escorts us to the elevator. He hands Elina a black card and this activates the seventieth floor button.

"We are going to the sky bar?" I grin.

"Yes. Ever been?"

"Never— Is this a date?"

"I like it when you get all giddy."

"I like that you like it." I wiggle my brows and she laughs.

The elevator opens and I turn my gaze to find quite a number of guests already in attendance. It is clear to me now that this is just another one of her business events and not a date. My smile shrinks with that realization.

"Are you ever not working?" I ask as we step off the elevator.

"Sometimes."

"Do you ever get sick of it?"

"Sometimes." She leans in and pecks me on my right cheek. "Text me your safe word if you can't take it anymore."

"Can't take wha—" I gasp.

191

Elina turned the nipple suckers on. ***Fuck!*** They are remote controlled? I squeeze her gown, unsure of what to do with the arousal coursing through me. My dick throbs in my cage and I swallow, trying to tame it. She holds my gaze for a few seconds before turning it off and I exhale with both relief and excitement, letting my gaze fall to her smirking lips, contemplating kissing her.

"Khun Cheng, sawatdee krap," a gentleman interrupts the intense moment we were sharing and Elina turns away.

"Sawatdee kha." They exchange bows.

"Very honored by your attendance, Khun Cheng. We have your table ready."

"This is Khun Sutthaya, my associate. He'll be joining me tonight."

The gentleman and I exchange bows.

"This way please." He leads the way.

Several guests bow to greet as we walk across the lounge. Some rise from their seats to exchange pleasantries with Elina, and every single time, Elina introduces me.

We arrive at her table and the people seated welcome Elina with cheerful words, air kisses and bows. The exchange of pleasantries and my introduction is short, they waste no time getting down to business talk and smoking. Apparently, these people just can't have a decent business meeting without alcohol and cigars.

Elina's left hand has remained on my right thigh below the table since the talks began, leaving her right hand free to smoke and chat. The conversations has barely shifted from negotiations, there seems to be a tussle on who gets what. I'm starting to realize why she left me on another table the first time she brought me along for an event. I'm not bored; the conversations are invigorating. However, I have nothing to contribute. The food arrives and I refrain from eating, waiting patiently for Elina to begin in respect to our rules.

"Please, let's not keep you waiting." Khun Ariya, one of Elina's business associates, points at my food.

Elina doesn't look my way, but I know she's watching me. I smile at Khun Ariya and pick up my spoon, tossing the food around the plate, still waiting for Elina to start eating.

"So, Khun Sutthaya, what do you do?" asks Khun Rama, a chubby cute man with soft eyes and handsomely styled hair.

"I'm a child psychologist."

The table swoons, as if I just announced I invented the Hubble telescope.

"We respect a medical man," Khun Ariya says.

"Do you have your own practice?" Khun Mook inquires, a middle-aged woman who since we sat has not stopped swooning over Elina, and as it seems, Elina holds her in the same regard.

"Building an app of some sort? The medical field is booming with apps for mental health these days, I'm always getting investment pitches," Khun Rama expresses, his champagne to his lips.

"I did consider private practice but would love to work in public health for a time being."

"A humble man," Khun Rama states.

"He is trying to save humanity." Elina leans back into her seat.

"Last I remember, Khun Cheng, you are a pessimist," Khun Ariya recalls.

"I consider myself a realist. But I do have a lot of respect for souls that can still dream. We could all use a little more faith." Elina turns to me with a smile.

"A Photograph, Khun Cheng?" A press man arrives.

Elina nods and a quick photograph is taken.

"Do you think you can achieve great change in public health?" Khun Rama continues his questioning.

For a man that has barely spoken since the negotiations began, it seems for some reason, he has taken interest in me.

"Of course, great change to me means connecting with children on a micro-level. The way we treat toddlers and pre-teens needs to evolve to match the current state of our society. Which is a far cry from the society our parents and their parents were brought up in. To me it means..." I slur my words when the nipple suckers begin pulsing suddenly. "It means..." I stifle a moan.

"Are you okay, Khun?" Khun Rama asks.

"Yes. Yes, I am." I fist my palm, unable to concentrate as the pleasure travels through me. "I was erm... Great change doesn't have to be flamboyant." I rub my forehead.

"Well," Khun Ariya raises a glass. "Cheers to that."

They all raise their glasses and I struggle to lift mine without shaking the glass. Elina finally begins to eat, and the rest of the table goes back to business chatter, but my focus stays on keeping it cool. Just when I think I can finally take it and maintain a calm exterior, the butt-plug comes on and I almost gasp, trembling and squeezing my trousers. I cover my mouth with my hand and squeeze, adjusting in my seat.

I'm losing self-control.

I can barely breathe.

My legs won't stop shaking under the table.

I feel myself begin to leak and I squeeze my trousers harder, stealing a glance at Elina whose focus has not once shifted to me.

"If you would excuse me?" I rise from the table, trembling. Elina's focus on her business talk doesn't falter at my request.

I find a waiter and ask him for directions to the bathroom, he points and I hurry into it, bursting through the door as I whimper. I check all the stalls quickly, making sure no one else is present before turning to the mirror and letting myself moan louder with my eyes shut.

"Holy fuck," I mutter, squeezing the sink. "Elina..." I move to the wall, gripping it tightly and stomping my feet. "Please... Argh... Fuck..." I slide down to my knees. "Mhm... Argh... Elina... Elina..." My moaning grows louder as the pleasure overwhelms me.

I grip my hair as my skin burns. My dick is trying hard to break free from its cage. I've gone too long without having an orgasm. It feels as though all my body wants to do is cum. It's a frustrating, sensual and deeply arousing feeling. There is an insane craving to cum for Elina's viewing pleasure, but at the same time I want to remain in this continuous state of desperate longing.

After a long twenty minutes, the nipple suckers stop and so does the butt-pug and I sigh out loud, gasping for air and shivering. I stretch my legs, relaxing them on the floor, weakened. Every inch of me is extra sensitive, I'd cum if Elina simply touched me. I shut my eyes and remain on the floor, trying to regain my senses. Minutes pass before I stumble up and find my flushed reflection in the mirror and the horrific situation of my once perfectly styled hair.

I try to clean the pre-cum off my cage and briefs but it's a struggle. I always clean my cage under the shower, taking my time with soap. I can't use the hand soap in the toilet, and I certainly cannot put my dick directly under the running tap. At any moment Elina might turn them on again, there really is no need for this excessive cleaning, but it's an effective way to avoid returning to the table too soon.

A ton of tissues later, most of the stickiness is gone.

I wash my hands and begin fixing my hair when the door swings open. Khun Rama walks in and we exchange nods.

"Taking your time in here," he says with a soft smile.

Now standing, I can see the difference in our heights. I tower over him easily.

With a little smile, I turn back to the mirror. He doesn't move, he doesn't speak, just stands, staring at me with the lingering stare he's had all through dinner.

"Do you mind?" I furrow my brows at hm, making my discomfort of his constant gawking more apparent.

"You don't remember me, do you?" he asks.

"Should I?" I turn to him, letting my hair go.

"Three years ago, February, Valentine's week, New York. You and Lamon Asnee."

It takes me a moment, but the memory of the events of that week rush back and the embarrassment sets in.

"You were at the Winston party in New York?" My eyes widen.

"Yes."

I sigh. "Dear Buddha..." I look away.

"Please, no need to feel embarrassed." He grins, flashing pearly white perfect teeth.

"I am—very."

"You shouldn't be."

"Not a lot of people have seen me naked, especially in that way."

"You looked... magnificent." He holds my gaze. "But I could tell you didn't want to be there."

Breaking our stare, I look down at my shoes. "It was a different time."

"Of course." He moves to the sink and pumps some soap into his palm. "But it seems you have a type." He turns on the tap.

"A type?"

"Women that could wreck you."

I exhale a laugh. "Elina is nothing like Lamon."

"Interesting. I do hope you are right about that."

"You've known her for a long time."

"Correct." He picks a paper towel, drying his hands.

"You knew Kiet?"

"Ah... Of course. You sound curious."

"Elina is not particularly an easy person to know."

"And yet, you swear she is nothing like Lamon."

I eye him, shaking my head with a smile. "What were they like... Elina and Kiet."

"One time, she described him to me as the bane of her existence. She said and I quote 'When he stops breathing, I'll stop living'. They were an incredibly passionate pair."

"I see— How do you two know each other?"

"She is Elina Cheng, knowing her is part of work, she runs the biggest investment firm in Asia. Going to events like this is also work, and during events like this, you hear things, see things."

"So you aren't a friend."

He makes a face. "Khun Cheng doesn't make friends. But I'm not a foe either. She invests in companies, I own a company, just business."

"Right."

"Must be intense to have her as a Domme."

"To say the least."

We share a soft laugh.

I raise a questioning finger. "Are you—"

"Oh no... not anymore. I thought I was a Dom once, but quickly realized I was horrible at it. I do like to just watch every now and then... like that night at the Winston party."

I nod, catching his gaze once more. "I should probably get back in there."

"Of course. Listen, if you ever start that private practice." He pulls out his card, handing it over to me. "Call me, I know a lot of investors and medical professionals in your field."

"Khun, can't take that."

"It's just for work."

"We both know that's not true." I smile.

He smiles back, passing a nod and tucking the card back into his wallet.

"She's lucky."

"I think I am the lucky one. See you back in there."

I walk out of the bathroom, hands in my pocket as I re-enter the party. It was a surprise running into a walking reminder of the time I spent with Lamon. A bit embarrassing to think he remembers me that way: on all fours, taking it at the command of Phi Lamon. But I could care less about that. What he said makes me boil with envy. *'Her bane of existence'?* How can I ever compete with that?

Elina turns to me as I approach the table, a smile on her red lips. It's raining, La Vie En Rose is playing on the piano. Her emerald green dress makes her glow in a sea of black and white hues. I smile back at her, holding her gaze.

"What took you so long, Handsome," her voice is velvety smooth.

"Can I steal you for a moment, Elina." I stretch out my hand.

The table quiets down and without hesitation, Elina slides her palm into mine. I help her rise to her feet then turn, guiding her to an open empty space by the tall windows, where the whole of Bangkok appears to be below our feet. A spectacular view. I twirl her and pull her into me and she laughs. We begin to sway, her hands on my shoulder, mine on her little waist. I take her right hand and kiss it gently. My smile broadens when I see she is still holding the remote control to my nipple suckers and butt-plug.

"So, it's, 'Handsome' when we are with your friends?" I raise a brow.

"Just making sure you're comfortable."

"Elina, I like what you chose to call me, it doesn't matter in front of who. Unless... it's uncomfortable for you?"

"No."

"So..."

"Noted." She leans into me. "My Pretty Thing."

I grin. "Everyone is watching."

"It will be in the papers tomorrow morning. 'The Black Widow of Chiang Mai Claims Another'," she says mimicking the tone of TV announcers.

We both laugh and I drop her at the tune of the music, bring her back up and twirl her once more before pulling her back into me.

"Did you take it?" Elina asks.

"What?"

"Whatever Rama offered in the bathroom."

"Will I be punished if I did?"

She raises a brow at me with a fond smile.

"You enjoyed watching him watch me, didn't you?'

"Yes."

"Did it make you jealous?"

"Do you want me to be?"

"Maybe—Yes."

She pulls me into her and the nipple suckers start working my nipples again. I shudder, holding onto her tight.

"That is cute." She rubs my back.

I latch onto her, struggling to keep swaying amidst the immense pleasure. Knowing everyone is watching while I'm being pleasured is a different kind of arousal I can't explain.

Elina knows how to set me ablaze with desire. She takes the lead, swaying me as I try to collect myself.

"Did you get my playlist?" I manage to ask.

She turns off the suckers.

"I sure did."

"Did you like it?"

She leans back, letting me take the lead once more.

"I did. I was surprised by your choices."

"I was trying to impress you," I say.

"I am impressed."

"Good."

I have always wondered what the most beautiful moment in my life would look like, and I think this is it. No other moment has ever topped this, and I'm tempted to say no other moment ever will. However, my journey as her submissive has just begun. I have a deep feeling, with Elina Cheng, there will be many more euphoric moments just like this one. Moments when I'm blown away by simply holding her in my arms.

Elina calls it a night and bids the table a good night but I'm not ready for tonight to be over. I could dance forever under this stunning silver chandelier, watching the rain and holding her close.

I could dance with her forever.

NINETEEN
A SHADE BRIGHTER

As soon as the elevator door closes, Elina turns on the butt-plug again and I fall against the wall with wobbly legs. In silence Elina watches me struggle for a few minutes before turning it off. I exhale, taking a deep breath and standing up right and it starts all over again. I let out a loud moan just when the elevator door opens, forcing me to curb it. Two middle aged women and a man step on, talking casually. The elevator begins its descent and Elina increases the speed. I gasp a moan and clench my jaw.

They all turn to me.

Elina smirks.

I bow in apology, faking a cough, but I can tell they think I am a creep. I pin myself to the wall, shoulders tensed as I squeeze my trousers, trying hard to contain myself. We arrive at the ground floor and Elina turns it off, giving me a break.

The drive through the rainy dark city is quiet. Elina continues to work on her iPad, as if she didn't spend the entire day doing just that. Sometimes I think she uses work as an excuse not to exist in the moment.

"Khun, do you mind pulling over here?" I ask, just as we come up on a bridge.

"What for?" Elina looks up at me with overworked eyes.

"You'll see." I smile.

Khun Toh pulls over and I get down from the car, standing on the sidewalk.

"What are you doing, Wine? You'll catch a cold."

"Dance with me, Elina," I plead as the rain soaks me.

"In the rain?" There is laughter in her throat.

"Yes... in the rain."

For a moment she hesitates, staring at me with tired eyes as she contemplates. I reach out to her and she takes my hand, stepping onto the sidewalk. I squat and take off her shoes so she doesn't slip while we dance, then take mine off and slip them onto her feet before taking off my suit jacket and hanging it over her shoulder.

"We don't have any music!" Elina says.

I take out my air pods. One in her left ear and one in my right ear. We begin swaying in the rain.

The cars blowing past us are not loud enough to quiet down the sound of Elina's joyous laughter when I almost slipped. We continue to dance on the bridge until shivers from the cold start to creep in.

Elina let me cuddle her the rest of the ride back to Lucifer's mansion. She called me 'My Pretty Thing' more times than I can count. It's rewarding to see her free and vulnerable. That sadness in her eyes melted away. I'm thankful I am the reason.

"You should come in," I say, getting down from the car.

"Get some rest."

"Please, Elina, come in. Even if it's for a second."

"Wine—"

"Please."

"You are a handful; do you know that?"

"You said it was okay for me to be needy."

She laughs and I join.

Elina caves, taking my hand and I guide her into the mansion, our clothes dripping water onto the marble tiles as we enter the house.

"Hey!" Lucifer appears, surprising me.

"Luce? I thought you were spending the night at Po's"

"Change of plans... Khun Cheng."

"Sawatdee kha." Elina slightly bows.

"Sawatdee krap." Lucifer returns the bow. "Welcome to our home. This is very shocking, very shocking—"

"We'll be in my room, if you need anything, do not knock," I warn him with my eyes.

"It's a lovely house," Elina says as we walk past a still surprised Lucifer.

We enter my room and I hurry to the closet to find her a change of clothes: big sweaters and sweatpants, clothes that will completely conceal her body so she's comfortable. I walk back into the room and pause when I find Elina staring at a picture of Po and me.

"It's from five years ago," I say.

She turns to me. "You look happy."

"For a time being, I was." I approach her with the clothes. "You should change, so you don't catch a cold."

"So should you."

"I'll change here."

She nods, takes the clothes and heads for the bathroom. I watch her disappear behind the door and hurry to change into my own clothes. I don't want to give her the impression that I want anything other than her company tonight. I find my shorts and hoodies, forcing myself out of my suit, stumbling here and there.

I rush to sit on the bed. Not sure what to do next so I stand, then sit again. Nervous about the way I am presenting myself. I probably shouldn't sit on the bed, that would make it look like I am expecting something sexual to happen. I hurry over to the couch, pick up the book I was reading earlier: *Lore and Lust*. I'm on my second read. Will it make me look smart? The is also quite suggestive.

I'm smart, I have a PhD, I don't need to prove that to Elina—she knows that—but I should probably hold up the Handmaid's Tale or something in the dark academia section. Everyone thinks dark academia readers are smart.

Yes. That's better.

I rise to grab it when I hear the bathroom door open. I fall back into my seat; Songs of Achilles will just have to do.

"Take out my toy," Elina commands as she re-enters the room, dressed in a bathrobe.

I really wanted to see her in my clothes. My hoodie would look so good on her. I'm a bit disappointed.

"Wine."

"Yes! Sorry." I pull down my shorts, letting out my soft caged dick.

She tosses me a blindfold, and I slip it on, my heart racing. I hear her steps inching closer and I swallow, already excited by the thought of sliding into her. She climbs over me, running her hands through my damp hair. I cannot touch her until she has given me the permission to do so. Instead, I squeeze the helm of her robe. She unlocks me and I moan, aroused by the feeling of being freed. My cock instantly hardens.

Elina tilts my head to the left, allowing her suck and bite me all over my neck and shoulder. I let out soft winces as she bites me. Each bite is more intense than the last. She guides my hand to her left boob, and I squeeze gently, shivering at how soft it feels. It's my first time touching her bare breast. Elina leans back and I lean forward, latching onto her nipple and sucking. Gently, she takes her boob out of my mouth and guides my lips to her right boob.

The second my lips touch her right nipple, she shivers, letting out a soft moan. Good to know that's her sensitive nipple. I continue gently fondling her left boobs as I suck her right nipple, enjoying the soft moans she rewards me with.

"Pull my panties to the side," Elina commands and I obey, freeing her breast from my hold and taking my hands in between her legs.

It fills me with so much pleasure to discover her panties are practically soaked, and not from the rain, the wetness is warm. Elina grips my dick, playing with it as she rubs the tip all over her clitoris.

I stop sucking to catch my breath and she shoves my head back into place, making me take her nipple back into my mouth. Her body trembles as she picks up the pace, rubbing my cock all over wet clitoris while digging deep into my neck, sucking, kissing and letting out deep erotic moans that are driving me wild.

"Two fingers, go slow," Elina commands, letting go of my dick.

I swallow, already reaching inside her.

I had hoped she'd let me inside her and use my dick till she cums. Making her cum with my dick has been the center of my fantasies for weeks now. Imagining her use it for her satisfaction and the intense orgasm that will follow when she lets me cum.

I slide two fingers into her and she winces. Her body makes a little jerk, a sign it hurts a little, so I go slower. My fingers are engulfed by her warm slippery self. *Oh fuck!* What I'd give to replace my fingers with my dick. I begin with a little thrust when my fingers are fully inside her. She pulls my chin up away from her nipples and kisses me.

205

"A bit faster," Elina whispers with our lips still touching and I pick up the pace.

She moans, holding me close and pulling my hair. Her scent occupies my lungs, drowning me in desire. My lips find her right nipple again, and she quivers, moaning out loud to my soft sucks. Once again, I'm leaking, aroused by her pleasure.

"There... there..." Elina whimpers. "Your left... yes... argh... argh."

I keep my fingers steady, thrusting and rubbing a warm soft spot inside her that seems to make her tremble with pleasure. I apply a little more pressure, and pick up my pace, thrusting evenly, trying to give her the best finger fuck of her life. She squeezes me close, digging her fingers into my skin, showering me with warmth as she cums. Her moans are intense, quiet, and lewd.

"Good boy," Elina mutters and I gasp, biting my lower lip.

The lustful smell of her fills the air, making me hunger for release even more. I leave my fingers in her, trembling in ecstasy. Feeling her cum as she calls me that is enough to drive me to the very edge. Whimpering, my body nears an orgasm.

"Know your place, Pretty thing," Elina whispers and I bite my lower lips harder and squeeze my eyes shut, thinking of dead rats and worms to help stop me from cumming without her permission.

It's not working.

Our heavy breathing fills the room as I slide my fingers out of her and deep them into my mouth, licking her sweet wetness. "Elina, can I—"

"Yes," she replies. Getting off me and guiding me to the bed.

I plunge between her legs, taking her warm wet haven into my mouth, pleased with its luscious softness and taste. I would love to take my time, inhaling as much of her as I can, but I set my tongue to work immediately, softly sucking and flickering her clitoris with my tongue. Her soft moans cause me to shiver, goosebumps spread vastly across my body. I focus on flicking her clitoris steadily with my tongue, slowly increasing my speed when I feel her waist move in demand for more.

I want her cumming and shaking with pleasure because of me. I want to taste her cum and I want my reward. I want it all, I am starved of her and I can't get enough.

Elina digs her fingers into my hair, pressing me deeper. Her legs hang over my shoulders and her thighs gently squeeze me as she wriggles in pleasure. I can tell she is close just by the way her waist moves. I keep my tongue moving steadily over her clitoris. She deeply groans, pulsing and jerking lightly. As she cums, an amazing feeling of warmth rush through me. I dig my tongue into her wet hole to lick as much of her wetness as I can, whimpering and moaning as the satisfying taste hits my tongue.

Elina pulls me away from her pussy, holding onto my hair and I swallow. I can hear her quietly breathing, still catching her breath and I remain on my knees, waiting for her next command. A few seconds pass and I'm still shaking, still tethering along the lines of an orgasm.

She pulls me back in and I give her whole pussy a big lick. My hands find her firm nipple and squeezes gently. She rewards me with a deep sensual moan, twitching. I dig my tongue into her, licking her cum; savoring the taste. She moans deeper and I begin to play with her clitoris, in hopes of getting her to cum again.

She rubs herself against my mouth, pulling my hair harder. I suck her clitoris, then flicker it, then suck. My fingers still rubbing her nipples. I can tell she is about to cum again, I can smell it. Her moans intensifies and she squeezes my head with her thigh, cumming once more. I keep flickering her clitoris with my tongue until I'm sure she is done cumming. I hear her moans die out into quiet whimpers and I spread her legs, trying to lick all the cum leaking into her ass. It is mine to claim and I am greedy with it.

She lets me have my moment, breathing softly as she recovers from her orgasms. I continue to lick her, kissing her at intervals. It's sensually satisfying. I feel like I'd burst with euphoria anytime soon. I could lick her the whole night.

"Wine..." I hear her mumble.

I don't want to stop, this is where I belong, in between her legs. If I could just make her cum one more time—if she could just let me taste it again. I squeeze her thighs in need and dig my tongue into her. I licked all the cum too soon, now I'm left digging for leftovers.

"Hey baby... I've given you enough," she says faintly.

"Can I have one more... please?"

I lick her and start sucking her clitoris again.

She rises and pulls me away from her, then holds my face up by the chin.

"Cum," Elina commands.

It feels as if I've been on pause forever and finally, I can press play. I gasp and whimper, shutting my eyes. An intense shiver travels through me and I begin to cum. She digs a finger into my mouth, letting me suck on it as I cum.

Exhausted and pleased, I lean forward, resting my head on her knees and trying to breathe. It's the first time I have experienced an orgasm without needing direct stimulation.

Elina rises from the bed, pulls me up by my collar and roughly pulls down my shorts, shoving me undo the bed, I arrive on my stomach. She runs her warm hand over my butt, and I shiver with excitement, holding onto the sheets. She squeezes each butt gently, before traveling in between my ass and tracing a finger round the entrance of my hole. I moan as she takes the butt-plug out of me, then rubs me.

"Look at your pathetic little hole. So eager to be fucked like the worthless slut you are," she speaks calmly but firmly, and her words excites me further.

Yes, I am a slut. But I am only a slut for you, Elina.

A gentle smack arrives on my right butt. I smile, rubbing my face over the sheets.

"I'm going to spank you. Fifteen times. And you're going to count, do you understand?"

"Yes—Elina." I swallow.

Spank! The first one arrives, barely hurting. I quiver. "One." ***Spank!*** "Two." I exhale, biting my lower lips. ***Spank!*** "Three." ***Spank!*** "Four." ***Spank!*** "Five." I squeeze the sheets, whimpering. ***Spank!*** "Six." I moan out loud, the tingling sensation spreads through my ass. She kisses the area she just spanked, rubbing my left butt cheek in preparation to spank it, I know it will be harder. I pray it is. ***Spank!*** "Seven!" A warm rush travels through me. ***Spank!*** "Eight." It's harder and more intense. ***Spank! Spank! Spank! Spank!*** I count in accordance, breaking into heavy tears. The release I feel is deep in my soul, I can't hold anything back. "Twelve." I say amidst tears, gripping the sheets tighter and wriggling. "I'm... sorry... I'm so sorry." The tears pour heavily down my cheeks.

"What are you sorry for?" Elina tenderly asks.

"I did something." I tremble. "Something terrible. I know it. They won't tell me what... I can't remember."

The room falls silent leaving behind the sound of my sobs.

"Wine... do you need a break?" Elina asks, stroking my hair.

"Please, Elina, punish me." I sob.

"Let's take a break."

"No... please, Elina. You can use whatever, I don't care."

Elina drags me up, takes a moment to tie up her bathrobe and yanks off my blindfold. "Wine! Stop! Look at me!"

I open my eyes slowly, my view still foggy from all the tears. "Elina... I am sorry."

"You don't have to be—Wine, it's okay."

Elina pulls me into a hug, letting me cry more on her shoulders.

It takes almost thirty minutes to collect myself. The emotional release I felt is nothing like I have ever felt. It was freeing and overwhelming at the same time.

"I don't mean to be that kind of submissive, Elina," I say with my head resting on her chest.

"What kind of submissive?" she asks patting my hair.

"Overbearing."

"She must have done a number on you."

"Who?"

"Your previous Domme."

I remain quiet.

"Why aren't you running out the door— When I break, they always run."

Her heart continues to pound rhythmically in the silence.

"I think about drowning a lot," Elina says, shocking me.

"Why?"

"The peace that comes with the quiet being underwater provides. Whenever I feel overwhelmed, I think about drowning."

"Elina..." I raise my face to look into her eyes and she looks down at me with a smile.

"You wanted to know something real about me."

"Yes."

"It scares me."

I sit up, looking down at her. "Drowning or just dying?"

"The peace I find in both."

I can't look away from her, wondering how my outburst was any different from the last one. It's moved her to the point of opening up to me in a way she never has.

"Have you ever done it?" I ask.

"Try to drown?"

"Yes."

"A couple of times," Elina continues.

"And?"

"Your body eventually goes up, even when you try to hold it down. It just won't let you." Elina pauses, adjusting her head in a manner that hides her eyes away from me. "At one point I was sure... very certain I would not come up—but my body, on its own accord, rose to the surface. My brain overrode my instructions so it could survive—and I lost."

"Maybe, you didn't want to stay down."

"I did," Elina insists.

"If you wanted to drown, Elina, you are a woman of means, you would have. You waited, giving your body time to make a decision for you, knowing it will save itself. You could have let the water in at any time, you could have let go, Elina."

She lifts herself off the bed and kisses my cheek tenderly. A faint smile finds home on my lips as her kisses travel to my neck, then shoulder. She slides her hand down to my exposed thighs and traces a circle using her index finger. It is beautifully soothing. I lean over and kiss her forehead then place my palm on her cheeks, burying my thoughts in her sad brown eyes. They are speaking an inscrutable language.

"You can use me again if you want," I whisper, in hopes of being a useful distraction for whatever haunting feeling she has going through her soul.

"So needy," she teases and we both giggle, letting it die down into the quietness. "Move back in."

"Will you sneak into my room at night and steal kisses?"

Soft laughter returns to the room as we hold each other's gaze fondly. She turns away, gets out of bed and walks towards the bathroom.

"Did Hathai see you?" I ask and she turns to me. "The night you tried to drown yourself."

"No. It was way past her bedtime. But Martha... she watched."

"Watched?"

"I'm sure she hoped I drowned."

"Why?" I shake my head.

"She really loved Kiet."

Elina walks into the bathroom and returns with her gown. She pecks my left cheek. Her free hand slides under my sweater and plucks each nipple sucker off me, making my body twitch.

"I'll see you tomorrow, Pretty Thing," she says softly and begins walking to the door.

"You're still in love with him?" I ask. She turns, holding my gaze.

Another silent minute passes.

"Yes. I am."

"You miss him."

"I do."

"Do you think you could ever love someone else, the way you love him?"

She doesn't look my way, she doesn't move. Just breathing, quietly.

"You should restart therapy, Wine."

"The wall is back up, huh?"

"There is no wall, Wine," she says, leaving the room.

TWENTY
JUNTA

Elina was not wrong about the tabloids. The next morning, her face was splashed across every major tabloid and news network.

THE BLACK WIDOW OF CHIANG MAI MAKES GRAND RETURN TO BANGKOK'S HIGH SOCIETY.

THE BLACK WIDOW ATTENDS PARTY WITH MYSTERIOUS STRANGER.

IS THE BLACK WIDOW DATING AGAIN? WHO IS HER NEXT VICTIM?

My face was always blurred out, or the pictures perfectly angled to hide my identity. Elina's doing. For the past three weeks, it has continued in a similar manner. During the week. Elina takes me along to brunches, games, meetings. During the weekend we grace parties of all sorts: movie premieres, fashion shows, night clubs.

I have never worn so many crop-tops my whole life. When we go to clubs, I'm mostly dressed in sheer tops or crop tops that expose the entirety of my abs, paired with lots of silver jewelry: rings, bracelets, necklaces. She hired a personal stylist just for that and sometimes she puts eye make-up on me. I think that's her favorite part.

Elina uses me whenever, wherever, however she pleases. My body is at her disposal, and I am obsessed with her dominance. I fear sometime soon; I will not be Kiet enough for her. As the weeks fly by, our playroom sessions have become increasingly intoxicating. I travel to a new world in the playroom. A world where I am not in control of anything. A world where her pleasure and satisfaction are all that matters to me. In it, I feel the safest. Sex in submission to her is nothing short of mind blowing, and in times when all she has given is her dominance not an orgasm, I have found completeness.

There are hickeys and bite marks all over my body. Her new favorite places to bite me are my thighs and back. All week, I have confined my body to turtleneck shirts, tops and scarves in a bid to hide them away from my interviewers, Khun Kittibun and Lucifer, but most importantly, Hathai. She'll surely grind me for an explanation if her eyes ever sets upon them. Hathai can never know.

I love that Elina leaves marks on me. They are like her stamps of ownership only I know exist when I am in public. However, wearing scarves and turtleneck clothing with Bangkok's weather is no easy feat.

The last time Elina opened up to me about her past suicidal thoughts is the only time she has. I yearn to walk a mile in her world, fade completely into it, allow her worries become mine, decipher her secrets, keep her eyes glowing with joy and her mouth filled with laughter. But that wall she claims is not there has grown taller.

Her not-so little revelation gave me a rather significant insight on my next approach with Hathai. It filled me with so many theories, including the possibility that

215

Hathai might have seen her once unknowing to her. The effect that would have on such a young mind, it perfectly tallies with Hathai's reclusive lifestyle.

Hathai and I are similar in many ways, it's almost impossible for me not to get attached to her. Unlike her mother, she's been opening up to me like never before. To everybody except her own mother. A mystery that has continued to prove difficult to crack.

My progress with Hathai is what fortified my confidence to begin pursuing more jobs away from Elina's prying eyes. When I'm not being used for Elina's pleasure, I'm out attending interviews with some of the wealthiest families in Bangkok Khun Kittibun lined up for me. He has always treated me like his own son from the second Plerng introduced me to him, way before Lucifer joined our friend group. Every time he bought something for Plerng, he bought for me too. When I needed a door opened with internships, he was there to support me. He made attaining a visa easy and supported me with living expenses while I was in the United States. He is the second parent I always wished I had. There was a time I secretly envy Plerng. I'd sometimes internally curse at her for being such a brat to her own father. If only she knew what it was like to wish for a parent you cannot have; I'd say to myself.

But that's the gift, isn't it? The gift of being a child to a parent who adores you unconditionally, holds you so close to their heart and wants to give you the world. You can take it all for granted without feeling guilty.

All I have done this week is attend interviews. After the interviews, it would look very promising, the parents would swoon, then the next day I'd get a call, informing me they decided to go in another direction with their choice. It has become a bit frustrating.

216

I don't need the extra income, but I do need more experience and something to make myself scarce around Elina. I never want to see the day when Elina tires of me and they say absence makes the heart fonder.

***

I step into the house and Phi Lamai welcomes me with a bow.

"A package came for you, Nong. It's in your room," she says, and I nod, moving to walk past her. "There is also a guest waiting for you in the kitchen."

"The kitchen?"

"She insisted on pouring herself wine, serving herself. She's walking around like she owns the place, it is very annoying."

I smirk–*Elina.*

"Sorry, Phi. Thank you."

I toss my bag to a chair and hurry to the kitchen in excitement. I haven't seen her in two days, my deliberate ploy to make myself scarce has left me in a constant state of longing. As I step into the kitchen, a putrid awful smell hits my nose and I scrunch my face. The sight of Hathai and Junta Cheng who is dressed head to toe in a red and gold Thai siwalai attire, sitting by the kitchen counter, eating durian and chatting takes me by surprise.

"Phi!" Hathai hurries over to me with a glowing smile, and we share a short hug. "Sawatdee kha. Your house is very nice. It's not as you described it."

"This isn't my house. Belongs to a friend." I pat her shoulder, settling my gaze on Junta Cheng. "Surprised to see you here, Khun Cheng."

217

Hathai drags me by the arm to the kitchen Island.

"I am full of surprises, Khun Sutthaya," Junta replies, adjusting the Sbai on her shoulder.

"We went to the museum, then we went shopping at the local market. I haven't visited one in such a long time. We bought so many things, we bought lots of fruits for you too." Hathai's happy face is pleasing to the eye.

"It seems you do not favor durian?" Junta asks, sitting poised.

"No, I do not. But I am grateful for the gesture."

"We got mangos too, and dragon fruit. Do you like dragon fruit?" Hathai looks up at me with happy eyes.

"Yes, I do, Nong. Thank you." I pat her head.

"This young woman here has filled my ears with stories about you."

"bpâa..." Hathai tugs on Junta's sleeve. "Don't tell him." She pouts and Junta smiles at her.

"I'd love to hear everything," I say.

"I'm sure it's nothing you aren't already aware of." Junta rises from her seat and sniffs Hathai's forehead before turning to me. "Do you mind if I steal you away for a moment, Khun."

"Not at all."

She washes her hand to get the durian scent off. That will be far from enough. By Buddha I hate that damn fruit.

"Lead the way," she says.

I turn and we exit the kitchen. I have an inkling whatever she has to say will be words Hathai must not hear. I lead her into the lower floor study and shut the door behind us.

"Please make yourself comfortable," I say, walking over to a sofa.

"This will be brief."

"Oh?"

"I am going to need you to stop fucking my sister."

Her sudden words pierce through me like a sharp knife, and I freeze in my stand.

"Excuse me?"

"My niece seems to be in awe of you. I would have insisted that you resign, seeing how disorderly your behavior is for a man of your profession. Hathai hasn't liked anyone the way she likes you in a long time—so—I will play nice. However, if such behavior doesn't cease; Thailand will become a very, very tiny box that will hardly contain both of us."

"With all due respect Khun Cheng, what your sister and I have does not interfere with my professional responsibilities. I care about Nong Hathai, she is finally opening up and I am seeing significant improvement."

"It is my job as the overseer of my family's institutions to protect the sanity of my sister from the likes of you—"

"Likes of me?"

"Khun Sutthaya, I know where you're from, courtesy is a faded tradition, but when someone is speaking, you let them finish."

"Apologies."

"I traveled back home because I'm set on making sure my sister's naiveness and elusiveness does not once again put her and this family in disarray. So yes, the likes of you. Peasants some might say and—"

"Ah! That's where Hathai learnt that from." I chuckle in my throat.

Naiveness and elusiveness are words I'd never describe Elina by. I have struggled to see her from Hathai's perspective and now I am being shown a third side? How could all three of us possibly have different perspectives of the same woman?

"I was made to believe you are being paid handsomely. I urge you not to reach for more of my sister's kindness."

"Are you insinuating I'm a gold digger?"

"No such words left my lips."

"It didn't have to. If I may—"

"You may not."

"I don't care. You've called me a peasant and now a gold digger which is very presumptuous of you. I've never asked Elina for anything more than she's willing to give."

"That is the beauty of my sister, isn't it? You don't have to ask." Junta turns to leave.

"Do you know she knows?" I draw back her attention. "Hathai knows how difficult your family made it for her parents to share a relationship and marry. And now, her father, the one that was fought off by this family, is dead. Leaving her alone. Do you know what that does to a child? Watching all of it unfold and then saying goodbye to him forever?"

A glint of fury flashes through her eyes as she clenches her jaw.

"You do not know him!" Junta huffs, springing forward towards me with a pointed finger. "You know nothing about what he was like! He was weak! Pathetic! Vile! He was...." She pauses, glaring at me and then turns away. "Hathai is better off without him—she never had a father as far as I'm concerned. Now, Khun, I hope I've made myself very clear about where I stand with your relationship with my sister."

"Yes, you did, Khun. But that isn't your place. If we discontinue, it'll be because we choose to do so."

"It's going to be so much fun, making your life very miserable in this country."

She turns away, heading for the door once again.

"Khun Cheng."

She halts at my call. Not turning back. "What!"

"Are you by any chance free on the twentieth?"

She turns halfway, narrowing her cold eyes at me. "Why? Do you intend on seducing me and chaining me up."

It comes as no shock to me that she knows about her sister's bedroom escapades. However, I am amused at the thought of me chaining Elina up.

"That is... usually not how it goes. But no, Khun Cheng. Rather, I'd like to invite you to a birthday party." I step forward.

"Is this some kind of sick joke?"

"Not at all. My friend, Plerng... Plerng Kittibun—"

"You know the Kittibun's?"

"Close friends for years. You and I briefly met at the Lamai Foundation's brunch."

"You were there?"

"Right in front of you."

"Your kind sure loves to lace their lives with the wealth of others and pretend like they don't want a scoop."

"Give me a break, Khun Cheng. Free on the twentieth?"

"Depends on the next thing you say."

"Plerng... for some reason I cannot possibly fathom, adores you, in a very... very peculiar way, and you gracing us with your presence would help scrap my friend and I's name off the bad friend's list. There will be a boat, what do you say?"

"Don't tell me you are trying to whore me out, just so you can get back in good graces?"

"I wouldn't... use that word... per say. But seeing as you're still standing here, I take it you aren't completely repulsed by the idea?"

"Khun Sutthaya, I will step away now to avoid committing an atrocity across your face."

"Probably a good idea."

Heels clicking against the marble floor, Junta Cheng storms out of the study.

I think we might be close friends in another life time, Junta and me. I find her humorous and endearing. Smiling sheepishly, I turn to the window to take a moment and absorb the ridiculousness of the conversation we just had. It's amusing, yet very foreign to me. Avoiding and running away from conflict comes natural to me. All through university Plerng and Lucifer were my shield. I wasn't in trouble often, but every now and then our peers would try to take advantage of my passiveness and I would let them before either Lucifer or Plerng swooped in.

It does feel good to talk back. To say exactly what I am thinking the moment I think it. Maybe if I hadn't waited all these years to ask Po about the incident from my childhood that still haunts me, it wouldn't have gone the way it did. The last time I even dared to bring it up was the day I graduated university.

He took me drinking, for the first time ever. He was genuinely happy, proud. We got drunk—mostly him. It was at a roadside bar, a stone throw away from home. Po wasn't guarded, he wasn't his usual distant self. He cracked a few nasty jokes and laughed his heart out at every one of them.

That night, he felt like the father I grew up with. The older the night grew, the more the urge to ask welled up inside me. Then the moment came, the moment I should have asked. I parted my lips, the words were right there—but then he did something he had not done for ages. He hugged me. And I shrunk. It lasted just about a minute and soon after, we were ready to head home. I did not ask the question, I did not want to ruin the moment.

I rejoin Junta and Hathai in the kitchen and after a short chat with Hathai, I bid them goodbye.

As I ascend the stairs, heading to my bedroom, a thought travels through my mind. It must be her, it must be Junta. Taking away all my potential clients, making it difficult for me to find a job. Is this her own way of making my life miserable? *Junta—fucking—Cheng!* I sigh.

TWENTY-ONE
BROKEN ROSES

For three days, I have been absent from Elina's presence—three long grueling days filled with thoughts of her hair, her smile, the little freckles across her left cheek that are lined up in a way that resembles a constellation. It's very pretty. My heart, my soul, my body are all jumping in excitement to see her today.

As the driver pulls up to the gate, a mailman arrives. We exchange greetings and he tells me he has mail for Elina. I receive it on her behalf, signing before continuing into the mansion grounds.

Elina stands in front of the mansion's door, her hands in her pockets, her eyes fixed on the car as we arrive, filled with sparkles. She's dressed in a dark blue Shirt, her sleeve rolled up to reveal the diamond bracelet around her wrist that matches the silver pearls around her neck, paired with free-flowing black trousers and my favorite thing: the belt. Her hair is slicked back away from her face, smooth and straight.

The car comes to a halt, and Elina opens the door for me, flashing a pretty smile as I step down.

"Why are you out here?" I laugh in my throat, butterflies already swirling round my stomach.

"I have missed you," she says.

224

I flush. "It's only been three days, Elina."

"You're slipping away from me."

There is no way I could have predicted this adorable coyness oozing from her face. Her eyes and smile are tender, and she keeps looking at me like—like she likes me, for me. I shouldn't think about it, but I can't help myself.

"Even if I tried, Elina Cheng. I could never slip away from you," I say.

Her smile broadens. She steps forward and slides her hand across my waist. I step backwards, cautiously looking around.

"Don't worry, Hathai isn't home. Spending all her time with Phi Junta it seems."

I nod. Relieved.

"Oh." I fish out the letter. "This came for you. I ran into the postman at the gate."

"Thank you."

She pulls the letter out of its envelope and unfolds it.

As her eyes scan the letter, the smile on her face begins to fade. Her once bright gaze sinks into painful despair. Her lips quiver, her hands shake, it is clear she is holding her breath. I furrow my brows in confusion and lift my hand to touch her and she backs away.

"Elina... what's wrong?"

Elina takes a deep breath and exhales loudly as she backs further away from me, her body trembling. She tosses the letter to the ground and turns, storming towards the gardens.

"Elina?" I pick the letter up.

Just like the other letters I had seen in her office, it is stamped with **EK**.

Beautiful Mistress,

*Happy anniversary. You make me whole. My life is
nothing without your dominance and unending love. Please
wear a smile today, because your smile shines brighter than
ten thousand dying stars.*

Your loving husband and slave.

From Kiet? How is that possible? He's been dead for
years. I crinkle my forehead. Khun Toh dashes out of the
mansion and snatches the letter out of my hand.

"Shit," he swears under his breath and turns away,
chasing after Elina.

I follow, my heart racing, my eyes frantically
searching for her as she disappears at a distance.

What have I done? Dear Buddha, what have I done?

We walk past the fountains, a few gardens, then arrive
at a familiar pathway, leading up a little hill. We arrive at the
pink garden—the one Kiet built—the one Hathai adores. My
eyes widen with fear when I see Elina ripping the flowers out
from their roots in a fit of pure rage. She lifts the garden
seats, smashing it into the ground until it shatters. It's an
excruciating sight. A ringing noise grows louder in my ear,
my hands and feet run cold, my stomach feels as though it is
fighting against gravity.

Elina screams and wails as she uproots and destroys
as many flowers as she can. Her hands are covered in blood.
Does she not see it? Does she not feel it?

"Elina! Stop!" I plunge forward and Khun Toh holds
me back.

"Leave her," he urges with an unsettling calmness. "If
you want to help, leave her."

I swallow and stand back, watching the sad sight. For three minutes, she goes on and on, destroying everything she can with her bloodied hands. Khun Toh and I look on in silence. His expression is cold, respectful, distant, almost like this is a sight he is accustomed to—but I cannot mask the fear and contain on my face.

With a loud cry, Elina falls to her knees, sobbing and punching the ground.

A few minutes pass and everything quiets down, giving way to whooshing sounds of the breeze blowing, the cawing birds in the sky. In any other circumstance, this would be a delightful moment. We could be laying under the warm sun, taking it all in the bosom of each other. We could be running our fingers all over each other's body, studying it like a map. The only thing I hear is the sound of my heart breaking. The air is stiff, the pain is felt everywhere on my skin. Seeing Elina in peril hurts in ways I could have never imagined.

She lifts herself off the ground and begins to limp towards us, rubbing her forehead with the back of her hand, covered in sand and blood.

"Khun Cheng." Khun Toh bows when she arrives in front of him.

"Take it all down— No more," her voice is a deep growl.

"Yes, Khun." He keeps his eyes lowered.

Without sparing a fleeting second to look me in the eye or even in my direction, Elina limps past me. I fist my palm, holding off following her to give her some space.

"Next time you see mail, you do not receive it. I run this household, you come to me," Khun Toh warns, his demeanor calm but his eyes filled with anger.

"I'm sorry, Khun. It will never happen again."

"Good." He turns to leave.

"What just happened?"

"You are closer to her than anyone else. You should ask her yourself." He continues down the path.

I take a hard long look at what used to be a full rich pink paradise, wondering what it would take for someone to feel that much pain—what it would take, to feel the kind of love that allows a person to feel that kind of pain.

I am no stranger to pain, emotional or physical. However, rage, as a result of pain, is new to me. I live in my head, I lock it all in. There are moments when I'd rather lash out and be free of it, moments when I'd rather scream and yell, but it never ends well. I hurt people—Just like Po.

But what a beauty it would be to be able to feel rage and lash out without a care in the world about how others perceive you. It might be a strange thing to say in the face of such a moment, but I wish it were me—raging.

**

I knock and walk into Elina's office, a nurse is tending to her wounds. I waited for hours to see her, watching the house keepers go in and out, as if a protocol had been put in place for times like this. Now I'm here, words fail me. The nurse finishes and packs up his box. He bows to Elina before walking past me and exits the office. I remain standing by the door, not knowing if I should go to her or wait.

"Don't hover, Pretty Thing." Elina chuckles.

I walk to her, arriving beside her seat. The corner of her lips slightly curves up at the sight of me. My gaze falls to her bandaged hands and my heart sinks. She still looks distraught. Her hair and clothes are covered with sand and petals. She has not let anyone except the nurse touch her.

"It doesn't hurt," Elina says. "Did you have lunch?"

I shake my head.

"Can I?" I reach out to touch her and she takes my palm, rubbing it all over her left cheek.

"Let's have lunch together," she says.

I kneel beside her and kiss her bandaged hand.

"Elina... Why won't you talk to me about him?"

"Wine—"

"Elina, please."

"I need you," she caresses my face, "to be a good boy and not push this any further."

"Please don't do that... do not use your dominance over me to push me away."

"I... I wasn't..."

"Elina—I. Want. In—I want in on you."

Her empty sinking eyes stare back at me. I can't read it. There is no sadness in them but there is also no joy. Just empty—like she feels nothing for my plea—nothing for anything.

"No, Wine. You do not want in. You want to disappear into someone else."

Her words move through me like a speeding bullet. I rise up from the ground slowly and turn away, heading for the door. Elina will say anything to fortify the wall between us and in so many ways I feel useless. She will never let me give her a fraction of the peace of mind she has given me, and I don't know how to exist in her world with that reality. It's like standing behind a glass wall looking at the man I want to become and not being able to reach him.

"Wine!" Elina calls and I halt, turning sharply. "Please don't leave."

"I don't know how to be here for you, Elina. You won't let me—I wanted this, I know I wanted this: to be yours, completely. And I am yours. Every inch of me screams for you, aches for you. I am yours to own, to command, to use as you see fit. But my emotions are **MINE**. You do not get to tell me how I feel. Especially when it comes to you. You do not get a say." I inhale and exhale heavily.

We remain standing in silence for a long moment.

"I'm sorry. You are right. I'm sorry—don't leave, Pretty Thing. I do not want to be alone today."

I toss my bag and run to her in an instant, throwing my hands around her neck and kissing her cheeks.

"You never have to be alone, Elina. You never have to be alone." I hold her face up to look into her eyes. "I'll walk every path you walk, and I'll follow you to the depths of hell if you'd let me."

She chuckles, holding my gaze.

"Don't be dramatic," she says.

"I mean every word, Elina."

I can tell the way she is looking at me is not from disbelief or lack of comprehension of my words. Rather, some kind of curiosity.

"What can I do for you? In what way can I be here for you? Tell me. Would you like a massage? I can run you a bath, I can read to you."

She lowers her gaze.

"I won't be in there with you, I'll wait by the door." I nod in plea.

"Ok." Elina raises her brows in approval and a weak smile travels across her face.

The playroom has become more than a place to indulge our sexual kinks. It's also the place where we joke around, where I see her smile the most, where we talk about art, music, life. The place I see shades of her the rest of the world does not get to see. Our little safe space.

Elina sits on the sofa, and I begin with her hair from the tip to scalp, trying to get it as petal and sand free as possible. I start massaging her forehead after I'm done, then move to the back of her neck, rubbing and pressing as she exhales with satisfaction. My hand travels to her shoulders and I continue to press. I can't massage her body the way I'd love to since I'm not allowed to see her naked, but her foot is an exemption. I excuse myself and fetch some warm towels and massage oils.

Upon my return, I get on my knees and take off her shoes like I always do, then wipe the dust and sand off her feet with the wet warm towel. I pour a little sandalwood oil and begin massaging slowly. Her eyes are closed, and her head is thrown back. She lets out satisfying cooing sounds.

When I am done with her feet, I run a hot bath and she moves to the changing room to put on a bathrobe. I pour some lavender oil into the water and make sure it's running at a decent temperature, which for Elina means scorching hot. When she walks in, we share warm smiles.

"I will be right outside, okay?" I say.

She nods. I walk over to the door and turn around.

"I'd love to read a poem that's a personal favorite I think you'll love."

"It's a soundproof bathroom."

"Easy fix." I hurry out of the bathroom, retrieve our phones from the bed and as I walk back into the bathroom, I call her number and pick it, handing it over to her.

"Creative." She nods.

"Thank you." We laugh softly. "You can lock the door."

"Okay."

I exit the bathroom and the door locks behind me.

I raise my phone, waiting to hear her step into the bath. When she does, it gladdens my heart. I retrieve the kindle from my bag then go back to sit on the floor in front of the bathroom door. Elina exhales and I hear the water swirling around.

"Does it feel nice?" I ask, pulling up the poem.

"Yes."

"Good. I'll begin with one of my favorite parts from the story of Phra Abhai Mani by Sunthorn Phu."

Elina laughs.

"You've read it?" I ask.

"It's a classic, who hasn't. Such a beautiful poem, please go on."

"You know, reading this for the first time when I was fifteen is when I realized how much I wanted to be dominated by a woman."

Elina laughs wholeheartedly and the water splashes around.

"It's barely a Femdom romance novel," she says.

"Barely? Have we read the same book? A pretty prince who plays the flute is banished by his father, the king, then kidnapped by a giantess who imprisons him in her cave and forces him to have her son. Elina?"

She laughs harder.

"It doesn't get any more Femdom than that," I conclude.

"And then he escaped and impregnated a mermaid. I always wondered how they had sex on that beach. She was half fish," she says in a soft tone.

"He could have had such a beautiful life with the giantess," I reply.

"Maybe... but he wasn't running away from his life like the rest of us. He wanted to live under the sun." She inhales. "Would you have preferred that kind of dominance from me. Leather, captivity, total control."

"I had that. I was gravely unhappy. In total honesty, I have imagined what it would feel like to experience that world with you. I think it would have been different."

"Why?"

"You have more compassion and empathy than my previous Domme— I rarely got after care."

"Aww... Pretty Thing." The comforting compassion in her voice fills me with warmth.

With a smile, I fold my legs. "It's ok. I'm over all of it now."

"Took you a long time, didn't it?"

"Longer than it should have. We were never going to work."

"Why did you stay?"

"Fear. Validation. I'm not certain."

"Fear of what?"

I breathe. "Being alone."

Goosebumps spread across my skin. It was not the answer I was expecting to leave my lips. I've only ever felt it, but never said it out loud. Ever. Elina says nothing and I wonder if I ventured too off course.

"So, back to Phra Abhai Mani? Hathai won't shut up about it either." I giggle. "She has this theory that the giantess was the victim in all of it. She thinks because the flute had magical powers that put humans to sleep, it worked differently on the giantess because she was also a magical being. She says the giantess was bewitched by the flute, that's why she kidnapped him. She hates how easily the giantess son turned against her when she presented herself in her true form and claimed another woman as his mother. How she had to die of heartbreak and turn to stone while the man with the flute went on to fall for other women. Hathai has a lot of theories. When you look at the story from her perspective, it's indeed a tragedy for the giantess."

"Sounds very much like her."

I let out a quiet laughter.

"How is she doing?" Elina asks.

"Great actually. She's talking more, being more vulnerable—I think your sister being around brings out the best in her."

"Oh." Elina swallows and remains quiet.

"Elina... I didn't mean..."

"I totally understand—thank you for doing a good job with her."

"She loves you deeply, Elina—she does."

Silence.

More silence.

Elina sniffs.

Elina sighs.

Elina sobs.

"I know," she says. "I know," her voice cracks.

I say nothing, resting my head on the door as I place my hand on it to be as close to her as possible. If only I could hold her, the way she holds me when I break.

I say no words of comfort, because sometimes, pain is meant to be felt, completely and without reserve.

TWENTY-TWO
DINNER TABLE

Elina slept next to me for the first-time last night. I haven't taken my eyes off her. I feel as though if I blink too much, it will all be over. I don't think I have ever noticed just how perfect her lashes are. They are long, straight, and compliment her little freckles. She appears very vulnerable, fragile, angelic.

She rubs her nose a lot when she sleeps. I checked several times to see if there was something crawling around, disturbing, but there wasn't, it's just her sleep thing. I rest my head on her shoulder and curl up next to her, intertwining my palms with hers. She adjusts, digging her nose into my hair and I hear her swallow.

"I was starting to think you'd stare at me forever," Elina says with a groggy deep voice, and I chuckle. "Did you get any sleep?"

"Some."

"Hungry?"

"A bit."

"Almost time for dinner. She might not come."

"She'll come," I say.

Elina inhales my hair and begins leaving tender kisses on my forehead. She caresses my cheek, leans over and kisses my nose then my lips.

"Elina..." I mutter.

Her lips sink into mine, kissing me as she rolls me onto my back and climbs over me. Her kisses travel to my cheek then my neck, sucking gently and spreading warmth over me. She bites me and I wince, wriggling my toes. She rolls my shirt up and continues with my nipples, sucking and biting as I squeeze the sheets. Three days away from Elina has made me sensitive to her bites all over again. I was beginning to get used to them.

Satisfied, she lifts herself off me and slides off the bed.

"Get ready for dinner," Elina says and heads for the stairs.

I watch her leave before falling back into the bed. She sure knows how to torment me.

After taking a long cold shower, I march over to the closet to get dressed. Elina stocks all my skin and hair care beauty products so it's easy to get ready after play sessions. All done with skincare, I move to the closet and pick out a black trouser. When I reach for one of my white shirts, my gaze flutters to Elina's section and her forest green shirt I have admired countless times, hangs in between a set of other shirts. I take it down and inhale her scent before slipping it on.

"In that shirt, your mouth won't be eating rice for dinner." Elina says, arriving by the door.

She leans against the door panel, wearing a gorgeous wine red gown and pearls.

"Good. I was not trying to impress the rice."

Elina rolls her eyes and by Buddha, I swear her cheeks turn pink.

"I'm sorry, are you blushing?" I smile, cocking my head to the side.

"I applied some blush earlier."

"Mm hmm."

"Shut up."

I breathe a laugh. "You look wonderful," I say.

"Thank you." She beams. "Dance with me." Elina walks in stretching out her hand to me.

I take it and twirl her as she chuckles.

It only lasts a few minutes before we have to leave for dinner. But nothing ever feels like a few minutes with Elina Cheng.

***

We enter the bustling dining room with the same joy and laughter we shared in the playroom. Phi Nam and the housekeepers are busy setting the table. Elina is trying too hard to impress Hathai with this dinner. It's the first dinner they will be having together since Kiet passed away. Even though she is doing an excellent job at masking it, I can tell she is nervous. She opens her mouth to speak when Hathai walks in.

"I wasn't aware she was joining us," Hathai says, pinning her eyes on me.

"I did say it was a family dinner," I reply.

"Which is why I invited Bpaa." She walks over to her seat with a sigh.

"You invited Khun Cheng?"

"Of course!" Junta enters the room, dressed in a black and white Chanel ensemble and a hat bigger than the whole dining table.

"Phi, this is a surprise, shouldn't you be on your way to Paris?" Elina asks.

"I moved things around, I couldn't possibly turn down my dearest niece." Junta winks at Hathai.

I pull out a seat for Junta and she sits, adjusting to her comfort. I do the same for Elina, then take my seat opposite Junta, beside Hathai, whose face is rumpled into a frown. Elina seats on the single seat facing us all and we steal glances at each other.

"Let me know if you need anything else." Phi Nam bows and leaves.

"What happened to your hand, Nong?" Junta asks.

"Nothing to worry about. Minor accident." Elina sips her water.

"You've always been clumsy. I'll call War, he is the best plastic surgeon in the country, you cannot afford to scar."

"I have his number, Phi."

"Yes, but you'll never call him. I'll take care of it. You're my first baby girl after all, even though you don't let me take care of you anymore. You need someone to take care of you, Nong. You need—"

"Phi," Elina's call is sharp, but she doesn't look Junta's way.

Junta swallows her words and breathes, pausing for a moment.

"I cannot remember the last time we all shared a meal together. Though, I would've preferred it to be a family affair." Junta directs her stare at me, raising her wine glass.

"Be nice, Bpaa," Hathai cautions.

"I am the nicest person." Junta smiles at Hathai.

"When are you leaving, Phi?" Elina inquires.

"Nothing needs my immediate attention."

"Neither do I."

"Don't get defensive, Nong."

"I don't need you hovering over me. You asked to see the books and you have. You should return. This is my territory. I don't step foot in your waters uninvited."

"I am not in exile, Nong. I can visit my country whenever it pleases me. Besides, Europe is boring."

"Did Po put you up to this?"

"Contrary to your belief, Nong, I do make most of my choices outside of Po's influence. And maybe if you heed his advice every now and then, we wouldn't have to pull you out of uncanny situations so often and I—"

Hathai drops her cutleries, the clanking noise silences Junta. "Stop it," Hathai demands, looking down at her plate.

I turn and catch a glimpse of her face then gently pat her back. She picks her cutleries back up and everyone continues eating in silence.

Dinner isn't as chaotic as I imagined, I hoped there would be more words between mother and daughter to get them talking and sharing. But this is a step in the right direction.

"Do you have family dinners with all your clients, Khun Sutthaya?" Junta breaks the silence.

"If I think it necessary, yes. It can create a safer environment for the child to share."

"Any family I know of?"

"At the moment, Hathai is the only child under my care."

Junta smirks and we hold each other's gaze in spite.

"That is interesting—I looked at your credentials, so many certifications, so little experience. One might wonder why you got this job."

"Phi." Elina glares at Junta.

"It's very telling, is all I'm saying, Nong."

"You only get experience by experiencing, Khun Cheng. And Hathai has been the most pleasing first experience." I smile at Hathai, she smiles back at me.

"One might say you should spend more time experiencing some things over other things. They say the first time is the shortest time one should spend learning."

"I have never heard of such a saying," I reply.

"Then you should read less romance books."

I open my mouth to retort when Khun Toh makes an entrance.

"Sorry to disturb dinner." He bows.

"You should join us." Junta waves him over. "Haven't seen much of you."

"Thank you, Khun, but certain matters need my attention." He smiles at her and turns to Elina. "Khun, the landscapers are here, just checking in to see if you'd like to make any last minute changes?"

"Not at all. But do request for the landscape papers."

Khun Toh bows and leaves.

"Landscapers? Doing some renovations?" Junta asks as she chews.

"Yes," Elina replies.

"Hmm, making your stay here permanent, finally. The pool?"

"One of the gardens."

"Ah. Ironic isn't it, you never wanted to live here in the first place." Junta laughs, turning her attention to me. "Po had to drag her by the hair, screaming and kicking, to make her move in here."

"Phi, stop it," Elina warns with her eyes.

"Alright, alright." Junta goes back to eating.

I bite down my smile. It is very new to me, hearing stories about Elina from the past. I lift my eyes to her and the side of my lips twitch, she knows I am looking. It's making her shy. I'd laugh if we were alone. *I'd laugh very hard.* My gaze shifts to Hathai and find her staring angrily at Elina.

"Which garden are you renovating?" Hathai asks.

I don't think I've ever seen or heard her speak to Elina directly.

"The one up the hill," Elina says.

"That is Po's garden."

"I know."

"What do you want to change?"

"Everything," Elina replies and picks up her wine glass.

"You can't do that. Why would you do that?"

"We have multiple gardens, Hathai. It's in our best interest—"

"No, it's not! It's in your best interest, everything is in your best interest."

"Hatty—" Junta furrows her brow.

Hathai springs up from her seat, slamming her hand against the table.

"Why do you always take away things that mean something to me! If you really despised him that much, why did you fight so hard to marry him! You've erased everything! Killing him wasn't enough for you!"

"Hathai Maryann Cheng!" Junta scolds. "You will speak to your mother with respect!"

"She is not my mother!" Hathai turns red. "She's a murderer!"

Junta springs up from her seat. "Go to your room right now, Hathai!"

"Khun Cheng," I intervene, "it is best to let her speak what's on her mind."

"I think it best you stop interfering with my family," Junta retorts.

"That is exactly my job, Khun."

"Arghh!" Hathai screams, pulling back her hair and the room falls silent.

"Hathai, it's okay," I say, rising from my seat. "Tell your mother why the garden is important to you."

"She knows—she always knows what is important to me, then she finds different ways to destroy it!"

Elina's eyes stay lowered, fixed on her plate.

"Why do you think that?" I ask.

Her eyes glisten with tears she won't let fall.

"In the left-wing.... there is a room." Hathai sobs. "It's empty... but there is a rope hanging loose from the ceiling... a stool under it..." Hathai's voice is shaky and heavy.

Trying to keep my orderliness, I slowly turn my gaze to Elina. Her eyes are squeezed shut, one could assume she is in physical pain from how tensed her body appears to be. From the corner of my eyes, I can see Junta's anger turning into surprise.

"She puts the rope around her neck... and stands there." The tears finally roll down Hathai's cheeks and she exhales. "She just stands there.... why would you just stand there? Over and over! and over again! Kick the stool already! Let it be over!"

"Hathai—" I call

"You don't want to be here! You don't want any of it! Any of me! Everything irritates you! Kick the stool!"

"Bunny..." Elina begins to speak but it's shallow. "You should have never seen that." The words roll off her lips and so do tears down her cheeks.

"Don't call me that! You aren't my mother!" Hathai screams, running to Elina and begins smacking and punching her. "Give me back my mother! Give her back to me!"

I try to pull her away, but she clings onto Elina's pearl necklace, ripping it apart when I am successful.

"Hathai, look at me!" I shake her as she cries. She tears away from my grasp, running out of the dining room.

"Is this true, Elina?" Junta asks, an intense frown on her face.

Elina goes back to eating like nothing ever happened. It infuriates Junta even more and although I have so much to say, I go after Hathai.

***

A single knock and Hathai opens the door, almost like she was waiting for me. She turns and walks back in, I follow, taking a deep breath. It's the first time she's let me into her room, a well spread out pink decorated fortress, exactly as I imagined. Very whimsical and elegant. So many plushies are placed on her bed. That was unexpected.

We sit on the window seat, her legs are folded onto her chest as she hugs them. Her red face is covered in tears and sweat. We sit in silence, but I don't take my eyes off her, letting her know I am only here for her, and she can choose to talk or not.

"I was not going to yell at her," she says, her voice cracking. "I really wasn't."

"No one's judging you Hathai. I am only here to listen."

"Please don't let her take away the garden." She sobs. "There are no more pictures left of Po, and she took away his guitar."

I take out my phone from my pocket. Open up my photo gallery of Kiet and pull up my favorite picture of him.

"Do you like this picture of him?" I hand the phone over to her. It's a picture of Kiet at a carnival in a bunny costume. She giggles and looks up at me. "You can swipe, there is more." I point and she continues, her face brightens up as she swipes. "If there is anyone you want, I can print it out, and we can hang it up on the wall."

"You can?" she asks. I nod with a smile. "She'll take it down."

"She won't. I promise."

She turns the phone screen towards me. "I like this one."

It's a monochrome picture of Kiet, laughing while clinging onto his guitar.

"Good choice." I nod and she returns my phone. "About the room... with the rope..."

She begins to sob again. "I am sorry."

"Why are you apologizing, Nong?"

"I know I'm not allowed in the left-wing. I just... I thought..." She cries heavier. I cup her cheeks, then pull her close, trying to get most of the tears off her cheeks. "I don't know what happened to Mae... I just want her back, she wasn't always like that."

I feel as though I am looking at myself through a mirror. We were taught to keep our own emotions in check during moments like this, to prioritize the feelings of the child and not our own emotions. But here I am, a tear in my eye, my heart sinking. I embrace her to comfort her, but also to hide my own tears.

She cried in my arms for as long as she could before sleeping off, then I tucked her in. I have never felt more like I have no clue what I'm doing—*I suck at this job.*

I step out of her room and Junta sits on the hallway bench, pressing her iPad. She lifts her head at the sound of the door opening.

"Is she asleep?"

I nod in response, still standing by the door.

"She's a strong kid," I say, sensing how concerned Junta is.

"I've always warned her all that snooping will get her in trouble. She loves to spy on people."

"I know."

Junta and I share a smile and she looks away.

"Why do you hate him so much?" I blurt out. "They both seem to be bound by their love for him."

My question is unexpected, for both me and her. It wasn't my intention to ask, but I know there is a part of the puzzle I'm missing. I fold my arms to brace myself for whatever she might spew.

"He was a great father, he really was—but a horrible person—and Elina, what binds her isn't love." Junta breathes and takes a long pause. "I thought she was doing ok. I thought it was all over—how bad is it?" She turns to me.

What else could possibly bind Elina to Kiet after all these years of his death if not love. Her unwavering loyalty in her love for him has been the driving force of our sexual relationship. I find it difficult to believe it can be anything else but that. I join Junta on the hallway bench.

"I don't think she wants to kill herself," I say.

Junta chuckles. "You must not know her as well as you think you do then."

We remain quiet for minutes.

"She tried once. Three years ago. Slit her wrist, sat and waited—I had never seen that much blood in my life. It just kept coming."

I stare into Junta's cold eyes that combated me a week ago, they are only filled with fear, and I feel every bit of it. Fear of losing her sister, but something else lurks behind her eyes that I can't quite make sense of. The thought of Elina attempting suicide sends a dark chill through my soul.

"I'm sorry, Khun," I meekly say. She exhales and gets up, packing up her bags. "Khun Cheng." I rub my sweaty palms against my knee, and she turns to me. "Hathai... She doesn't have to be a strong kid. She shouldn't have to. She's not a broken kid either, it's the world she's living in that's broken. I think she deserves a place... a home, where she can be just a kid—I think that home should be with you."

"You want me to take custody of her?" Junta squints at me with an expression that makes me feel like I have committed an abomination just by the thought of it.

"Just until Elina figures it out. She might not be trying to kill herself but she's destroying Hathai."

"She is a great mother," Junta says with a force in her voice.

"I know."

"She's a really great mother."

"I know."

"She loves that child, you should have seen her... you should have seen her before it all began."

"I don't doubt it for a second. But right now, she's not her mother. She's a broken woman, trying to hold on."

Junta hisses, turning away. A few seconds pass and she begins pacing around in a circle. The sound of her heels clicking fills the air.

"She'll never let me take her, even if it's temporary. Elina... you don't know her, she'll fight."

"If we work together, we can make it easier. Elina needs help. Hathai needs a home."

Junta pauses, looking at nothing in particular.

"I can see you are trying to help, Khun. I think... you may be a better man than he ever was. But I have extreme difficulty in trusting anyone my sister brings into this family, you have to understand. I will take my time to come to a decision."

"Of course."

"Watch over them," Junta says, reaching for her bag.

Before I can reply, Junta is walking down the hallway.

The very second those words left my lips, I felt as though I had betrayed Elina. I now think it was inevitable. The day Hathai appeared in front of my room the morning after I passed out, all teary eyed, with so much emotion and sympathy, I knew it wasn't her that needed fixing, she was simply mirroring. It would be a lie to imply the thought of separating them hadn't crossed my mind several times prior. But I chose to hang onto my own selfish desires—for far too long.

I think back to the cold nights I spent on the floor in my room, absent of my parent's touch, devastated and alone. If I moved in with Yaa at the countryside, surrounded by nature and her undying warmth, I might not have grown up with so much resentment for myself—so much fear, an emptiness I cannot explain. Hathai can have that—she should have that.

Yet, I know when I look into Elina's eyes tonight, all I'll see is the reflection of the man who just took her daughter away from her.

***

Without knocking, I walk into her office. The moonlight streaming in through the tall windows illuminates the room alongside a few yellow lights. Elina sits behind her desk, her chair turned around to face the tall window. I haven't seen her smoke in a while. I stand for a few minutes, watching the smoke from her cigar rise above her silhouette and disappear into the air before taking steps towards her.

"How is she?" Elina asks as I arrive, not looking at me.

"Asleep. Tired."

She blows smoke into the air and puts out the cigar in an ashtray beside her as she gets up, staggering over to me. Her hands slide across my waist, and she places her head on my shoulder, letting out a loud sigh of relief. The heat from her body warms me and there is a flowery scent coming from her hair. I put my right hand on her lower back to embrace her, but she lifts her head and kisses me. Strong hard kisses of frustration. I kiss her back, but do not invest in it, just waiting till she's had her full and pulls away. When she realizes, she stops and leans her whole body on me, pinning me against the window. I squeeze her in a hug, gently swaying her in silence.

"I would love nothing more than to be an object for your distraction tonight—but that would be extremely selfish of me, Elina," I say in a low tone.

It starts as a simple smile, but soon grows into loud laughter, mocking me as she steps away. The sight of her laughing so painfully, with no cause for amusement, stills me.

I wonder who she saw when she looked into my eyes, who she wanted to bury her aches in. If she saw me, then maybe she also saw the lingering guilt from my fresh betrayal. And if she saw him, did that make her feel safe enough? Not that I'm willing to be any of them tonight, I'd rather disappear under her dominance. However, the woman that stands before me isn't the woman that dominates me. After a few minutes, her laughter dies down. She tousles her hair and draws a deep breath, exhaling loudly.

"I want to make you cum— If you can't give me that, you should fuck off."

"Elina—"

"Selfish? Wine? You think that's extremely selfish? Everything I do is for you!" Her eyes glow with fury. "From the moment I set my eyes on you! I've seen you! Wine! You've never seen me! That's what's selfish!"

"You won't let me! When have you ever confided in me! Have I not asked! Have I not pleaded with you!"

"With you I have only two options! The version of me you need me to be and the version of me I cannot stand! Look me in the eyes, right now! Tell me you want to know! Tell me knowing won't crack the bubble you so desperately crave! A place to run away from your life, to feel something aside from pain and fear!"

My lips part in shock. I can't make sense of the words she's forming. I begin to say something to deny her accusation but none of my words are audible. My lips betray me. My heart aches from the weight of unspoken words.

I take a step forward, stretching out my hand and she takes a step back. We stand, as though challenging each other, not moving. Her breathing is loud and though the room is dim and she is a few steps away, I think I see a tear. She storms out of the office, slamming the door.

I don't follow her, I don't chase after her. I have no understanding of the events that just unfolded, but I know she doesn't need me hovering.

TWENTY-THREE
SHADES OF MEMORY

The mansion is over nine thousand square feet, but it felt too small to contain Elina and I tonight. There was a stiffness in the air, a weight on my soul. I couldn't breathe. It felt as if the walls were judging me, suffocating me.

When I left the mansion, my intention was to return to Lucifer's home, and maybe drink myself to sleep—not that alcohol has ever helped. But instead, here I am, standing in front of my childhood home, tired and conflicted. This house—it follows me everywhere. No matter how far or how long I stay away from it, the memories it's stolen from me haunt me, and eventually, I yield and return.

I pull the gate apart and enter, walking stealthily. It's just past 9pm, I know Po is still awake, but I hope he isn't sitting in the parlor watching TV, which he does most evenings before bed. His plants are doing well. I take a minute to smile at them and run my fingers through a couple before entering the house. The sitting room is empty, he must have retired for the night.

I continue in, and when I turn into the passageway and my eyes fall on that door; the door at the end of the hallway that has remained unopened most of my life. I keep my eyes fixed on it as I walk to my room. I haven't thought about it once since I left home, there was no room for it, not in Elina's world, not under her dominance.

After hesitating in front of my room door for more than a minute, I turn towards the door, fidgeting as I walk to it. I turn the door knob, just to check, and to my utmost surprise, it's unlocked. Gripping the knob tighter, I take a deep breath and push the door open.

I cannot remember what it was like to walk within these walls as a child, yet, everything is familiar. The room is super clean, not even a speck of dust. The bright blue colored walls, with rainbows and clouds painted on them don't appear to have aged or deteriorated over the years. The baby's cot is well arranged with baby blankets neatly folded into a pile, cute toys surround it. The rocking chair Mae always sat in is still by the window. I watch as the white cotton curtains are lifted by soft breeze blowing in from the ajar window, making them float over the rocking chair. A vague memory of Mae, rocking my little sister in that chair, while I played with trains on the floor beside her flashes through my mind and I let out a small gasp.

Recollecting childhood memories never happens to me.

"Witthaya."

I shudder at the sound of Po's voice, turning sharply to his direction. His dark silhouette stands in the middle of the passageway. I didn't close the door behind me when I entered, Elina is rubbing off on me. I wai in greeting and he walks over, stepping into the nursery and stands beside me. Both of us look down into my little sister's cot in silence. I expected him to be upset, ask me to leave, scold me even, but he doesn't.

"She really liked this one." He picks up a small blue dinosaur toy and hands it to me. "It was her favorite."

"You've been cleaning her nursery?" I ask, taking the toy from him.

He nods. "Have you eaten?"

"Yes."

"Are you back for good?"

"I think it's best if I keep staying at Lucifer's."

"Well... this house is in your name. Don't abandon it for too long."

It takes me a second to understand what he means.

"My name? Po, why would you—"

"You are going to inherit it anyways, why later when it can be sooner."

He walks to the rocking chair and sits with a grunt. I reach over and pick up the little baby shirt on top of the pile of blankets, running my finger over it.

"You keep every memory of her alive. I thought you wanted to forget all about her. You act like she never existed."

Po says nothing. The creaking sound from him rocking the chair fills the nursery. I don't want to look into his face, it will take away whatever courage I have mustered from this grueling night to ask. It's always in his face, that scared look that warns me off.

"Po—"

"Witthaya, some things are better left unsaid, buried and forgotten."

He knew it was coming, the question. I'll be honest, I have been afraid of what he will tell me. What if the truth is so ugly, too ugly to look at? What if Po is protecting me by not telling me? Whatever he says to me will be the reason Mae left, it will be the reason why he changed, the reason why there is a big hole in my heart I cannot fill. There is no way it's going to be pretty and because of that, I've run from the truth many times. But Po has always been so good at stirring me away from it.

"None of it is buried or forgotten, Po. I have always been scared of this room, the memory of her." I take a deep breath. "What did I do? You've never forgiven me for it, why?"

"I hold nothing against you, Witthaya."

"I barely remember her, but I remember what you were like before she was gone. You hugged me a lot, told me how much you loved me all the time. I'm not saying you didn't deserve to hurt or grieve—but I was your child too, Po, and I was alive—I am alive. Yet, I still live in her shadow. You've never loved me as much as you love her memory and Mae... well, she just couldn't stand me after her."

Po exhales and stops rocking the chair. I squeeze the toy in my hand, tensed at the thought of him actually revealing it all to me, what it would mean.

"It was never my intention to make you feel unloved, Witthaya. You are my son, my love for you is bound in blood."

"I wish it was bound with words and actions."

He peels his gaze away from the window and turns it to me.

"I know this is not what you want to hear—but—I did the best I could. I am human, and maybe I was weak, and you got hurt, but it really was the best I could do."

I swallow. "So, I did something?"

He nods.

"To my sister?"

He nods.

"Po, you have to tell me. I need my life to stop feeling like I'm walking under water all the time, over something I cannot remember."

"It won't change anything if you know. Instead that water you've been under will choke you. Witthaya, please, start therapy again."

I laid in bed all night, watching the fan spin, round and round and round. Po was right. I am a twenty-eight-year-old man, carrying around the ghost of his sister whom he doesn't remember. What if it's something I can't live with? Something that will broaden the hole I already feel.

I wonder if Elina would be able to look her struggling daughter in the eye and say, 'I did all I could do'. She is exactly the kind of Parent Po was to me when I was Hathai's age. There but not there. I don't think Elina has done all she can do. She gave up too soon, and so did Po.

The night was long and filled with thoughts, but I still managed to squeeze in a few hours of sleep, waking up to the smell of Po making breakfast and a panic attack, two things I am all too familiar with. I rolled out of bed, went straight to the kitchen. Po and I made breakfast in our own fashion: in silence.

I have another interview today and then I have to head over to Lucifer's office. Plerng's birthday is just four days away and I have barely been of any help. Maybe there is something I can do to help before returning to the mansion to check on Hathai—and only Hathai.

I fix my hair in the mirror; it is due for a cut. Po walks in and stands by the door, his hands on his waist as he watches me. I don't look in his direction, only watching him from the corner of my eye, waiting for him to speak, but he doesn't.

"Po, what is it?" I smile. He clears his throat, but I know it's false. "Po?"

"Do you have a boyfriend?"

I snap my head towards him.

"No! What! What gave you that idea?"

"Girlfriend then?"

My gaze falters and I look away.

"You are a grown man, Witthaya. I don't mind, just asking."

"Of course not, Po."

"Then, who is sending you two dozen red roses by 9am?"

"What?"

He shrugs and points towards the living room, walking away. I follow him. The living room is stacked with buckets of red roses, two dozen worth. My lips part in surprise and my heart begins to race in excitement. Of course, I know exactly who it's from.

"They just dropped it off. It came with a note. Your name is printed on it—in gold letters. That's a lot of effort for a non-boyfriend."

He hands me an envelope and I begin to open it. I don't try to hide my eagerness and excitement from Po, I forget he is standing next to me. I take the note out from the envelope and Po cranes his neck to see what's written inside. I lean back and he leans in, I move away, and he moves to my corner.

"Po!"

"Who is he?"

"I don't have a boyfriend, Po."

"No one sends a man roses just cause, Witthaya."

"Po, can I have some privacy?"

He laughs and walks away.

Smiling sheepishly, I open the note to read. It's handwritten and the paper is lavender scented.

My dearest beautiful boy,

Last night scared you, but don't hide away from me.

Sincerely, Elina.

I place my palm over my lips as a broad smile spreads across my face. Surrounded by roses, I feel like a prince being wooed into marriage. It's ridiculous, I know, but that's how I feel. My smile starts to fade when I realize she doesn't know yet.

If Elina knew how hell bent I am to see Hathai taken away from her and placed in another person's care. She'll never forgive me, even if that person is her sister. She'll never look at me the same way. This is the first time in my life anyone has sent me flowers, and it feels so wrong. I feel so guilty.

***

All day I have thought about the roses, trying to allow myself enjoy the sentiment. I want to pick up the phone and call her; hear her voice and let her hear mine, but I can't get myself to. I'm staring at the lovely parents interviewing me and all I'm thinking about is Elina.

I wonder if Elina is holding her phone close by, waiting for me to call and tell her I'll be in her arms by dusk. If I had known yesterday would go the way it did, I wouldn't have bothered trying to make myself scarce. I would have spent every moment I had to spare under her whip. I miss her already, but for the life of me, I cannot look into her eyes today.

The interview ends and I bid the lovely parents goodbye and head over to the mansion. I don't intend on staying long so I ask the driver to wait. I hurry in and check on Hathai. As expected, she's preoccupied with classes. We exchange smiles then take a moment to chat. Hathai has always been so good at bouncing back—or rather, masking her pain.

I'm certain Elina knew I was in the mansion, and I'm glad she chose not to come see me. The rest of the day went by, and then the next and then the next. Every day I wake up and swear this is the day I'd call Elina, and every day I don't.

I hoped Junta Cheng would've called me by now and shared her plans so we can begin the process of separating Hathai from Elina—*Ugh, the Cheng's.*

TWENTY-FOUR
DEAR FRIEND

Today is Plerng's birthday, a very welcome distraction. I have missed her company and cannot wait to hear loud laughter and ramblings again.

We have a solid surprise plan. Khun Kittibun told her he's bringing her aboard a yacht for an evening meeting. Plerng is not expecting a party, and to top it off, neither Lucifer nor I called or texted her birthday messages. I'm sure she's fuming and cussing us out.

I arrive at the dock where Lucifer's two deck luxurious yacht is packed and waiting, a little later than I should thanks to traffic. It's already past 5pm and Plerng is set to arrive at seven. As I approach, I see the server's loading drinks onto the boat and Lucifer hurrying them. He sees me and rolls his eyes. I laugh.

"I'm sorry! I'm sorry." I shake my head, putting my palms together in apology.

"What the hell bro! You were supposed to be here an hour ago!"

"I know! Traffic! Sorry, where do you need me, Mmh?" I hug him and sniff his cheeks.

"It's all done anyways, come on." He drags me onto the yacht, eager to show me what he's done so far.

It's an all-white party as we planned. The yacht is packed with women—lesbians to be precise—so many lesbians. I can count the number of men I've seen since I stepped into the yacht. There are strippers walking around wearing dildos and bras that barely conceal anything. So many boobs, I don't know where to look without being disrespectful, they are just... Everywhere.

Over the years, we have always planned our birthday parties together, and sometimes we just keep it within ourselves. Small and fun. Either way it's never this flamboyant and lewd. I am staring down at a vagina shaped cake. It's just so... *Why Lucifer?*

"What do you think, huh!" Lucifer beams with pride from his accomplishment, chewing his gum loudly.

"You should have just painted the lesbian flag on the yacht."

"Oh fuck! That would have been amazing, Wine!"

"That was a joke, Luce, are you kidding me? Plerng doesn't know half these people."

"You'd be surprised! You were gone two years, Wine, she got around. She doesn't know all of them but most of them, sure."

"Remind me never to ask you to plan my party."

"Hey, don't hate the vibe! Be right back." He disappears into the yacht.

I don't hate the vibe, it's not so different from the raging gay parties Lucifer would drag us to during our university days. Naked bodies scattered around, everyone checking out everyone. I cringed hard at it then and I'm cringing hard at it now. The only difference would be how no one has hit on me yet, or even looked at me like I'm a piece of dick. The women are preoccupied with each other. To my right, a small circle gossips about celebrity news, and to my left, global warming.

It doesn't take long for a bunch of strippers to drag me into their company and bombard me with questions. They fill my ears with stories about their best and worst experiences on the job, ex and present lovers. In a short span of conversation, I have learnt their names, where they are from, their personal goals and soon I am lost far deep into conversation to care about the vagina shaped cakes or the massive dildos some of them have on.

"They're here! They're here!" Lucifer quietly screams and the lights of the yacht go off. We all fall to the ground, crouching.

The plan was to have Khun Kittibun text Lucifer once they arrive at the boat club's parking lot so the lights could be off just in time, and we can all hide. Very young of us, I'm loving every second of it. I crouch on the ground next to Nong Mook, a stripper I just met and we giggle. I can hear Plerng and Khun Kittibun arguing as they enter the yacht. Plerng is displeased with her father's spontaneous meeting.

Once they are close enough, the lights come back on, fireworks go off and simultaneously we scream happy birthday with cheers and claps. Balloons shaped like breasts are released into the air and Plerng stands with her mouth ajar. I rush to hug her and so does Lucifer. All three of us laughing in our embrace, but soon she begins punching us for not texting her a happy birthday.

As expected, Plerng forgot we existed after the party got heated. She moved to the upper deck with her friends, leaving Lucifer and I on the lower deck. We don't mind it. It's her night and we are back in her good graces.

"Do you wish he stayed?" I ask and sip my drink.

"My boyfriend?"

I nod.

"Well yeah." Lucifer laughs.

"How does it make you feel? He's too old for scenes like this, don't you have to attend most parties alone?"

"He's not too old for scenes like this, he's just forty-nine," Lucifer says and we both laugh. "I have always known dating someone older would come with a different lifestyle and that's fine. I get to go home and dance with him later tonight— But you know what's cool about being in a relationship with someone older?"

"What?"

"The emotional security. He just lets me be and I find that very rejuvenating. I always used to have to explain everything, but now, I spend more time telling my partner about my day rather than explaining my day, you know?"

"I think I get it."

Lucifer laughs. "We are getting old too, Wine, you're twenty-eight, I'm twenty-nine in a few months..."

"Somehow, it feels good."

"What feels good?" Plerng stumbles over, falling beside Lucifer.

"You're wasted!" I tease.

"Not yet! But I'm heading there." Plerng laughs and we join her. "I really needed this."

"Luce did most of it, I just showed up."

"I hired a party planner, I just showed up too."

"Well thanks to both of you and the party planner." Plerng squeezes Lucifer with a side hug. I join, squeezing him tighter. "But if you guys ever cut me out again, our friendship is over, I mean it."

We break away from our group hug.

"I hate that you both feel you had to hide things from me. Luce, I don't care you took the company, I care that you let fucking Po tell me and Wine, I want to clap for you if what you have with your boss works out or lend you a shoulder if it fails. Doesn't mean I don't get to say what I think, that's what best friends are for. Don't... lock me out of the boys club."

"I promise there is no boys club," Lucifer testifies.

"It felt like there was, ok? So, no more."

I pull her into a hug. "No more boys club."

Lucifer joins in the group hug, and we chuckle. With Plerng now in the middle, we squeeze her even tighter.

"What the fuck did you do to Darika," Lucifer asks and Plerng pulls away with a sigh.

"Nothing."

"You fucking Liar." Lucifer shoves her. "She just magically happens to be in the middle of a criminal investigation right after meeting you?"

"She is getting what she deserves."

"Oh come on!" Lucifer and I sigh in unison.

"Did she do the crime or is this just some sick way of getting into Junta's pants," I ask.

"She dates people like us, convinces them to invest in her fashion company that till date has only accumulated one-hundred dollars in revenue, sounds a lot to me like a thief."

"Sounds a lot to me like they gave her the money," Lucifer says.

"It is about the intent, Luce."

"How do you know all this stuff?" I ask.

"I know a lot of stuff, Wine. You have to have your claws out while dealing with these people. That's why I didn't want you in this, you're too nice and people are devious." Plerng sips her wine.

"People are devious whether they are billionaires, millionaires or poor," I say.

"Yes, but at least with poor people, it is expected. People will do crazy things to survive. With the rich, you never see it coming." She leans back. "So... what's the sex like?"

"Don't start, Plerng." I laugh.

"What? If you're going to fuck your boss—"

"She's not my boss, she's my client."

"You both are all over my daily tabloid feed."

"Plerng, it's your night, we are not talking about my sex life," I insist.

"Oh please! That's all I live for! Do tell already!"

I eye her and Lucifer joins her in staring at me, waiting for an answer.

"It's... really good."

They tease, making ridiculous noises.

"Is she kinky? Rumor has it, the woman likes to whip things." Plerng pokes my sides and I laugh.

"She's—interesting."

"Oh my God, Wine, you've been holding out on me." Lucifer ruffles my hair.

"Luce, don't, don't encourage her," I beg.

"Aren't you going to go say hi?" Plerng asks.

"Hi?" I narrow my eyes.

"I'll give it to her, she can pull off white."

"Oh shoot, Wine, don't look up," Lucifer says.

"Why?" I sit up.

"It's just sex right, it's only physical?" Plerng holds my hand. "You don't like her... like her."

I gulp, slowly nodding and Lucifer exhales.

"Good, cause she's here with a date," Lucifer says.

"What?"

"Do you guys have some sort of arrangement with dating other people?" Plerng asks.

"W... what do you mean she's here?"

Lucifer nods upwards and I look up to the upper deck. There is a clear view from where we sit on the lower deck and I see Elina, leaning against the railings. The foreigner from her office has his hands around her waist, smiling and looking into her eyes. All of a sudden, the air around me is sucked away.

"Wine?"

"Mmh?" I turn to Plerng.

"Did you not know she was coming?"

I gulp my whole drink down. "No."

"I sent her an invitation, thought she'd mention it," Lucifer says.

"I'm just glad she brought Junta," Plerng chuckles.

"That was literally the reason we decided to invite her." Lucifer breaks into laughter and Plerng joins.

"She's barely spoken to me, but I will change that by the end of tonight." Plerng wraps her hand around my shoulder. "At least one of us will be in a Cheng sister's bed by the end of tonight." She grins.

Plerng and Lucifer continue to chat but my eyes find Elina again, and I stare. I hate that his hands are there, around her waist, where I have touched, squeezed, kissed. I hate the way he looks at Elina. It's the way he looked at her in that video, with desire, like he wants her, like Elina is his— *she's not*.

"Where are you going?" Plerng calls as I rise from my seat.

I ignore her and push through the dancing bodies, making my way to the stairs. I skip a few flights of stairs in a hurry to reach the upper deck. The upper deck is more crowded, it's where the party is. They're all the way on the other end. I keep pushing, and soon I'm in front of them.

"Elina Cheng!" I call sharply in annoyance, and she turns.

She doesn't look the least bit surprised to see me, she knew I'd be here.

"Wine." We hold each other's gaze as she smiles.

I look down at her waist, the foreigner's hand is still around her, driving the sanity out of me.

"I think we've met before?" the foreigner says, his voice deep and solid.

"This is Khun Witthaya Sutthaya, Hathai's psychologist. This is Louis Andersen, a dear friend."

Louis greets me with a slight bow. I ignore him, leaving my gaze on Elina.

"I didn't know you'd come," I say.

"Phi Junta insisted. She's been cracking down on my personal space recently. Suicide watch," Elina says so casually with a laugh.

"And you brought your... dear friend?"

"She never takes me to parties like this," Louis says. The sound of his voice irritates me. "Was surprised."

They both laugh.

"Are you on a date?" I squint.

"Sometimes I date, Wine, but—"

Without thinking I plunge forward and kiss her with a fierce passion. She doesn't resist my kisses, she doesn't move, my lips tell hers how to move and I keep kissing her till I feel whatever Anderson's hand slide off Elina's waist. He steps back, watching. I let go of Elina, my heart racing as I stare into her eyes.

"No the fuck you're not," I say.

TWENTY-FIVE
A DATE IN SPACE

I turn around and begin to exit the upper deck.

Damn it! what was I thinking kissing her like that! In front of everyone! *Damn it! Damn it! Damn it!*

I hurry down the stairs and arrive back on the lower deck. Lucifer drags me into a corner, surrounded by dancing strippers and shoves a drink into my hand.

"What was that about!" he asks at the top of his voice to beat the loud music.

Without saying a word, I gulp down my drink, sparing not even a drop. I don't know what that was about either. I don't know what to tell him. He gives me a pass and doesn't push the question any further, refilling my drink as we dance alongside the strippers. I won't call what I'm doing dancing, more like swaying with no rhythm to the music, trying to calm the nervous jitters and quiet down my thoughts.

I smell Elina in the air, her tobacco scent. It must be from when I kissed her. I was close enough. I stop swaying when I sense it getting stronger, closer and closer. It's her, Elina is close. I hold my breath, pinning my gaze to the ground.

Her warm hands slide across my waist from behind, commanding a shivering sensation to travel through me. She pulls me close to her, burying her face on my right shoulder and I close my eyes as the richness of her scent travels up my nose. Her hands continue upwards, slithering under my light cotton shirt.

Gently, she sways me to the rhythm of her body, leaving a trail of warm breath on my neck. Her hands run free over my ribs, making me flush and shiver with desire. She turns me around and our noses touch. I rush to kiss her, but she pulls back. I leave my eyes closed, scared to open them and find out this is all a figment of my overactive imagination.

She lifts the drink out of my hand, placing it in a corner I cannot see, then takes my hands and slides them across her waist. I squeeze her gown and her lips find my right ear, kissing it. She throws her hands across my neck, allowing me to sway her in whatever direction I please. The world around me vanishes, only her and I remain.

I open my eyes and find her stunning brown eyes staring back at me. A little joy dances inside me. Elina smirks playfully and pulls my nose with her fingers. I look away. She takes my hand and leads me away from the company of Lucifer who has been pretending not to stare. We walk to the Back of the yacht where there are just a handful of guests kissing or chatting.

When we reach the end, she lets go of my hand and leans on the railings with her elbow, watching the water splash against the body of the yacht as the breeze ruins her bouncy curls. I stand still in awe, watching her watch the water. It's a view, worthy enough to be etched into artistic history by the finest of painters. I take a few steps forward, sliding my finger over the railings.

"You can't have other subs," I say. "If you won't share me, I won't share you either."

"He doesn't submit to me. He's a friend." Her voice is as smooth as the surface of the ocean when there is nothing to ripple it.

"He's in love with you."

"Yes."

I shrink, taking a step back and fisting my palm. "You know?"

"Yes."

"Is that why you brought him here, to make me jealous?"

"Making a man jealous is not something that is worth my time, Wine. He wanted to come, so he came. Somehow, this party became a must attend event for many."

"You are leading him on—do you like him?"

"He's a grown man, he can handle it. The real question is what are you so insecure about?"

"I'm not."

"Insecurity is not a good outfit on a man."

"I'm not," I insist, lowering my gaze.

"Come here." Elina flicks a finger at me, and I obey, advancing forward.

She runs her hands through my hair, then my cheeks, relaxing me and wrecking every nervous cell in my body.

"I'm sorry," I mutter.

"Not yet—but you will be." Elina smirks devilishly and it takes everything in me to not kiss her. "Come on." Elina turns away.

I follow and she leads me back to the yacht's entrance, a speed boat hangs by the corner.

"Are we leaving?"

She nods. "Get on."

"I have to say goodbye to my friends."

"Ok, I'll wait."

I hurry back into the boat.

Lucifer's yacht isn't parked far from the dock. In less than five minutes, we have arrived. The area her car is parked is laced top to bottom with bodyguards.

"They follow you around town now?" I ask.

"Phi Junta's doing. Pay them no mind."

They open the door for Elina and I and we get in. When Elina takes off, a car follows behind. It doesn't take long for her to start speeding and I hold onto my wits. Elina hasn't mentioned where we are going, and I could care less. I know the night will end with me under her and I relish in that thought.

We arrive in the empty parking lot of what appears to be some kind of entertainment center. It's past 10pm, the lights are on but there is no way it's still open.

"What are we doing here?"

"Come on." Elina takes my arm with a chuckle, dragging me into the building.

A tall attendant welcomes us at the reception and we exchange greetings. She leads us down a hallway that looks like something out of a futuristic sci-fi film. Pitch black walls, silver marble floor, led lightning pointing where to go lined on the wall. She leads us into a room that has a long, widespread counter and they both disappear behind a door while I wait, admiring the cool sculptures and futuristic monochrome design.

I fold my arms across my chest to help curb the chills I'm getting from the heavy air conditioners. I'm dressed for the warm Bangkok weather in a light cotton shirt and trousers. I did not expect to end up in the middle of the North Pole.

"Here we go!" Elina says, dragging my attention away from the unique ceiling lights I was admiring. The attendant places two sets of roller skaters and winter jackets on a steel bench.

"We're skating?" I giggle.

"You'll see," she replies, sitting on the bench.

I get on my knees and unbuckle her sandals, then kiss each foot before sliding on the roller skates. I help her put on her winter gear, our gazes locked on each other. Maybe if she'd stop smiling, I'd stop too.

Once I'm done with her, I start with my own shoes, then my winter jacket. When I reach for my gloves, Elina collects them, and I offer her my hands. She slips them onto each one and pats my hair.

"Let's put Yuzuru Hanyu to shame," I say and Elina chuckles.

We help each other to our feet and the attendant leads the way through a thick black door. The lush smell of candy runs up my nose as the freezing temperature hits my skin. Aside from the sparkling white floor that is covered in a rising fog, I can't see anything else. The whole hall is pitch black. The only lights are the ones around the ice. It's incredibly beautiful but at the same time, scary. Anything could be staring back at us from the darkness, it feels like we are on an alien spaceship.

Elina puts one foot on the ice and then another, holding onto me. Once I am sure she is in, I follow. But when I take a second step forward, I slip and stumble over, taking Elina to the ground with me. We burst into wheezing loud laughter.

"Can you even walk on ice?" Elina groans as she picks herself up.

I remain on the floor, taking a moment to enjoy how at ease I feel, laying in such a big rink and looking up into the pitch-dark ceiling that appears endless before trying to get up. Elina gives me a hand up and when I am on my two feet, I cling onto her, not moving, just holding her tight in a hug.

Can I stand by myself? Yes. Do I want to? No. She's so cozy. She lets me hold onto her for a few minutes, hugging me and patting the back of my head.

"So needy," Elina whispers and that's enough to force me out of her arms.

She laughs as I skate away, catching up to me and takes my hand, leading me to the center of the rink.

"Is the ground going to open up and suck us into another dimension?" I say in a whisper as if there are aliens listening in from the darkness.

"Wait for it," Elina whispers back.

"For what?"

She places a finger over my lips, a proud smile on her face as she leans in and kisses me. I close my eyes, not kissing her back, just letting the softness of her lips rest on mine. And then I feel it. A gentle gust of chilly wind. I furrow my brows and begin opening my eyes when the wind's pressure doubles, blowing as if we are in the middle of a massive storm.

"Holy fuck!" I gasp, shivering.

Elina laughs, skating away.

All the lights on the floor go out and an ultra-immersive open space simulation appears. My jaw drops. I look up to the ceiling and there's nothing but the moon, hovering as though I am standing on top of earth.

Elina skates past me, stars swirl around her, she looks like a fairy in her white winter jacket. I skate towards her.

"What do you think? It opens in a month."

"It's breathtaking, Elina Cheng."

"Second time you've called me that today." Elina skates away and spins around in a circle, making the stars swirl around her.

I can't tell if it's the pure oxygen being pumped into the building, the fact that I'm literally walking in space in the middle of Bangkok, or the way Elina skates in such an angelic manner. But right now—in this moment—I'm happy.

"Ok... check this out," she says, skating back to me.

She pulls out a remote and presses a button and we are teleported into another planet. It looks like the planet from the interstellar movie. An endless ocean with a heavy storm raging, one can feel the vibrations from the floor. As we skate, the holographic simulation of water ripples. I know it isn't real but sometimes when the storm roars I get jumpy.

From planets to planets, prehistoric earth to the time of dinosaurs, we skate. Every single simulation is just as thrilling and exciting. We skate until our legs can't take it anymore and our lungs are worn out from laughing and screaming.

Exhausted, we lay on the ground in the middle of a planet that is designed to look and feel like the biblical Garden of Eden. It's quiet, serene, green and rich with beautifully designed butterflies. You can hear the running of water, the chirping of crickets, fluttering of wings. It is almost therapeutic and soul healing.

Elina's head rests on my shoulders as I play with the butterflies. She shares with me what inspired the project, her expansion plans and extremely annoying board members, and I talk about my winters in Boston, the friends I didn't make, my favorite professors and what I miss about being a student. One look at us and you'd think we've been best friends for years and it's beautiful.

"How many apartments do you have in the city?" I ask as we step into yet another penthouse Elina owns.

"A couple."

"Define a couple?"

"Ten."

"You own ten penthouses? Why do you need ten penthouses?"

"Billionaires should own things in tens," she says. I laugh. Can't believe she held onto that. She leans in. "Ten different places you'll beg to taste me," she continues, her voice mellow and sultry. I swallow as my cheeks warm. She smiles. "Go clean up. I have to make a call. Your room is that way." Elina points and walks towards the balcony.

I move to the bedroom, taking my clothes off tiredly and marching to the bathroom. My gaze falls to an enema laid out on the sink and my heart jumps. This is it! Elina is finally going to peg me! I giggle, picking up the enema and lube. It's been forever since I douched, the part of bottoming I am usually not ecstatic about. I begin to lube it up when Elina walks into the bathroom, startling me. I hide it behind my back.

"Elina!"

"Why are you hiding the enema?"

"I... it's..."

Douching is not something I was allowed to talk about with Phi Lamon, one of her rules. Out of sight, out of mind for her. Sometimes, I felt bottom shamed and truthfully it worked with my kink for humiliation. But unlike Elina, Phi Lamon always wanted to peg me. She loved it. She loved doing it to me and she loved watching others do it to me, and every time, she needed me to douche. It left me with a bad eating habit, starving half the time.

"Sit." Elina points to the edge of the bathtub and I obey, walking backwards.

As I sit, Elina reaches behind me and snaps the enema out of my hand. I open my mouth to protest but she shushes me before the words form. She retrieves a shaving blade and cream from the cabinet and my brows elevates at the sight of it.

I have always kept myself hairless for Elina, both on my groin area and in my ass. Why does she want to do this now! I clasp my legs tightly together and look away.

"You're funny." A subtle mocking laughter escapes her. "Open your legs, Wine."

I press my lips together, unable to look her in the eye. Ignoring my resistance, Elina gets down on her knees and forces my legs apart. My heart sinks and I squeeze the bathtub, ashamed.

She applies some shaving cream to my groin area, then takes a blade and starts shaving me in even long straight strokes. She remains quiet and focused. As the minutes pass by, my anxiety fades away. Sometimes, she looks up at me and smiles and I'd force a smile back, still trying to relax into it.

I never thought being shaved by my Domme would make me feel so wanted, cared for and desired. The act is one of complete service. Just watching her treat my body in a non-sexual manner although am completely naked, makes me feel uniquely validated. Occasionally, her hand would graze my dick, or she'd lift it to get a clear view and my dick would respond to her touch, hardening. She doesn't react, simply keeps going, shaving off every single hair.

All done, Elina rises from the floor, wipes me and washes her hands.

"You should know, Pretty Thing—you are perfect," Elina says, holding my gaze while drying her hands.

She leaves the bathroom, shutting the door behind her and I sit in silence, my gaze pinned on the door, overwhelmed by her acceptance.

It is one thing to see yourself, know yourself, desire yourself, and it is an entirely different thing to be seen by another, known by another, desired by another. She wasn't wrong—*Elina is good with her hands*. I bury my face in my palms and shed a few tears. I can't help but wonder—what do you give to a woman that has everything; including the person she loves? What a gift it'd be to be loved by her.

***

I step into the walk-in closet after thirty minutes of begging the water to run clear. I don't want to say I hate douching because the reward is worth it. But by Buddha I hate douching, especially when it takes so long!

"Shit," I mutter when I see a pink short skirt, lace stockings and a sissy bra, hanging in wait for me. Elina is feminizing me tonight.

In all the months we've been together, Elina has not once forced-feminized or sissified me. Just when I thought I was in the clear for my behavior earlier. I wear the skirt and it barely covers anything. A little tilt forward and my whole ass is on display. I slip on the lace stockings and then the sissy bra.

I take small steps back into the bedroom, feeling both ready for whatever punishment Elina decides to administer, and powerful in my femininity. Elina sits in her bathrobe and pajamas at the edge of the bed, a book in her hand, something by R. F. Kuang. Her new author obsession lately.

She doesn't lift her gaze to me, she doesn't give me any attention whatsoever as I inch closer.

"On your knees," Elina commands, flipping a page of her book.

I obey, keeping my eyes low as I descend to the ground. I steal a glance at her book, it's The Burning God. I should read that next so we can talk about it over tea, or in a bath if she ever lets me bathe her.

For thirty minutes I have remained kneeling while Elina continues to read, taking a sip of her red wine every few pages. My gaze stays lowered, in wait for her, running different scenarios of how else I will be punished through my mind.

The wait is more mental than physical. Most times I'm tied up and blindfolded, left on the ground in complete submission without her dominant presence. It forces my mind to wander into places I dread entering: my feelings of worthlessness, self-hate, guilt, they all stare back at me in the darkness. Sometimes I see Mae's face through the eyes of my inner child: her judgmental stare, her disapproval, her abandonment. I have a hate–love relationship with *the wait*.

Elina rises from the bed and instantly every hair on my skin stands. My busy mind is quickly replaced by a deep sense of servitude to her.

With every step she takes towards me, my cock hardens and sinful desires creep into my mind. I impatiently wait for *her touch, her command, her will.*

She lifts my face up and holds me firmly in her gaze for a few long seconds before lowering herself to kiss me. I part my lips, and when her lips touch mine, she presses my jaw, forcing my mouth to open wider allowing her spit cold wine into my mouth. As I swallow, Elina licks my lips, making me shiver with longing. I squeeze the helm of my skirt and she smirks.

"You wanted control, didn't you?" Elina asks, elevating her right brow. I shake my head, lowering my gaze. "Ah ah ah..." Elina forces my face back up with a finger. "Eyes on me, Pretty Thing. Don't be shy now." She moves a stray hair from my face and rubs my cheek. "What are you?"

"Elina Cheng's slut," I mutter.

She leans in closer. "I didn't quite catch that."

"Elina Cheng's slut," I repeat, my skin warming.

"Good boy." She straightens up and walks away.

It only takes a few minutes for Elina to return. She tossing me a bottle of lube and what seems to be a fifteen-inch dildo, thick as a coke bottle, capable of sticking to the ground. I exhale at the sight of it, leaving my mouth open.

"Go on... fuck yourself. Show me how in control you are."

TWENTY-SIX
PLEASURE & PUNISHMENT

"It's... it's huge," I say, pouting.

I have never had a dildo this big inside me, let alone an actual dick.

"I don't remember giving you permission to speak," Elina says.

I lower my gaze and reach for the lube and dildo. I stick the dildo to the ground and begin to lube it up. Then pour some into my fingers and lean forward to stretch myself.

"Turn around and put on a show for me," Elina demands.

I obey, turning around on my tired knees and leaning forward, making it easier for my fingers to slide into my hole. I close my eyes and let the tight pain simmer through me. Trying to finger myself from this position is uncomfortable, but it isn't just the angling that makes it so, it's the absence of Elina's control of my body. Even when I'm inside her, I'm never in control of my own pleasure.

I continue fingering my ass without her help, getting it as stretched as I can, till it is dripping with lube. I lift my ass and try to take the dildo inside me. I shudder and a little gasp escapes me when the tip pierces through me, sending a quick sharp pain through my hole. I lower myself onto it,

278

gripping my butt cheeks, spreading myself to allow more penetration, but it is quite tasking. I let go of my ass, crouching lower onto the floor in hopes of being rescued by Elina. It would be easier if Elina was in control, my body would not push back so much.

I wait for a few minutes on the floor, but Elina doesn't come for me. With a wince, I rise, whimpering as I continue to lower myself onto the huge dildo.

I let out a loud exhale when half of it is finally inside me, taking deep breaths as I prepare myself to ride it. Slowly, I start bouncing my ass on the dildo. The first few thrusts were so difficult and uncomfortable, but now I feel my hole adjusting to it and pleasure seeping in. I let out quiet moans, gently stroking my dick.

Finally, Elina rises from the bed and every footstep she takes towards me, drives me wild with servitude and intense lust.

"Look at you. My glorious little slut." She kneels by my left side and rubs my sweaty bouncing hips with soft hands. Her touch triggers goosebumps all over me, making my moans grow louder with excitement. "You're leaking." She runs her hands all over my thigh. "You like this feeling, don't you? Having your ass stuffed, stroking your cock, pleasing yourself without me?"

I whimper, shaking my head.

She holds my jaw and turns my face to hers. I leave my eyes lowered, afraid I might cum if I stare in her eyes too long. I can't cum, she needs to know my pleasure is worth nothing if she isn't in control of it.

"Speak, slut."

"I only want to be fucked by you, Elina."

"But here you are, leaking like a little bitch."

She slides her hand up my sissy bra and runs her palm all over my chest.

I moan quietly, but when her lips touch my nipple, it sets me off.

"Argh! Elina..."

My moans grow louder with each suck. She draws a circle around it and sucks more of me, caressing me all over my thigh, hips and neck. Finally setting it free, she leans back, lifts my little skirt and grabs my ass, squeezing it as I bounce on her dildo. She is ravishing me with her scratches and claiming me with her sucks.

"Stroke faster," she demands.

I obey, moaning.

"Focus on only the tip." She fondles my balls.

I obey, stroking my tip faster. My body is a mess, my mind is a fog. I turn to her, trying to get more of her scent in me.

"You should cum if you feel like it."

"Only at your command, Elina," I reply, breathless.

"You are in charge."

"Please... Elina, I only want to cum for you."

She gives my hair a strong pull backwards and the pain shoots right through me, forcing me to dance along the edge.

"Elina... please..."

"Give in to what your body wants, Pretty Thing."

"Do I have your permission?" It is not a question; I am begging for it.

Ignoring me, she bites my shoulder, squeezing my ass and I tremble, gasping from the intense sensation and losing control. In seconds, I'm cumming, falling forward to help curb. Having an orgasm outside Elina's command is deeply unsatisfying, I feel nothing, even though my body is reeling from the sensations. It feels just the same as having my orgasm ruined.

"Was it everything you dreamed? Being in control?" Elina asks, helping me sit back on my legs and driving the dildo back into me.

I drop my head in frustration. "I am so sorry, Elina... it will never happen again."

She lifts my face to hers, and I struggle to keep my eyes open.

"You will be a good boy?"

"Yes."

Elina kisses my cheeks, then my shoulders, sliding her hands to my groin and taking hold of my semi–hard dick. She fiddles with it for a bit, letting our foreheads touch. In no time, I am hard again, praying she doesn't make me do it again.

"Do you know how wet you've made me?"

My eyes lids fly open. "Really?"

She nods.

"Did it please you?"

She nods and arousal shoots through me like explosive fireworks.

"Do it again," Elina demands, letting go of my cock.

Without hesitation, I take a hold of myself and start stroking, letting out tiny moans. I move to begin riding the dildo, but my waist and knees are too weak, I can barely give it a good shake. I lean forward, placing my left hand on the ground to support myself.

Elina runs her hand from the base of my neck to the tip of my butt crack, as if trying to study every vibration and movement. She moves behind and grips my waist, giving me ample support to bounce on the dildo and my pace picks up, accompanied by loud moans and strong trembles.

"You torture me with your waist, Pretty thing. What am I supposed do to with the waist of a whore?" Elina says, squeezing me tighter. "A slutty little whore that needs to be filled with cum and abandoned to leak for days." Her hand grips my ass. "That's all you are good for, Pretty Thing. To be used, fucked, stuffed and tossed, like the pathetic little hole you are."

"Argh! Argh! Fuck!" I curse. My eyes shut to help contain the ecstasy I'm rolling in.

"I could watch your ass bounce forever," Elina says, rubbing my waist and I whimper and moan like a little bitch for her.

She holds up my skirt and it drives me into sinful lust, knowing she is staring at my hole while I get fucked by her dildo. I work hard at taking all of it, making sure I am fully stuffed for her viewing pleasure. I know it will hurt later; her dildo is too much for me. Her hands continue to give me support and every now and then, I get a rewarding gentle spank.

Elina pulls me back by my waist and I fall into her, the back of my head rests on her chest. I can feel the softness of her breasts behind my neck. She leans over and gives me an intense upside-down kiss, digging her tongue into the farthest part of my mouth and sucking my lips with fiery passion. She reaches for the lube, fills her hands with it and begins stroking my cock, her toy. I whimper and wriggle on her body, my legs spread apart, my hands clinging to her arms with my eyes tightly shut, only opening it a few times to look down at her toy and the view is incredibly erotic. Seeing Elina completely in control of my dick, stroking it, rubbing the tip as she squeezes my free nipple is administering unbearable pleasure to my being. It is the kind of vanity I never want to end.

"Oh my God!" I gasp. "Argh! Mmh! M... mommy... Please..." I moan. She digs her nose into my hair, stroking my tip faster. "Mommy..." I cry out, overwhelmed.

"Yes, Pretty Thing." She kisses my forehead. "Is it too much for you?"

"Yes... please..." I curl my toes.

"Then you should cum." She squeezes my nipple, while licking my ear. "Do it for me," she whispers.

My body tenses up. I moan, wriggling and jerking in her arms as I cum all over myself and her hands.

"There you go..." She pats my hair as I whimper, still rubbing the tip of my cock and making me jerk. "Such a good boy... good job." She lifts her cum covered fingers to my lips and I latch on, licking off every drop of my cum. "Take care of the mess you made in between my legs," Elina commands.

I rise from the softness of her breasts and turn around. She tosses me a blind fold, I slide it on and surrender myself in between her legs, reaching for her pajamas and sliding it off her in haste, desperate to taste her.

The smell of her pussy fills my lungs and my mouth waters in need. My lips touch her lace panties, and I am pleased to find her soaked with wet goodness. Impatient, I pull it to the side and begin licking her, squeezing her left thigh.

I lick her selfishly, until all that is left is the smell of her pussy, then I take off her panties and begin sucking her clitoris, flickering speedily with my tongue as she whimpers. Elina's moans are soft and sweet, showering me with warmth. I hold up her legs, wondering what it'll feel like to take a long hard stare at her mesmerizing vagina while worshiping it.

"On your back," Elina commands.

I obey.

She sits on my face, allowing my mouth serve her and all her wetness drips into me. I waste no time feasting on her clitoris, sucking her, pushing my tongue into her. She grinds and rubs herself all over my mouth. If only I could see her tummy and boobs from this angle, watching all of it jiggle.

It's easy to tell when Elina is about to cum, the best part about eating her out. She unleashes her full body weight on me, her thighs squeeze my head, she lets out a deep sensual erotic moan, pulls my hair while jerking, then finally, she cums. A few seconds later, wetness drips out of her. I continue to lick her till she is perfectly clean.

She gets off me, breathing quietly as I lick my lips, savoring the taste of her. She rolls me over, making me lie on my tummy, allowing her to slide the dildo out of me. My body tenses as she does, some pain following.

"Arch your waist," her tired voice demands, and I obey, raising my waist and widening my legs to give her the full visual of my exposed hole.

She cups each butt, squeezes and then slides her fingers into me, making me twitch and whimper. "You should see your hole, well stretched, begging to be fucked even after taking all of that." She slides in a second finger, thrusting faster and my moans grow louder. "I should keep you here for days. Keep your worthless hole used, until you can't walk to one of those interviews." She spanks me, and I groan, biting my lower lips. "What do you think about that, Pretty Thing?"

"Whatever you need, Elina."

"So obedient all of a sudden, aren't you sore?"

"I'm yours to use, Elina."

She increases her pace, thrusting hard and fast, and even though I am completely soft, I begin to leak.

"That was not the question." Her free hand grips my soft cock, stroking it while simultaneously fingering me, making me tremble and quiver against the floor.

"Yes, I am, Elina."

"But I can't get enough of you, Wine."

"Then please keep using me till—"

She bites my butt, hard. I squirt out cum involuntarily. It was difficult to anticipate and control, it came out of me in a rush, overwhelming me.

"Fuck," Elina mutters.

""I... I'm sorry... I didn't mean..." I groan.

She lets go of me and I fall into my own poodle of cum.

Her hands continue to rub all over my body, touching me tenderly.

"You are so beautiful—yet so painful," Elina says as I whimper on the floor.

She curls up beside me. A few minutes of silence pass. Just when I think she's done and resting, I hear her touching herself. The squelching sound ripples through me, making me hunger to please her once again.

"Elina, let me do it for you."

She ignores me, moaning as she masturbates.

"Elina please, let me touch you instead. I'll be really good with it."

She pulls me close by the jaw and my lips find her breast.

"Suck," she commands. "That's where I want you."

I take her firm nipple in my mouth, sucking while squeezing and playing with the other breast. The sound of her masturbating is sensually arousing, but my body is too weak to harden. She kisses my forehead and buries her nose in my hair. I continue sucking and playing around with her breasts, feeling her toss and wriggle in pleasure.

I love that she can't stay still, I love how she pets me while I suck her. She grips my hair tighter and cums with a guttural moan, breathing heavy. I continue sucking just because it's quite relaxing for me.

Gently, she lifts me away from sucking her. I wish I had more time with her breasts. It is not often Elina lets me play with them or suck them. It was wonderful to do so.

I find her fingers and suck the wetness off them before crawling in between her legs. Her weakened body remains unmoving on the floor as I slowly pry her legs open and get to work, licking every drop of her cum, until the only wetness on her is the one from my tongue.

We laid there in utter silence, saying nothing, feeling everything, until sleep came. The rising sun, piercing through the skyline window gradually wakes us. Elina kisses my forehead before exiting to the bathroom and I stay behind and clean up all the mess from the night prior. After a shower, I join Elina under the heavy comforters.

"Lay on your tummy," Elina says, eyes closed.

"It's ok, I'm fine."

"I was not asking."

I obey, turning slowly. It even hurts to turn. When I'm finally on my tummy, I let out a sigh of relief, squeezing my pillow. Elina moves closer, wrapping her arms around me, completely engulfing me.

"Does it hurt so much?" Elina asks.

"It feels better this way—thanks for holding me. You smell wonderful." I feel her smile and so do I.

"Shut up and sleep."

I breathe a quiet laugh and she kisses my cheeks.

A few minutes pass and we do nothing, listening to each other's breathing.

"How long have you known about the interviews?" I ask.

"A week."

"I thought you stopped having me followed?"

"You interviewed with a family that knows me, they called for a recommendation."

"You gave them?"

"Yes."

"But you don't want me working for someone else."

"That didn't seem to stop you from interviewing."

I remain quiet. She chuckles after a few seconds.

"I'm fine with it, Wine. You weren't mine then, now you are."

"I have this thing I'm working on... a way for parents to identify and track early signs of autism in kids, trauma as well, but I need more data."

"Sounds interesting."

"It's a bit intimidating."

"Everything always is until you do it. And I have no doubt you can do it. You should see how your eyes light up when you talk about kids. You care—you genuinely care. That's why you will win."

The smile on my lips stretches and I fold my arms into hers, lifting it onto my chest. "Thank you, Elina."

"You're welcome—and, Wine?"

"Yes."

"Keep things away from me again and you will be severely punished."

"Yes, Elina."

She digs her nose into my hair, inhaling me deeply.

"When you said, 'I have never seen you'—what did you mean?" I ask.

She squeezes me tighter. "Doesn't matter, I should have never yelled at you."

"I don't care about the yelling. I just don't understand."

She kisses the back of my neck, sniffing me.

"You don't have to—I like that I am where you come to when you need to disappear—I won't crack again."

"What if I want you to—what if I want to see it—all of it."

I turn to face her, groaning softly from the pain shooting through me. When our eyes meet, we both smile. She kisses the tip of my nose.

"Wine."

"Mmh?"

"Move back in."

"Okay, Elina," I reply without hesitation.

I have had enough. I don't want to be away from Elina, there is no point in trying to pretend it doesn't kill me to be.

She pouts, leaning in for a kiss. Her lips serenade mine for a few seconds before she kisses me tenderly, as if my lips are made of glass and would shatter if she kissed me harder.

TWENTY—SEVEN
WHEN YOU HOLD ME

The rest of our morning was spent in bed, arms wrapped around each other.

I slept off and when I woke up five hours later, Elina was working on her laptop and a full buffet was waiting for me. After the late lunch, I took another shower and sat across from Elina on the balcony, sharing conversation about the current political climate in the country and then we played chess. She must have taught Hathai because she's phenomenal at it. When she went back to work, I resorted to caring for her toe nails: cutting it, cleaning it and then painting it a light shade of pink. The rest of the weekend continued in the same mundane manner, doing simple things when we weren't sleeping or eating. Although I wanted Elina to do more with me other than just kiss and cuddle, she refrained from any other sexual acts because I was still sore. Nonetheless, it was the perfect weekend for two very imperfect people.

I'm restless with excitement as I pack to return to the Cheng mansion. Maybe she'll finally let me see her room. I know it's her most private and intimate space aside from the playroom. I imagine it's completely draped in hues of gray.

289

"We've missed you all weekend," Lucifer says, entering the room and falls into my bed, licking ice cream.

"How did the rest of the party go?" I ask.

"I barely remember half of that night."

We both laugh.

"That's a lot of fun. Did Plerng get to speak with Junta?"

"Yes, and she won't shut up about it. She hasn't been blowing up your phone?"

"It's been turned off since Friday, I'll call her in a bit."

"Are you packing?"

"Yes, moving back into the Cheng mansion."

"What! Since when?"

"Since now."

"Aren't you staying for Sunday dinner?"

"Of course, I'm leaving tomorrow. Po... I mean... your boyfriend would kill me if I don't stay."

"This is about Khun Cheng, isn't it?"

"Mainly about her daughter, remember? The one I'm hired to care for?"

"Right. How serious are both of you?"

"Luce, stop asking the same question over and over."

"You're sure this is purely physical, and you aren't falling for this woman."

"I like her... but no, I'm not 'in like' with her."

"Is she falling for you?"

I chuckle. "No, she isn't."

"What if she is?"

"She's not, trust me."

"But what if she is?"

I stop packing and fold my arms across my chest.

"She's... in love with someone else."

"Wine! What the hell are you thinking?"

"Don't Lucifer, please. She is everything I need in my life right now. I feel... a special kind of safe with her. When she holds me... everything else just... it all fades away and I'd rather a piece of her than none."

I go back to packing but I can feel Lucifer staring at me.

"Wine," Lucifer breaks his long silence. "It sounds to me like you are falling in love with her."

"Trust me. I'm not."

Lucifer doesn't know the whole picture. He doesn't know about my submissive lifestyle and what it means to me. I'm not ashamed of it, but in some way, I think letting him see it all will make my two separate worlds collide and I prefer them to be as far apart as possible.

***

I waited till 3pm to leave Lucifer's home, just around the same time Hathai wraps up her classes. I'd love to surprise her with my return, watch her try to hide how happy she is.

The taxi driver lifts my three boxes one by one out of the car and I drag one along into the mansion. The housekeepers help with the others. I head straight for the stairs as I enter.

"Khun Sutthaya."

I turn at the call and there stands Junta.

"Khun Cheng, sawatdee krap."

We both exchange the wai in greeting.

"Sawatdee kha, glad you're here."

"Do you mind joining me in the tea room?"

"Sure." I nod and hand over the bag I'm holding to a housekeeper before joining Junta.

My eyes fall on Elina as we enter the room. I smile but she doesn't return the gesture. She sits legs crossed in a single arm seat. Her chin rests on her fisted palm with a stern expression.

"This is Dr. Chulajavana and Khun Klanarongran, one of the family lawyers," Junta introduces me to the middle aged man and woman and we exchange the wai in greeting. "I brought them in to help with Hathai's transition."

"Hathai's transition?" I furrow my brows.

"Yes, into my care," Junta replies.

"Khun Cheng... This is not how we were supposed to do this. You should have come to me first."

"Dr. Chulajavana has over thirty-five-years of experience with children just like Hathai. I think he is better equipped to handle this situation."

"You are removing me from Hathai's care?"

"It's not because I don't trust you, Khun Sutthaya. I think there are too many conflicting interests here and I want the best for her."

"Removing me is the worst thing you could do to her right now. I know her in ways that will take anyone months to even get their foot in the door. I deserve to see this case through."

"Khun Sutthaya—"

"Phi," Elina interrupts. "You are not taking my daughter. That is final."

"It's only temporary, Nong. You need help. You need to take care of yourself, you are not helping her this way."

It isn't supposed to go like this. I had a plan. A good plan, involving a deep well-structured conversation with Elina and Junta. Junta blind-sided me. I fist my palm and bite down my anger.

Junta keeps talking but Elina's fiery gaze shifts to me. The resentment and fury in her eyes crush me and my stomach turns, my heart sinks into it. I should have been more prepared, I should have been ready. *Oh... my Elina.*

Ignoring Junta, Elina springs up from her seat, grabs me by the arm and pulls me out of the tea room, into the hallway and up the stairs, straight into the left wing. I follow. I don't resist, I don't stop. She's furious, I get it.

We travel down another flight of stairs I have never seen before and she takes another turn into a narrow passage, arriving at a door she simply kicks open, dragging me inside an abandoned unpainted room with only one window.

"The only thing! Standing between me and that fucking rope! Is Hathai! And you! You dare to take that away?"

It takes me a moment to grasp this is the room Hathai talked about. A rope hangs off the ceiling, a stool below it, that's all there is in this cold, unpainted, deserted room with one window and a ton of cockroaches.

"Elina—"

"You could have told me! You could have come to me!"

"You'd never listen." I shake my head, avoiding her gaze.

Elina punches the wall and I leap towards her at the sight of the blood spewing from her knuckles. I take her hand and she pulls away.

"Don't fucking touch me! I brought you here to help her! Not steal her away from me! She's my daughter! My little girl!"

"I know that, Elina, but you are destroying her! You are breaking her with your pain because you are too cowardly to fight for yourself! To heal yourself! You are killing her with your grief! And she deserves more! She deserves peace! Stability! Warm love! Everything good a parent has to offer! You cannot give her that!" I scream back.

"Cowardly you say? You stopped therapy, you stopped trying, don't fucking lecture me on how to be brave!"

"I never said I was! I don't have a twelve-year-old who needs me! Stop whining! And grow the fuck up!"

"What do you want from me!" Elina's eyes fill with tears.

"Step off the stool, Elina! Or give her back her mother! You don't get to wallow anymore! He's been gone for five years, Elina! Move on!" My voice thunders in this prison of a room, melting away into damning silence and creating space for our heavy breathing

"You're fired—I don't want you around my daughter, and I don't want you around me."

SPECIAL CHAPTER
YOURS, ALWAYS

I open the door and step into Elina's sun-filled office. We have plans today. Playroom plans. It's the reason she chose to work from home today and the reason I've been giddy since dawn.

She's on a phone call so I hover around the door, watching her pace back and forth by the tall windows in a dark green pantsuit. She flips her hair, placing her hand on her waist and the sun falls to her bouncy curls and caramel skin. I smile. My fairytale of a woman.

I take more steps in, dropping my bag on the couch before advancing towards her table. She slams her phone on the table and I jerk lightly, watching it tumble to the ground.

"Stupid fuckers," she says under heavy breaths, shivering in anger.

I swallow, taking another step closer. She hisses, picking up her iPad.

"Hey," I say.

"Hey," She replies, not looking in my direction. "Did you have a good day?"

"Yes. It seems that is not the case for you?"

She sighs, turning back to the table. "Going home?"

"Can I ask you to talk about it?"

"It's just work stuff. Going home?" she repeats.

"Umm... just wanted to see if you need me for anything."

"No," she says sharply. "Go home."

"Anything?"

"No."

I nod. "So I can go home?"

"Yes."

"I can?"

She lifts her gaze to me and exhales. "Yes. Go home, Witthaya. I don't want to talk about it and I don't need you here."

"I can listen. Or just, massage your feet."

"I said go home, Witthaya!" she snaps at me and my heart jumps.

I walk back to the couch, pick my bag up and exit her office. Once the door is shut, I quietly exhale. Jitters from being nervous spread across my skin and anxiety sets in.

It's not often I get to see Elina angry, she is quite skilled at keeping her feelings a distance away from me. I'm not unfamiliar with that. People leaving me in the dark seems to be a frequent occurrence in my life. There is a certain type of loneliness that comes with being treated that way. I have not felt this way in a very long time.

I take a seat on the hallway bench and wait. I'm not quite sure what to do to help, but I know if I leave, I won't be able to stop thinking about Elina. I won't stop replaying the look on her face when she snapped at me. How fierce her eyes were, the brassiness of her voice, the way my heart sank. That'll be the only thing consuming my thoughts. I wish she'd just let me be there, whatever it is, I can just be there.

I hate this feeling.

An hour passes by and then another hour. I lay on the bench, waiting patiently for when she is done with her day. Maybe she'll be in a better mood and we can have dinner together, or she can let me rub her feet, comb her hair, whatever she needs.

Another hour comes and she's still in the office. It's just past 8pm. Maybe I should knock? She might be in a better mood. I rise and walk to the door. My hand is lifted and ready to knock but I pause. It was still her command that I leave her office.

I sigh, taking a step back with my eyes on the door before I turn and return to the bench, laying back down tired and drowsy, hoping she opens up soon.

Sleep takes me before I know it.

***

I smell Elina. My skin remembers the warmth of her touch even in my sleep. She is caressing my cheeks. Now she is running a finger over my brow. She runs the same finger down to my lips, gently touching. I smile, my eyes slowly fluttering open. Her wholesome honey brown eyes stare back at me with the utmost care.

"Hey, Pretty Thing." Her lips curve into a vibrant smile. "You were supposed to go home." She nuzzles her nose against mine.

My smile broadens with a soft purr in my throat. "You scolded me," I say against her lips.

She leans back and stares at me with softened, warm eyes, her hand still patting my head.

I sit up and pout. "Done for the day?"

She nods, taking a seat beside me on the bench. "This is an uncomfortable bench to sleep on."

"Yes. My back hurts."

We both breathe a laugh.

"I'm sorry you had a bad day," I say, turning to her. "Did it get better?"

"Not really." She exhales. "Sorry I snapped."

"It's okay to be angry, Elina. I get it, I might even find it hot."

We smile at each other.

"It's not okay to push me away when you're upset. It's very triggering for me."

She slides her hand over mine, taking my palm and intertwining our fingers. "It is?"

"Yes." I breathe, leaning back on the wall. "I was on a high school excursion sponsored by the school to the Khao Yai vineyard. The moment I laid eyes on all the beautiful green, I knew it'd become my favorite place. I snuck away and began to wander the fields alone. For hours I wandered through the grape vines, just taking in the scent and the breeze. Eventually I found the perfect place to lay down under the sun and read my book. It was peaceful, quiet and serene. I could only get through a few pages before sleep came.

It was dark when I woke to the sound of voices screaming my name. I had fallen asleep under a thick grape vine and they thought I lost my way. The vintner found me, but instead of scolding me, he conveyed how worried they were and why it was important to follow rules when on excursions. Afterwards he took me to his home. He lived a walking distance from the vineyard. That night, I shared dinner with his family, his wife, two sons and their grandparents before they found me a place to sleep. It was the first time I realized how different I was from other kids with a full home. They touched each other, hugged each other, played and laughed together.

The next morning Po came to get me. He didn't speak to me for three days after that. The silent treatment was Po's way of letting me know I was being punished. And then there is Mae. One day she was there and one day she wasn't. Never gave a reason either. I hate it." I sigh, taking a long pause. "I understand that you have your secrets, things you are not ready to share yet. I am okay standing by the door. Just... please don't shut the door in my face." I turn to her.

"Come here." She pulls me into her embrace, resting my head on her shoulder as she rubs my back. "You won't go home today."

"Okay."

She kisses my head. "How about dinner and a bath?"

"Okay."

***

Dinner was chicken curry, after which I took a long warm shower that helped with my jitters then slipped into one of my pajamas from the collection of sleeping wear I have in the playroom closet.

It's been twenty minutes and I have remained seated by the edge of the bed, watching Elina pace back and forth while on a phone call. I really need her attention today. I want her to talk to me, cuddle me and sleep with me. While the first two might be possible, I know the last one will probably not happen.

I turn away and crawl into bed, sliding under the soft duvet.

"Thank you, Nong... ok... alright." She hangs up and turns to me. "Going to bed?"

I nod. She puts her phone down on a dresser and climbs into bed beside me. "Still jittery?"

I smile. "A little. It'll pass. Sweet dreams." I kiss her cheek and turn the other way, pulling a pillow to cuddle.

"Wine," she calls. I turn.

"Mmh?"

She cups my cheek, gently caressing me with her thumb. "You have to ask if you want it," she says quietly.

I swallow. My gaze falls to her breasts and I look away instantly.

"It's okay," she croons.

"Can you hold me?"

She stares at me for a moment and nods before joining me under the blankets. I curl into her bosom, resting my head on her chest. Her skin is warm, supple and smells of lavender and jasmine. I exhale, rubbing my cheeks all over her chest. She pats my back soothingly, her chest rising and falling as she breathes.

"Elina," I call.

"Mmh?" she replies softly.

She sounds tired. Maybe I shouldn't ask. I slide my hand across her waist and squeeze her close, inhaling her sweet scent as much as possible. A moment passes before she pulls me back a little, lifting my face to hers. There is only a glint of light falling across her face in the dim playroom. It's enough to allow me feel her soft gaze on my skin, guiding my lips to say the words resting on them.

"Can... I umm..."

"Go on."

"Can I suck your breasts?" I hold my breath, swallowing hard as she doesn't flinch at the question. "Please?" I press my lips into a thin line.

"There you go." She smiles at me.

I look away, smiling to myself, my heart racing a little as both embarrassment and shyness runs through me. She slips out of bed, walks to the closet and returns with a blindfold and lube bottle. As she climbs back in, I lie on my back, holding my shirt at the helm of my sleeve.

She reaches for my waist, rubbing gently before pulling down my trousers and stripping me naked. Then she pulls the blanket up and slides the blindfold over my eyes. Her hands slowly guide me back into her bosom and I feel her unbutton her shirt, letting out her breast. She guides me by the jaw to her nipple and I latch on with ease, feeling her body lightly tense up from the sensation. Her moan of relief is a soft exhale.

Blood immediately rushes in between my legs and my dick hardens.

I slide my hand across her waist, sucking her firm nipple with great tenderness, teasing softly with my tongue as she pets my hair. She moans a bit deeper, making me shiver and I suckle harder, whimpering from the satisfying pleasure of hearing her moan.

I reach in between her legs, sliding my hand into her trouser, then her panties, till there is warm wetness soaking all my fingers. Licking her clean after I cause a mess is my duty and right now there is so much wetness for me to feast on when I'm done with her breasts.

I begin massaging her firm clitoris and her moans grow. I need her to cum, fill her delicious pussy with more wetness for me. She moans, digging her finger into my hair and I go a bit faster, sucking and whimpering.

She guides my hand away from the joy of bliss resting in between her legs and leads it onto her other breasts, making me fondle and play with it while I suck her.

"Just like that," she says in a rare seductive pitch.

301

Elina's breast fill my hand. Soft, squishy, bouncy breasts.

Her lubed hands reach inside my trousers and grips my erection, stroking me as my sucking grows more needy and my whimpers grow louder.

This is so intimate. Being cocooned in Elina's warmth, sucking her as she strokes me. My body tenses up and I squeeze her breasts greedily, wanting to suck both of them at the same time. She runs her hand through my hair, patting me, soothing me. I moan. Wriggling in pleasure as my toes curl. She is slow with my cock but the pleasure from each stroke is heightened by the pleasure of sucking her breasts. I run my hand around it, squeezing as I switch from her right breast to the left. She presses the tip of my cock and I stop sucking to draw breath.

"Mommy..." I manage to call out. "Mommy... I... I can't..." I shiver.

She guides my lips back to her breast and I go back to sucking and wriggling against her body.

"You will cum hard for me, won't you, baby?" she whispers, stroking me steady. "I want all of it."

I moan loudly with her breasts in my mouth, squeezing her as the blazing pleasure shoots through me. My legs are shaking as I cum, my mind is in a fog, none of which distracts me from her breast. Every suck is a gift I'll cherish.

This orgasm is different. It feels like a warm blanket, like I am being swaddled and rocked to sleep. Warm tender pleasure flows through my skin and so do goosebumps.

"You did so good," Elina whispers, rubbing my back with her free hand. "Mommy is proud of you," she croons.

Something in my soul gives away. I curl myself against her, holding back tears of validation as my heart bursts. I never want to let go, I never want to free myself of this comfort. My body feels like it's recovering from emotions I can't remember. She kisses my forehead, gently removing her breast from my mouth and tucks it back into her dress before removing my blindfold and kisses me, wrapping me tighter in her arms.

"Elina..." I call softly, my nose buried in her collarbone.

"Yes, Pretty Thing?"

"I am yours, always."

She breathes a tired laugh and remains quiet for a moment.

"You are mine, always."

TWENTY—EIGHT
BREAKING ME

ONE MONTH LATER

The warm afternoon sun pours into my room as I wake. I feel the gentle breeze, I hear our neighbors laughing, I smell the jok Po left in my room an hour ago. I leave my eyes closed and squeeze my pillow because I can smell something else. I can smell her. I can smell Elina. Her hand touches my back, but only a little. I feel her breath on my neck and shift. A smile forms on my face but I'm too much of a coward to let it bloom. It cannot be her; I know it isn't.

"Elina..." I whisper. "Are you real? Are you there?"

She giggles. "Open your eyes and see, Pretty Thing."

I swallow and squeeze my pillow hard, taking a deep breath. I open my eyes—slowly—then I turn—she is not here—she never was. Something breaks inside me that is already broken.

When she left me. Joy left with her. Color left with her. Beauty left with her. Peace left with her. I am abandoned in a sea of nothing, drifting away into oblivion.

Plerng and Lucifer keep bickering about something trivial as we push our shopping carts down the aisle, filling it with groceries. I like that they are, it makes me feel less alone. One of my favorite things about their company is how they don't always need me to get involved. We are very good at being alone together, I love that about our friendship.

I come across a magazine rack and stop at the sight of the headlines on most of the tabloids.

CHIANG MAI'S BILLIONAIRE FAMILY BATTLE OVER CUSTODY

THE CHENG SISTER'S AT WAR

THE BLACK WIDOW DRAGS FAMILY TO COURT

Elina and Junta's face are splashed on every cover. I stop and stare. When it leaked a week ago, the press tore into it, exploiting any clue they could find. Junta filed for legal custody of Hathai a week after I was fired, citing mental health problems as the reason Elina is not suitable to parent.

It will not be an easy feat to prove, there is nothing physically wrong with Elina, she appears completely fine, very capable, intelligent, smart. Hathai is well taken care of, no sign of neglect. You'd have to look beyond her perfect grades, well slicked ponytails, her elegance in ballet and magnificence at the piano to see how much damage Elina is causing.

I'm set to be deposed by their lawyers tomorrow. If this goes to court, I'll be asked to testify—I dread it. Po insisted I get a lawyer to be present and I have to meet him later this afternoon.

"Stupid," I mutter to myself as I stare at Elina's cold expression on the tabloid cover. I hate her for putting me in this position, for putting Hathai through this.

I smack the magazine and the whole rack comes crashing down. It was not my intention, I believed it to be drilled into the wall. I stand looking at the scattered magazines.

"Wine?" Plerng calls as she and Lucifer hurry over. "Are you ok?"

They must've not seen me knock it over.

"Yes, sorry, I was just..." I squat to pick the magazines, Lucifer joins me.

"I'll find an attendant." Plerng runs off.

Lucifer takes notice of the tabloid covers and looks over at me. Our eyes meet—he knows—he looks away. I'm thankful he doesn't ask. The attendant arrives, in no time the rack is back up and the magazines are well stacked. We move to the register to pay for our groceries.

Being stuck in traffic usually irritates me, but not today. I don't want to be at home with Po. I don't want to be in Lucifer's home which is where we are headed. I don't want to be anywhere. I want this car ride to take as long as it can, caught in the middle, not going forward, not going backwards.

"Wine," Plerng calls as she slurps her milk tea.

"Mmh?" I reply, not turning my gaze away from the window.

"Do you need us to come along tomorrow?"

"No."

"Why not? It'll be good to have some moral support."

"I don't need you guys there."

"Well, I want to be there regardless, so I'm coming."

"And so am I," Lucifer includes.

"Plerng, I just told you no!" I scold. "Don't you have other people to nag! Eyebrows to wax or something?"

"Hey! Don't yell at her, Wine! She's just trying to help."

I can see Lucifer's frown from the rear view mirror. "I didn't ask for the fucking help! Don't shove it down my throat."

"Wine, cut it out!" Luce continues.

"We'll come, and we'll sit in the lobby and wait, because that's what friends do. And when you step out, we'll give you a damn hug," Plerng's states in an authoritative tone. "Don't be that guy, Wine. The guy that pushes his friends away when they want to be there for him. The guy that doesn't know how to ask for help. He ends up alone, angry at himself. That guy is pitiful, that guy never wins." Plerng's tone grew softer with every word and so did my anger.

We sit in silence in the car, listening to the humming sound of the engine, the honking cars in traffic, the bustling of the city. I feel sick and heavy. I feel like a failure at everything, and I loathe this feeling. Losing a Domme—especially one as precious as Elina—cuts deep into you. It feels as though a part of my soul has been sliced off and I can't function.

***

I arrive home to find Po watering the plants and he welcomes me with a half-smile. I greet him with a wai. It's almost time for dinner so I move to the kitchen to get things ready. I wash my hands, then set out ingredients.

"I bought herbal tea," Po announces as he enters the kitchen. "One of the monks recommended it for sleeping." He lays it out on the counter. "Three tea bags before you sleep. It has chamomile too, strong stuff he said."

"Thank you, Po."

The nightmares are back. I haven't been sleeping as much, barely even. Sometimes it's the nightmares that keep me up, other times it's the constant obsessive thoughts of Elina.

"Any news about the interviews?"

"No, Po."

"That's fine, it will come at its own time," Po encoura-
ges

I nod and start chopping the onions.

"Are you anxious about tomorrow?"

I shake my head. "No Po, can't wait to get it over with."

I'm so anxious. Each time I think about seeing Elina's face in person for the first time in a month, my stomach turns. But I don't want Po worrying. He takes out fresh fish from the freezer, placing it on the kitchen table.

"You made a good choice, Witthaya. I hope the family does what's best for that child. These wealthy people, they'll probably manipulate the law like they always do."

I don't respond, I wish everyone would stop talking about it already. Lucifer, Plerng, Po. It's all they've talked about for weeks.

"Come with me to the temple this Friday, it will be good for you. I don't like forcing you to come to the temple, but prayers won't hurt, Witthaya. Make merit with me, mmh?"

I nod. I can't say no. I have no more excuses left in me, heck, I need as many prayers as I can get.

I couldn't get any food into my system during dinner and Po let me get away with not eating. I did the laundry and retired to my bedroom afterwards with the magical herbal tea Po bought. After a few sips, I crawl into bed with the same book I have been reading since I moved back home. I'm barely halfway through. I'd read a few paragraphs and then stare at the pages for hours on end.

I'm twenty-eight, unemployed, can't get a job, can't date, can't sleep, can't do anything. I miss being dominated. I might suck at everything else, but I was great at submitting. Everything was perfect, now everything is gone. The thought of finding another person to dominate me makes my skin crawl, but I need it and I need it from only one person whose name strikes pain in my heart when I whisper it.

I'm tired. I want to sleep—cry—cum.

I miss her.

Everything about her, including Kiet.

What strength do I have to face her tomorrow? I would not be able to look her in the eye. Does it break her as much as it breaks me to be apart from her? Probably not, she'll find someone else who looks just like Kiet, and I'll be replaced.

I sip the rest of my tea which is now cold and turn off the bedside lamp, placing my book beside it. I'm waiting for the tea to kick in and for sleep to take me, but I'm also afraid to sleep. I don't want to dream. I don't want to see Mae's face, that goddamn knife, the sound of my dead baby sister's cries—I don't want any of it.

I rose with the first ray of sunrise. Po's tea might have worked if I didn't fight off every urge to fall asleep. I had no intention of letting him know I didn't sleep, so I laid in bed all night, trying not to move as much. I swear the man can hear through walls.

"Don't skip breakfast, you're starting to look malnourished," Po complains as I head out the door. "Eat it on the ride over." He hands me a box.

"Po, it's a brief meeting, I'll be home before noon."

He puts it into my hand, ignoring my protest. "Eat it," he says and pats my back before heading back into the house. I giggle at his efforts then join Plerng and Lucifer in the car and we are off.

***

I have never been inside a law firm this big. Thirty flights high, very modern, very sleek. The front desk receptionist issues us ID passes—the only way to get through security—then gives us direction on where to go: the last floor, the thirtieth floor.

The elevator slides open, and an assistant already waiting leads the way to a conference room big enough to seat twenty people. My lawyer, already seated, waves me over and we exchange bows in greeting. I bid Luce and Plerng temporary goodbyes as they return to the waiting area.

I take a seat beside my lawyer, backing the skyline view and facing the tall transparent glass walls. We exchange further pleasantries. He already walked me through what to be prepared for yesterday and it sounded simple enough, however, I'm still nervous, my palms are sweaty. Amidst all the chaos, I am dying to see Elina in person, hear her voice, smell her scent.

The door flies open and my heart jumps. It is not Elina, I exhale. We rise and exchange the wai with the three suited men and one woman who made an entrance. Junta dressed head to toe in white follows behind. As we conclude pleasantries, the door flies open again and my heart leaps again. Two suited men and two women make an entrance and finally, **Elina**, dressed head to toe in darker hues of gray.

My eyes follow her as she sits on the opposite side of the table, three seats down to my left. She doesn't look my way, she's engaged in a hushed conversation with one of her lawyers. My body shivers in respect to its owner. I'd lay down all that I am to be touched by Elina again.

The conversation with her lawyer breaks and she looks away, but not in my direction. I turn away from her as introductions begin to fly across the table but pay no mind to them. I won't remember them anyways once I leave here.

"Shall we begin?" one of Elina's lawyers inquires and my lawyer nods. "Please state your name for the record."

"Witthaya Sutthaya."

"How long were you under Khun Cheng's employ?"

"Seven months."

"How would you describe Hathai Cheng the first time you met her?"

"Umm." I swallow. "She was very territorial."

"With what exactly?"

"Everything. She was... closed off, didn't want me in her life."

"Because you were a stranger?"

"That's what I thought at the time."

"And later?"

"Hathai didn't want me or her getting hurt."

"You?"

"Hathai believes walling yourself off from affection is the best way to survive. In some way, she thought she was protecting me."

"Protecting a stranger?"

"She cares deeply for people."

"All that care must have come from a lot of love don't you think?"

"Yes."

"Love that her parents must have provided for her?"

"Yes."

"But you claim Khun Cheng is not a fit parent?"

"Right now, yes."

"At what moment would you say she was a fit parent?"

"I think... any time before her ex-husband passed away."

"You think?"

"Yes, I think."

"Have you ever witnessed Khun Cheng physically assault her daughter?"

"No."

"Has she ever denied her basic needs, a good education, proper feeding, clothing?"

"No."

"When Khun Cheng hired you, she described Hathai as an overly confident genius, interested in classical music, arts and mathematics, with a lack of socializing skills, lack of empathy, very introverted, accurate?"

"Yes."

"What has changed or improved since then?"

"Not much on the outside. Her environment won't let that side of her I see blossom."

"The same environment she's been showered with love, The one where she's getting a great education and has a very privileged lifestyle."

"She also does not have any friends her age, avoids getting close to people, does not see her own mother unless something tragic is happening or she is forced to."

"That was not the question, Khun, please stick to the questions I ask."

"There was no question, you made a statement and I replied with a statement."

The boardroom stays quiet for a cold passing minute.

"Khun Sutthaya, from the ages of fifteen to twenty-one, you received therapy and when you returned from the United States you started therapy again and suddenly stopped."

I intertwine my palms under the table.

"Therapy is good for everyone."

"Of course. Pardon me, but does the death of your sister have anything to do with why you've been in therapy for so long, on and off?"

I tighten the grip on my hands.

"Irrelevant, next question," my lawyer intervenes.

"Would you say grief deeply affects a person?" Elina's lawyer continues.

I take a deep breath. "Yes."

"So, it can leave lifelong emotional scars on the grieving person?"

"Yes."

"Except when the person is a parent, then of course they should be up and going as soon as possible."

"I don't see the question."

"Would you say your mental health is in a good place?"

"Next question, my client would not be answering that question," my lawyer says.

"What type of relationship did you and Khun Cheng have to help you come to the conclusion she's unfit to parent?"

"Do you actually have a decent question for my client?" My lawyer sits up.

"Here's a good one, did you have sexual relations with Khun Cheng?"

"My client will not—"

"Yes," I interrupt my lawyer. He glares at me. I ignore him. I knew the question was coming. I dig my nails into the back of my palm. "My relationship with Khun Cheng did not influence my assessment of Hathai."

"Did you at any time prior to your sexual relationship with Khun Cheng inform her of your assessment."

"Yes, I mentioned Hathai was mirroring her behavior and she needed to make changes."

"And what happened next."

"Nothing."

"You entered a sexual relationship with Khun Cheng and decided not to push it further."

"That is not a question, don't speak for my client," my lawyer cautions.

"After you began your relationship with Khun Cheng, did you bring up any other concerns in regard to her daughter?"

"No."

"So, your sexual relationship with Khun Cheng did influence your assessment of Hathai."

"Again, you're speaking for my client."

"Khun Sutthaya, who initiated the sexual relationship between you and Khun Cheng?"

"Relevance?" my lawyer leans forward, visibly pressed.

It was brutal.

I felt like a pig being gutted for spectacle. My head and heart ached alike. I stole a few glances at Elina, but she never once looked my way. Her eyes remained lowered. If they knew all that, it's because Elina told them, and she told them with the sole purpose of winning. Her lawyers treated it like it was just another day at work and not my life they were tormenting. The second it was over, they smiled, shook hands with Junta's lawyers and my lawyer who went on to compliment their office and the view. Elina was the first one out the door, but Junta took a second to share a smile with me before leaving.

"I know that was tough, they are just throwing darts, discrediting your assessment or ability to give said assessment is a good strategy, I'll admit. But most of these questions won't actually be asked in court if they make it to trial. Remember, you aren't on trial here, it's their case, you're just a guest, don't let it get to you," my lawyer consoles me.

He pats me on the back and heads out the door.

Still not ready to move, I remain seated, looking down at the back of my palm slightly bleeding from having me dig my nails in over and over again. My whole body still shivers from the anxiety.

I step out of the conference room and into the waiting area, where Plerng and Lucifer are seated. They spring up at the sight of me, waving shaved ice and some snacks. I smile, glad they chose to be here.

TWENTY-NINE
WISHING ON STARS

Plerng opens her arms and I fall into them, squeezing her as Lucifer caresses my back.

"I don't want to be here," I say in a feeble tone.

"Let's go wherever you want," Lucifer says.

I let go of Plerng and nod.

Their expressions begin to change, from beaming sympathetic faces to uncomfortable frowns. I turn around and Elina stands in front of me. A wave of anger rubbles through me.

"Wi—"

"Fuck you, Khun Cheng," I curse.

"Khun?" she says with a sad tenderness.

I turn swiftly, heading for the elevator with heavy strides.

I press the elevator button multiple times at an alarming speed as if that will hasten the elevator's ascension. When the elevator door doesn't open, I slam it harder. Lucifer grabs my hand and I take it back, stepping away from the door. Finally, the elevator door opens, I rush in, pressing the ground floor button with haste.

As it closes, I can still see Elina standing in the same spot, looking at me with those heavy eyes. I don't want to see her face, I don't want to see her, smell her, hear her, because

316

my heart doesn't care what I want. My heart has forgotten how ruthless her lawyers tore into me and it wants to run to her, it wants to be hugged by her, caressed by her.

Tomorrow, it will be Junta's lawyers. I hate this, but above all, I hate that at the end of the day, I won't kneel under her whip.

***

Three days of depositions, lawyers, suits, grueling questions and her heavy eyes I pretended not to see, and finally, it is over. I'm wishing on every star this doesn't go to trial, I can't sit through this again. Hathai must be a mess internally, the tabloids won't shut up about it.

I slide my shoes off and step on the hardwood floor of the temple, following Po in.

The temple is serene, not a lot of people come here since it's far from the metropolitan area. Sometimes, I think Po doesn't want to go on his worldwide cruise because he doesn't want to be too far away from the temple, it's almost like a part of his soul.

Prayer is centering. I feel collected for the first time in a long time. I feel more than myself, my worries, I feel humbled. I spend a lot of time in my head, loathing myself, and these words make me feel arrogant for not being grateful enough. Not being grateful for Po, Lucifer and Plerngs' undying love. It's asking me to look at everything good in my life, it's asking me to search my soul. I'm moved to tears, but these aren't tears about everything that's wrong with me, rather everything that's right.

Po and I decided on a walk back home after our visit to the temple, apparently this is also the best time to chew apples according to Po. He bought some from a street vendor and has been cutting them piece by piece and handing them over to me or shoving them into my mouth. At first, I found it a bit embarrassing but then Po said, "It's not embarrassing, you are embarrassed, they're not the same thing."

It's a carefree walk while eating. We aren't talking about much but his little snappy comments at things we see as we walk is an earful. I like today. It is the perfect relief from the week I have had. As we approach home, I see Plerng and Lucifer sitting by the gate, they wave at us and we wave back with smiles.

It's been a while since they've been in my home. I'm not surprised they showed up, they've been hovering around me all week and I'm grateful for it.

We made lunch together. It's the noisiest the house has been since I got back. Po resorted to sharing his childhood stories which brought a lot of laughter to our lips. I'm grateful for how supportive he's been this week, in his own non-hovering way.

After lunch he dragged Lucifer and Plerng to the backyard to show them his new pottery works, and I stayed behind to clean the dining table and then proceeded to do the dishes.

"Hey slugger, need help?" Plerng asks, entering the kitchen.

"I got it, thanks. Is he done bragging?"

"He's definitely earned bragging rights! His work is spectacular!"

She takes a dish rag and starts drying the dishes I'm putting away.

"Wine—I have to tell you something."

"Okay."

"Junta Cheng is taking me to dinner."

"What!" The plate falls off my hand into the sink, splashing soapy water all over the counter and my shirt. "Shit!" I reach for a rag. "Plerng! That is amazing! When did this happen... how did this happen?"

"A few days ago."

"Oh my god! You fucking whore." I shove her with my shoulder, and she laughs.

"Are you sure you're ok with this... with everything happening with the other Cheng sister."

"Plerng, don't be ridiculous. I'm happy for you."

"Are you sure? I mean—"

"Plerng, I really don't care, as long as you're happy. You've wanted this long before I ever met Elina."

"Cool."

"What's she like?"

"She's so sweet. I like her cheeks."

"Her cheeks?" I raise an eyebrow.

"I'm saying... this could be something."

"Do you want it to be exclusive?"

"We haven't even kissed yet—or touched."

"Okay... but do you?"

"Junta doesn't appreciate neediness or quick attachment. As of now, I want nothing aside from dinner. I should play hard to get for a while, don't you think?"

"Don't try to be calculative about it, you'll spend too much time in your head and for what? Be needy, and if she doesn't like it then her loss. You shouldn't have to be anyone other than yourself when it comes to matters of the heart."

"Hmm... since when are you such a hopeless romantic?" Plerng pokes my side and I wriggle away. "You should go to the temple more often, this you is good."

I laugh, drying my hands, then pull her into a hug, kissing her forehead.

"I love you," I say. "Thanks for being here all week."

"I love you too, buddy."

***

The new week is here, I can finally put all of last week behind me. I need to get my life back on track. I mean, it was never on track, but still.

I fold the laundry and proceed to do some cleaning. I've been cleaning the nursery once a week, taking over from Po. It's lessened the anxiety I feel about this room but hasn't eradicated it. I think about her with less fear now, and I find that more memories from my childhood are coming back to me.

My phone rings and I pull it out of my pocket. It's an email from the Suwannarat family. I have been expecting it since my promising interview with them. The email informs me they aren't interested in hiring me, no surprise there, Junta really set things in stone. Until now, I have not given it much attention, everything began to unravel quickly. But now, I have all the time.

I arrive at the Suwannarat mansion a few minutes past noon. They aren't expecting me. I ring the bell and a housekeeper answers the door. We exchange greetings. She's hesitant to inform Khun Suwannarat of my arrival, but I'm persuasive. She concedes and shuts the door. After a few minutes, the door re-opens and Khun Suwannarat appears with a smile.

"Khun Sutthaya, sawatdee kha."

"Sawatdee krap." We exchange the wai. "Apologies for visiting unannounced."

"No worries. It was my belief you received an email?"

"Yes, I did, and I want to know why."

"I'm sorry?"

"I'm over qualified for the job and you and your husband seemed to love me during the interview. I just need you to tell me why you won't hire me."

"Khun Sutthaya I—"

"I think you should give me a fair chance based on what you think, not what other people are telling you. And I know you probably have a good relationship with Khun Cheng, but I assure you—"

"Khun Cheng? Elina Cheng?"

"Junta Cheng, Khun. I believe she put a call through to you and—"

"Khun Sutthaya, would you like to come in for juice?"

"Yes, absolutely." I nod.

She leads the way into her splendid extravagant home.

"I have met Junta Cheng at a few galas, charity events, but we are barely friends," she explains as we walk into her kitchen. "Please sit."

I sit, watching her retrieve a glass.

"She didn't call you?"

"Not at all." She begins pouring orange juice into a cup.

"Then why won't you hire me? I'm sorry, I respect your decision, I just need to understand."

She pours herself a drink too and takes a sip. She takes a moment to smile at me before sitting.

"I did receive a call, but it wasn't from Junta Cheng."

My curiosity peaks and I squeeze my forehead. She sips her drink again and takes a seat, leaning forward.

"They said they were a close family member and pleaded with us to not hire you."

"What?" I narrow my eyes.

"Khun Sutthaya." She swallows. "We are still open to hiring you and we'd very much love to see you back at a hundred percent, you have such big promise. You should take your time with healing."

"Healing from what?"

"We were informed you lost a family member and you've been struggling to cope. When I lost my grandmother, I was totally devastated. It was a difficult time for my family and the pain still lingers."

"Khun Suwannarat, I can assure you the death of my sister does not affect my work at all."

"We were told you were in therapy and decided to quit because of work. You shouldn't, it's something you should do."

"Khun, that's not... I mean..." I adjust in my seat. "My sister died when I was five."

"Five?" She cocks her head to the side in surprise. "That's not what she said."

"She?"

"Khun Sutthaya, I'm sorry. I'm not quite sure what's going on here. Let's say in a month, if I'm still hiring, let's have another interview?"

I take a moment, then nod. She gets up from her seat and escorts me to the door.

"Thanks, Khun, for your time."

"You're welcome." She smiles, turning to close the door.

"Khun," I call. "Can I have the number?"

"Of the caller?"

I nod.

"I doubt I still have it but let me have a quick check." She disappears into the mansion.

I swallow, strumming my fingers on my thighs. It would have been easier if it was Junta, it's unnerving not knowing who or why. It doesn't take long for her to appear and hand me a card with a number written on it. I thank her with a bow.

Halfway home and I am still staring at the card, trying to decide if I should wait till I'm home to call the number, or make the call now. I lean forward, placing my forehead on the back of the seat in front of me, taking deep breaths in thought. My anxiety is getting the better part of me.

I pull out my phone and dial the number. It rings. I grip my phone tighter.

"Yes," a familiar voice comes through the phone.

I jolt backwards. I can no longer feel the cool air coming from the air conditioner. My skin burns hot, my eyes are filled with warm tears ready to drip down my cheeks without my consent. The sound of her voice was a beacon for my innermost fears, I did not get a chance to tame them like I always do, they raced to the surface and spilled all over my skin in form of a cold sweat.

"Mae?" I manage to mutter.

She sighs. "Witthaya," she calls softly.

I squeeze my trousers and shut my eyes tight.

THIRTY
STRANGER

It hasn't rained in a while, I can smell it coming. The cloud already turned a darker shade of gray.

I chose to sit by the window so I'd have something to distract me from her face if necessary. Through the window, I see children playing on a swing, some others on the grass. One of the kids playing on the grass has a pretty pink shoe on. He looks cute in it and won't stop showing it off to his friends.

A waiter arrives with my warm cocoa. I thank her but I'm in no mood to drink. I only ordered so I don't look like a creep, sitting alone in a cafe, staring at children playing on a swing.

I didn't tell Po about today, I'm certain he would've found a frivolous reason to stop me from meeting Mae. And maybe I should have let him, maybe he would turn out to be right. She walked out, never looked back, never wanted to have anything to do with me. But after hearing her voice three days ago, it was impossible to not crave seeing her face and remind myself what she looks like.

It's better to know right? Tell me I'm right please. Tell me I am not a complete fool. I'll leave if you tell me I'm wrong.

Even after she heard my sobs, even after I whispered how much I missed her—she didn't ask to see me. She didn't ask how I've been. She didn't ask if I was loved or hurting. She would have hung up if I didn't insist on meeting.

I sigh, readjusting myself in the hand woven rattan chair, turning to the entrance. Two pretty young women enter. I turn my gaze to my cocoa drink, stretching my hands to lift it up when it dawns on me. I return my gaze to the entrance, one of the two women takes a folder out of her bag, hands it to the second lady before turning to scan the room.

I see her face and for a second my heart stops. Mae has not aged a day. Though I haven't seen her since I was a boy, I remembered her instantly. She looks elegant, beautiful. Her hair pinned up, clothed in a white pantsuit. We have the same eyes, the same nose too.

She sees me, flashes a smile and waves. I stand up and wai. She begins to walk towards me. I should be nervous, I should be an internal wreck, but I'm not. I'm calm, centered, prepared. She arrives in front of me.

"Witthaya," she says. Her voice is stronger than I remember, over the phone it sounded softer. "Should we sit?"

I nod and we sit. I keep my eyes on her. I can tell she is uncomfortable; she hasn't looked at me for more than five seconds. "You haven't aged a day, Mae."

She smiles. "Thank you. You look taller up close. That's good. You were a tiny little boy. I was pleased to find out you sprouted." She laughs. "Love the new hair color, also the length. You've always kept it short, but this suits you."

I touch my hair, pursing my lips as I smile. I don't know her, she's a stranger to me, nothing but fragments of memories. But it feels good to hear her compliment me. I feel like a little boy all over again.

"Thank you, you seem to know a lot about me."

"I do." She holds my gaze for a fleeting moment. "You already got something to drink. Would you like anything else? I'll tell Nong Mook to bring it over."

"Nong Mook?"

She points to one of the servers.

"You must be a frequent customer here if you already know the server's name," I say.

She chuckles. "Not exactly. Haven't been here in a year, but I figured since you wanted to meet, it might as well be at my own café."

"You own it?"

"Yes. I own a chain of café's from here to Korea."

"That's great." I gulp. She nods.

I feel a sting of jealousy. She seems to be doing so well. A part of me wished she was in a difficult place in her life and that's why she didn't want me or try to reach out to me.

"So, Witthaya. How can I help you?"

"Help me?"

"You wanted to meet," she replies. I can hear the disinterest in her voice.

"Mae, aren't you even the least bit excited to see me?"

"It is good to see you, Witthaya."

Her countenance tells me otherwise. I intertwine my palms under the table, irritated.

"You don't look like it. You don't sound like it either."

"I'm sorry to disappoint you."

I lower my head, nodding. She doesn't sound sorry, she sounds like she wants this to be over, quickly.

"Mae, why have you been calling people and telling them not to hire me?"

"Because that's not what you need right now."

"What I need?" I blink. "You don't know me, you don't know anything about what I need."

"Fair enough, but you need to restart therapy."

"You've been stalking me all these years?"

"Your father and I—"

"Po? Po knew about this?"

"Why did you have to choose child care, Witthaya. Out of all the professions?"

"Why not?"

"Witthaya, you need to let the guilt go, move on, do something useful with your life. Look at the mess you caused with the Cheng family, and you've barely even started with your career... I am trying to help you, give you a chance. I'm trying to fix things, why can't..."

The more she speaks, the more resentment I feel. She knows everything, she's known all this time and chose to not reach out to me?

"How did my sister die?" I cut in.

The question quiets her and her shoulders tense up. She tucks her hair behind her ear, shocked or surprised by it.

"Why can't you just let this go? Why can't you just move on."

"I can't move on from something I cannot remember— You want to help? Then I need to know. Po, he won't tell me for reasons I cannot comprehend, but it's destroying me, and I don't even know why."

She waves over the server and requests for a glass of water with three ice cubes, weirdly specific. She turns and looks at me, the first time she's held my gaze for more than a few seconds. I refrain from speaking, I'd rather she takes her time and only speaks when she's ready. We sit in uncomfortable silence till the water arrives and she gulps down half the glass.

"Nobody blames you, and it isn't your fault."

"Blames me for what?"

"Your sister's death. Nobody blames you anymore, we've all found a way to move on, but you seem to want to keep punishing yourself, running around this circle—"

"Why was I blamed in the first place, what did I do?"

She leans forward, furrowing her brow.

"Just now, I realized... your father never told you."

"What?"

"The accident, you don't remember any of it? I cannot believe Tanawat didn't tell you, all this time? I thought he did, he told me he did."

"Mae! Tell me what?"

"Witthaya." She sighs, shaking her head. "You don't remember how your sister died?"

"No, Mae."

She presses her lips into a thin line and leans back into her seat, turning to the window and staring at the children. She's stealing my distraction and I am growing impatient by the second.

"Your father had just started working at this new company and I was taking some time off work because your sister was sick. It was just me and you both most days—and you both we're a lot." She chuckles, taking another long moment. "I was giving you both a bath... you loved to play with trains—God you loved that thing—you took it everywhere." She takes a deep breath. "Your sister was in this cute floater in the bath... I asked you to watch her... for just one minute..."

My heart begins to sink into my turning tummy. I know where this is going. I tilt my head in sympathy for me, it already hurts. She exhales loudly, shaking her head and looks down.

"When I came back, your sister was face down in the bathtub and you were playing with trains on the floor."

I dig my nails into the back of my palm.

"She had been drowning for fifteen minutes and you just sat there... playing with that goddamn train."

I hold my breath and we stare at each other for what feels like an eternity. I turn my gaze to look out the window, it's finally beginning to drizzle.

A couple of parents dash out to bring the kids in, some of the children are hesitant, choosing to play in the rain.

"Listen, Witthaya—"

"I was five years old, Mae... I was a child."

"You could've called out for help, Witthaya. You could have run to me, you could have—"

"I was a child, how could you and Po ever put that on me. I have gone my whole life, thinking that I smoldered my own sister in her sleep or stabbed her to death, did something horrific, and you are telling me I did nothing?"

"You never liked her, you never liked having a sibling, you complained all the time—"

"I was a child! Mae!" my voice thunders and I feel every head in the café snap towards me. "You and Po were the parents. You and Po were responsible. And you both neglected your children. I have gone all my life, thinking I cannot be loved, thinking I'm undeserving because my parents wouldn't spare me a single hug! You both treated me like I died with her."

"Witthaya—"

"At least Po stayed. But you walked away! Left me alone to deal with the grief, the pain, the guilt. How could you both ever put that on me!" I spring up from my seat, heavy with anger. "I will never forgive you and Po. My whole life is a haze, and you chose not to be in it. Stay the fuck away from me! Don't try to help, don't send me notes, don't ever show up, ever again. You wanted out, so stay the fuck out!"

I dash out into the rain, folding my hands across my chest, my heart pounding, my body trembling. I am a cup filled to the brim with sizzling hot water. I have no destination, just walking blindly in the rain. For the first time in my life, I don't feel guilty about having an outburst, I feel cheated.

The rain comes down heavier. I have been walking for more than twenty minutes now with no sense of self or direction. I'm soaked, drenched. I put out my hand, hailing taxis, but none would stop, cars fly past me in the street. A random stranger finally pulls over and offers to drop me off at the nearest bus station.

He was kind enough to not try and make conversation. After exchanging pleasantries, we sat quietly until we arrived at the bus stop. I thanked him and got down, pitying his soaked car seat. He nodded it off and told me not to worry. Once at the bus stop, finding a taxi driver was easier.

All I could think about in the strangers car was Hathai—but now, only Elina occupies my mind. I need to see her. The urgency takes over me, so I change my destination from Lucifer's home to the Cheng mansion.

I press down the bell a few times and Khun Toh's voice comes through the intercom.

"Khun Sutthaya, I—"

"I need to see her."

"Khun—"

"Just tell her I'm here and I'm not leaving until she shows up."

"Khun Cheng isn't here."

"Where is she?" I ask, shivering, the cold is starting to get me. He doesn't respond. "Phi... please."

"Her penthouse."

"Which one."

"The last one you visited."

I rush back into the car and the driver takes off.

It's already dark when I arrive at the apartment complex. I hurriedly alight from the taxi and dash inside. The receptionist, startled by my appearance tries to warn me off but I'm persistent, asking her to let Elina know I'm here and I need to see her. She doesn't budge. Soon the security is upon me. Backing away, I pull out my phone and begin texting her.

"I need to see you, I'm in the building."

"Tell them to let me up."

"I won't fucking leave until you let me up."

"You fucking coward! Let me up!"

"Just one fucking minute, Elina!"

I'm in the middle of typing another message when I am called back in by security and directed to the elevator.

Still shivering, I fold my arms, holding steady as the elevator ascends. I make it to her floor and then to her door, taking a deep breath before knocking. She opens, a glass of scotch in her hand, a wine red robe wrapped around her. My eyes size her up from head to toe. Her eyes are just as heavy as the last time I saw them during the depositions.

"You're drunk," I say.

She laughs and takes the final gulp from her glass. "Yes." She holds my gaze. "Damn it, Wine, you're drenched. Come in, I'll dry you up."

"I don't want to come in."

She leans against the door. "Why did you come?"

"I met my mother today."

"Wow, that's umm... How did it go?"

"I thought I murdered her you know? My sister... I thought the big secret was that I killed her."

"You didn't?" She cocks her head to the side.

I shake my head. "They... they made me believe I... Elina, you have to let her go."

She stands erect, shaking her head as she turns away from me.

"Look at me, Elina, look at me." I tap my chest. She turns back and I see the tears in her eyes. "If you can't love her—this is who she'll become. She'll never be happy. She'll always think it's her fault and it'll wreck her." I take a step forward and hold her face with my palm. "She wasn't made to be a cushion for your pain—please, don't put this on her, don't make her cry herself to sleep for the rest of her life. Let her feel love, the good kind of love—for her own sake. Don't be the mother that puts her fear before love. You'll hate yourself for it, you'll never forgive yourself." I put my forehead to hers and her warm breath brushes against my cold face.

She swallows and I swallow.

I let go, turning to leave.

"Pretty Thing," Elina calls. By Buddha I have missed hearing that. I turn around. "I'm sorry about the deposition," she says, letting the tears in her eyes drop.

I want to reach over, wrap my shivering self around her warm, soft body, inhale her sweet jasmine scent. But I'm so angry. I feel too much, and I'd rather feel it alone. So, I nod and continue down the hallway to the elevator.

Tears won't come to me, maybe I'll feel some relief if I cry—crying has always come easy to me, but not today, the day I need it the most. I don't know how I can ever look at Po the same. I have so many things to say, so many questions, but when has he ever given me any answers?

The rain has finally let up and the ride back to Lucifer's home seems to be taking a lot of time thanks to the traffic. I don't mind it, however I think a walk will better help clear my head.

It takes me almost an hour, but I arrive at the bridge—Elina and I's bridge. The one where I danced with her in the rain because I never wanted that night to end.

I'm worn out and cold, but still not ready to be around anyone. I don't want to explain my feelings or talk. I'm overwhelmed by the amount of work I have to do on myself. I wonder if the nightmares will stop now that I know. I wonder if I'll finally stop being so hard on myself. Will knowing take away all those years—all that loneliness I felt as a child. I sigh, leaning over the bridge and staring into the dark vast water, my thoughts reflecting back at me. It's comforting to know I once laughed and danced on this bridge. A good memory to tangle along with all the bad ones.

"You're not going to jump, are you?" a voice startles me.

Immersed in my own thoughts, I didn't notice the man standing a few feet to my right.

"Do I look that miserable?" I say, keeping my eyes on the water.

"Well, my brother celebrated his child's fifth birthday, all smiles and happy, then the next day he jumped off this bridge. You don't need to look miserable," the calm voice says.

"Dear Buddha. That's depressing."

"It sure is."

"Did you come to jump?" I ask, still not looking in his direction.

"God no, I am not a desperate attention seeker like my brother."

"Oh, he definitely did it for the attention."

"Of course, what a diva."

We remain silent for a few seconds. I snort a laugh, and so does he, our laugh growing louder.

"Not a lot of people get my dark sense of humor; your life must be really fucked up," he continues.

"I found out today I didn't murder my sister. My parents are just really messed up people." A shiver runs through me and I hug myself tighter.

"Parents huh, they're the worst."

"Yeah, we should get rid of all parents."

"Exactly, cleanse the world of their evil."

We both laugh.

It dies down and we continue to stare at the water. I thought I wanted to be alone, but his presence and dark humor is comforting.

"You miss him?" I ask.

"Terribly. He was the best. We were best friends. I don't know what went wrong, he didn't even leave a note."

"Are your parents okay?"

"It's been six years. I think they found a way to live with it. But these things, you never really get over it. Today is Arm's birthday so it's hard on everyone. It always is on his birthday."

"Arm?"

"My nephew, he just turned eleven."

"He's a man now."

"Yeah." He scoffs. "Your parents, do you hate them?"

"I really want to. But I don't. There is this feeling, like I miss having parents even though they are right there. At least one of them."

"That's so sad."

"Is it?" I turn to him and our eyes meet.

"Your eyes... Wow," he says with a grin. I look away, flustered and he chuckles. "You've always been shy."

I turn back to him sharply. He takes a few steps closer and a clear picture of his rather handsome chubby frame, tucked underneath a black casual outfit ensemble emerges.

"Khun Rama?" I lean off the railings.

"Khun Sutthaya." He now stands so close. We hold each other's gaze for more than a minute before sharing subtle laughter. "Would you like to see a photo of my nephew?"

"Oh yes." I'm still shocked. What are the odds?

He pulls out his phone to show me and I lean closer.

He smells like bubblegum and vanilla, must be from the birthday party. The picture of his adorable little nephew holding a cake pops up and he swoons over him in the most heartwarming way. As he swipes and brags, there are more pictures of the boy, with family members and friends. He seems loved, happy and safe.

"Oh. Looks like we have company." He points.

I turn around in search of what company he's referring to.

"Khun," he calls back my attention. "I mean, you're crying."

I touch my cheeks and it's wet. I sigh, relieved. "Was searching for those," I say, staring at my wet fingers.

Khun Rama lifts his hand to my face, wiping the tears off. His touch is comforting.

"You're soaking wet. Can I drive you home?" he says calmly. "Will it be against her rules?"

I smirk. "Can you feed me first?"

He lets out a toothy grin. He has lovely teeth, and a beautiful smile I didn't quite notice the first time we met—rather the second time seeing as I was too busy to take notice of him the first time.

"Do you like fried bananas?"

"Yes," I reply.

"I know a place, come on."

He leads me down to where his car is parked, making light conversation as we walk. A driver waits for him upon arrival, tossing his cigarette away and rushing to open the door. It's a really nice car, the type I've seen Elina drive on occasion.

"Nice car," I compliment, standing by the door. "You aren't by any chance a billionaire, with a dead ex-husband and a child that needs care."

"Umm..." He laughs. I think I've freaked him out. "No, I don't have an ex-husband or a child."

"Just a billionaire then."

"Hopefully one day. Why? You have a thing for billionaires?"

"Well, I have been called a gold digger."

"Hmm... What else have you been called?"

"You tell me—what do you see when you look at me?"

He takes a long hard look at me and leans in closer.

"A man I'd like to kiss by the end of tonight."

THIRTY—ONE
A NEW KIND OF DESIRE

"Goodness, the grandpas love him," Plerng says, lifting her champagne to her lips.

"Don't call them that," Lucifer protests.

"Literally all of Po's friends have grandkids, Lucifer. What am I supposed to call them?"

Lucifer rolls his eyes and I snort a laugh. It's his birthday. He decided to trade his traditional birthday style, filled with extravagant partying and drunken nights, for the calm setting of a dinner party, so his boyfriend could attend. It's a lovely gesture, and he seems to enjoy the more laid back setting. It also allows us to perch on the wall and gossip without interruptions.

"He's so your type. I mean look at him, chubby squishy cheeks," Lucifer says.

"He's definitely your type," Plerng adds. "You love mama's boys."

"He's not a mama's boy," I disagree.

We watch as Rama spins the grandma's around, they laugh and giggle.

"He's a mama's boy," Plerng and Lucifer say in unison.

"I bet his dick is big," Plerng says.

"Plerng don't start," I beg.

"Mama's boys have big dicks," she continues. "Does he fuck or does he fauckkk?"

"He does have a great ass," Lucifer includes. "They are begging to be squeezed."

"Ok! Both of you stop being weirdos! This conversation is gross, and no we haven't had sex! What do you think I am? I just met the guy three weeks ago."

"And yet you invited him to my party, which means it must be some form of serious, right? What's the deal?" Lucifer asks.

"He's nice, an open book, we've been on two dates this week, it's sweet."

"Uh, huh." Plerng squints at me. "Have you kissed him yet?"

"Yes, it was a great first kiss."

"He's lying," Lucifer accuses. "You're such a horrible liar."

They begin to laugh and I drown my shyness with champagne.

Rama and Khun Kittibun walk over, laughing arm in arm. Khun Kittibun falls into Lucifer's arms, giving him kisses all over and Plerng groans.

"He's a keeper," Khun Kittibun winks at me before dragging Lucifer to the center of the sitting room to dance.

"So... Rama..." Plerng says, lifting herself off the wall to start what I know would be an outrageous and uncomfortable conversation.

"Plerng..." I warn with a stern stare. I don't need her grilling him tonight.

"Got it." She moves away.

Rama laughs at the gesture, replacing Plerng on the wall beside me. The past three weeks with Rama have been the complete opposite of the last eight months of my life. His life isn't all candy and rainbows, he has experienced the loss of a brother and is the definition of a self-made multi-millionaire, clawing through the dirt to get to the top. Yet, he still holds his innocence, and is optimistic about life.

In a way, Rama breathed fresh air into my life. Every time I say something negative, he counters it with sweet positive words. I'd forgotten what it felt like to look at life that way, or maybe I just got comfortable in the mess of it all. It's tougher to look at the beauty of life when everything feels like shit, but he does it with ease.

He often babysits for his sister in-law who is a cardiologist and is the sweetest uncle. If you ask me, I think a little too sweet. He spoils the boy. Once, he brought me along for a school run and we just hung out at his nephew's badminton practice. His life feels real. I don't try so hard, it's simple.

"Dance with me." He takes me by the arm to join the rest of the dancing family and friends.

The music is groovy, but our moves are slower. He rests his head on my shoulder and I lead our steps. I can smell his coconut scented conditioner, it's refreshing. I look over at the other end of the room, Lucifer and Po are smiling at me. Lucifer proceeds to make the blowjob sign with his hand and mouth and Po smacks his hand. I grin.

We exhausted ourselves dancing before Po pulled us all into a game of charades. Rama and Po are on the winning team and Plerng and I are losing miserably without shame. Po's friends are all hyped up and so is Lucifer who is hellbent on beating his boyfriend. It's a funny sight, I didn't think I'd enjoy the company of grannies this much.

My phone buzzes in my back pocket but I'm too invested in the game to pick it up, I ignore it a few times. It buzzes the fourth time and I reach for it. I raise a brow, surprised by the name on the screen. I excuse myself and hurry to the dining room, away from the noisy chatter. My eyes remain fixed on the screen. I take a deep breath and pick the call.

"Hi," I say.

"Hi," Elina's groggy soft voice comes through the phone. "How are you?"

"I'm good, I'm good, you?"

"Good. You didn't want to pick my call."

"No, sorry. I was umm... I was... There is a game thing... it wasn't on purpose."

She laughs but it's so low I can barely hear her.

"Ok. Sorry I'm calling so late."

"No need to be, it's fine."

I wait for her to speak, but she doesn't. I lean against the dining table, lowering my head.

"Elina?"

"Yes."

"Why did you call?"

"Right, umm... I'm handing over custody to Phi Junta."

"Wow, that's great, Elina... really good for Hathai. Thanks for letting me know."

It's been a month since the deposition, and I had long come to terms with going to court. I'm happy for both Hathai and myself that this isn't moving to trial.

Another round of silence spreads and we quietly listen to each other's breathing over the phone. More minutes pass by and it's now beginning as if she is really here, right next to me. I can almost smell her, feel her warm breath on my neck. I gulp down and slowly close my eyes. Her breath gets warmer, and so does my whole body. I part my lips, letting out a silent exhale of frustration and longing I didn't realize my body still feels.

Loud cheering noises comes from the sitting-room and I throw my eyes open, the warmth leaving my skin as I rise and walk into the kitchen.

"You're with company?" Elina asks.

"Yes, it's Lucifer's birthday, a little get together."

"Wish Lucifer a happy birthday for me."

"Alright. Um.... Elina, I have to get back and—"

"Sure, I just wanted to tell you she's moving to Europe next Wednesday. Paris with Phi. Just in case you'd like to see her before they leave. She'd really like to see you—she's missed you."

"I'd love to Elina, what time is she leaving?"

"12pm."

"I'll be there by 10am."

"Great. Enjoy your party, Pretty Thing."

Goosebumps spread across my skin at the sound of her saying those words and the warmth from before returns hotter.

"Sweet dream na kha."

"Sweet dreams na krap."

She hangs up.

I exhale, lowering myself over the kitchen counter, stomping my feet on the ground to fight off the unwanted feeling of arousal that has met my body. I should keep my eyes open, it will help. But I also want to hang on to this feeling for as long as I can. I leave it closed, sinking deeper into the fading sensation.

"Hey." Rama enters the kitchen and I spring up from the counter.

"Hey." I cross my legs just in case I'm showing.

"You abandoned the ship."

He moves closer and I move backwards, turning to the fridge to take out sparkling water, taking my time.

"Sorry about that, parched."

I keep looking into the fridge although the water is right there in front of me. Just waiting till I'm completely soft.

"You have very lovely people in your life," he says.

I reach for the water and turn. If I stand in front of the fridge any longer, it'll look weird.

"Thanks, they are adorable."

I pour myself a glass, asking him if he wants some but he waves it off.

"I have to call it a night. I have this crazy important meeting with a potential investor tomorrow morning. Sorry I can't stay much longer."

"No, you were amazing tonight, thanks for coming."

"Can I?" He points at my cheek, I nod.

He gives me a gentle peck. Rama is soft that way, very courteous for a tech guy.

"Sweet dreams na krap, handsome," he whispers in my ear. The same ear I had my phone placed on a few seconds ago, the same ear I felt Elina's breath on while she said the same words. It sets me off.

I smile at him and he turns to leave.

"Rama," I call, just as he arrives by the door.

Before he can fully turn, I am upon him, dragging him by the collar and slamming him against the wall, kissing him, running my hands through his thick hair. My kisses are fueled by desire, my desire is fueled by starvation. It's been so long since I've been touched or kissed the way I yearn to be touched and kissed.

His hands slide under my shirt, holding me close to him. I haven't given either of us a moment to catch a breath. We shuffle around the kitchen sucking each other's lips like it's the last time and he wastes no time catching up. His hardened cock against me arouses me further.

I reach for his belt, unhooking it before unzipping his trousers, eager to feel his hard hot cock in my palms, stroke it, lick it, suck it. My hand begins to travel down his trousers when he stops me, breaking away from our passion filled kisses.

"Here?" he asks, his breath labored.

I nod, shoving my lips back into the warmth of his mouth, reaching for his cock again.

"W... what if someone sees."

"So what?" I reply, my lips mere inches away from his.

He nervously chuckles and I can tell he's uncomfortable.

I had forgotten for a moment he wasn't Elina. Elina wouldn't have cared. I bet she would have let me lick her off in the middle of the kitchen just a few steps away from the guests. She would have cum so hard making sure my mouth was filled with her juicy cum after riding it. She probably would have thrown me over this counter and fingered my ass till I was dripping and begging.

"My room?" I ask and he nods.

We run up the stairs like horny teenage boys, giggling and laughing till we burst into my room, our lips already reaching for each other. Rama's hands hang around my neck as I shut the door with my left leg. Not looking towards it, I lift him up and carry him to bed in a rush. I get on my knees, pull his trousers and take his beautifully structured cock in my mouth.

I love how he feels, so many veins, rock hard and hot. I hold onto his waist as I suck him off and he moans rather quietly, almost like he doesn't want people to hear. I suck more of him, licking him from his balls to his tip and then his quiet moans explode. He digs his fingers in my hair, pulling. The pain excites me further.

"Fuck, I'm sorry," he says between breaths.

343

"No, it's fine." I take his cock back in my mouth. He doesn't reach for my hair again, but I need the pain.

Sucking his tip while fondling his balls forces him to fall back into the bed and his moans grow deeper. Reaching for my hair again but this time, gently. I press his hand, signaling him to pull, but he doesn't.

"You can pull if you want to, don't worry."

"Won't that hurt?" he asks, rising from the bed to look into my eyes,

"Yes." I lick him. "I like that, remember?" I smirk.

I go back to sucking him off, taking him all the way into my throat. He moans harder, trembling, I can tell his close. He pulls my hair a bit harder but not as hard as before. Nonetheless, my cock hardens, now I need to fuck him. I keep sucking him off to drive him over the edge and he taps my shoulder.

"I'm... I'm..." he tries to speak, but his cock is deep inside my mouth, driving him insane.

He attempts to pull me away from him and I pin his hands down, sucking him until he cums. He moans loudly, tossing around. The feeling of his cock pulsing in my mouth as he orgasms deepens my desire to fuck him hard.

When I'm done licking all the cum, I lift my face to look at him, watching him relish in the pleasure as he comes back to his senses, his expressions are pleasing.

"Sorry, I tried to warn you," he says with labored breaths.

"It's okay, I like to swallow," I reply.

His cum tastes just how a normal healthy cum should taste, salty and bland. I don't mind it, I do like to swallow, but its taste is a harsh reminder that it wasn't Elina's pussy I just sucked off for the past ten minutes. He blankly stares at me for a few seconds before flashing a smile. He pulls me up from the floor and onto the bed, climbing over me and begins undoing his shirt, kissing my neck, then my cheeks and then my lips.

As his kisses come, I move his hands to my sensitive nipple, hoping he sucks them too and he does, only for about five seconds before traveling down to undo my trousers' button. *Fuck, I'm getting soft.*

He takes my semi hard dick into his mouth. It does feel good, but I'm too focused on staying hard to really enjoy it. I reach for him and pull him up, kissing him.

"Tell me all the nasty things you want to do to me," I beg.

"Oh erm... like what?"

"Just anything, anything... I'm I a good boy, Daddy?"

"Umm... Yes?"

Oh dammit! Not what I was hoping for.

"Why?" I ask, pulling him close and kissing his chest.

"Umm." He moans. "You have really good hands and uh... good skin."

"You think I'm a nasty whore, don't you?"

"What!" He leans back. "No, I'd never think that." He cups my face, looking down at me with concerned eyes. "Why would you think I think that?"

I pull his hands down to my cock which is almost soft, staring desperately into his eyes.

"Rama, please call me a nasty whore," I beg.

"Oh," he mutters, the realization hitting him. "Umm... you're a nasty whore."

"Good good good, what else?"

"You're so, so bad, so bad, so nasty—I'm sorry, I'm sorry." He pulls away, getting off me and fixing his clothes.

Finally, I'm thinking with my head, realizing what just happened. I'm embarrassed and the guilt sets in. He must have been so uncomfortable.

"I'm so sorry, that made you uncomfortable."

"More like, insecure." He chuckles. "You seem very experienced. That was the best blowjob I've ever had."

"It was?"

"I'm a tech nerd stereotype, ok? I didn't lose my virginity until I was twenty and I didn't come out until I was Twenty-five. I'm horrible at dirty talk. The one time I tried being adventurous with sex, I ended up at an orgy and it scared me for life."

I smile.

"I am part of the one percent of humanity that loathes porn. I... I usually just lay there." He turns to me. "I can learn if you're patient with me, I really can. I just don't think I have the confidence to verbally abuse someone. I mean, when I stand in queues, I let people jump the line when really, I want to scream at them." He looks away.

I haven't stopped staring at him since he began speaking. Every word he says makes me feel guilty about thinking of Elina tonight. He's been nothing but warm and welcoming and I've taken it for granted.

"You think I'm a loser," he says.

I turn his face to mine and kiss him.

"Rama—I could never think that. When the time is right, I'm going to fuck you. And when I do, you won't just be laying there, you'll choke me, scratch me, spank me, pull my hair, call me every nasty thing you wanted to call those losers that won't just stand on the damn queue, until my cock has pleased you to your satisfaction and you've covered me with your cum."

He stares at me, his eyes widening with every word. I can't tell if he is surprised or intrigued. He gulps and I smirk, looking down at his once again hardened cock.

"Looks like someone agrees with me." I sit back. "Now give me a command and when you do, add pervert at the end."

He hesitates, taking his time to exhale his nervousness. I wait, not breaking eye contact. I feel him squeeze the sheet and I smile at him to put him at ease.

"Suck my dick... pervert," he commands.

I grin, getting on my knees and taking him back into my mouth.

THIRTY—TWO
LIKE THE FIRST TIME

Before Lucifer's birthday, I pictured a scenario where Rama would freak out about my need for pain. The reason why the night we met, I held off on kissing him, even though all of me wanted to. It was a beautiful night, sitting by the roadside having dinner under the bare sky. But if anything, it's made dating Rama more exciting and fun. He sends me a list of degrading insults, pictures of cuffs, whips, things he is thinking of buying. It created room for a lot of laughs during the few times we've tried play sessions. We both aren't ready for penetrative sex yet and that's fine. Besides, I can't get enough of his cock in my mouth.

The man bakes and cooks. Each time we go on a date it's a three course meal. This past week is what the hopeless romantics call a whirlwind romance.

I decided to apply for jobs at private institutions that specialize in social work. I don't want to work in a major hospital, I want an environment that allows me to get as up close and personal with as many children as possible: non-profit foundations, pediatric centers or even schools. There are so many applications to get through and when Rama isn't working, he's helping me fill them out.

His apartment is a gorgeous modern decor bachelor pad that faces a massive body of water and city bridge. From his kitchen counter where I'm seated, you can see all of that water. I still haven't gotten used to the view.

"Next Friday, my partner and I are throwing a networking party, you should come," he says, stirring the soup on the stove.

"Ugh, I'm tired of sucking up to rich people." I pout, chin in palm, exhausted from filling out applications.

He chuckles. "They're not all rich you know, besides there is only one investor I need my boyfriend to suck up to. I have worked hard to get her to show up. If she invests in Rigital, breaking into the rest of Asia will be easy peasy," he explains, prancing back and forth in his cute little apron.

I sit back, smiling to myself.

"Boyfriend?" I ask.

He freezes in front of the stove, turning around sharply with his mouth wide apart.

"I mean... shit. I'm a blabbing moron. Just... I have boys who are my friends, and you happen to be one of them. That came out wrong. I mean, you are definitely more than a boy who is my friend, seeing as you have erm... I probably shouldn't complete that sentence."

"Rama."

"Yes." He clears his throat, taking a few steps forward.

"The food is burning."

"Oh shit!" He runs back, opening the oven to bring out the burning roast.

The smoke overwhelms him, and he falls back coughing. I rush over as he coughs, take out the food from the oven and turn off the stove. I retrieve a bottle of water from the fridge and hand it to him. He gulps it down, with red, watery eyes. I pull him close, wiping the tears away and laughing.

"Wine, what I meant to say was... I'd very much love to be your boyfriend," he says with his cracked voice and teary eyes.

I take a second to take in the moment before pulling him into a hug, holding him tightly. From the moment we met, everything about Rama has brought me comfort and joy, this moment is no different.

"Thank you," I say, rubbing his back.

"Is that a 'no thank you' or 'a yes thank you'?"

I smile, breaking our hug to look into his expecting eyes.

"It's a 'I've never been asked to be anyone's boyfriend before thank you'. I'm glad you asked."

"Then say yes."

We both chuckle.

"Rama—it will break me if I hurt you."

"And if you don't?"

"And if I do?"

"Wine, we can stand here wondering or you can say yes and find out."

"It's only been a month, how do you know?"

"How does anyone know?"

I raise my hands to his head, patting him before making our foreheads touch. His hands wrap around my waist, and we remain silent in the stuffiness of the smoke filled kitchen.

***

I arrive at the Cheng mansion just a few minutes past 10am, staring out the window as the taxi pulls up. Khun Toh is waiting for me, arms crossed behind his back.

"Khun, welcome back." He bows and so do I in greeting.

"Thank you."

"You're well?"

"Yes," I reply with a grin.

He leads me into the mansion, filling my ears with how the rest of the household missed my company before leaving for his office. As I climb up the stairs, familiar memories and emotions flash through my mind and body. I welcome them all with a smile.

I arrive where I once stood as Khun Toh warned me not to enter the left wing for the first time. I take a moment to stare, wondering if she's in there. Is she in the dining room? Her bedroom I never got to see? Her office? That office. I sigh, remembering all that transpired within its walls. Only for a few minutes do I linger before turning into the right wing.

Hathai's door is wide open, so I poke my head in. The floor and bed are littered with boxes. One of the housekeepers walks out of her closet carrying clothes. She gasps, startled by my unforeseen presence.

"Khun Sutthaya?" We exchange bows. "Sawatdee kha."

"Sawatdee krap, sorry for scaring you."

"Not at all! It's been too long, good to see you."

"You too, Phi Chailai. Where is she?"

"Her favorite place." She smiles at me.

Thanking her with a bow, I head over to the music room. I can hear the sound of the piano as I approach.

I arrive by the door and stand by it watching her. Her sophisticated taste in fashion has not wavered. She sits in front of her piano dressed in a two piece Chanel outfit, her hair in a ponytail, her legs tucked into a black hose. The view is straight from the first time I met her. I clear my throat to alert her of my presence.

"Phi!" Hathai springs up from her seat and runs towards me with the biggest smile on her face.

I open my arms and she falls into them, hugging me with a hard squeeze. I laugh, lifting her up from the ground and giving her a quick spin.

"I heard you missed me so much," I tease.

"It's a lie."

"Oh? But just now you almost squeezed me to death."

"Hand spasm." She turns away and we both laugh.

"That piece you were playing, it's really good, never heard you play it before."

"Yes. I just learnt it. Mae taught me."

"Mae?"

Hathai nods. "She's been teaching me new music. Would you like to hear more of it?"

"Sure."

She returns to her piano and begins to play. It does sound like music Elina would write. Very melancholic.

Hathai plays for about fifteen minutes, and I listen, watching her get lost in the sad melody whenever she closes her eyes. Moments spent watching her were some of my favorite moments with her. It's the way she carries life in her words and movements, it made me reflect on my life, and in many ways, brought me comfort.

We sat and began chatting about simple things. She doesn't want to leave Thailand but Junta had promised her it would only be for a year so Elina could sort things out. Hathai does not believe it would only be for a year. She ended the sentence with, "If staying away will make Mae laugh again, I'll go far away."

Telling her it wasn't her fault how much Elina is hurting didn't seem to liven up her solemn mood. I don't even know why I thought it would, it never worked on me as a boy... still doesn't. But I want her to know the responsibility of her mother's happiness is not hers to bear. I want her to find a way to be a kid again, to cry when she needs to and laugh when she needs to. It's tough when for years, dealing with your emotions alone is the only way you've coped. It will be a hard change, one I'm uncertain Junta can ease her into, but I know Junta is full of love, and I think that is enough to guide her decisions.

Elina is teaching her the violin and chess again. It's a good start... a great start. I would have loved to see it. Sit across the room and look into Elina's eyes as they play, just to see what she feels. There is a lot of agony between them and even though now she speaks about Elina with less contempt, I feel it.

"Can I ask you a question?"

Hathai nods.

"Why do you think she's a murderer?"

She smiles at me. "She'll tell you one day, if you stay."

I stare into her sad eyes for a long second.

"Hathai, you know I'm only here to say goodbye. My work with you is over for now."

"Phi... We both know it was never just about your work." She holds my gaze.

She knows. She's always known. She leans in and hugs me.

"Did you make merit?" she asks in my arms.

I nod. "Yes."

"Good. I'm proud of you, Phi."

I breathe a laugh. "I'm proud of you too, Nong."

"You two are peas in a pod," Junta's voice separates our hug. "Hatty go check on your bags, make sure you have everything."

Hathai hurries out of the music room, and I rise, picking my bag up.

"She'll love Paris," I say, stepping forward.

Junta nods. "I hope so. Onto the next client for you?"

"We will see."

"Khun Sutthaya, I never got a chance to thank you for Hathai. And I'm sorry about that shit show of a deposition."

"It's fine."

"No—it wasn't," she says.

With a smile, she turns and leaves.

I helped with a few traveling boxes, stacking up the vehicle and decided to wait by the car. Hathai and Junta went into the left wing to say goodbye. Elina knows I'm here, she doesn't want to see me, or rather, she knows I don't want to see her. They walk out the door and I lift myself off from the car, opening the door to let Hathai in.

"I almost forgot." I pull out a package from my bag and hand it over to Hathai.

With a big grin and fast hands, she rips open the brown paper, gasping at the picture in the frame.

"You made a print of Po!" She beams.

"I promised," I say.

She hugs me once again, shaking me this time. I look over at Junta who nods in approval.

Our goodbye is short and fast. One minute I'm ushering her into the car, next minute I'm waving and in a blink of an eye, she's gone. Hathai is particularly good at goodbyes, didn't even look back a second. I decide upon a stroll to the pink garden we once got lost in, the one that served as a happy memory of her father but a harsh reminder of pain to her mother.

It's all gone, Elina took it down.

I walk around what is now an open space covered in grass. I'm reminded once again why life with Rama is simple.

354

All week long, the institutions have been replying my applications and scheduling interviews. I haven't seen Po since my encounter with Mae. He is used to me disappearing by now, he hasn't called once and I don't want him to, I don't need any more explanations from him, I don't need anything.

I shop, I drink wine with friends, I laugh a lot more these days, sleep has not yet found me, but the sight of Rama sleeping next to me is just enough.

***

Rama was right, they aren't all rich people, most of the guests are regular employees from different companies, looking to find co-founders, investors, or a listening ear to their brilliant idea. It isn't difficult for me to ease into conversation about tech, agriculture or Thailand's robotics future. I expected a bunch of egotistical men who needed to prove how smarter than you they are, but I have found decent visionaries who actually seemed to care about the soul of their tech.

The conversations are free flowing. I mentioned what I do to the little group I have been chatting with for a while as Rama and his partner networks, and I'm introduced to another tech guy whose app wants to help track mental health problems in toddlers. We dive into a rather intense conversation about the psychology of children and I'm loving every second of it. I feel stimulated intellectually in a way I haven't been in a long time, sipping wine overlooking the Bangkok skyline.

"Hey honey," Rama interrupts.

"Hey hey." I pull him close by the waist. "This is my boyfriend, Rama. This is Awut, he's building an app that helps parents track the mental illnesses in children!" I make an explosion sound with my mouth.

"Big fan of your app, Khun," Awut says, shaking hands with Rama.

"Thank you, mind if I borrow him for a second," Rama asks.

Awut smiles and nods.

"I'll find you," I tell him as I turn away with Rama, moving my hands to his shoulder and shaking him. "I'm glad you dragged me here, this is great! This is really good! I feel revitalized with these people and when I tell you it isn't my scene, I mean it is not." I laugh.

"Ok, pipe it down, you'll implode," he jokes, and I laugh some more.

"What do you need, gorgeous boyfriend?" I lean in for a kiss and he covers my mouth with his hand.

"The investor I told you about, she just arrived."

I grumble into his palm before he releases my lips.

"Do you really need me there?"

"No." He giggles. "But I'd love to have you there, you're my lucky charm."

"That's adorable, I can't say no to that." I smirk.

He pulls me along and I follow, playing with his hair. This night has brought me nothing but excitement, I'm ecstatic.

"You like me, right?" Rama asks.

"That's random. But yes, you're my favorite person."

"Don't get mad."

"Mad about what?"

As we approach, two people stand, their backs to us, facing the skyline. It only takes me a second to recognize that back, those shoulders, that alluring beautiful frame, a beautiful blend of masculinity and femininity, that villainess aura. My breath shortens and my heart begins to race, trying to convince me otherwise. My gaze travels to her waist. I recognize the belt across it, I'd recognize that belt anywhere. I used to yearn for it, beg for it, it used to drive me wild with desire.

The cool rooftop breeze blows hot against my skin. I'm only a few steps away from her but I can smell it, the smell of cigar, mixed with the sweetness of jasmine, the scent that drove me to insanity, the one that consumed me. I gulp.

"Did I cross a line?" Rama asks.

"I... umm..."

"Rama," the man standing next to Elina calls. Rama's business partner.

She turns, lips redder than they have ever been, deep brown gorgeous eyes that meet mine instantly. I dare not take any more steps further. I'd lose control and crumble into mush. She doesn't take her eyes off me, melting my soul with her stare. I'm reminded of the first time I set my eyes upon her, how those eyes had me too weak to speak or walk. I lower my gaze in respect, as if I'm still under her dominance.

"Khun Cheng, glad you could attend." Rama bows. "You remember Wine Sutthaya."

She stretches her hands out to me for a handshake.

How dare she—she knows what her touch does to me—she knows how much of me she controls. I can't back out, not because I don't want Rama to see what she turns me into, but because my whole body and soul are dying to feel her.

I reach for her, sliding my hands into her smooth firm palm. Every part of my body she's touched, kissed, whipped, squeezed, shivers in response to its owner. It all flashes before my eyes, what it felt like to hold her, to be held by her, the perfect world she created for me in the playroom, the taste of her lips in my mouth—the taste of her in my mouth.

I take my hand back in a rush, taking a quick glance at Rama, whose gaze has been on me the whole time. I flash a nervous smile, he doesn't smile back but turns over to Elina and starts speaking words I cannot hear. Elina won't take her eyes off me. I wish I'm uncomfortable. I wish I wanted her to stop. But I don't. I have missed those eyes, that scent—I have painfully missed her.

"The first phase will roughly be an 80 to 250 million dollars evaluation but that's with expansion," Rama explains. "We can have all of Southeast Asia locked in by the first two years, the numbers are—"

"It's yours," Elina replies.

"Excuse me?"

"Your first phase investment," Elina finally moves her gaze from me to Rama. "It's yours. Call my desk on Monday," she says.

Rama chuckles.

"Khun Cheng, I think we should take a few steps backwards here, I'm glad you're eager to come on but I'd still love to show you the framework first."

"Good, then come to my office on Monday."

Elina returns her gaze to me, and I look down at my drink, squeezing the cup.

"I'm going to use the bathroom," I say.

"Sure." Rama leans in to give me a peck and I step back.

As I turn to leave, my eyes find the blazing stare of Elina. The side of her lips twitch. I tremble, squeezing the side of my trousers.

Just like the first time we met, my legs wobble.

THIRTY–THREE
ADDICT

I dip my hand under the running water, letting it run over them as I stare at my reflection in the mirror. My heart is still racing.

I rub my wet hands around my neck, then my face, trying to cool my burning body. Why would Rama not tell me? How do I go back out there? It would be impossible not to stare at her belt and crave it. Rama would see. *Oh fuck.*

A knock comes at the door, and I ignore it. It comes again.

"Occupied!" I scream.

"Honey it's me," Rama says. I throw the door open and pull him inside. "You're angry."

"You bet your ass I am! What is this?"

"You never talk about her and when I try bringing it up, you act like I'm committing a crime."

"So instead you ambush me?"

"I was not trying to. I wanted you to meet all the people I work with. We've been pursuing this deal with Khun Cheng long before I discovered you were in a relationship with her."

"I was not in a relationship with Elina, we had an arrangement."

"Ok then, in love with her?"

359

"What? Rama... she was my Domme, nothing more."

"Right... that's why just now you trembled at her touch."

"I... Rama... I wasn't..."

"Wine, I don't care... I get it, you shared a strong bond with her, and maybe... I might never get a chance to experience that with you—"

"Rama—"

"Wine, just don't be mad at me, okay?" His voice grows soft. "I didn't mean to throw it in your face like this. Please don't yell, I can't take it." He takes a few steps forward and I pull him into a hug.

"Sorry for yelling."

He kisses me. Soft kisses that are quick to grow into fierce passionate kisses. I pin him against the wall, sliding my hands under his shirt and he giggles at the coldness of my touch.

"Sorry," I whisper, kissing his earlobes. "Turn around for me, gorgeous," I say, and he obeys, turning and placing his hands on the wall.

I tilt his neck and kiss it, sucking hard intentionally to leave a hickey as my hand slides into his trousers. He winces and moans, reaching behind to grab my hair.

"Enjoying that control, Pretty thing?" Elina's voice echoes in my head and I leap backwards, breathless and shaking.

"Why did you stop," Rama asks, turning around.

"Umm... we are moving too fast..."

"It's okay, I'm okay with it." He moves closer. "You can touch me how you want." He kisses me. "As rough as you want," he says against my lips.

"You're cute." I chuckle.

"That is not a very sexy thing to say... I can be hot too." He takes my lips back into his mouth, squeezing my chest.

"We are in a public bathroom," I say.

"I thought you like that."

"Yes. I do."

"So?"

"You have a long night ahead, you should be out there."

"It's fine."

"Rama... there is always tomorrow." I wipe his mouth with my thumb and kiss his cheek. "I'll go... I'll call you tomorrow?"

"Stay."

"I... I think I got a cold anyway... been getting shivers all night. I promise I'm not running away."

He touches my forehead. "Oh. Okay." We smile at each other.

I exit the party, walking to the elevator in a rush.

This night has been rollercoaster. I'm afraid if I spare a second, I'll look back, my eyes will find Elina and I won't be able to leave. What if she tries to speak to me? What if her fingers accidentally touch mine? What if... Nothing can happen... So yes, I'm running away. I'm running away because at the end of it all, I care too much about Rama.

I approach the elevator with my head lowered, slipping on my jacket. It's taking more time because my hand is stuck on something in my sleeve, I'm struggling to push it through. Finally succeeding, I straighten my jacket and look up. The sight of Elina standing in front of the elevator watching me startles me, I freeze.

I look back, contemplating pretending I didn't see her, but that's not possible, no one else is trying to leave the party. I turn back to her icy gaze, smiling as I take more steps towards the elevator. I arrive a few steps away from her. The nostalgic feeling of her jasmine perfume hits me, triggering something at the core of my being.

"Running away too I see," Elina says.

My eyes remain fixed on the elevator door, watching the numbers showing on top of it change as it ascends.

"Just leaving," I say. I have no doubt in my being she knows that's a fucking lie. Elina knows exactly what I am running from.

I see her forming an insidious grin from the corner of my eyes. She turns to the elevator door and we both watch in silence. Away from her view, I squeeze my trousers. *Fuck.* I can't stand her perfume and there is this warmth coming from her body even though she is steps away from me. Once again, my heart has begun its marathon.

"He's good with you," Elina says.

"Yes." I turn to her. "Why do you want to invest so fast? I hope it has nothing to do with me. Rama likes to earn things on his own merit."

She turns to me, meeting my gaze and I return my gaze to the elevator to avoid a prolonged stare.

"I knew him before you, Wine. My investment advisors already did evaluations on his company and tech. I wouldn't be here if I wasn't already prepared to invest."

I nod and she takes a step towards me.

"I told you, Wine. I don't mix business with pleasure."

I nod again and falsely clear my throat, turning to meet her eyes. This time I leave my gaze on her, allowing her shower me with jitters and shivers. Holy fuck, she got prettier. Her brows have grown a bit more, her cheekbones are well contoured, her lips are perfectly lined, showing every curve. I wonder if her lips still feel the same, taste the same.

She takes another step closer, and I turn to her fully. I like her new curly hair. Her eyes have always been tender with me. It's magnetic. The elevator dings and opens, we both turn to it. She steps back, placing her hand on the elevator door to stop it from closing too soon then gestures me in.

"Aren't you leaving too?" I ask.

"Yes, you go down first."

"We can share an elevator, Elina."

"No. We cannot, Wine."

"Why not?"

"Because, Wine. I won't give a fuck about your boyfriend when I do things to you in it."

I gulp. I should step in, fuck I should.

"Things like what?" I ask.

With every passing second she stands staring, saying nothing, my imagination fills in the blank with lewd images. I watch her clench her jaw, a quiet grunt escapes her.

"Get in the elevator, Witthaya," Elina commands.

I obey, walking into the elevator. She lets go of the door, keeping her gaze on me as it closes. I sigh, falling against the wall with my back, placing my hands on my knees, trying to catch my breath.

The building is a skyscraper, there are still so many flights down, I can't wait, I'm heavily turned on and showing. I stop the elevator only three flights down, getting off in search of a bathroom.

There is one down the hall. I dash into it, checking every stall to make sure no one is in them before locking the bathroom door. I pace back and forth, those lewd images won't leave my mind, I need to get rid of them, I know I need to, but my body... my body wants to relish in them, sink into them. Her voice is stuck in my head and each time I close my eyes, I see her lips.

I take out my phone and open up a picture album I created for only Elina's pictures. Pictures of her I secretly took for months: her sleeping, eating, laughing, working out. Other pictures are from public pages. I haven't opened them since before the deposition. I haven't had the need to till now. In most of her official photos, Elina is formally dressed, except for my favorite where she opted for a long sleeve dark blue turtleneck top. It brings out her eyes. I have often fantasized of her dominating me while dressed like that. It's the perfect image of her for me to masturbate to.

I take another long hard look at my reflection, then back to the picture. I put my phone down and begin to unhook my belt in a rush. A message arrives, I can see it's from Elina. I pick my phone up.

"Don't," the message reads.

I scoff. "Don't what?" I text back.

"Masturbate to thoughts of me."

"Is that a command?"

"Do you want it to be?"

"Yes," I reply almost as soon as her message arrives. Silence.

"Please?" I text again.

I wait Impatiently for her reply, but it never comes.

Elina ignored me, left me pacing back and forth in a public bathroom like an addict, in desperate need of a fix. *Her dominance.* Maybe it was the realization of what I was doing, betraying Rama with a simple text message, or the way she commanded my attention and then discarded it. Maybe it was both, but soon I was soft and back to my senses, feeling pitiful.

I took a long cold shower as soon as I got home and climbed into bed, hugging my pillow. I have remained in the same position for almost three hours now, feeling somewhat guilty. Thoughts of Rama and his chubby cheeks, worrying over me flash through my mind. He's kind and sweet. When I look into our future, I can see babies, cute little chubby babies with deep brown skin and thick hair like his. I can see Sunday dinners, play dates. I can see a home filled with love. The kind I never had. *Why can't that just be enough?*

"Wine," Khun Kittibun knocks and opens the door. "You have a guest," he announces, and Rama pops up from behind him, walking in. Khun Kittibun shuts the door.

"It's past 1am." I chuckle. "What are you doing here?"

He arrives with a big grin.

"Got you soup. You didn't think I was going to leave my sick boyfriend alone all night, did you?"

He sits on the bed, unwrapping the dish and I move down to the edge of the bed, sitting beside him.

"You didn't have to. I took pills, I'm better."

"Ahhh," he mouths, lifting a spoonful of soup to my lips.

I open up, allowing him feed me repeatedly. Not because I'm hungry or because I want to make him feel useful, but it's a genuine joy experiencing the care on his face. He wipes my lips with his thumb, and I lick it off his fingers.

"I'm full," I pout. He puts away the dish and hands me a bottle of water which I gulp down easily.

"Can I stay and watch you sleep off before leaving?" Rama asks.

"Leaving? Stay the night, Gorgeous. It's late already."

"Really?" His eyes widen.

"Of course." I have no clue why that surprised him. Maybe because we spend more time at his apartment than in Lucifer's home. "We should find you something to sleep in." I rise from the bed.

"Okay."

He follows me to my closet. I fish out different t-shirts and sleep wear and we laugh at some, making jest of the designs on them.

"That one! It has bunnies!" He points at my oversized gray shirt with purple bunnies printed on them.

"You like bunnies?" I reply, handing it over to him.

"Love them. Would love to adopt some one day, but I don't want to do it alone." His eyes are bubbly as he finishes the sentence.

I ruffle his hair and kiss his cheek.

"Go change."

He goes into the bathroom, and I fix up the closet before returning to bed, staring blankly at the bathroom door. As I lay in bed waiting for him, my guilty conscience pricks me even more.

It doesn't take long for him to return with my T-shirt on and his adorable Star Wars briefs. I chuckle at the sight of it but refrain from making any silly comments, I don't want to make him more shy than he already is. I lift the blanket and he slides under, wrapping his arms around me. I kiss his forehead, rubbing his back as we lay in silence.

"So, about the bunnies, do you like bunnies?" he asks.

I smile into his coconut scented hair.

"I don't particularly have an opinion on rabbits."

He doesn't respond, only squeezing me a bit tighter.

"I don't mind," I continue. "If you want them, I'll love to be part of it."

He looks up at me. "You would?"

I nod. He smiles at me, his fluffy adorable cheeks puff up. I smile back, it's such a warm moment. He puts his head back on my chest and I continue to rub his back. My mind is blank, he feels good to hold. He took a shower with my soap, it's satisfying having my scent all over him.

"Want to hear a secret?" Rama says.

"Yeah."

"I kind of… got ready."

"For?" I ask. He raises his head to look up at me, giving me a corny look with his lips pressed into a thin line. "Oh—*OH*."

He lowers himself further down my chest with a soft laugh, hiding his face from me.

"I thought, we could celebrate after the party if I got the investment and… I mean you're sick, I'm not asking you to, we don't have to do anything. I just remembered and wanted to tell you."

I gently pull him away from my body to get a better look at his face before leaving soft kisses on his lips, really soft kisses, because that's how he makes me feel, soft like a dumpling.

"Congratulations on your investment, sorry I didn't say that earlier."

"It's ok, I'm just glad you were there."

I slide my hands under his T-shirt to continue rubbing his back and our eyes meet.

"I'm going to make love to you now," I say.

"I didn't say it so you would."

"I know."

"We probably shouldn't. I can't satisfy your kinks anyways, at least for now."

"I don't need you to do anything, you can lay there if you want to, hold me if you want to, whatever you want. Tonight—you're my kink."

I raise his chin and lift his lips to mine. I roll him over, placing myself on him but making sure my weight isn't pressing him down. From his cheeks to his neck, my lips travel.

"I like that you're wearing my shirt," I say, kissing his neck. "I can't wait to take it off you."

He laughs. I take another moment to look at his smiling face before continuing my journey down his body. He lets out small cooing noises as I kiss and caress him. I slide his shirt up and kiss his chest, tracing my lips to his left nipple as I stroke his right with my fingers. His whimpers grow louder.

I'm hard—*awfully hard.*

Tonight, I'm going to please every bit of him to his satisfaction.

THIRTY–FOUR
MOVING ON

I retrieve a condom and a lubricant bottle and hurry back to bed, kissing him as soon as I arrive. My hands slide down to his waist, pulling down his briefs before I throw his legs over my shoulders, kissing his legs, ankles, then his feet.

"Open it." I toss him the condom then reach for the lube. I squeeze some onto his cock and begin rubbing it.

I watch him bite his lips as his gentle moans grow stronger. He keeps struggling to open the condom pack since he can't focus and it's cute. From this angle, looking down at him, I can see everything: his body trembling, his chest rising and falling rapidly as I stroke him, every expression he makes on his face. Fuck! It's enough to keep me hard for hours on end.

I pour more lube on my fingers and slide it into his ass, spreading his legs to get more access. I keep adding more as I go, fingering him as he struggles to open the condom. He pauses every second to try and catch a breath. Now I realize the lube might have been too much, it's dripping all over.

"Rama?"

"Mmh?" he answers with a moan.

"Are you ever going to open that condom?"

My fingers haven't stopped stretching him, it's made it difficult for him to speak. He gives me back the condom. I chuckle and collect it, tearing it open with my teeth and sliding it onto my hard cock. I'd rather stretch him with my dick.

I press against him, and he winces. It's cute, his cheeks are red. I smile at it.

I press and retract my dick, then use my fingers to stretch him further. Just a few thrusts and his hole is ready for me. I don't take my eyes off him till I'm deep inside him.

He lets out a beautiful moan of relief, making me giggle. He joins me for a second, but I'm quick to shut him up with a thrust. He loves it, rewarding me with erotic moans that fill me with lust. I continue with slow gentle thrusts, listening to him make sounds I have never heard him make before. He finally looks at me, holding my gaze as he moans, biting his lips, enjoying every sensation my cock is inflicting on him. I look away, I can't stand it, I'd cum within minutes.

The pleasure radiates through me, and I tighten my grip on his thigh, thrusting harder and quickening my pace. The sound of our bodies against each other, alongside our loud moans, drives me wild with pleasure. I go harder, faster, loving every fucking bit of it. I want to last as long as I can, so this feeling doesn't go away. But I already know soon I'd cum.

The harder I fuck him, the better it feels, but it's been a few minutes and I haven't heard him moan. I open my eyes, still fucking him hard and fast but one glance at him slows me down. His face is scrunched, his lips are pressed into a thin line with his shoulders tensed.

"Rama, are you ok?" I ask between heavy breaths. He nods. "Do I need to go slower?"

"I can take it," he mutters.

I cease thrusting, lowering myself over him as I bring my face close to his.

"I don't want you to take it, I want you to enjoy it. You can tell me to slow down if you need me to." I kiss his lips. "Ok?"

"Ok," he whispers, and I smile at him, wrapping myself around his soft body.

He kisses me deeper like he's been waiting to be kissed for too long. His kisses command me to begin thrusting again, gentle deep thrusts. In no time, his beautiful moans return, right next to my ear. It warms my heart and my cock alike.

He squeezes me tightly, his hands in my hair as he moans. He holds my face up and looks into my eyes as I fuck him. I kiss him instead, so I don't have to, I'd cum if I do. He pulls me back, staring at them anyway.

"You should know—your dick is so pretty," he says, his eyes sultry and calm.

I gasp at his words, dropping my head back on his chest as I tremble.

"And... you feel so good," he continues, grabbing my ass, squeezing as I fuck him. "Your ass is so soft."

I moan into his neck. His words though simple drive my body into another kind of pleasure. It builds up more intensely as I thrust in and out of him.

He whimpers. "Faster."

I pick up my pace at his gentle command and he squeezes me, pressing me against him. He throws his head back into the pillow, gasping for air. I surrender my body to the pleasure running through me.

"You're going to make me cum," he cries.

I need to see it, all of it. Every expression on his face, every wriggle his body makes, watch him struggle to breathe, bite his lips, squeeze his eyes. I've seen him cum loads of times but not while my cock is inside him, pleasing every nerve in his body.

"Would you like to sit on my cock?" I ask.

"Yes please," he mutters.

I roll over, placing him on top of me. I spread his ass, guiding my dick back inside him. Slowly, he sits on it, shivering as it sinks into his depth. He whimpers from how deep I am inside him and I smirk with satisfaction from the view.

"Does that feel good?" I ask, partly to make sure he is ok with the depth, but mostly because I want to hear him shower me with more praise.

He lifts my palm to his lips, kissing it before sliding my hands down to his waist.

"You're doing a good job with me. Don't stop," he replies between moans.

He starts riding me, his little bounces are so arousing to watch. His cock flaps around as he bounces and I reach for the lube bottle once again, squeezing some into my hands and begin stroking him. He releases his lower lip, moaning louder with each stroke, trying to keep his balance. Overwhelmed by the pleasure, he falls forward and I take over fucking him, fast but not hard. He hasn't opened his eyes once, moaning deeply into my mouth.

His warm cum spreads over my tummy, driving me wild with lust as the expression on his face reflects the ecstasy his in. I keep fucking him, shutting my eyes and letting my body feel every sensation

"Mo... Daddy," I stutter.

"It's okay, darling. You can cum. You've been a very, very good boy."

He swipes his cum off my body and inserts his finger into my mouth. I latch on sucking, fucking, moaning.

"Such a good boy," he whispers into my ear. "Cum for me."

Without hesitation, I begin to cum, holding him close as my body shivers in the bliss of an orgasm, moaning with my eyes closed shut, fucking him fast.

"Good job, gorgeous," he pats my head.

I hold onto his body, kissing him as I moan. He slides off me and I fall back into the bed, breathing heavily from exhaustion and pleasure. My eyes struggle to stay open as I watch him take his T-shirt off and wipe the cum off me. I smile at him, too exhausted to move.

"I never got to take it off you," I say, and he smirks.

"Some other time."

He takes off my condom, tosses it to the ground then uses the shirt on himself too before pulling me onto his chest for a cuddle, making sure I'm well covered under the duvet. His lips on my forehead, my hand around his body, soaking up all the warmth I can get. In silence, I listen to the rhythm of his heartbeat, soothing me to sleep.

I've had it wrong all this time. My submissive lifestyle isn't more important than him. I should have kissed him sooner, made love to him sooner. If I did before that phone call with Elina, I would've been able to see him—for him. Instead of shoving my past before him. What I had with Elina, is nothing compared to what I have with Rama. What we have is real. I can easily see myself sinking into his world. What he'd create for me—what we'd create together—it'll be magical.

***

I don't recall the moment I fell asleep, one minute I was listening to his heartbeat, the next minute I'm waking up. I lay still, recollecting the memories of last night. With a big grin on my face, I roll over, laying on my back and stretching. I rise, glancing around, he isn't here. I get down from the bed, strolling to the bathroom lazily. My phone dings and I lift it off the wall chest. It's a message from Po.

'Witthaya, I spoke to your mother. I know none of our actions make sense to you, life is complicated. I await your return, there is much to discuss.'

I don't want to go home, see him, or talk. They took things from me, precious things. It will take me a lifetime to recover what I've lost. I meant every word when I said I wasn't going to forgive them for it. None of them ever forgave me either. It's only fair that for once, I put my own well-being first.

I return to my inbox to see if there are any other messages, and there is another, from Elina. Now she responds? She took things from me too. I'm tired of people taking. I delete the message and block her number. I don't need to know what she has to say, we are over—*really over.*

I swallow at that thought, taking a moment before continuing into the bathroom to take a piss, a quick shower and brush my teeth.

THIRTY–FIVE
HONEYMOON

I jog down the stairs and walk straight into the bustling kitchen. Khun Kittibun, Lucifer, Plerng and Rama are all laughing and chatting as they make breakfast. Of course Plerng is in a corner sipping wine by 10am.

"There he is!" Khun Kittibun walks over and pats my shoulder. "Your boyfriend makes cupcakes." He cheerfully squeezes my cheeks.

He walks away and my eyes find Rama. He winks at me, making me smile. Our gazes stay on each other. He's more handsome in the sunlight, in a sunflower printed apron, smeared with flour.

"The rest of us are here by the way," Plerng says.

"He doesn't care," Lucifer includes.

I keep flirting with my eyes, undressing him, lusting over him. I can hear Plerng and Lucifer, but they are only background noise to my selfish desires. Rama breaks our stare, turning to the oven, releasing me from his charm.

"I think it's a fabulous idea, but you'd have to come in for a few board meetings to get approval. It's how things are done," Khun Kittibun says, piling a set of dishes.

"I have never needed the board's approval for a sponsorship, Po," Plerng complains.

"Don't hassle me, talk to Nong, he's the C.E.O."

"What? Don't put this on me, I too have to answer to the board," Lucifer says.

"What are we talking about?" I ask.

"Plerng wants a charity sponsored," Lucifer states.

"Isn't that what the foundation is for?"

"Took the words right out of my mouth, Wine," Plerng says.

"It's in Europe," Khun Kittibun says. "We are focused on Asia."

"So? It's time for us to expand."

Khun Kittibun and Lucifer chuckle.

"Plerng stop looking for an excuse to go to Paris with your girlfriend. Pick up the phone, call her, tell her you're coming," Khun Kittibun persuades, his mouth stuffed with blue berries as Lucifer won't stop feeding him.

"You're moving to Europe for Junta?" I ask, taking some blue berries for myself.

"No, I'm not moving across continents for a woman who by the way, stood me up. I just think sending young talented fashion students to Paris to study under some of the greats will be a great feat for the country,"

"You're a humanitarian now?" Lucifer raises a brow.

"If that's what you want to call it, Lucifer. I will be there to oversee and make sure the students are well taken care of and things run smoothly— "

"You hate charity work," I interrupt.

"No, I don't. I just think most of the people who do charity are pretentious pieces of shit."

"Plerng, it's too early for all the cursing, let's have this conversation at dinner when you can freely grace us with your wonderful words," Khun Kittibun says.

Plerng doesn't back down, they keep going at it, so I return my gaze to Rama who is still standing by the oven. He laughs and I join him.

"Anyway, how did the networking party go last night?"
Khun Kittibun turns his attention from Plerng to Rama.

"It was good, might have sealed our Series A funding.
I like the odds."

"That's impressive. You see what happens, Plerng,
when you pitch ideas?"

"Po, don't compare me to your golden boy, some
people will call that bad parenting."

"Some people don't have you as their child. Write a
proposal, pitch it to the board, get approval, it's not that
hard."

"It's really not."

"Shut up, Lucifer," Plerng retorts.

"Who is the investor, I can put a call through and
make further recommendations on your behalf," Khun
Kittibun says, turning to Rama.

I stand upright at the question.

"That'd be great, you probably know them too, Cheng
Global," Rama replies, removing the cupcakes from the oven.

Everyone freezes.

Lucifer and Plerng turn, throwing treacherous stares
at me. I shrug. It's too early for me to be getting judged.
Rama turns back to us with a big smile on his face, holding
freshly baked cupcakes that smell heavenly.

"I certainly do," Khun Kittibun squeezes a response. "I
will put a call through."

"That'll be amazing, thank you."

"Whatever you need, Nong. You're part of the family
now."

"Ok, Po, let's not scare my boyfriend away."
We all chuckle.

"Wine, let's chat outside for a moment," Plerng
suggests.

"No, I'm good here, Rama might need my help."

I don't want to have the conversation they are about to bring up. I want a simple morning, breakfast, sex later, then lay in bed all day with my boyfriend. I'd rather nobody mentions Elina this morning, tomorrow, or the day after.

"I don't, I have it covered," Rama says, trying to be a sweetheart.

"Let's go buddy," Lucifer drags me along.

I turn around and mouth save me to Rama. He smiles.

"I saw that," Plerng who is following behind says.

They drag me outside and I begrudgingly follow, grumbling as we arrive by the poolside.

"Guys listen, I promise this isn't a big deal," I say.

"Your ex is investing in your boyfriend's company, it's a big deal!" Lucifer says.

"It's not serious."

"Does he know?" Plerng asks.

"Yes, he's known Elina for years."

"They are friends?"

"Casual business acquaintances."

"Whoa, Wine, that's just..." Lucifer shakes his head. "What if she invested because of you?"

"She didn't."

"How are you sure?" Plerng asks.

"Because of the way she looked at me when she saw me. She also told me."

"The way she looked at you? You spoke to her?"

"Both of you stop, what happened with Elina and I is over and done and I'm moving on, you guys should too."

"You were devastated after it ended, Wine, and that's me putting it lightly. She wrecked you and now you're just going to be okay with them working together?" Plerng says with disgust glowing in her eyes.

"How did she look at you?" Lucifer asks.

I open my mouth to speak but pause to collect my words.

"She was excited to see me."

"Excuse me?" Plerng narrows her eyes at me as she folds her arms.

"If she knew I was dating Rama beforehand, she would have been cocky... very cocky. But she wasn't, she was excited... And nice."

"Does Rama know the extent of your relationship with her, how badly you were hurt? How things ended?"

"I don't think it's necessary to share that information."

"This isn't good, Wine. This is classic you, it won't end well," Plerng continues.

"What is that supposed to mean?"

"You never address things head on. The man is in your kitchen baking blueberry cupcakes! Blueberry cupcakes, Wine! Tell him!" Plerng scolds.

"Ok, this is turning into something else, I'm going back inside." I walk past them heading for the entrance.

"Wine," Lucifer calls.

"The lack of trust coming from both of you is disappointing."

I know I've given Plerng and Lucifer enough reasons not to trust me with my own heart. I haven't always made the right choices when it comes to relationships, but Rama... I just know it in my bones, he is the right choice, and I don't see any reason why I should risk losing him.

I walk back into the house and re-join Khun Kittibun and Rama in the kitchen. Soon after, Plerng and Lucifer return. We carry on with breakfast. There is still some tension between Plerng and I. She has been avoiding speaking, rarely looking in my direction. I'm agitated by her lack of trust, but that's just Plerng, always has to be right, wearing her truth on her sleeve.

As soon as breakfast was over, I dragged Rama back to my room and resumed what we started the night before. I had him naked all day, cumming. Our first time having penetrative sex unleashed a part of me that was eternally hungry for him. And all weekend he let me have anything I asked of him, but it was never enough, I always needed more.

The new week came by, and Rama went back to work, while I started going in for interviews. We saw less of each other during the day, I found myself craving for the weekend again. I missed him. When he wasn't cooked up in a meeting or working on something important, we'd text. Those moments weren't as many as I'd hoped. Not when all I thought about was him.

The weekend returned, and once again, he was all mine. He made up for all the moments he wasn't there, asked all the questions, checked in with me, cooked, bought me adorable gifts, and the sex—the sex was perfect. I loved every second. I cursed Monday when it returned, at least until I got the call asking me to come in for a second interview.

The Thawon Children's Center is one of the top three children counseling institutions in the country. I applied with little faith in getting an interview, and even less faith in getting a second interview or being shortlisted. When the call came through, I was cleaning Rama's house which is a complete mess ninety percent of the time. I did a weird dance at the news and rushed to call him but could only get to his assistant. I called Lucifer and Plerng instead to scream my heart out and we went drinking.

Lucifer and I are supposed to return home together, but I made him drop my drunk ass off at Rama's. Even after the long night, I still very much want to celebrate with him.

He opens the door at Lucifer's second knock, and Lucifer hands me over to him.

"All yours," I hear him say.

"Is he okay? What happened?" Rama asks.

"He likes to drink these days when he's happy, don't worry about it. See you tomorrow, Wine." Lucifer kisses me on the cheek and walks away.

Rama helps me inside and shuts the door.

"Let's get you some water."

He leaves me on the kitchen counter, fills up a glass with water, and hands it to me. I gulp it down in one go.

"That is the best water I've ever tasted," I say.

Rama scoffs, taking the glass to refill.

"What were you guys celebrating?"

"I got a second interview from the Thawon Center, it's like a formality. Usually means you have the job."

"What! That's great, honey." He cups my face. "Why didn't you call me?"

"I did, your assistant answered."

He kisses me. "So, we couldn't celebrate together? I'm sorry."

"We still can." I throw my hands over his neck and pull him close.

I've been turned on from the moment the alcohol began to kick in. My thoughts went straight to him, my body needed his touch. I kiss him deeper, ruffling his hair, already moaning into his mouth. I unhook my belt and slide it off me.

"I want you to fuck me... hard. As hard as you can," I whisper into his ear, placing the belt in his hands. "Tie me up with this."

"You are so drunk." Rama chuckles.

I pull back to look at his face. "Not as drunk as you think. I've always wanted to bottom for you. Haven't you ever wanted me to?"

"No. You're really good with me."

"You can be very bad with me." I lean in closer. "As bad as you want." My hand slides down his trouser and grabs his dick, kissing, licking his ear

"Wine," he calls, pulling me away. "How about a shower, Mmh?"

I smell myself and he laughs.

"You won't have sex with me cause I'm smelly?" I pout.

"I just want you to feel better, come on." He takes my arm, steering my half-drunk self up the stairs to the bedroom.

I rushed through the shower, stepping out with only my towel around my waist, still tipsy. Rama sits on the bed, working on his iPad. I take it away and climb over him, dripping water from my poorly dried body onto him. I cup his face and kiss him.

"You didn't dry your hair," he mutters in between kisses.

"Please take off my towel."

"Wine... Wine." He pulls me back. "I'm sorry, honey... but I have to be up before six. I have this very important meeting."

I untie my towel so he can see my hard dick, eager to please him.

"That's not fair," he pleads, leaning in and kissing my waist. He traces his lips down to my groin and then takes me in his mouth, giving me a few sucks, before maneuvering me and placing me on the bed.

"Can't you be a little late, mmh?" I say.

He smiles at me and kisses my cheeks. "You are so needy." He giggles.

Those words render me immobile. I lay frozen under the weight of his body for a moment, watching him laugh before gently pushing him off me and turning away, pulling the duvet over my damp body.

"Hey." He spoons me. "I'm sorry, I wish I could move the meeting. Don't be mad."

"I'm not, I'm just going to bed." I turn off the bedside lamp.

I'm not pissed because he won't have sex with me, it's the first time he has ever turned me down and I understand his reason. In the future there will be more moments like this, we are slowly slipping out of the honeymoon phase and settling into a domestic relationship. I feel grounded by it. I'm pissed because for the first time in weeks, I just thought of Elina. It was a fleeting thought at the mention of that word: **needy**. But it was still—a thought.

THIRTY—SIX
AN ELEVATOR REUNION

I was offered the job at the Thawon Center immediately after the interview, I'm set to begin next week Monday. I called Plerng and Luce the second I left the building, they screamed with joy, but made it clear they weren't in the mood to go drinking tonight. Neither am I.

I need to tell Rama too, but I gave him the cold shoulder last night because I was pissed at myself for thinking about Elina, and this morning because I was pissed at myself for giving him the cold shoulder last night. I'm not particularly the best at using my words.

I ordered Rama lunch from his favorite restaurant, so I can surprise him at work and apologize. It's something I knew I had to do even before I was offered the job. I have never been to his office, but I have been dying to see it. The place that steals him away from me all week, the place he calls his second home.

I arrive at the front desk and the well suited, cleanly shaved gentleman welcomes me with a plain smile.

"Sawatdee krap, Khun," he greets, and we exchange bows. "How may I help you?"

"I'm here to see Rama," I reply with a smile.

"Rama Ruangwiwat? Our C.E.O?"

"Yes please."

"Do you have an appointment scheduled?"

"No, but I'm sure if you inform him I'm here he wouldn't mind."

"Sorry, Khun, he never takes unscheduled appointments."

"Can you just inform him a Wine Sutthaya is here?"

He pulls out a paper and slides it over the counter.

"You can fill out this form. In one to two weeks, a member of the PR team will contact you about the possibilities of scheduling a meeting."

I scoff, shaking my head as I place the meals on the counter.

"Listen. Your boss is my boyfriend. I just want to surprise him with lunch, why not do me a favor and call his office."

"Khun, you need to step back from the counter and exit the building."

"Are you even listening to me?"

"I will call security if you don't step back."

I sigh, stepping away from the counter.

"Can I at least sit and wait?"

"Khun—"

"Thank you!"

I walk over to the waiting lounge. He ignores me as I take a seat, throwing a distasteful glance my way every chance he gets.

The waiting lounge is quite comfortable. There are several bean bags, sofas, some stuff that look like giant toys. Two women and a man sit across the lounge, sipping drinks as they type on their laptops like mindless zombies. I leave my gaze on one of the girls, she looks a bit too young to be working in a company like this.

"Prolonged staring makes me uncomfortable, Khun," she says, not looking away from her laptop.

"Oh sorry." I glance at the ID hanging over her neck. "You work here?"

"Yes."

"Isn't this the waiting lounge?"

"We have an open working space policy."

"Meaning?"

"We work wherever we want."

"Right."

I keep staring at her, she really looks like she belongs in a high school, learning math or something, not the four walls of a multi-million dollar company, working.

"Khun?" She glares at me.

"Sorry." I turn away.

It isn't a horrible wait. I have been procrastinating cleaning out my email, arranging documents in my folders and deleting dated files. I get to it, barely noticing the hours fly by. Different employees walk in and out of the lounge at separate times and everyone mostly minds their business.

"Darling?" Rama calls and I look up at the sound of his voice.

"Hey!" I spring up from my seat.

"What are you doing here?" he asks with a smile and concerned eyes.

"Can't I visit?"

"Of course, but you could've come to my office or called." He pecks me.

"I wanted to surprise you but wasn't able to get past your front desk guy. Are you surprised?"

He chuckles and nods, then takes me by the arm and leads me back to the reception.

"Luke, did you leave my boyfriend in the waiting lounge?"

"Sir, erm... I was not sure who he was and—"

"Don't ever let it repeat itself," Rama says in a stern tone with an expression I scarcely see on his face. It's sexy.

"Yes, Sir." He bows in apology to Rama. "Sorry, Khun." He bows in apology to me.

"Have security activate an express card for a Witthaya Sutthaya, we'll pick it up on our way out."

"Yes, Sir." He immediately starts to dial.

With our palms still intertwined, Rama leads me into the company building.

"What's an express card?" I ask.

"It allows you get to anywhere in the building, so you can surprise me anytime." He beams. "A tour?"

I nod. He slides our intertwined palms into his jacket's pocket and drags me along.

I don't know which one makes me more smitten: the way he proudly introduces me to his employees as his boyfriend, or that my hand is inside his pocket while he does. Not to mention the occasional cheek sniffing.

The working environment of his company is pretty laid back, which I think is also a reflection of his chill personality. Everyone is dressed in sneakers, shorts, polos and tees, and there are workstations with swings. It looks like a children's playground which is befitting for how young his employees are. They all seem to like him a lot, and for some reason I find that super sexy.

We make it to his office, it's not that different from his home office, they both look like gaming stations. Ironic, since Rama doesn't play video games that much. It isn't hard to feel at home in his office, that has less to do with the familiarity of the décor, and more to do with his soft kisses and warm embrace.

Lunch was already cold, but he ate it anyway, citing it was the thought that counted and when I told him about my new job, he popped a bottle of wine.

The genuine excitement in his eyes stirs joy in my heart as we share conversation sitting on the floor by the window. It's the kind of evening every boyfriend dreams of.

"What are you doing tomorrow?" Rama asks.

"I could be laying naked in your bed if you'd like." I crawl to him and lie on his laps. He lowers himself over me like he's about to kiss me, but instead slaps my forehead. I groan and he laughs.

"My parents are having the whole family over for dinner, I'd like you to come."

"Meet your parents? Are we there yet?"

"Don't overthink it, a lot of people meet my parents. I could introduce you as a friend if you feel uncomfortable."

I lift myself off him. "A lot of people? Ex boyfriends?"

"Jealousy is cute on you."

"How many boyfriends have you introduced to your parents?"

"Not that many."

"How many is 'not that many'?"

Rama laughs. "Two."

"That is a lot... that is a lot," I say with a laugh, pointing at him.

"Would you like to come?"

I nod, laying back down. He pats my hair and kisses my forehead.

"About this morning..." I begin to apologize when my phone rings.

The number isn't a familiar one, it's also not saved on my phone. I answer anyway cause I'm tipsy and could care less.

"Yes."

"Hey bro, how are you doing?" a familiar voice comes through the phone.

"Awut?"

He softly laughs. "You didn't save my number, did you?"

"I'm sorry, no I didn't... Sawatdee krap."

"Sawatdee krap. Listen, I was wondering if you're free tomorrow. I have this pitch next week with my co-founder, we'd love to pick your brain on some issues regarding our app."

"I see, I'm sorry but tomorrow is—"

"We really need your input, it could make all the difference in our pitch, and we need someone in the medical field on our advisory board. It would help with how we build our interface, what do you say? Forty-five minutes tops, we can come to you."

I look over at Rama and he nods me on.

"What time is it?"

"5pm is when the team can get together."

I place my hand over my phone, lowering it away from my mouth. "What time is dinner with your parents?"

"7pm but we can be late," Rama replies.

"Ok, 5pm sounds good, text me an address, I'll come to you."

The call ends and I wrap Rama's hand around me. We continue to watch the sunset, talking about nothing in particular.

We lazy around his office for a few more hours before he drives me home and kisses me goodbye. As soon as Rama's car is out of sight, I sprint to Lucifer's bedroom and invade his closet. I have nothing befitting for meeting the parents of my first partner for the first time.

"A suit maybe?" I suggest. Lucifer is quick to banish such ideas from my head.

"Parents love white, you'd look pure, like you've never sucked a dick in your life," Lucifer says, fishing out every white clothing he can lay his hands on.

It took an hour but we finally picked an outfit, and for over thirty minutes I have remained in front of the mirror, having a fake Q&A session with my reflection, pretending my reflection is one of Rama's parents bombarding me with questions. Most of the questions are over the top, I know they'll probably won't ask these. However, the lack of parenting figures in my life has left me with the need to overcompensate and appear capable. I don't want to be pitied or seen as incomplete when the question "tell me about your parents," comes up. I don't want to be caught off guard.

I wore myself out with the marathon of ridiculous questions and lost track of time, falling asleep in the clothing ensemble Lucifer so graciously put together for me.

I woke up late in a rumpled outfit with not enough time to wash it and return it to its former glory from last night, so decided on a traditional V-neck oversized shirt and some loose pants. You can't go wrong with simple.

First, I stop by a supermarket to pick up wine, fruits, chocolates, gifts for Rama's parents. I might not have enough time after my meeting with Awut to stop by and pick them up. The address Awut sent is the same one from weeks ago. The skyscraper building where Rama's company held the networking event. Apparently, that night Awut was able to meet the owner of the penthouse where the event was held and shared the idea behind his tech, piquing their interest.

The whole meeting is a big fluff to my ego. For the first time in a long time, I feel like I have actually earned my degrees. The kind of questions they are asking, the flaws I'm pointing out in their interface, you'd need to really understand a child's psychology to give the kind of feedback I'm giving. Haven't felt more proud of myself than I do right now.

I glance over at my phone and realize it's past six and Rama already left two missed calls. I got carried away with all the big ideas being thrown around. I inform Awut of my need to leave and he insists we schedule another meeting to discuss bringing me on officially as an adviser for their company. I thank them for the consideration with a wai and bid them goodbye, hurrying to the elevator. It opens almost immediately after I press the ground floor button and I get in. I dial Rama's number and he picks.

"I have been trying to reach you," he says.

"I am so sorry, forgive me, rushing over, I got carried away," the elevator stops, "it was such a great meeting, they want me on their advisory board. Crazy right? I absolutely love..."

I look up and freeze at the sight of Elina dressed head to toe in a bright red ensemble, her face lowered, having a conversation with a way taller broad man. There is a rare smile on her face as she steps on. She doesn't look up, she hasn't seen me frozen against the elevator wall. I lower my face, trying to hide away from her. Suddenly, the air is too thick.

"Honey? You were saying?" Rama calls back my attention.

I'm too scared to speak, she might hear me, she'll know I'm here. *She can't know I'm here.* I lower the phone and end the call, turning off my phone so Rama can't call back, the ringing might trigger her to turn. If I had just left an hour earlier like I was supposed to. *Oh fuck*. There are still so many flights to go.

"Mike, can you do me a favor?" she asks the man standing next to her.

"Of course, Khun Cheng?" he replies.

Elina presses a button and the elevator stops, the doors slide open.

"Please get off here," she politely asks.

I lift my head and turn to them. "Please don't," I say.

The man turns to me, but Elina doesn't, she leaves her eyes on him with a confident smirk. He glances back and forth, from me to Elina, then me again. He lets out a soft chuckle and steps off the elevator, bowing to Elina. Elina presses the button and the elevator door closes. I pin myself to the wall, as far away from Elina as possible. She says nothing, just stands there, staring at the door as the minutes fly by.

"You never texted back," Elina breaks her silence, keeping her gaze on the door.

"I never read it—I blocked your number, Elina."

She exhales, taking her hands out of the pocket of her long red coat and turns to me. I keep my eyes on the ground because if they meet hers, it would be my undoing.

"It was about Hathai, she sent you mail."

"You can send them over to Lucifer's house."

"I already sent them to your home. Your father is a very sweet man."

I turn my gaze to her, squeezing my forehead. "You met my father?"

"Yes. We had tea."

"What were you thinking! I never said..."

She steps forward.

"Don't come any closer, Elina."

She continues advancing towards me, her scent getting stronger.

"Elina, please don't come any closer," I say, my tone giving my weakness away.

She keeps advancing, closing every inch of space between us. With every step, the smell of her perfume overpowers my senses, and I part my lips to breathe a little easier. Her warm breath brushes against my flushed cheeks, and every hair on my skin stands. She's been smoking. There is that familiar scent of cigar on her breath, it's enough to send tingles across my body. I loosen my grip on the plastic bag and it falls to the ground.

Her hands gently grip my waist, and I let out a small whimper, looking into her eyes with my heart racing. She slides her palm under my shirt and lowers her face to my neck, tracing her breath around my neck. I swallow, trembling under the heat of her body. My nipples brush lightly against my shirt and a warm sensation spreads through me. Her hands keep traveling upwards. I try to fight my body's submission to her, but it feels like I don't get a say. My body wants something, my heart seeks the same thing too, and I'm losing, like I always do when it comes to Elina. She brings her face closer to mine, and I stare into her deep brown sad eyes, already feeling myself relinquishing control.

"What. Are. You?" Elina asks against my lips, and I quiver.

"Elina... please..."

Not today—Today I meet my boyfriend's parents. Today I'll sleep in his arms... Please Elina.

"What. Are. You?" she asks again.

I lower my gaze.

With a finger, Elina lifts my gaze back to hers, commanding every bit of resistance I have left to melt away

and something snaps inside of me—something gives away—
and my soul surrenders in submission.

"Elina Cheng's slut," I whisper, and gasp at the sound
of my own voice conceding.

She blinks, and I see her basking in the glory of her
dominance—and she is—***glorious***.

"Beg," Elina commands in a husky tone.

My gaze falls to her lips, and I bite mine, whimpering,
squeezing her coat in need.

"Please—kiss me."

THIRTY-SEVEN
LIFTED VEIL

Her lips brush against mine. I leave them slightly parted, waiting for her to consume all of me. I'm dying of thirst... thirst for her, the kind of thirst only her lips, her hands, her body, her soul can quench.

Elina tortures me, leaving me in drought, dangling it in front of me but refuses to make it all stop. She's proud and pleased with my desperation. The obsession I see glowing in her eyes makes me swell with the need for submission.

"Please," I beg.

In no rush, Elina sinks her lips into my mouth, and I hold my breath. Our eyes stay open, fixed on each other as her lips suck mine. I squeeze her coat, holding her close as her tender kisses begin to overwhelm me. My skin burns at her touch. My soul melts into hers. I yearn to give her all of me, be the only casualty of her explosion. I want it all to consume me until there is nothing left.

She shuts her eyes and I shut mine, letting my body ignite with every kiss, every touch. She presses me harder against the wall, licking me and leaving soft bites as she descends to my shoulder. My whimpering sounds fill the elevator, I cannot tame them any longer. My hands slide under her coat, squeezing her shirt. I want to touch her bare body, feel her heartbeat under my palm, but I still remember all the rules.

She lifts my shirt with her right hand, squeezing my ass with her left, then gives my nipple a lick, and I moan. She finds my lips again in an attempt to quiet me down, kissing me wildly, leaving her fingers on my wet sensitive nipple.

The elevator comes to a halt and my eyes fly open, we aren't at the ground floor yet. The door opens and a middle aged woman tries to get on. Shocked by the sight she stands back, staring. I give Elina a gentle push and she pins my hands harder to the wall, kissing me, having her way with me.

I share a short stare with the woman from behind her overpowering kisses, alerting her of my inability to stop her. She steps back shaking her head in what I believe is disgust. The elevator door closes. Just as I return my focus to the sensations overwhelming me, Elina takes a break from my lips to look into my eyes.

"I. Missed. You," Elina says, stressing every word. The raging lust that once lingered in her eyes has turned into wounded desire. "Tell me you missed me too."

I hold her gaze, gathering my breath, my legs ready to give away. I slide my right hand over her neck and cup her face.

"There are no words, Elina. There are no words," I say, in a shaky whisper. "I. Need. You."

She pulls me back into a kiss and I guide her hands back to my chest. I never want her to stop. My mind is empty. The only thing left is my hunger for submission. The elevator door opens again, and we break away. Elina takes my hand and leads me past the number of people waiting to get on.

A valet brings forth her suede black Porsche convertible. I've never seen this one, but I'm sure there are a number of her cars I've never seen. The color and added designs, all make it look like a Bat-mobile.

Elina takes off in a flash. I smile at the thrill of it, the familiarity of what a rush riding with her felt like hits me. Her hand slides over my thigh, I gulp, pressing my lips into a thin line.

"You need me?" she asks, her eyes on the road.

I place my hands over hers, squeezing before lifting my gaze to her.

"You took it away—my submission—your dominance," I reply meekly. Her expression softens and she turns to me.

"It will never happen again," Elina says, staring into my eyes.

"Eyes on the road, Elina." I smile.

She smirks and turns, lifting my hand to her lips and kisses it. I leave my gaze on her, in awe of her beauty and effortless seductiveness.

We arrive at the mansion, I step down, so does she. I walk to her and she slides her hand across my waist, kissing my cheek as we walk into the mansion. It's different stepping into the mansion this way, so openly, not a single care in the world. Her eyes on me, mine on her, soft smiles on our lips.

Every step I take lights up the way as we descend into the Playroom. Rivers of excitement rush through me. The familiar smell in the air hits me, triggering so many memories. The sight of all the instruments of pain and pleasure she once used on me. The bed that was home to our sweat and cum. All of it welcomes me and I sigh a sigh of exhilaration.

"Nothing changed."

"Yes," she replies from behind me.

She takes the helm of my shirt and lifts it over my head, tossing it to the ground. I hold my breath as she slides a finger across my waist, walking to the front of me. Our eyes meet under the dim lights for the first time, and we smile at each other. I lower my gaze, watching her fingers untie my trousers and letting it fall to the ground before she slides down my briefs. I take a step out of them.

She takes a step back, studying me like she hasn't seen my naked body a gazillion times. Her expressions are never easy to read, but unlike the first time I entered her playroom, I don't feel nervous, shy or uncomfortable standing naked in front of her. I feel safe in her thoughts. I feel admired. I feel beautiful.

"The male form—it's an incredible piece of art don't you think?" she asks.

"Maybe—sometimes it appears more phallic than artsy."

Elina smirks, takes off her coat and tosses it to the bed before sitting down at the edge of it, leaving her legs slightly parted. She taps her thigh and flicks me over with a finger.

"Come here, Pretty Thing."

I take small steps towards her and arrive between her legs.

"What? Scared to sit?"

I laugh softly and so does she.

"Don't worry, I work out," she says, sliding her hands up my thigh and grips my waist with much tenderness.

I climb over her and she helps me sit on her laps comfortably. It's difficult to avoid her eyes from this angle, especially when she is deliberately trying to look into mine.

"You should see how stunning you look when your cheeks turn pink under that brown skin," she says, brushing the hair away from my face. "Don't be shy, look at me."

I fold my lips and lower my gaze further, my face getting warmer by the second.

"Please, baby, look at me." She traces a finger from my jawline to my chin and gently turns my face to her gaze.

Coyly, I raise my eyes to meet her gaze and she smiles at me. "Good boy," she whispers and goosebumps spiral across skin. "Now kiss me."

I lower my lips to hers, holding her gaze. I squeeze her trousers as my lips sink into hers and kiss her, feeling her lips stretch into a smile. She rubs her hand all over my back as we kiss. Growing bolder, I cup her face and kiss her deeper and she lets me. Her hands cup my ass cheeks and I arch my back like I always do when she squeezes them.

"Elina," I mutter, in between kisses.

"Yes." She leans back to look into my eyes.

"Nothing."

"Nothing?"

"Yes. I missed saying your name out loud."

We both chuckle.

"What else did you miss?"

"Everything—I missed your eyes—your smell—your laughter—your pain."

She kisses my chest and squeezes me close to her. "That's cute," she says, a purr in her throat.

I lean back and take her face in my palm.

"All this time... I thought I was feeling. But all I ever felt was your absence— It did not feel good, Elina, it did not feel good."

She elevates her brows, as if surprised.

"Why are you surprised? Have I not shown you I am yours, in every way?"

She smiles and I swallow.

"I'll wait, Elina... I'll wait until you can love me the way you love him."

We hold each other's gaze for a few seconds, and I lean in and kiss her, rubbing her cheeks.

"Sometime tonight, Pretty Thing, I'm going to fuck you," she says against my lips.

I smile and she kisses my cheeks before sliding me off her and getting up.

"But first." She holds up my chin. "We should get you cleaned up."

My eyes widen. "You want me to bathe you? I mean... are you now okay being..."

"I want to bathe you is what I meant," she clarifies, and I nod with disappointment. "I'm sorry, Pretty Thing. I'm not ready for that yet."

"No, Elina, take your time. I told you I'd wait."

She stretches out her hand and I take it.

***

It's one thing to be under her dominance while blindfolded, and an entirely different thing to be able to look in her eyes while being dominated.

Elina is flawless in her domination, she savors every moment, her eyes glow with satisfaction. Each time I wince or moan from the pain, she closes her eyes for a second, relishing in the sound of my exhilaration. There are expressions on her face I've never seen before. She looks just as addicted to my submission as I am to her dominance. It's like experiencing her for the first time. Exhausted as I am, I could keep going for hours if she wanted.

"Are you okay?" she asks, unchaining me and I nod.

With a warm towel, she wipes the lube and cum off me. I get down from the strap table with a groan and she lifts my face up and kisses it, then hands me a wine red robe to match hers.

"Come on," she says and takes my hand.

She leads me to the wall that hangs all the whips and chains, retrieves a remote from a shelf and clicks a button. The wall slides open and my lips part in surprise. She leads me through a short pathway, into a small elevator. It doesn't make any sense how this fits in here or why it's here. It escalates and opens up to a whole new world.

"My bedroom," she says.

The walls are tall and so are the windows. The massive king size bed is covered in silver silk. Most of the decorations are silver and black, a few shades of gray and dark red. The curtains are long and thick. It's not void of warmth as I had previously imagined, but everything is over the top; my whole sitting room back home would fit into the bedroom's sitting area. I walk around with a smile, my eyes scanning everything. I never imagined she'd be the type to leave flowers in her room but here it is.

"Not what I thought it'd be," I say, standing in front of her rather meticulous arrangement of a set of tiny art on the wall.

"Of course," she replies, walking over to her bed and slides under her sheets.

"It's beautiful."

"Thank you. Come join me."

I turn and walk to her.

I have never felt sheets so soft; it feels like sliding into heaven, and smells like what I imagine angels smell like. She pulls me into her embrace and kisses my forehead.

"It's your room too now," she says.

I look up at her to ask what she means, but her eyes are closed, her breathing soft, she is exhausted. Smiling to myself, I squeeze her. Whatever it means can wait. Right now, I'm in her arms again, that's all I care about. I'm letting myself enjoy the comfort of her bosom because it tends to slip away from me.

I'm awoken by sweet pleasure shooting through me. I shift and feel something in me. My ass is exposed, and my hips are elevated with a pillow. I am blindfolded.

Elina is fingering me.

I smile to myself. She is gentle with me, stretching me, lubing me up and making me wet. She rubs my ass as she fingers me, gently massaging it. I try not to moan even though that is all I want to do.

She kisses my right butt cheek, then I feel the tip of her dildo pierce my entrance. I stifle a groan, trying as hard as possible not to move. It's finally happening! Elina Cheng is going to peg me! ***Thank you! Thank you! Thank you!***

I press my lips together the deeper she slides into me, squeezing my pillow. Elina spreads my legs and drives her strap into the very depths of me and I squeeze my eyes, biting my lower lip.

"Arch your waist for me, Pretty Thing," she says with a velvety smooth voice.

I obey, lifting my ass and she makes the first thrust. I exhale in pleasure, digging my face into the pillow. She lowers her body onto my back and digs her fingers into my hair, pulling it hard and lifting my face off the pillow.

"Your ass is mine to fuck. I will not go easy on it. I will not be kind with it. You can cum when you feel like it, but I'll just go harder. If you stop moaning, I'll stop fucking. When you start crying, I'll just go harder. Do you understand?"

I nod, squeezing the sheets.

"Use your words."

"Yes, Elina," I reply in a trembling voice.

"Repeat the first part to me."

"My ass is yours to fuck."

"Good boy." She frees my hair and slides her hand under my jaw, holding it tight as she begins to thrust, increasing her pace as my moans grow louder. "Did you fuck him?"

I whimper, shivering from the growing pleasure.

"Did you?" she asks again.

I nod, biting my lower lip.

I have no time to spare and feel guilt, the pleasure grows more intense by the second. It's a different kind of pleasure getting fucked in the ass, every stroke is maddening.

"How many times?"

"Elina..."

"How many times did you fuck him?"

"I'm... I'm not sure... I can't... I can't remember."

She releases her grip on my jaw, leans backwards and lifts me by the waist to my knees, my chest pressed to the bed. She pours more lube onto my hole, fingering me a bit more and spanking me hard.

"Hold onto that pillow, Slut. So help me God, I'm going to fuck every memory of his body off you."

In one thrust she shoves all her dick back inside me and I gasp, whimpering.

I bury my face in my arm, and she begins to pound me—hard. I could never fuck her this hard, her thrusts are deep, quick and precise. My knees shake as the pleasure becomes overwhelming; I moan louder. She squeezes and slaps my butt whenever she pleases, hard slaps that sends a rush through me. Pre-cum begins to leak as I groan from mind shattering pleasure.

Elina lifts me backwards into her arms, making me sit on her dick as she fucks me. Her right hand finds my cock and strokes it from behind while her left squeezes my nipple. The tears leaving my eyes are from being over stimulated, I can't take anymore, but I never want her to stop. Getting fucked by Elina is a dream come true.

"When you need to get fucked—you come to me," she says against my cheeks. "When you need pain, you come to me—when you need to be treated like a whore—you come to me." She throws me back into the bed, turning me around to face her.

She raises my legs over her shoulder and continues fucking me hard and fast. With no pillow to quiet me down, I'm moaning like a little bitch—*Elina's bitch*. She lowers herself onto me, runs a finger over my lips then digs it into my mouth, keeping her pace. An intense orgasm shoots through me and warm cum leaks from me, pouring over my belly. *She doesn't stop, she doesn't care.* I groan and shake, rolling my eyes back. She slows down her pace and I know she is watching me tremble. Her touch is filled with greedy desire and lust for me. I let myself get lost in it.

I am hers. I belong to Elina Cheng.

"When you need to fall in love—you come to me." Her voice is a sweet tenderness.

Something takes over me when those words leave her lips and before I can form the words, she pulls back, and continues her deep thrusts, leaving no chance for me to understand what she means. I can't think, I can't talk, I can only moan. She fucks mercilessly, everything my body needs to escape, her dick has provided.

I reach for her hand, lifting it off my nipple and sliding it up to my neck.

"You can call me by his name," I say between heavy breaths.

"What?" she asks.

"Kiet... You can call me by his name."

I never thought I'd be able to say those words out loud. My resemblance to Kiet has been an open secret between us. I've always known Elina picked me because of him, I don't want her to have to hide that anymore. I wish to wholly dissolve into her fantasies. I'm hers in every and any way she wishes me to be hers.

"Kiet?" she mutters, I nod. "Kiet," she says again. "Kiet."

I smile, letting her know it's okay.

"Yes, Elina. I will be him for you... I will be anyone you want me to be."

She fucks me harder with a growl. I throw my head back, losing myself to her desires. I'm hard again. Her grip around my neck tightens and I hold onto the sheets, crying from the intense pleasure, inching closer to an orgasm. It almost feels like an out of body experience, knowing when she looks at me, she sees him. The more pleasure I feel, the more difficult it is for me to breathe, her grip tightens with every stroke.

"Kiet," she mumbles.

She keeps repeating his name as I sink deeper and deeper and deeper into her world. It takes me a few minutes to realize I cannot breathe; her grip is too tight around my neck. I begin gasping for air, trying hard to pull, her grip is tight. To no avail, I try to alert her by shaking my legs, struggling to call her name but she can't hear me. I yank off my blindfold and find her cold empty eyes staring back at me with no expression. I can tell she is not there, only an empty vessel, repeating Kiet's name over and over and over again.

"Cross!" I manage to let out, tears gushing. "Cross!" I scream again.

Everything is starting to go black; my head is heavy and feels like it is ready to explode. I hold her hand, struggling to free me from her grip.

"Cross..." my voice fades and my body starts losing its battle, my vision goes black.

In the darkness, I feel her grip begin to loosen. My sight begins to clear up. There is a ringing noise in my ear. I can hear her from a distance screaming my name, though she's right on top of me.

"Wine!" Elina shakes me. "Wine! Wine! Please!"

I cough uncontrollably, not yet aware of myself.

"I'm so sorry! I'm sorry! Wine! Breathe! Oh my God! Breathe!"

With my vision still blurry, I can see her teary face, her scared wide-open eyes, she looks like chaos, I can feel every ounce of the fear she feels. I continue to try breathing, gasping for air. My whole mouth and throat hurts and it's so difficult to swallow. She jumps off the bed, running to the closet.

"E... Elina," I try to call, but my hoarse shallow voice cannot get anywhere.

I get off the bed, only taking a few steps before I fall to the ground. Everything is spinning, my mind is in a fog, it all hurts; but I have to get to her, I need to get to her, look her in the eyes, hold her, let her know it's okay. I start to crawl to the closet, falling over every now and then till I find my balance.

I arrive at the closet's door and pull the doorknob, but it won't open. I begin banging the door, hitting it hard. It takes everything in me to rise to my feet.

"Elina! Open the door!" I scream, hitting and kicking the door. "Elina!" my voice cracks. "Elina! Open the fucking door!" I fall on my knees, crying without ceasing as I lean against the door. "Elina, please... open the door," I sob. "Talk to me."

I remain leaning against the door for the better half of an hour before trying to get up, my body and mind exhausted, yet the tears haven't stopped coming.

"Elina... Please," I beg.

I grab the door handle in a fit of rage, pulling it and banging the door then I hear it unlock. I didn't notice the press on the handle all this time. Sobbing, I open the door and enter. The closet is big enough to fit another bedroom. I start to search for her, it is like a little maze.

I find her seated on the floor, curled up against a wall beside one of the many wardrobes. Her hands squeeze her folded legs as she trembles. Elina appears small, defeated, broken. She looks up at me and I see her red sunken eyes. More tears pour out of me. I do not have the words, I do not understand this emotion. We hold each other's gaze, nothing but sobs and heavy breathing can be heard. I take a step towards her, and she shudders, squeezing into herself. I step back, slowly descending on my knees. It devastates me to see her this way, I can't bear to look at her, but I also cannot bear to remove my gaze from her.

"Why do you love him so much," Elina whispers.

"Who? Rama?"

"Kiet."

I narrow my eyes, confused.

"I... I don't, Elina, I..."

"You adore him. No matter what I do, it's only his world you want to exist in. Why can't I ever be enough!" she screams, forcing me to fall back in shock.

"Elina," I call shakily. "I... I thought... Isn't that..."

"Do you ever think how it makes me feel, watching you fall in love with him! And he's not even alive!" her voice cracks. "He took everything from me... and it doesn't matter how hard I try, he keeps taking."

"Elina." I stretch out my hand.

She springs up from the floor, taking her robe apart, then her shirt, revealing her naked body to me. I gasp at the sight of her body, covered in heavy burns and what seem to be knife scars, long deep knife scars all over her chest, arm

407

and belly. There are burns on her shoulder, abdomen and thighs. It is a gruesome sight, my lips are still ajar, and my vision is blurry with tears. She continues, takes off her strap and her panties. There are deep wounds around her panty line, like she's being burnt there.

"Elina... w...who did this to you?" my voice is wounded and weak. The tears welling up in my eyes pour down.

"Kiet."

"I... I don't understand, you... you were so in love with... I thought you loved each other. Was it a mistake? Were you his submissive?"

"No, I was his Domme. When has that ever stopped men from making women kink dispensers?" She slumps on the ground. "The playroom was the only place I had control at first, and it was beautiful. He was beautiful. The first time he hit me... I ended up in a coma for a week. He didn't tell anyone I was there. And when I woke up, the first thing he said was. 'Look at you... so weak, can't even take a little beating'. What kind of person says that to someone they almost killed?" She shakes her head and looks down at her fingers. "He always wanted something from me, a new kink I needed to satisfy, I didn't know any better. I was too young. Too naive. I... I thought that was my job... as his Domme... you know? He made me feel like the worst Domme in the world when I didn't meet those demands. I loved Doming so much, especially with him... I loved him and so I let him take chunks of me... chipping away bits of my soul until there was nothing left. And I thought, this is it, I would never feel again—and then you—your wonderful flawed self, walked through my door—and I felt everything, after years of feeling nothing. It was like being awoken from the dead." Elina smiles painfully. "But you just wanted to disappear. It feels like the price of having you is reliving his memory and I...

I..." She adjusts to her knees, and I lower my gaze, shaken up by the sight of her tortured, burnt and bruised body. "I thought I could take it all for you, My Love—I know you're hurting too, no one's ever thought I'm a safe haven before. They all think I'm a doormat. I wanted to take it all, just to see you smile. But you are crushing my soul into pieces—it's like you are the enemy of all things right about me. The enemy of joy, happiness, love. Sometimes I think I'd let you burn right through me. But, My Love, I am barely hanging on."

My tears keep gushing, I keep sobbing, trembling. "I just thought... I thought you'd only want me if you saw him, but I have always wanted you."

"You do not want me, Pretty Thing. You want a place to runaway to, but I'm too weak."

"Don't say that, Elina, you're the strongest person I know."

"The only person who thinks that is you, because that's who you need me to be. Hathai, she knows me better, that's why she loathes me."

"She doesn't lo—"

"He was sick, but not terminal. I had to make a decision: keep him alive in a coma or pull the plug. All the doctors said he had a shot, they said he could survive, that there was gene therapy, bone marrow transplants, so many options. I took him where they'd do my bidding. He never had a chance. They turned off his support system and it was made to look like there was no other option. When I heard the flatline—my heart leaped with joy—so much joy, I smiled." She sobs with a painful smile that turns quickly to a frown. "I smiled—and she saw it. Hathai. I forgot she was there, and she saw it. She knew. She's never forgiven me for it, she never will, and she'd be right. I wanted him dead, not away in prison, not with someone else. **DEAD**. I really did. I was grateful. But when it was over, I was no longer me. I was not a mother—I was not a Wife—I was not a Domme—I was no one."

"Elina..." I shake my head.

"My Love." She crawls closer, takes my hand and lifts it to her chest. For the first time ever, I feel her heartbeat against my bare palm. "Did you ever once think maybe... I could love you... for you?"

I swallow, letting more tears run down my cheeks. "No," I whisper.

"Could you ever love me, just as I am?"

I cry harder, squeezing her chest.

"I don't know," I cry. "I don't know what I am anymore."

Elina sits, watching me cry my heart out.

THIRTY-EIGHT
THE GOOD ENEMY

"Nong Wine... Nong Wine," Dr. Rueng calls back my attention.

"Yes, I'm sorry." I exhale.

"That's okay. Where were you just now?"

"It's raining. The view is calming. Sorry, what was your question?"

"Didn't ask any, I was expressing how glad I am you decided to re-start therapy."

"Wish I could say the same."

"Why is that?"

"I've been in therapy for as long as I can remember. I'm never going to be... normal... It's never going to end."

"That's just the thing, Nong. Therapists are not surgeons. We don't go in to fix problems, because life is an unending maze. We help people navigate it, guide you, but in the end, it's all up to you. And sometimes finding a way out is a lifelong journey."

"Yeah."

As Dr. Rueng scribbles down on her writing pad, I lay down on the couch, snuggling up next to the cushions, watching her fingers dance over the paper with a light ache in my heart.

"We can finally begin working towards healing. We've pin pointed where your fear of abandonment stems from. You tried so hard to earn affection as a child that it... it..." She exhales, taking a long pause that conveys her worry. "Are you familiar with the term trauma bonding?"

I nod. "You think Elina stayed in the relationship with Kiet because she was trapped in a trauma bond?"

"I wasn't talking about Elina and Kiet."

"She was never abusive with me, that was an outburst," I say, my tone sharp and my voice deep.

"The misconception about trauma bonding is that it can only occur between an abuser and the abused. That isn't always the case. A trauma bond can occur between two abused people, easily mistaken as compatibility when in actuality, they are inflicting more wounds on their unhealed trauma. It feels good because they can both escape and validate their own trauma in the other person."

I scoff, turning to face the ceiling and a few minutes of mournful silence pass.

"I used to think everyone else was hurting me, taking from me. But all along it's been me, hurting them, taking from them—she did it all for me–everything—why couldn't I see it?" I swallow. "I am not the victim in this—I am the villain."

"And what makes you think you can't be both the victim and the villain? She did it for herself too, Nong. She escaped into your pain just the same way you did into hers." Dr. Rueng leans forward. "You don't think you deserve it do you? You don't think you deserve a happy ending, a life filled with laughter, joy, love."

The tears I've been fighting off for the past hour as I narrated the events of the last few months to Dr. Rueng finally rolls down my cheek. I turn to meet her sincere eyes.

"I remember my sister, faced down in the water. I could've gone to her—I could've—but my train..." I pause, taking a deep breath.

"Yes, you could have saved her. But you were not responsible for her, they were. They dumped it all on you so it could be easier for them, they robbed you of your chance to feel the pain, the grief and you've spent your whole life punishing yourself, denying yourself happiness because you don't think you deserve it. It's time to stop. You'll only keep hurting the people that truly love you if you do not."

"How?" I ask shakily.

Her face is scrunched and serious then she says, "Don't go to Paris, stay here, face her. It can be more than just pain. No one has ever seen you, the way she has seen you, and I think it's the same thing for her too. Face Rama, your father, your friends. Don't run away. Hold yourself accountable and them too."

I turn my gaze to the ceiling.

My Sessions with Dr. Rueng make me feel worse, she says everything my soul isn't ready to hear yet. Wallowing in self-pity is easier. My days are the same: hiding under my blanket, crying myself to sleep, masturbating to feel something aside from pain, only showering or brushing when I need to leave the house which is almost never. It's so difficult to get out of bed and go about simple day routines, I had to turn down the offer at the Thawon center.

Every day I remember bits and pieces of my childhood. I remember my sister, *URAIWAN*. Her smile, laughter, how she wriggled in her blanket. I daydream of the woman she could have become if I had saved her instead of my train toy that got derailed off its tracks. I imagine she could have become a politician, or maybe Miss Thailand, eventually bringing home the Miss Universe crown. She might have also become a microbiologist, I bet she'd look great in a lab coat. She could have become someone's friend, girlfriend, wife, mother, aunty. But instead, she never even got to take her first step, run, go to school, discover her favorite color, the food she hates, learn to drive, kiss a boy, maybe a girl, have arguments with Mae about how short her skirt is before school, sneak out to parties. *She never got to be anything—anyone.*

For the first time in my life, I'm grieving her death, and it sucks.

I appreciate Lucifer and Plerng giving me my space, even though none of them know or understand what I'm going through. Unlike Khun Kittibun who hovers, checking in on me multiple times a day. I think the reason Khun Kittibun granted Plerng the sponsorship is just so I can have a change of scenery. He insisted I join Plerng in Paris, practically shoving it down my throat. Lucifer decided to spend a week with us too. I guess in a way we are finally getting the grand trip we planned since university.

A knock comes and the door opens, I never answer these days.

"Nong, you have a guest," Khun Kittibun says. I turn around. Rama stands next to him. "Got you some fresh juice." He places it down on the bedside table, then places his palm to my forehead. He keeps doing that, I don't know why. I'm not physically sick and he knows.

"So sticky, please take a shower, mmh?" His eyes are filled with worry. "Dr. Rueng said leaving your bed for at least five minutes a day could change your whole mood, why not take a walk with Nong Rama," he suggests.

414

I turn away from him, returning my gaze to the wall. A few seconds pass and I hear him get up from the bed and walk away, closing the door. I turn around thinking Rama left too but he's still standing in the same spot, by the door.

"Your room stinks," he says.

"You should leave."

He rolls his eyes at me, walks over to the single sofa and takes a seat. I pin my eyes on the ceiling to avoid looking at him.

"What kind of person breaks up over a text message?" he says.

"I'm sorry."

"That's not what I came here for?"

I turn to him, sitting up.

"Why did you come? Closure?"

"Well, Khun Kittibun won't stop calling."

I chuckle. "He's trying too hard."

"He is doing what parents do, worrying about you."

We hold each other's gaze for a few seconds, and I look away.

"You're in love with her," Rama says.

"I'm not in love with her."

"Stop... doing that, Wine. Lying to yourself is not good for anyone."

"This isn't about Elina, and it isn't about you either."

"You never even gave me a chance, you never even tried."

"I don't know what's wrong with me," I reply. "I hurt everything I touch."

"Don't give me that self-pity bullshit." Rama sighs.

"Why are you here?"

"I don't know." He exhales and rubs his forehead. "I haven't stopped thinking about you. I have tried." He smiles.

"You're my favorite memory—I miss you—I miss you so much."

"I am so sorry, Rama."

The room remains quiet.

"When are you leaving for Paris?"

"Two days."

He scoffs, gets up from his seat and paces around. My eyes follow him back and forth.

"Don't go."

"Rama, I—"

"Don't! Ok? Just don't. Whatever it is, I can be here for you. I want to be, just stay, let me help. You don't have to give me anything in return, Wine."

"I am incapable of being the kind of man you deserve."

"I don't need you to be anyone... just... Wine..." He walks over to me, taking my hand into his as he kneels in front of me. His compassionate eyes stare into mine. "I am over the moon and stars about you. I think I'm deeply in love with you." He wipes the tears already falling down my cheeks. "Wine, I love you—every inch of you. I'm not asking you to love me back. But please... please I'm begging you—don't take you away from me."

"Rama..." I squeeze my eyes shut.

***

Everything hurt more after that night. I wanted to hold him, hug him, kiss him, lay in his arms and let him soak me with his love. But I knew, I'd only be punishing him further. I wished I never met him that night at the bridge, all I ever brought him was pain and yet he looked at me like I was a ball of light. I do not deserve him—I do not deserve any of them.

The trip to the airport took longer than I expected, I slept through most of it. When I was awake, I listened to Lucifer and Plerng's gossip. Some of their choice of words forced a smile on my face but I kept my gaze out the window.

I cannot wait to be out of Bangkok, bid Thailand goodbye for the next few years or so. These past months since my return have been the most intoxicating, ecstatic, painful, eye-opening, thrilling, exhilarating months of my life. It gave me so much—Elina gave me so much. Maybe I'm running away, maybe I'm running towards. I'll know when I get to Paris.

We walk into the Kittibun private jet; our bags are being arranged by the flight attendants. Plerng and Lucifer begin to drink as I sit to send Po a message.

I've been looking at the blinking cursor on my screen, but nothing is coming to mind. Maybe it's best to send him a letter from Paris. A slight worry crosses my mind, I hope he is well, I hope he is eating, watering the flowers and keeping up with his pottery works and visiting the temple. I'd really hate for him to not at least have the routine that keeps him happy.

"Hey slugger!" Plerng and Lucifer walk over. "Are you sure you don't want a glass of champagne?" Plerng pats my hair.

"No," I reply with a smile.

"Sure?" Lucifer asks.

"No, I still have to take those sleeping pills."

"Alright then, if you do get bored and need to chit chat, we are here," Plerng says with a reassuring nod.

"Thanks guys."

Lucifer leans in and kisses my forehead.

"We will be in the air any moment, Khun Kittibun," the captain informs Plerng.

She thanks him and returns with Lucifer to her seat. They resume their gossiping.

I rest into my seat, contemplating taking the pills now or later in the middle of the flight. My phone dings and I look over, it's a message from Elina. I exhale, furrowing my brow. I haven't spoken to her since that day. Neither one of us tried to reach out to each other. Why would she anyway, after all I put her through. My heart begins to race as the anxiety kicks in and I swallow, opening the message.

As I read, tears run down my cheeks. Each word pierces through me, breaking me. I cannot hold the pain, I cry harder, holding my chest, it's just too much to bear. Lucifer and Plerng rush over. Lucifer pulls me into his bosom. I hold onto him tight as everything hurts.

"What do you need, Wine, tell us please," Plerng begs, getting on her knees so I can see her face.

"I miss her so much, Plerng," I scream between cries. "It hurts so much, but that's all I have now, it's the only kind of pain I have left."

"Who, Wine? Please talk to us, what's going on?"

I begin to spew; I am a cup filled to the brim. The words won't stop coming, I tell them everything—*everything*. It's just too much to hold in, I don't want to hold it in anymore. I want to be emptied; I want to pour it all out till there is nothing left.

My beautiful boy. My dearest beautiful boy.

*The sun may rise, and set a thousand times, but to me time stands still till you are back in my arms. Nothing will ever compare to the cherished moments we spent together, staring into each other's eyes. The second I set my eyes on you, I knew. It was you. The man I'll love till I draw my last breath. I have only ever seen you, My Love. I have only ever wanted you. And yes, you are the enemy, but My Love—you are the good kind. You are—**THE GOOD ENEMY**.*

DEAREST ELINA

My dearest Elina,

How magical it'd be to wander around the streets of Paris under the rain at night with you. Walk hand in hand in a sunny park early in the morning. Feel the atmosphere at les Quais de Seine on a Friday night. Discover our favorite terrasse on a warm Sunday afternoon with your friends. Paris would go so well with us.

Wouldn't it, Elina?

If you ever find it in your kindest heart to forgive me, please pick my calls or reply my email.

I took pieces of you, Elina. No. I stole pieces of you for myself. Words will fail to describe how my heart breaks. Maybe I have lost you forever. Maybe you'll never speak to me again. But Elina, I beg of you to forgive me. You never have to see me again, you never have to touch me again.

I should've run back into your arms that day after seeing your letter. But Elina, you do not deserve a man that cannot love himself. You do not deserve this version of me. I'll fix it. And if you'd have me, I'll return to you.

Yours, always.
Wine.

My dearest Elina.

I am drunk and deeply apologize for writing again. My lips are filled with words meant only for your ears and they ache to tell you so many beautiful imperfect things. But you are not here, so I write again.

Seven months in Paris. Dear Buddha. I miss you. I miss you so much it physically hurts. My skin is allergic to anyone's touch that isn't yours. I get sick from their touch. I get sick, Elina. I am so sorry about this letter. Have you seen any of my other letters?

Yours, always.
Wine.

My dearest Elina,

How are you? How are you? How are you?
I came across a little cafe and every table had a glass jar on it, carrying jasmine flowers. Fresh ones at that. The smell reminds me of you, so I decided to write you again and let you know there is a whole street in Paris that smells just like you, and it is the most beautiful street I have ever seen. All the buildings are aged with a few cracks but they are painted white with red roofing. There is barely any litter, barely any chatter too. I think you'd like it here, Elina.

Yours, always.
Wine.

My dearest Elina,

Junta finally let me see Hathai. In only a year, she has grown up so much, I almost did not recognize her in her new Parisian style. We talked about a lot of things. She deliberately did not bring you up, but I can tell she misses you greatly too. Do you ever intend on visiting Paris? Would you like to see me if you do? I often imagine what it'd feel like to see your face again. I would crumble into nothing at the sight of you.

Yours, always.
Wine.

My dearest love,

Elina, Elina, Elina. I miss saying your name out loud. Sometimes I whisper it to myself to give my life more meaning. Are you well? Are you eating?

I start at my new job next week. I am so nervous. I never thought I'd ever consider teaching at a university, but I am starting to think of it as another way of touching young minds. But it is scary. Standing in front of a class of over fifty people and talking. It's also pretty weird to think I am now the kind of guy that stands in front of people and talks.

Oh and I am watching birds. I am also now the kind of guy that watches birds.

Yours, always.
Wine.

ABOUT THE AUTHOR

S.N. JEFF is a Nigerian born over-thinker and certified procrastinator with a bad habit of laughing too loudly. She spends most of her time in her home, with her laptop that has a broken screen and her eyeglasses that is missing one hand. Apparently, if you tie a scarf around your head, it holds the glasses in place, so there is no need to get the other hand fixed—even though all it will take is one appointment. She also believes in karma, coffee, and chicken.

When she is not writing, she is thinking about writing while scrolling through TikTok. She also thinks her writing is awful seventy percent of the time. She is working at it, do not give up on her just yet.

She has a shit ton of stories to tell, and you can follow her writing journey on all social media: **SNJEFFAUTHOR**, or visit **SNJEFF.COM** and check out her upcoming works or sign up to her mailing list to get notified the next book for The Good Enemy comes out.

Printed in Great Britain
by Amazon

16853567R00249